Beginnings

I Found My Heart in San Francisco
San Francisco
Book Two

Susan X Meagher

BEGINNINGS
I FOUND MY HEART IN SAN FRANCISCO: BOOK TWO
© 2006 BY SUSAN X MEAGHER

ISBN 0-977088-52-9

THIS TRADE PAPERBACK ORIGINAL IS PUBLISHED BY BRISK PRESS, NEW YORK, NY 10011

FIRST PRINTING: FEBRUARY 2006

Acknowledgements

Thanks to the team who helped proof this edition. It took a lot of time and effort from all: Stefanie, Edye, Judy, Karen, Laura, Lori, and Elaine.

Thanks also to Carrie for every day she chooses to spend with me. I'm a very lucky woman.

Other books by Susan X Meagher

Arbor Vitae

I Found My Heart in San Francisco

Awakenings

Beginnings

Coalescence

Disclosures

Anthologies

Undercover Tales

The Milk of Human Kindness

Infinite Pleasures

Telltale Kisses

At First Blush

For further information visit the author's website

www.sxmeagher.com

Chapter One

"**A**re you sure I'm not dreaming?"

"Mmm, I can't guarantee anything right now. All I know for sure is that my dream just came true."

Lying on the sun-warmed boulder, one of two women laughed gently, her green eyes twinkling as she took in the beautiful sights that surrounded her.

From a purely artistic perspective, most would say that the stunning vista that spread as far as the eye could see was the most interesting feature of the landscape. The crest of Mt. Tam, a popular destination for bikers, hikers and naturalists, would top the list of the most beautiful attractions in the entire San Francisco Bay Area. And when one added a spectacular sunset, the vote would be nearly unanimous.

On this warm, dry April afternoon, the sunset did not disappoint. The usual fog bank had held off a bit this day, allowing the inhabitants of the area a magnificent and rare view of the crimson and gold orb as it sank into the sea. But the sunset lost some of its luster in the golden-haired woman's eyes; the spectacular display paling in comparison to the loveliest sight that her eyes had ever welcomed.

The object of her slavish devotion rolled onto her side, long, straight hair sliding along the warm rock. Blinking her eyes languidly at her admirer, her face broke into a dazzling smile, showing twin rows of bright white teeth. "Seven months. In seven months you've changed my life forever."

"It does seem longer, doesn't it?" The smaller of the two sat up and stretched a bit, filling her lungs with the cool, vapor-laden air. "It feels like I've known you forever, but at the same time it's like we just met."

Her companion pulled up into a sitting position and draped her long, muscular arm around her friend's shoulders. "I remember when we met," she said, chuckling to herself as the scene replayed in her mind. "We could have saved a lot of time if I'd acted on my first impulse." Her right eyebrow twitched in challenge and the blonde went for the bait.

"And that was?" she drawled lazily.

"I remember sitting at my desk in that psych class, and when the professor announced that my partner for class projects was Jamie Evans, I thought it might be a man. And that was *not* why I took a class called 'The Psychology of the Lesbian Experience'."

"You do pretty well in the androgynous name competition too. When I saw that my partner was Ryan O'Flaherty, I was totally bummed! I wanted to meet a real live lesbian!"

Ryan leaned forward, putting her smiling face directly in front of Jamie's. "Disappointed?"

"Never. Not then, not now, not ever." Her head inclined and nuzzled against Ryan's tanned neck as her friend moved to lean again her. "You?"

"No. No. And … no." Ryan's mouth found Jamie's ear and she hummed against the fine blonde hair. "Can I act on that first impulse now?"

Jamie sat up and tilted her head a tiny bit in question as Ryan's head dropped to meet hers. Their lips touched in a soft, gentle, languid kiss that slowly but inexorably began to grow in intensity. With a sharp intake of air Jamie pulled away and leaned her forehead against Ryan's. "I think I'd have learned everything I needed to know about lesbians if you'd done that."

"No way. Being friends first is what's let us be here today. And even though you've been through a lot of pain, everything that happened had to happen."

Now Jamie sat up completely and turned to watch the sunset for a few moments. "I suppose you're right," she said, "but I wish I hadn't had to hurt another person to get here."

"You didn't know how you felt when you got engaged. You're not the kind of woman who would toy with a person like that. And as soon as you knew it wasn't right, you broke it off."

"That's a bit of revisionist history, but I appreciate that you're my champion," she said as she turned to give Ryan a smile. "I did the best I could at the time."

"That's all any of us can do." They sat quietly for a few moments, each of them reflecting on the events that had led them to this mountain on this beautiful afternoon. Both of them were still raw from the pain they'd been through, and neither wanted to discuss the past in detail. And the joy they were experiencing made it hard to concentrate on anything but the present.

Even though the air was beginning to chill, the warmth of their burgeoning connection made them all but oblivious to the changing weather. "I don't ever want to leave," Jamie whispered as she continued to nuzzle Ryan's warm neck.

"I don't either. But moving to a nice soft bed doesn't sound so bad, does it?" Ryan grinned crookedly as she turned to steal several light kisses.

Jamie felt every molecule of breath leave her chest as the implication of that question hit her. Her months of often-painful indecision had finally culminated in her profession of love for the gentle woman at her side. Finding that Ryan loved her too was more than she'd dared hope for. She'd planned this day for weeks and had run through the scenario hundreds of times in her mind. But she now realized, to her horror, that she had never gone further in her planning than the initial revelation. She had absolutely no idea how to respond to Ryan's question, and the fear clearly showed on her face as Ryan once again took her in her arms and soothed, "Don't worry. We won't do one thing that makes you uncomfortable. We'll go at your pace. I swear."

"I ... I don't ... I'm ... I'm not sure ..." she stammered, feeling completely foolish and more than a little immature.

Ryan hugged and placing a tiny kiss on her forehead. "You're a precious gift to me. I'll do everything in my power to make you feel safe. Please don't worry about a thing."

"Thank you," Jamie whispered softly. As she lifted her head she took a quick glance at the darkening sky. "I *am* worried about one thing. I'm worried that we'll never get off this mountain if we don't get going."

Ryan looked around and took in the deepening gloom, seemingly for the first time. "Now that's a valid concern."

They rose and stretched for a few minutes before climbing astride their mountain bikes for the short trip to their destination. As they rode in the fading, watery light, Jamie reflected on the events that had led them to this day. She smiled as she considered that Ryan's offer to train her to participate in the California AIDS Ride had been the catalyst that had allowed them to come to know each other so well. Working with Ryan several times a week—in both the gym and on the road—had helped lay the foundation of a friendship that had steadily grown into something much more, and she thanked God that their paths had crossed and then merged.

They arrived at the small, elegant hotel as full darkness settled in. Ryan had seen the façade many times, but she had never ventured inside. As she did, she observed that the hotel was constructed in a style reminiscent of a sixteenth century English manor house. It was the type of place that she never would have selected on her own, but she felt strangely at ease with Jamie at her side. They were obviously not the first bike riders that had gotten stuck on Mt. Tam, since the courteous staff was attuned to their potential needs. Jamie efficiently handled the arrangements at the front desk while Ryan spoke to the bellman about securing their bikes. The staff didn't bat an eye when they indicated that they had no luggage, and the clerk at the front desk thoughtfully offered to send up a basket with essential toiletries. After their business was taken care of, they decided to walk along the beach as neither wanted to lose the ephemeral magic of the day.

When they reached the ocean, they both removed their shoes and socks and rolled their bike pants up to guard against a dousing by the shallow surf. Holding hands in the cool moonlit night they walked along, feeling the warmth of their new bond. "Do you remember walking along this beach at Christmas break?" Ryan asked, breaking the silence.

"Of course I do. And I always will. It's one of my favorite memories. Something changed for me that day, even though I tried not to face it."

"What do you mean?"

"It makes sense to me now, since I know I was falling in love with you, but I was confused by how warm and peaceful I felt when we walked down the beach together. I was having a really tough time at home and things were really bad with Jack, but after a few hours with you I felt whole again." She gazed up at Ryan with a peaceful smile on her face and closed her eyes as her tall partner bent to kiss her.

Ryan felt Jamie's cold skin and wrapped her in her arms. "You're starting to chill. It's time to go back." She noticed the reluctance in her partner's face so she placed her fingers on her chin and gently tilted her head back. "Remember my promise. Nothing will happen that you aren't comfortable with."

Jamie gave a slight nod and cuddled up against Ryan's warm body as they turned to head back to the hotel.

When they arrived back at the inn, Jamie stopped at the front desk and arranged to have dinner sent up to their room. While she was occupied, Ryan used her calling card at a pay phone to call home. "Hey, Rory," she said when her brother answered.

"Hi, where are you guys?"

"We're still in Marin. We got stuck on the top of Mt. Tam and didn't have time to make the last ferry. We found a hotel on Muir Beach so we're staying over."

"Do you have the money for that? I'm happy to come get you guys."

"No, I don't want to put you out; we'll stay over and go for another long ride tomorrow."

"I don't mind. I could be there in less than an hour."

"That's okay, Rory, we're kind of having fun," she explained rather lamely. "It's nice to stay in a hotel once in a while."

There was a moment of dead silence on the other end until Rory finally said, "Ryan, is that really you?"

"Of course it is," she laughed. "Who else would it be?"

"Uhm, some crazy woman who throws her money away on hotels?"

"Funny," she said with a short laugh. "Tell Da that we'll be home on the last ferry tomorrow night."

"Okay. Take care of yourselves. I love you."

"I love you too, Rory," she said, wrinkling up her nose at Jamie who was making eyes at her.

As she hung up, Jamie said, "I think that's so cute. I don't know anyone else who tells her brothers how much she loves them."

"Well, the boys don't do it to each other," Ryan replied with a goofy grin. "That would be odd even for us, but each one of them still kisses Da goodnight. It's always been cool for us to show each other how we feel."

"I think I'm gonna learn an awful lot from being around the lovin' O'Flahertys," Jamie said in a relatively poor Irish brogue.

Since they had no luggage, they showed themselves up to the room. As she opened the heavy carved door, Ryan stood at the opening and stared for a minute. Their room was absolutely adorable and much more elegant that any hotel room she'd ever been in. Ryan couldn't imagine that all of the rooms were this spacious and lavishly decorated, so she guessed that Jamie had secured one of the best. The big fireplace crackled with a recently lit fire, lending the room a decidedly romantic flavor. But even though the room was generously-sized, there was only one big bed in the center of the room. Ryan immediately noticed that Jamie was staring at it wide-eyed, and she nearly had to push her to get her to cross the threshold.

She didn't think she needed to repeat her reassurances since Jamie would obviously only be reassured by her actions. So she wrapped Jamie in her arms and said, "Go draw a bath to stretch out those legs. I'll wait for dinner to arrive."

Without comment, Jamie did as instructed. Ryan lay back on the bed and allowed the feeling of contentment and excitement to build. She wasn't at all sure what would happen between them this evening, but she knew that eventually her patient approach would reassure Jamie. *If it kills me, I'm not going to put one bit of pressure on her. I'm going to let her take the lead and go at her own pace.* While she reflected on the way Jamie's soft lips had tasted, she thought, *But just because I'm going to let her take the lead doesn't mean I can't hope she'll come out of that bathroom stark naked and ready for love!*

Even as Ryan was dreaming about the possibility of an intimate evening, her inexperienced companion was lying in the tub, her body shaking despite the warmth of the water. She knew that Ryan was a completely trustworthy person and that she would, without question, honor her pledge to go as slowly as Jamie needed. But as she shivered away, she realized the problem wasn't with Ryan, it was with herself.

I don't want her to think I'm a big baby, she thought glumly as she sat up to add more hot water to the tub. *I mean, I know that she's patient—God knows she's patient—but her opinion of me means so much … I don't want to disappoint her.*

The water was now so hot that she feared it might scald her, but still she shivered. *Come on,* she commanded, *get your head on straight. You should be enjoying every minute of this experience. Jesus! Lie back and let some of this in.*

She tried to do just that, spending a few moments doing some deep breathing exercises to help clear the stress from her body. Every anxious thought was intentionally put away as she tried her best to summon the joy and elation Ryan's acceptance had brought. *Okay … okay,* she mused as the warm feelings started to flood through her body. *This is working … this is most definitely working.* The warmth seemed to start at her toes and work its way up, spreading to her limbs, and lodging in her chest. The delight that she felt when Ryan had first acknowledged that she loved her started to grow and expand until it filled her chest to bursting. She had to stop herself from crying out in bliss as she recalled the mesmerizing power of Ryan's soft lips.

Mmm, soft isn't the right word, she mused as her tongue delicately traced her lips, trying to savor the remembrance. *Soft isn't nearly enough.* She searched her vocabulary for the correct term but quickly realized that she was unaware of it since she had never in her life felt anything so soft. *Soft … yet firm and resilient. Heat and warmth and softness and silky sweetness that … my God!* She cried silently to herself as she sat up quickly. *Thinking about her lips makes me more aroused than I can ever remember being.*

What will it feel like when she ... Oh shit! She thought as she started to shiver again. *Don't go there! You need to take some baby steps here ... enjoy what you feel comfortable with ... Ryan won't make fun of you ... she loves you!* That thought did the trick as the anxiety abated once again, and she sank back down in the tub to meditate on that one thought. *She loves me! She loves* me!

The food arrived and Ryan forged Jamie's name on the bill, adding a generous tip. She knocked lightly on the bathroom door and announced, "Dinner's here."

"That's too hard a choice," Jamie moaned through the door. "How can I decide between soaking in a hot tub and eating a delicious meal?"

"One fact might tip the scale," Ryan mischievously replied. "I'm alone with the food." She laughed out loud when she heard Jamie immediately get out of the tub. "I thought that might motivate you. Oh, and I found nice big robes in the closet," she said as she tried to open the door to toss the robe in. She was a bit dismayed to find that Jamie had actually locked the door. *God, does she think I'll molest her? Getting her comfortable might be a harder task than I thought!* Jamie opened the door a crack and accepted the robe, and Ryan politely didn't mention the locked door.

When Jamie emerged, all pink and scrubbed, Ryan was wearing the other robe and beginning to dig into a sumptuous dinner. "I guess I made it out just in time," Jamie said to her perennially hungry friend.

Her months of experience had prepared Jamie well for ordering dinner, and she was pleased to see that Ryan almost failed to finish every bite. Her friend's appetite was legendary and a chill ran down Jamie's back when she considered that Ryan's prodigious appetite wasn't limited to food. Even as she tried to dismiss this thought, Ryan was polishing off both plates as expected. After resting for a few minutes, Ryan went to take a soak while Jamie relaxed in one of the cushy upholstered chairs, fully sated and just a little nervous. The inn sent up toothbrushes and other essentials, and she set about washing out their under things in the sink adjacent to the bathroom. When Ryan came out of the steamy bath, the laundry was done and Jamie hung it over the shower rod.

She went to brush her teeth, casting sly glances at Ryan to see where she was going to sit. She let out a sigh of relief when Ryan chose one of the chairs, delaying the trip to the bed for another moment or two. When she had nearly brushed the enamel off her teeth, she reluctantly went back into the sitting area and took the other chair. The tension was rolling off Jamie in waves, but Ryan was unsure of how to calm her down. Finally she decided to broach the loaded topic. "Ready for bed?" she asked as neutrally as possible.

"No, no, I'm really not tired." Ryan nearly laughed when she took in the exhausted face, but she held her reaction in check to avoid embarrassing her friend.

"Would you like to lie down and relax?"

Jamie knew she couldn't delay the inevitable, so she screwed up her courage and said, "Ryan, I hope you're okay with this, and I really want you to tell me if you're not, but I'm ... uhm ..."

"What is it?" Ryan asked gently as she crossed over to her chair and squatted down to look into her eyes. "You can tell me anything."

All of a sudden Jamie was unable to meet the penetrating gaze that seemed to burn into her. She was embarrassed, but she knew she had to get it out sooner or later, so she decided to jump off the cliff immediately. "I'm not really ready to uhm ... love you ... ah ... physically, or, well ... at least completely," she stammered.

Ryan placed her warm hand on the even warmer cheek and leaned over to kiss her gently, "I think I'd be happy with nothing more than we had today," she said. "I love you ... all of you, and I'm willing to wait for however long it takes for you to feel comfortable with sex." She sat back on her heels and regarded her friend for a moment before she asked, "You *do* want to progress to having sex, don't you?"

"Oh, yes," she said as she nodded her head forcefully. "Of course I do."

Ryan leaned back in for another sweet kiss and asked, "Are you comfortable with my kissing you?"

"Very," she replied dreamily as she draped her arms loosely around Ryan's neck and kissed her back.

"Then I'm a happy girl. Remember that kissing is my favorite activity," the grinning brunette said with an eyebrow wiggle as she tweaked Jamie's nose. She got up and went back to sit in her own chair, noting with approval that Jamie looked much more relaxed. "Are you sure you're not just a little bit tired?"

Jamie's shy blush and sheepish grin were accompanied by a tiny nod of her head.

"Do you want me to call the desk and have them send a roll-away bed up?"

"Uhm ... do you think you could sleep with me and not ..." Jamie stammered as she glanced toward the bed nervously.

Ryan slowly blinked her eyes trying to understand the implication of this question. As it became clear, she gazed at Jamie with a hurt look in her eyes and said, "God, I know I've got a reputation, but I'm not a rapist!"

Jamie jumped from her chair and knelt down next to Ryan. She looked into her big, blue eyes and hurriedly explained, "I was only going to ask if you could sleep with me and not be too uncomfortable," she insisted. "I'm worried about pleasing you, and I'm really worried that you won't be able to be patient with me. But it would never cross my mind that you'd force yourself on me."

Ryan closed her eyes as she placed her hand upon Jamie's smooth cheek. "I'm sorry that came out like that. I'm nervous too, you know."

"*You're* nervous? What do *you* have to be nervous about?"

"Thanks," Ryan replied with a false smile. "Now I feel better."

"Well, I mean that you've been with ... you know ... uhm ... lots of ..."

"I know, I know," Ryan said with an embarrassed scowl. "That's exactly what I'm nervous about." She took in a deep breath and blew it out as she admitted, "I'm worried about your opinion of me. I know you've always considered sex to be a very big step and that it has to be part of a deep commitment for you. I'm worried about your opinion of me for having slept with so many women. Your respect means everything," she said as she looked up at Jamie with a fragile expression on her beautiful face.

"Oh, Ryan," she said as she reached up and wrapped her arms around her neck. "I respect you. You're one of the most moral and upright people I know." She sat back and added with a bashful smile, "I worry that you'll think I'm too inexperienced. Maybe we should get some of this stuff out in the open."

"Okay," Ryan said. "I'll start. This might take a minute, though. Do you wanna sit down?"

Jamie cast a quick glance at her chair, but all of a sudden it seemed much too far away. "Can I perch here?" she asked, indicating the wide arm of Ryan's chair.

"Of course," Ryan said, as she turned a tiny bit to make room. Jamie sat upon the arm and used the free space that Ryan had created to lean against the back cushion. It was uncomfortable, but she wanted to be close while still maintaining a little separation.

Ryan began, "I think that one of your most endearing qualities is your devotion— to people and principles. I admire that you decided you needed to only be sexual with people that you love and that you stuck with that decision even though you must have been pressured to give in. I didn't know Jack very well, but I can't believe he didn't want you to give in sooner than you wanted to."

"Well, in his defense, I have to admit that he never tried to talk me into it. He just gave me incredibly pathetic looks and sometimes made a show of how he couldn't stand up after we'd been kissing for a while."

"One more good thing about being a woman," Ryan said dryly, only her dancing eyes giving away her playfulness. "No obviously incapacitating signs of arousal."

Jamie laughed, then returned to the topic. "You're right about boys pressuring me. Especially in high school. I never felt physically intimidated, but one guy tried to force his hand down my pants after a party during my freshman year."

"And that didn't intimidate you?" she asked in amazement, knowing that it certainly would have intimidated her at that age.

"Nope. Just because I hadn't seen testicles didn't mean I didn't know where they were," she declared with a wiggling eyebrow.

"You didn't!"

"I most certainly did! And I acted like I'd inadvertently elbowed him right in the jewels so he couldn't even get mad. I've got to tell you, guys lose interest really fast when they're doubled over in pain."

Ryan crossed her legs exaggeratedly as she said, "Remind me not to make you mad!"

Jamie gave her a kiss on the cheek as she got up and returned to her own chair. "Are you done praising me?"

"Not by a long shot," Ryan replied with a brief shake of her head. "I could go on all night, but I'll try to keep it brief." She shot Jamie a sweet grin and continued, "I feel really special that you want to share your body with me. The fact that it's a big decision for you makes it even more precious to me. I guess that's part of my worry," she conceded. "I worry that you'll feel like I've demeaned or devalued myself by being so promiscuous."

"Okay, let's set some ground rules right now," Jamie said briskly. "I do not think of you as promiscuous. I don't think you're a slut, either. Have you enjoyed having sex with lots of women?"

"Yeah, of course."

"That's my point. You were doing something that you enjoyed, and I assume you didn't feel guilty about it at the time, right?"

"Right."

"So, you chose to be very expressive, with consenting adults, who you were up front with, and you didn't feel guilty about it. What's wrong with that? Just because that wouldn't work for me doesn't mean that I judge *you* for it. We're very different people with different sex drives. And I've got to admit, I'm pretty interested in tapping into some of your drive," she added with a slightly embarrassed grin.

"Are you really?" Ryan asked with her own little grin curling up the corners of her mouth.

"Well, yeah. I don't know a thing about how to love a woman. I'm scared spitless about what to do with you when we get to that point. Knowing that you've done just about everything reassures me in a funny way. It's kind of like when you taught me to ride your bike. You were so confident and gentle with me, and I have a feeling you'll be the same way with lovemaking."

"I'll always be gentle with you," Ryan promised, gazing steadily into her eyes. "Thanks for reassuring me. I was feeling insecure about your opinion, but you've really made me feel better."

"You're welcome," she said through a deep yawn.

"Still not sleepy?" Ryan teased.

"Okay, I am tired," she admitted, although she made no move toward the bed.

"Do you want to sleep together? If you don't feel comfortable, I don't mind asking for a bed to be brought up."

"I think I'd like to sleep with you, but I don't want to make you uncomfortable," she insisted.

"I'd be very comfortable sharing your bed. We've slept together a bunch of times. I'll just convince myself that nothing's changed. But what should we sleep in?" Ryan looked around the room for ideas.

"That's a very good question. I don't have the slightest idea. The hotel didn't happen to send up any underwear did they? All of ours is wet."

"Nope," Ryan said as she walked over to the sink and delicately sorted through the toiletries. "Maybe we could cover ourselves with toothpaste," she said helpfully as she held up the tiny tube.

"Well, smarty pants, does your pledge of chastity still hold if we sleep in that bed naked?"

Ryan's eyes grew wide as she stared first at the big bed and then at her friend, "Uhm, I've always found that sleeping in a big, bulky terry cloth robe is very pleasant."

Jamie smiled. "I really appreciate your patience. I mean, I know you have a strong ah … drive and I know this won't be easy for you."

"Well, I think I've done pretty darn well for myself this winter. How about a little appreciation for that?" she asked petulantly as she strolled back to her chair and flopped down.

"What do you mean?"

"I haven't had the companionship of a woman in … let's see … two months. And aside from that one little pressure release, it was three months before that."

"What?" Jamie gawked, a bit incredulous. "I mean I know you and Tracy didn't, but what about after her?"

"I told you about the night I went to visit Ally. But right after that, you told me how you felt about me. If there was any chance in the world that I could be with you, I wasn't going to blow it."

"But I wouldn't have known if you'd had casual sex, Ryan. And besides, I didn't have any claim on you."

Ryan leveled her gaze and stared deeply into Jamie's eyes for a long moment. "*I* would have known. Casual sex didn't interest me once I thought I could have a real relationship with you. Actually, Ally called me right after you told me you might be interested in me. I had dinner with her, but I told her all about you and explained that I couldn't have sex with her or anyone else until I knew where I stood with you. And let me correct one little detail, buddy." She crossed over to Jamie and kissed her soundly. "You've always had a claim on me. You just didn't always know it."

"Whoa," Jamie said as she pulled away from Ryan's smiling face. "I think we need to set some ground rules for the physical side of this relationship, because that kiss almost made me forget my principles!" Ryan returned to her seat as Jamie began, "Let's start with tonight. Will it bother you to snuggle in bed?"

"It'll bother me if we don't!" Ryan said with wide eyes.

Smiling winsomely, Jamie said, "You don't know how relieved that makes me. Part of the reason I eventually decided to sleep with Jack was so we could lie in bed and cuddle. But even though he did it, you could tell it wasn't his idea."

"You are in luck, Ms. Evans. I am a certified cuddleaholic. I absolutely, positively love to cuddle, and I do it with every person who'll let me. And it doesn't have to be connected to sex either. I cuddle Caitlin when we nap together, and I've even been known to snuggle up to Duffy when I'm feeling touch deprived."

"Excellent," she gleefully replied. "Since we're not going to have sex right away, I think we need to stay away from each other's uhm … erogenous zones," she said with a fierce blush. "Is that okay?"

"Jamie, do you really think I could touch your erogenous zones and stop there? That's an obvious rule."

"How about hugging?"

"I'm in favor of as much hugging as I can get."

"Done. What else should we cover?"

"How do you feel about indirect hugs, say for instance, sitting on my lap?" she asked with a crooked grin.

"Don't you mean sitting on each other's laps? Shouldn't this be an equal partnership?"

"That's a very good point," Ryan said as she walked over to the chair and climbed aboard Jamie's small lap. "Mmm, I like this," she enthused as she tried to ignore the strangled breath Jamie was trying to take. "How about you?"

"HELP!" she finally cried, much to Ryan's howling amusement.

"I weigh a lot more than you do. It makes sense that I'll be the sittee and you'll be the sitter. Let's switch."

As soon as they did, Jamie enthusiastically agreed that lap sitting was not only allowed, it was a clear requirement. "God, this feels good," she mumbled into Ryan's terry cloth-clad shoulder. The rhythmic trailing of Ryan's hand through her hair, the clean sweet smell of her skin and the warmth of the fireplace were combining to relax her so thoroughly that she feared she would fall asleep right where she sat. "We could stay right here," she sleepily suggested.

"I could do that," Ryan agreed as her fresh, minty breath ruffled the blonde hair hanging over Jamie's eyes.

"I've never felt safer or more secure. I don't think you could make me any happier."

"Mind if I try?" she asked with a dangerously raised eyebrow.

Jamie felt most of her sleepiness leave her body as she cautiously shook her head.

Ryan pulled her in closer and effortlessly stood. Jamie's arms tightened reflexively around her neck as they crossed the room to stand by the bed. Squatting down a bit, Ryan reached down with her free hand and deftly pulled the covers back. She leaned over and softly deposited Jamie right in the middle of the bed. As Jamie released her hold, she kissed her lightly and ordered, "Don't go away." Dashing around to the other side of the bed, she quickly got in and drew the covers over both of their bodies. She adjusted her robe and scooted over to the middle of the bed, enveloping Jamie in a tender full body hug. When it became obvious that Ryan was only planning on hugging her, Jamie felt all of the tension leave her body as she relaxed into the warm, reassuring hug. After a moment, she gave Ryan a sweet smile and said, "Now I really don't think you could make me any happier."

As Ryan bent to taste her lips she lightly rubbed noses and threatened, "Don't tempt me!"

They luxuriated in the tender embrace, soaking up the sensations of warm, clean, relaxed bodies, and gentle kisses.

Feeling a bit emboldened, Jamie slid her hand behind Ryan's head and pulled her close for a number of mind-numbing kisses. Ryan could feel her control begin to slip, so she regretfully pulled away and gasped, "We need some kissing rules and we need them quick!"

"Okay," Jamie agreed with a giggle. "What do you have in mind?"

"I think we need to stick to fairly chaste kisses," Ryan said thoughtfully. "I have lots of self-control if I don't get started, but it tends to fade away once my motor gets running."

"I can live with that. Let's make it a rule. Chaste kisses only," she said with a giggle as she practiced on a willing Ryan.

The first rule was shattered approximately three minutes after it was instituted. Ryan pulled back from a searing kiss and tried to focus her eyes. "What happened?" she asked groggily.

Jamie smiled sweetly up at her, "I got carried away?" she said by way of explanation.

"Do we try to live by the rule, or would you like to make a friendly amendment?" Ryan asked with a definite leer.

"I think we had better try to live with the rule, much as I hate to. I really don't feel ready yet and I want it to be special when it happens."

"Oh, I guarantee it'll be special," Ryan said with an even bigger leer as she broke the rule one last time.

After the lights were turned off, they moved around trying to get comfortable in their bulky robes. It was tough to find a good position, but they finally settled down with Jamie lying on her left side and Ryan spooned up against her back. Ryan's right arm was tucked around her waist, and their heads rested on the same large fluffy pillow. "You have the sweetest smelling neck," Ryan murmured sleepily as she felt some of the tension of the day draining from her body. "You're the first person I've ever met who could give Caitlin a run for her money."

Jamie smiled at the compliment, but Ryan couldn't see her face so she added a little squeeze of her hand to make sure she knew it had been heard. "This is an awfully nice way to sleep, isn't it?" Jamie asked a few moments later.

"The best," Ryan agreed as her warm breath tickled the back of her partner's neck. "The first night of many thousands."

Ryan felt her eyes grow heavy as Jamie's slow, deep breathing caused her to relax even more fully. But as she was about to drift off, she got a stab of anxiety in her chest, causing her to flinch perceptibly. "Are you okay?" Jamie's now alert voice asked.

"Yeah, just had that falling sensation I sometimes get when I'm half asleep," she said, partially truthfully. As Jamie settled back down, Ryan tried to slow her racing heart. *Yeah,* she said to herself, *this is about falling. Only this time the falling sensation is falling in love.* She reassured herself as best she could, but a nagging doubt was burrowing into her subconscious. *God, I know I could make love to Jamie a million different ways—and I'm sure that I won't have any problem pleasing her physically. But this isn't about that. I've been with so many women, but none of them really mattered to me.*

I tried to please them, but I concentrated on my sexual prowess to do it. I can't rely on that with Jamie, though. She's not gonna base her opinion of me on how many orgasms I give her. She's gonna love me based on the real me—on how open and connected and intimate I can be with her. She sucked in a deep breath as her stomach did a little flip. *This is scary!* She tightened her hold and nuzzled her head against Jamie's neck, willing the sweet smell to help calm her racing heart. *It's okay*, she repeated again and again. *She loves you and she'll help you learn how to be more intimate. It'll work out if you try hard enough. She loves you enough to take that risk.* She was still reassuring herself fifteen minutes later as she drifted off into an exhausted slumber.

Ryan's convulsive hold on her waist woke Jamie abruptly an hour later. *She's twitching as bad as Duffy does when he sleeps*, she mused with a little smile as she gently patted her arm. *Boy, I hope that's not a normal occurrence*, she added with a start. *I could get bruised from those big, muscular arms grabbing me all night.*

As soon as those words hit her brain, Jamie's stomach clenched nervously. *I can't get nervous every time I think of her touching me*, she complained to her balky stomach. *I want her to touch me. I really do! It's just that I'm anxious about the physical part.* After a pause she admitted, *Okay, okay, I admit that's a pretty big part. But I know I won't have much trouble loving her in every other way. She's so easy to love*, she thought with a contented smile. *She's so easy to talk to and share things with. I know we'll be okay as long as we can keep doing that*, she thought decisively. *She'll help me figure out how to love her physically.* She giggled quietly as she added, *At least I picked an expert.*

Just before dawn, Jamie awoke to feel the most exquisite sense of contentment she could ever remember. She was pressed up against Ryan's side, and she smiled to herself when she felt fingers tangled in her hair. Ryan was lying on her back and to Jamie's intense interest her robe had opened slightly during the night. The right half of her tempting left breast peeked out and nearly begged to be touched. She felt an overpowering desire to do just that and felt herself almost automatically give in to the pull. Her hand moved slowly toward its target, being careful not to wake Ryan. She cautiously reached out to move the robe a tiny bit further open. Then she slid her hand into the garment and was rewarded with a deep rumbling laugh. "I'm not going to vote for you as sergeant-at-arms," Ryan said as she turned to face the thoroughly embarrassed woman. "You obviously have no respect for the rules." She smiled while reaching up to lightly touch Jamie's lips with her own.

Jamie dropped her head onto Ryan's terry cloth-covered chest. "God, I'm so embarrassed."

"There's nothing to be embarrassed about. This is all new for you and you're just trying to feel comfortable." As she lifted Jamie's chin away from her chest, she said,

"If you want to touch me, it's perfectly all right with me. I won't even think of it as a sexual touch. It can be like a little science experiment."

"No. I … I … I'm too embarrassed now. It was only because you were asleep that I wanted to."

"Do you want me to pretend I'm asleep?" she asked, only partially kidding.

"No. I'm sure I'll have other opportunities."

"More than you will be able to count. I promise," Ryan said as she gazed lovingly into her eyes.

A few more minutes of cuddling and then they each took a long shower and got back into their bike clothes. After a delicious breakfast in the lovely little dining room they retrieved their bikes and took off.

Through the late winter and early spring, they had chosen Sunday as their big ride day. They started months ago at thirty miles and had slowly progressed up to seventy-five miles. As they pedaled away from the inn, Ryan asked, "Do you want to do our long ride today, or do you need a day off?"

"I think I feel pretty good. Yesterday was strenuous, but we didn't really ride that far. It might be good to stress ourselves today. Do you want to stay in Marin, or go back to the city and ride?"

"I'd like to stay over here," Ryan said with a shy grin. "It feels kind of magical. And besides, I already told Rory we'd take the last ferry back tonight."

"You are so sweet, Ryan O'Flaherty. Stop a minute so I can give you a kiss."

Ryan did. She stood waiting for Jamie with a completely open and willing smile on her face. Jamie got as close as she was able while straddling her bike. Leaning in, she wrapped her arms around Ryan while she stretched to her full height. She placed several gentle kisses on Ryan's soft lips and let the warmth of the hug seep into her. "It's so hard for me to believe this is really happening," she said as they broke apart. "I've wanted you for so long, it's amazing."

"Really?" A delighted smile stole across Ryan's face. "How long have you known?"

"I've known in my conscious mind since the day after Jack broke up with me." She was embarrassed, but she continued, "You were kissing Tracy goodbye in the kitchen, and I felt such a wave of desire for you that it just about knocked me out. And the whole time I was with Jack again, I was fighting to ignore my desire for you."

"What about your subconscious mind?"

"Anna and I talked about this a lot. Even when I didn't want to," she added, grinning. "My knees got so weak the first time I saw you. I remember it like it was yesterday. I still remember what you were wearing. You turned around in your desk and gave me one of those fantastic smiles. I think I was lost from that day on."

"I remember that day too," Ryan said. "When I turned around my first thought was, 'Wow'. But after studying you for a couple of seconds, I thought you were probably straight so I didn't think anything would happen. I do have a confession though," she said as she looked down at the ground.

"What's that?"

"I could tell how flustered you were and I was kind of playing with you. I thought it was so cute, and I thought, 'maybe she's not *too* straight'," she admitted with an embarrassed chuckle.

"I figured you knew," Jamie said as she gave her a squeeze. "I'm not very good at hiding my feelings." She looked up at Ryan in question, "But you stopped flirting right away. Why?"

"The next time I saw you was when we went for a drive in your car. You were so sweet to me; I just couldn't play with you. I liked you too much to risk hurting you."

"I'm glad you didn't play with me," Jamie said. "If you had, we probably wouldn't be here today. And I'm very glad we're here today." She gave Ryan one final chaste kiss in adherence to the rules.

They rode off into Muir Woods again, riding steadily for over an hour. They stopped for a water break and stretched a bit, but then got right back on and rode for another hour. Their goal was to ride for thirty-five miles before lunch and they were doing very well. They had a few energy bars left over from the day before and they munched on them as they forced more water down. After a quick trip to a nearby restroom, they started off again.

The terrain had flattened out quite a bit as they got closer to Mill Valley. The easy ride allowed them to converse as they rode side by side on the packed earth trail. "When did you start having feelings for me?" Jamie asked as she rode up next to Ryan.

"Well, I thought you were cute from the very beginning, as you know," she grinned. "But I really do have the ability to compartmentalize people. I removed you from the 'potential' category right away. To be honest, I never gave it another thought until your birthday," she said with a little smirk. "That friendly little kiss you gave me was a little friendlier than I expected."

Jamie's expression was a mixture of trepidation and embarrassment. "What did you think? Did you like it?"

"I liked it a lot more than I should have," Ryan said with a grin. "I actually had to give myself a good talking to in your bathroom. It was one of those nights that I wished I didn't have such a firm moral code."

"But that wasn't when you thought you might have feelings for me?" Jamie asked, confused.

"Well, yes and no. If you hadn't been who you were we might still be in bed, but I couldn't get past the fact that you were straight and engaged. But that was one of the first times I thought it was too bad we couldn't be together. The day I broke up with Tracy was when the idea really lodged in my brain," she said. "I was having dinner with Conor, and he asked me if I was interested in you. I gave him my usual spiel about not dating straight women, but he wouldn't let go of it. He asked if I'd date you if I could." She laughed at the memory. "I said I'd be all over you."

"So did you think about it again?"

"Yeah. Several times. The night we went bowling together for one." She laughed a bit as she admitted, "Remember when I almost took a header on the ball return?" At Jamie's nod, she said, "You and I had just made some strange, intense eye contact that totally threw me. I hardly knew where I was!"

"I remember that too," Jamie agreed. "I wasn't sure if I was imagining it or not, but it felt really intense. I think that's why I let the boys talk me into drinking so much," she said. "My emotions felt out of control that night and I think I wanted to suppress them."

"You should have seen me trying to ignore my feelings when we slept together that night," Ryan said, shivering visibly. "You really expected a lot out of me, young lady."

"You don't have to hide your desire any more."

"Hey, that's not the only time I felt desire for you," Ryan said. "The St. Patrick's Day massage was a night that will live on in my memory. I woke up that morning, and you were asleep next to me. I wanted so badly to reach down and kiss you." She blushed as she added, "I was leaning over to smell you when you woke up and almost caught me."

"You were … smelling me?" Jamie asked with a wary look on her face.

"Yeah. Smell is very powerful for me. I associate things with smell more than my other senses. I could get a little hint of your scent and I wanted more. I'm glad you didn't catch me, though. That's kind of a hard thing to explain, 'Gee, Jamie, I was just smelling you. No big deal.'"

"Smell, huh?" she said. "I think I remember touch more than smell. That's why I was trying to touch you this morning. I had the strongest urge to feel your skin."

Ryan slowed down and eventually stopped by a deep grove of redwoods. "Would you like to stop here and engage in a little sense imprinting?" she asked with a gentle, encouraging smile. "We could each indulge our favorite sense."

Jamie felt her mouth go bone dry at the look of raw desire on Ryan's face. Eventually she choked out, "We might as well stop, since I have no strength left in my legs." As she got off her bike, she looked up at Ryan in wonder, "How do you do that? I'm going along just fine and then you knock me out with one look."

"Hey, don't look at me. You started it! The look on your face when you said you wanted to touch me almost knocked me off my bike."

When they had walked their bikes deep enough in the grove to avoid detection, they approached each other hesitantly. Ryan took the lead as they removed their helmets and gloves. She approached Jamie cautiously but decisively and stood very close. Her eyelids fluttered closed as she tilted her lovely face just enough so that a shaft of light that had broken through the redwoods illuminated her features. The moment was fleeting, but in that single tick of the clock, Jamie was absolutely certain that the most beautiful woman ever created stood before her. It was all she could do not to reach out and touch that magnificent face, but she held back, afraid to ruin the moment.

Jamie felt her breath catch, and she stood completely still, except for the rapid thumping of her heart. Ryan moved another inch and took in a breath, starting just under Jamie's flushed ear. With a deliberate pace she started to move, one slow sensuous inch at a time. Her eyes were closed but her nose twitched slightly as her nostrils flared. The slow, seductive smile that curled her lovely lips gave clear testimony that she was enjoying herself, but as the smile grew wider Jamie's knees grew weaker. She had to close her own eyes as Ryan began to move around her body, sniffing behind her neck, the top of her head, each cheek, under her chin, down her chest and slowly back up. Their bodies did not touch at any time, but as Jamie felt that warm breath tickle her exposed skin, she was certain that she was being stroked with the gentlest touch on earth. The entire journey lasted only a minute or two, but Jamie had never felt more thoroughly loved. Her skin tingled with sensation and actually felt like it was glowing by the time Ryan was finished. Ryan's eyes remained closed as she raised her head and filled her lungs one last time. "I will *always* remember this moment," she promised as her eyes slowly opened to focus on Jamie's.

Jamie practically fell into her arms and she let her lips express the feelings welling up in her chest. Her heart felt as though it would explode with emotion, and she realized with a start that loving Ryan O'Flaherty was going to be a completely different experience than she had ever even dreamed of.

The mixture of their kisses and the display of Ryan's desire emboldened her, and she felt her hands move up to grasp the broad muscular shoulders. She closed her eyes and lightly ran her fingertips down the tops of her arms, coming back up on the undersides. She placed her hands on the protuberant collarbones and traced them through the jersey. Then slowly, hesitantly, she moved her hands downward, brushing along the tops of both breasts simultaneously, as she gazed curiously up at Ryan's face. She let out a small sigh as her fingers circled each firm mound, and then gently cupped each breast in her hands. Her eyes were closed again and Ryan's now did the same. She held the breasts gently, lifting them just a touch to feel their weight. Fingers shaking, she drew her thumbs up the center of each breast to lightly brush the now rigidly firm nipples. As she began to circle each point with her thumbs, Ryan sharply sucked in a breath through her teeth.

Jamie felt her burgeoning desire pounding through her entire body. She was completely unable to stop herself as she threw her arms around Ryan's neck and latched onto her mouth hungrily. She felt the warm lips part slightly and she allowed her tongue to slide into the inviting moist heat. She was shaking violently with a mix of passion and fear as all control left her. Her legs collapsed and she felt herself begin to sink to the ground, but Ryan resisted gently but firmly. Those strong arms gripped her around the waist and held her up until she could stand again. She hadn't let go of Ryan's lips, and she felt that sweet mouth break into a grin. "Are you sure that you're the one who wants to go slow?"

"No, I don't," she moaned as she rested her head on Ryan's chest. "I want to throw you down on the ground and ravish you for hours. I've never, ever come close to feeling like this before. I don't think I can stop!"

"There's no one I'd rather be ravished by," Ryan whispered. "But I want you to be certain before we go further."

"Oh, why did I fall in love with the voice of reason? You are so mature," she said with a hint of exasperation in her voice.

"Hey, I'm using every bit of self-control to stop myself from tearing your clothes off right here. But because I know that we'll have the rest of our lives to love each other, I can wait, even though it's incredibly hard. And I do mean *incredibly* hard."

"Do you really believe that?" Jamie asked softly with a look of wonder on her face.

"Believe what?"

"That we'll be together the rest of our lives?"

"Of course I do! Don't you?"

"Yes, of course I do. I just wasn't sure if you were able to commit to me that completely."

"Jamie, I wouldn't have let this get this far if I wasn't completely serious. I've never loved a friend only because friendship means so much to me. There's not one part of me that would jeopardize what we have just for sex. I can have sex with anyone. But I can love only you," she said softly as she placed a tender kiss on Jamie's quivering lips.

Now it was Ryan's turn to kiss the tears from Jamie's eyes. They kissed softly and held each other for long minutes before they finally broke apart. Ryan smiled and said, "We'd better find someplace to stop for lunch. I really don't think I can ride in this condition. This is payback for making fun of Jack's inability to stand up when he was turned on."

"Yeah. I don't think God had bike seats in mind when He designed a woman's sexual response."

They found a restaurant with an outdoor eating area in Mill Valley and they were contentedly eating their sandwiches when Ryan asked, "Do you ever think about why you took 'The Lesbian Experience'?"

Jamie laughed a little. "Is that a tactful way to ask if I had any glimmers of doubt about my avowed heterosexuality?" Upon Ryan's slight nod, she said, "I've talked about that a lot with Anna. I know I didn't think about it consciously, but I must have had some subconscious questions. I mean," she observed wryly, "there were a lot of classes offered at eight in the morning."

"You've never talked about any boyfriends before Jack. Did you date a lot in high school?"

"Yeah, I guess I did. I enjoyed dating when I was a sophomore. I went out with some guys I really liked, but a lot of the other girls were already having sex and the cool guys mostly drifted off to them. By junior year, boys were beginning to tire of the 'let's see who can deflower Jamie' game, and I was totally sick of it. I felt like I spent most of my dates fighting them off, and that wasn't a lot of fun."

"Did you wanna have sex with any of them?"

"I'd have to say no," Jamie replied thoughtfully. "I didn't feel that they were interested in me as much as they were in my body. I knew I'd feel shitty about myself if I gave in because they wanted me to, so I didn't do it."

"You were pretty mature for a high school kid."

"Partly, yes, I was mature. But in retrospect, I think I may have just not had any spark with them. On the other hand, I know that I never felt desire for any of my girl friends, either. So maybe I was slow to mature sexually."

"Were you attracted to Jack sexually?" Ryan asked carefully, wary of bringing up the topic.

"Yeah, I was. Well, at least more than I ever had been with a guy. But after a lot of thought, I'm beginning to think that maybe I was settling for Jack."

"What do you mean, settling?"

"I suppose the honest answer is that I liked him more than I'd ever liked a guy. I was sexually aroused by him ... at least I was before we started having intercourse." She rolled her eyes. "Should that have been a clue? Anyway, I think Jack might have provided me with an excuse to never have to date another guy. He was cute and smart, and I knew he'd be a good husband and a good father. My father was crazy about him, and it just seemed to fit."

"It sounds more like a merger than passion," Ryan observed.

"Ryan, I've already felt more passion for you than I did the whole time I was with Jack."

"Then *you* are in for a treat," Ryan said as she tweaked her nose. "You ain't seen nothing yet."

Jamie batted her eyes, charmed by the blatant teasing. "I can't wait."

"Uhm, I was wondering," Ryan started, uncharacteristically hesitant in her approach. "How have you ... well, what I mean is ..."

"What is it?" Jamie asked as she reached out and covered her hand.

"Well, I guess I want to know ... uhm ... how this is all sitting with you. I mean, I know you had a hard time when you were first aware that you were attracted to me ... and I uhm ..."

Now Jamie grasped her hand tightly, gazing into her eyes with unwavering attention. "I don't know what this all means," she said slowly. "But at this point, I don't much care. I've tried to avoid labeling my behavior or myself. I'm not sure that'll always be the case, but for right now all I know is that I love you and I want to be with you. That's enough for me."

"You want to be with me for ... how long?" Ryan asked, her eyes clouding.

Jamie's face lit up in a smile so contagious that Ryan's face matched it before the smaller woman said a word. "Well, I thought we could use this lifetime to get to know each other a little bit. Then the next two or three lifetimes could be dedicated to working out any little tiny problems that come up. Around the fourth or fifth …"

Ryan turned her hand and grasped Jamie's. "That's enough for now," she said. "We can decide on the fifth lifetime when we get a little closer. I don't wanna rush things."

After lunch they rode for another three hours, stopping for water and bathroom breaks only.

During one break, Ryan offered to stretch Jamie's back out. The smaller woman stood close and linked her hands behind Ryan's head.

As Ryan rose to her full height, Jamie chuckled as she said, "I'm awfully far from the ground. How tall are you, anyway?"

"Mmm, I'm not sure. The last time I was measured I was six foot two, but I think I've grown an inch or so since then."

"You're still growing!" the significantly smaller woman gasped as Ryan gently lowered her to the ground.

"No, not now," Ryan laughed. "It's been a few years since anyone had cause to measure me. It's not that important to me, so I've never bothered to do it again."

Jamie stepped back a few feet and gave the lanky woman a long look. "It's funny," she finally said. "You're in such perfect proportion that you don't look extraordinarily tall. But when I stand next to you, my face only reaches your … uhm … chest," she mumbled, a flush coloring her cheeks.

"All part of my plan," Ryan said with a mischievous grin as she and Jamie cast glances at the spot in question.

By five o'clock, they were back in Sausalito ready to board the ferry. "Do you think you could give me a massage on the deck?" Jamie asked as they climbed aboard.

"I'm happy to rub your legs if we can find a seat, but a complete massage might find us swimming back."

"Oh, I don't know," Jamie replied blithely. "San Franciscans are a pretty laid back bunch." She smiled at Ryan's grin and sat quietly for a few minutes, watching the other passengers get settled. "Can we sleep together tonight?" Jamie asked, breaking the silence. "I hate the thought of being away from you all night."

"Uhm … where do you want to go?" Ryan responded, knowing their options were rather limited.

"Can't we go to your house? Nobody needs to know yet."

"I can't, Jamie. Da has a rule that we all follow. No overnight dates in the house. He obviously doesn't mind if we sleep over at someone else's house, but he thinks it makes it uncomfortable for the others if we do it at home."

Jamie pursed her lips and nodded briefly. "I understand," she said quietly, obviously disappointed. "It's different now between us, isn't it?"

"It's a delicious difference," Ryan agreed as she planted a firm kiss on Jamie's mouth.

"Mmm ..." she mumbled as they broke apart. "People *are* staring."

A devilish grin settled onto Ryan's features as she stayed right where she was and said, "I'd stare too if someone as gorgeous as you was sitting next to me." But when Jamie didn't answer right away, Ryan immediately said, "Hey, I'm sorry if that bothered you. I wasn't thinking."

"No, no, don't apologize," Jamie insisted as she patted her on the leg and gave her a small smile. "This is so new ... I want to keep it between us for a while."

"No problem," Ryan said lightly. "Besides, if people see how good you kiss they might start a riot."

The grin that curled Jamie's lips was absolutely luminous. "Really? Are you serious?"

"About the riot? Absolutely!" Ryan replied with wide eyes.

"No, silly, about the kisses. Do you really like the way I kiss you?"

"This is important to you, isn't it?" Ryan asked gently, searching Jamie's eyes for confirmation.

"Yeah, it is."

"Okay, I'll tell you," Ryan said, furrowing her brow for a minute. "Now remember, we've only been doing this since yesterday afternoon."

"I know," Jamie replied tentatively, now upset with herself for asking the always-forthright woman to reveal her true feelings.

"And it generally takes a while for people to get used to each other physically," she warned, still thinking.

"I know," Jamie said, her voice tremulously rising in pitch.

"Okay," Ryan said as she turned to gaze directly into moss green eyes. "I'd have to honestly say that the first kiss you gave me on Mt. Tam was more pleasurable in every way than the sum total of every kiss I've ever been given." Seeing the relief flood her partner's face, she continued, "And every subsequent kiss has caused my appreciation of your technique to grow exponentially."

"Oh, Ryan," she said with a shaky voice. "I know you mean it when you use math terms to describe something."

"I most definitely mean it," she vowed, her eyes fluttering closed. "And if we weren't on this ferry, I'd beg you for another example."

Before her eyes could open, Jamie's soft lips captured hers for a long, emotion-laden meeting. "Let 'em riot," she purred as she punctuated her statement with a final buss.

"Wow," Ryan breathed rather helplessly as she collapsed back against the hard plastic seat. "A lifetime of those might be more than my body can withstand."

"We'll train constantly to keep those little lips in shape." After a moment she asked, "Will you tell your family about us?"

"Sure, unless you don't want me to. I don't keep a lot of secrets from them, and knowing Da he'll figure it out pretty darned quick anyway."

"No, it's fine with me if you tell them. Do you think he'll be happy?"

"I guarantee he'll be happy. As will each of the boys. They're all crazy about you. Not that I blame them," she added with a big smile. "I guess we can't sleep together at your house either, huh?"

"No. Not until I want to tell everyone. Cassie would figure it out really fast. You know, I think she was the first one to really suspect something between you and me. I guess I owe her an apology for telling her how wrong she was."

"You most certainly do not owe her an apology," Ryan said indignantly. "She wasn't trying to help you figure out something, she was trying to pry into your personal life. She's not a friend."

"I guess you're right. Luckily she's going to New York for the summer. Her dad got her an internship with *Time/Life*. I think I'm going to tell her that I don't want her to come back to the house when she returns."

"How will your parents and Mia feel about that?"

"I don't think Mia will care. She's pretty sick of her, too. I'm leery of telling my parents, though. They'll want to know what's up."

"Do you think you could stand her for another year?"

"No, I don't. She'll be in the way of you spending time there, and I'm not going to give that up for anything."

"I guess this is another good reason to delay having sex. Once we start, I know I won't want to stop. And having to search around for a place to be together is too stressful. It makes it seem like we're doing something wrong, and I don't ever want you to feel that way."

"Hey, I thought you weren't going to date any more girls who didn't have a place where you could go?" she teased.

"You're the exception to a lot of rules," Ryan grinned as she kissed her on the tip of her nose. "Is that okay?" she asked referring to the tiny kiss.

"No problem. Half of the people are staring at us openly and the other half are trying to figure out how to toss me over to get their hands on you."

"Wrong! They're trying to figure out if these muscles are just for show before they make their move on you."

"You're too cute," Jamie said as she patted her thigh. "After Cassie leaves will you sleep over sometimes?"

"Of course I will. As much as you want. I have to make sure you're getting your daily cuddle quotient."

After they disembarked from the crowded boat, they walked through the parking lot of the Ferry Building, slowly making their way to their cars. Ryan helped load Jamie's bike on her Boxster, and Jamie returned the favor with the truck. There was nothing to do except say goodbye, but neither could bear to make that move. "We could sleep in the bed of the truck," Jamie said as she looked longingly at the six-foot long surface.

"It's really going to be hard for me to let you go," Ryan said with a catch in her voice as she wrapped Jamie in her arms tightly, secure in her actions since no other people were close by.

"We could get a hotel room," the smaller woman mumbled into her chest.

"For how long?" Ryan asked gently as she ran her fingers through Jamie's hair. "We have to come back to reality sooner or later. It might as well be sooner."

Jamie snuggled closer letting herself be enveloped by the strong body. After a long while she raised her head and Ryan leaned down and kissed her sweetly. They finally drew apart and hugged each other for a long time. After one more lingering kiss, they got into their cars and started to drive off, but Jamie immediately beeped her horn. Ryan hopped out of the big truck and ran over to the Boxster. Jamie didn't say a word, but she pulled Ryan's dark head down and tasted every millimeter of her soft lips. She gently patted her cheek and quickly put the car in gear before she could talk herself out of it.

Ryan pulled up in front of her home at eight o'clock. She was exhausted from the long day, but completely energized at the same time. Conor was alone in their father's room watching TV. She wanted to go downstairs and collapse, so she made her expression as blank as possible when she entered the house.

"Hey, that was some bike ride, huh?" Conor greeted her with a hug and followed her into the kitchen.

"Yeah, we got stuck so we had to stay over. I didn't want to ride down Mt. Tam in the dark."

"Rory said you had to stay in a hotel. Did you have enough money for that?"

"Ahh … so it would seem," she drawled.

"We would have been happy to come get you, Sis."

"I know, but it worked out fine. We got a good ride in today too." She went to the refrigerator and got a big glass of milk. "I'm going to bed. See you tomorrow."

As she turned to walk down the stairs, a smiling face leaned over the staircase chanting, "Ryan's got a girlfriend, Ryan's got a girlfriend."

Chapter Two

Monday morning, Ryan leapt out of bed practically singing. She dressed quickly and snagged Duffy for an energetic run in the neighborhood, and was dripping sweat when she jogged back into the house. Conor was the first to greet her. "So, I'm right aren't I?" he said with a twinkle in his eye.

Ryan brushed past him to get a glass of juice. She tried to hide her smile, but was quite unsuccessful. "C'mon Ryan, talk to me," he pleaded.

She turned the tap on and stuck her face under the cold water for a moment. Grabbing a kitchen towel, she dried off and turned around, regarding him with a stern look on her face. Seeing his grinning visage caused her to break into a wide smile. He threw his arms around her and squeezed her as he spun her around the kitchen. "I'm so happy for you!" He lowered her to the ground, giving her a kiss on the cheek. "Tell me what happened."

"I guess I can give you the expurgated version," she said with a laugh. "We went to Mt. Tam and Muir Woods to ride and we spent the whole day hanging out and talking. We were up on the top of Mt. Tam at about four and we realized we couldn't make it back without really rushing. Jamie got on her ever-present cell phone and found us a great room at the Pelican Inn."

"Not too shabby," he said with approval.

"Not shabby at all, in fact," she replied. "Anyway we were able to stay and watch the sunset, and out of the blue Jamie told me that she loved me." She held up her hands and shrugged.

"So ... you said ..."

"I told her I loved her too, which I do. But how did you guess?"

"Well, it wasn't really all that hard. The look on your face when you admitted you'd like to go out with her was a pretty strong signal. And since no woman in San Francisco is safe once you get her in your sights, I knew it was just a matter of time. Then, when Rory said he offered to pick you up but you chose to stay in an expensive hotel ..."

"So my chronic cheapness did me in, huh?"

"Pretty much," he admitted. "But the kicker was those bee-stung lips you had last night," he laughed as she reached up with her fingers to feel the body part in question. "You looked like someone had been sucking on your face for hours."

"Great!" she muttered.

"Uhm ... I guess I might as well tell you before Rory does ..."

"Tell me what?" she said threateningly as she began to advance on him, knowing that he was only hesitant when he had done something wrong.

"Rory and I had a little bet on who'd win Jamie's heart. I bet on myself as you can well imagine. Rory, of course, bet on you. So even though I'm really happy for you, you did cost me fifty dollars."

She wrapped her arm around his neck and proceeded to thump his head with her other fist. Just then Martin came home from his shift, laughing at the antics of his children. "So this is what happens around here while I'm off at work, eh? What are you little hooligans up to now?"

"Ryan's got a girlfriend, Da," Conor shouted out before Ryan could say a word.

"That's nice dear," he said as he went to put water in the teapot. "Will we get to meet this young lady?"

"You already have," Ryan said as she blushed furiously.

He put the pot on the stove and turned to look at his only daughter. He folded his arms and regarded her blush and Conor's smile before he shook his head and laughed. "Well aren't you the lucky one, Siobhán. I couldn't be happier for you, darlin'," he said as he wrapped her in a hug. "How did this all come about?"

Ryan looked at her watch and said, "I'm going to be late if I don't get in the shower. I'm totally stoked, but Conor's gonna have to tell you all the details." She gave them both a kiss and ran downstairs to get ready for school.

Before she left the house Ryan called Jamie's cell phone. "Do you still love me?" she asked in her best sexy voice.

"I'm not sure. Does this sound like love? I went to sleep thinking of you, I dreamt of you all night long, I woke up thinking of you and you've been on my mind every minute since. I've been waiting to call you since six this morning, and if I don't see you soon I'm going to scream."

"Well whatever it is, it's contagious, because I have the same symptoms," Ryan replied seriously. "I think we should get together to compare notes."

"I think the only time we're both free today is at four for our workout."

"We both have eight o'clock classes, right?"

"Right," Jamie replied.

"I'll come over and walk you to school. It's not much, but I have to see you before four o'clock. Can you wait for me?"

"Always," she replied firmly.

Ryan flew across the Bay Bridge, mostly due to being allowed to ride in the car pool lanes because of her bike. She arrived at Jamie's at seven-thirty, just time enough to get to their classes if they hurried. Jamie was sitting on the porch with a big grin on her face when Ryan pulled up.

She hopped off the bike and ran up the sidewalk, grabbing the front door as she passed by her startled friend. "I need something from your room. Come with me," she demanded.

Jamie looked at her quizzically, but dutifully ran after her. Ryan nodded to Cassie on the way up the stairs and closed the door after Jamie. "What did you ne —" Jamie started to ask, but her lips were otherwise occupied for several frantic minutes.

"I have never, in my entire life, needed to kiss someone as much as I needed to kiss you," Ryan whispered into her ear. After several more gentle kisses, she smiled and asked, "Ready?"

"Yeah, but not for school," Jamie replied huskily as she wrapped her arms around Ryan and began to return the affection. But Ryan gently extracted herself and asked, "You free for dinner?"

"For you, anything," she replied breathlessly as she looked up at Ryan in a state of helpless devotion.

They walked together in the cool mist, hardly even noticing where they were. As they walked by the plant genetics and biology building Jamie looked up at her quizzically. "Isn't your morning class in Koshland Hall?"

"Yeah," she replied with a sigh, "but I need a few more minutes with you. I'll walk you to your class."

"Ryan, don't be silly," Jamie said, her good sense returning for a moment. "That'll take you twenty extra minutes if you run all the way back!"

"Your point?" the thoroughly besotted woman asked.

Jamie couldn't help but give her a very wide smile. "My point is that you are quite possibly the sweetest woman on earth, and if we weren't in public I'd kiss you until you cried for mercy."

Ryan matched her smile and slowly shook her head. "That will never happen," she vowed. "I love your kisses better than chocolate."

Jamie stopped in her tracks and stared at her in amazement. "Now *that* was a declaration of love!"

Ryan showed up every morning at seven for the rest of the week. They would spend a few minutes in Jamie's room kissing and holding each other then they would stop at a coffee shop and get breakfast, which they would eat on their walk.

To create more time alone, Ryan had come up with the deviously brilliant idea of spending their lunch hour in the small observatory on campus. The intimate space was always dark and usually empty during the middle of the day. Comfortable, theatre style chairs ringed the small room providing a perfect secluded spot for a half-hour or so of quiet intimacies.

They spent every evening together. They were both wary of spending too much time at the house so they generally ate at local restaurants. Then they would walk around Berkeley or stroll through the campus until Ryan had to leave. This was the hardest part of each day for both of them—their need for each other was growing stronger day by day and parting was becoming more and more difficult.

Their partings were not often passionate. They were heartfelt expressions of the depth of their connection, a manifestation of their growing dependency. They would hold each other tenderly for long minutes, letting the emotion seep into their bones. Then a few gentle kisses as they parted for the night, with one of them often rushing back for one more hug.

On Thursday night, Ryan had her companion backed up against the stone surface of Haviland Hall when a group of students exited right next to them. It was obvious to the young men that the women had been locked in a passionate embrace, and as they passed Ryan stood at her full height and raised her arms to shield Jamie from their stares. They weren't obnoxious guys, but their snickers obviously affected Jamie. After they had passed, she leaned her head against her partner's chest and sighed deeply. "This is really getting to be hard for me."

"It's okay," Ryan soothed. "They didn't mean anything. I'm sure they would have done that if I were a guy, too."

"That's the problem," she insisted. "I don't feel comfortable with a lot of public displays of affection. I wouldn't have felt comfortable kissing Jack like this in public either."

"God, Jamie, are you doing this just to please me? I … I thought …"

"No, no, Ryan, please don't even think that. I need your kisses desperately, but it's hard for me to feel like we have to sneak around to be close."

"Ah, damn," Ryan said as her shoulders slumped in defeat. "This is exactly what I was worried about. I never want you to feel like our love is anything to be ashamed of."

"I'm not ashamed, I'm really not. But I feel like our love is a very private thing. I'm sure I'll loosen up with time."

"I don't want you to loosen up. If you need privacy to feel comfortable, we'll figure something out. Your comfort means a great deal to me, and I'll do my best to make you feel safe."

"Thanks," she said as she hugged Ryan firmly. "Let's go get your bike," she suggested as she took her hand. They walked back to Jamie's street where Ryan had started to leave her bike in the morning. To avoid detection, she parked a full block away, which was where Jamie now said her good-byes. "Don't worry, Ryan, we'll figure out a way to get all of our needs met," she promised. But Ryan was more than a little disappointed when their good-byes were much more chaste than normal.

On Friday evening, after a short debate, they decided to attend a movie. They wanted to see a quiet little picture about a farm family in the south of France, but once they entered the theater they were dismayed to find that the last three rows were filled. Neither of them had any real desire to see a movie at all. Watching a film was just a façade to disguise their true purpose—needing a place they could attend to their growing needs. The only theater in the complex with seats available in the rear was *I Still Know What You Did Last Summer* since most of that audience liked to sit close to the screen. As they squirmed around in their narrow seats trying to make every minute count, Ryan had a very unpleasant flash. *I'm sitting in a tiny little chair trying to make out with my girlfriend with a horror movie blaring in the background. This is truly getting ridiculous. I feel like we're twelve years old!* She found herself beginning to resent Cassie and Mia, then her own family, and finally Jamie for putting her in this situation. *If she weren't so fucking afraid of her dumb ass roommates, we could be at her house right now. Hell, if she weren't so afraid of her roommates, we'd be having hot sex right now. Damn it, damn it, damn it!*

Long before the movie was over, Ryan indicated that she had to leave. They walked along the quiet streets, hand in hand as usual, but neither of them spoke. It was obvious that the strain was wearing on both of them even though less than a week had passed. She walked Jamie to her door and gave her a friendly hug. "We'll figure this out. I promise."

She was home by a little after nine and after a rousing welcome from Duffy, she shuffled into the living room. "Hi, Da," she said wearily.

"Hello, sweetheart. Did you have a nice evening?"

She flopped down on the loveseat and gazed at him glumly. "No, I would have to say this was not a nice evening."

"What happened, dear? Did you have a row?"

"No, nothing like that. We spent a dreadful hour at an insipid horror movie."

"You took Jamie to one of those things? I wouldn't have guessed that was her style." She gave him a look that included one raised eyebrow and a smirk. "Oh, I see, the movie wasn't the attraction. But why spend your evenings that way, darlin'? Doesn't Jamie have her own home?"

"She does, but she has a roommate that doesn't like me. Jamie doesn't want her to know about us, so we can't spend much time there. And we can't really be too affectionate around campus or even out in public. Jamie's not ready for the world to know about us so we have to be pretty careful." She turned to smile up at him, "I guess it's making me cranky."

"Be kind to yourself, Siobhán, falling in love is not the easiest thing in the world, in the best of circumstances."

That brought a small smile to her face. "I guess that's part of it," she replied. "She's all I think of, Da. I've never been like this about anyone."

"She's really special to you, isn't she?"

"She's the one, Da. I've never said that about anyone before, but I know it's true. She's the one for me."

He looked at her for several minutes, neither gaze wavering in the slightest. "I believe you, sweetheart. I know that determined look, and when you have it there's no doubt in your mind."

"None whatsoever," she agreed with a beaming smile.

"You know, darlin', the reason I've always asked all of you not to have your girlfriends over here is because I felt that it created a tense atmosphere for the others. But maybe we have to look at this issue again for you."

"Why just for me?"

"Well, honey; you're the only one who can't get married to your love. It hardly seems fair to stop you from being with the woman of your dreams simply because you can't make a public commitment to each other."

She got up from her chair and crossed over to him to hug him soundly. "When was the last time I told you that you were the best father in the whole world?"

"You show me every day, sweetheart. You don't need to tell me," he said as he gave her a kiss on the forehead.

She sat back down and tried to explain the current state of their relationship. "I can't tell you how much I appreciate your willingness to change the house rules for us, Da. And we will get to the point that we're ready to take you up on the offer. But we're not really there yet," she said with a thoughtful look on her face. "We're both very committed to one another, but Jamie has some issues to work out concerning ... well ... sex," she said with a blush.

"Well, I'm one of the world's poorest resources on that topic, but I'd be happy to talk to you about it if you need to."

"Thanks," she said with a grin. "It's not really all that big a deal. Jamie has never been with a woman. She wants to take it slow so she can feel comfortable. She likens it to dating for a while."

"Oh," he said, "So you've not ..."

"Right," she agreed. "We've not."

"Ahh, that must be quite a sacrifice for you, darlin'. I know you're not used to a celibate life," he said with a chuckle.

"Y ... Y ... You know about my ...?" she stammered.

"Siobhán, just because I haven't been with a woman in seventeen years doesn't mean I don't understand the urge. It's been obvious to me for years that you greatly enjoy the company of women."

"Does that ... did that bother you?" she squeaked out.

"Well, I'd be lying if I said I would have chosen that path for you, or for any of your brothers for that matter. I'd prefer that you found someone to love and shared yourself with them alone. I've always considered it a blessing that you're a lesbian, though," he added wryly. "It's been a weight off my mind not to have to worry about you getting pregnant!"

"One more benefit of lesbianism," she agreed wholeheartedly.

Chapter Three

Ryan was on the phone as early as she thought polite on Saturday morning. She had gone on a long run with Duffy and felt fully rejuvenated after her talk with her father and a good night's sleep. "Are you in the mood for a hot date tonight?" she asked when she reached Jamie.

"Sure. You sound like you're in a good mood. What's up?"

"I've decided that we've been going about this togetherness thing all wrong. We're trying to fit our little square pegs into round holes. It's time we refocused our energies."

There was an air of mystery to her voice that Jamie found fascinating. "What's the plan?"

"I'm not telling. All I'll say is that you'd better get your homework done, because you won't get another chance. I'll be there at six."

"You really won't tell?"

"Nope. Not a word."

"Hmm … Then I just have three words for you. Bring your jammies."

"Damn, those are the nicest three words I've heard since you said 'I love you.'"

At six sharp, Jamie ran down the stairs to answer the door. The stunning vision that greeted her nearly knocked the breath from her lungs. Ryan was wearing her most faded jeans, an even more faded jeans jacket and a skin tight white tank top. As Jamie pulled her into the house, she slid her hands into the jacket and ran her hands up and down the planes of her back as she stood on tip toes for a kiss. Ryan gave her a sexy grin, stretched to her full height and settled her shoulders, adopting a pose that nearly made Jamie melt. "Like the look?" she drawled.

Blinking her eyes to clear her vision, Jamie could only nod mutely. Her ability to speak had been stripped from her when her hands discovered that the only material covering her lover's gorgeous torso was the thin ribbed cotton of that painted-on tank top.

"Thanks for the compliment," Ryan murmured as she pulled her close for a longer, hotter kiss.

Jamie fanned herself, still trying to form a sentence. "You look so …"

"Yes?"

"So hot," she finally decided, pacing in a circle to admire the vision from every angle. "And sexy." She ran her hands down Ryan's broad shoulders, feeling the muscles hidden under soft denim. "And tough," she growled as she slid her arms around Ryan's waist from behind and pressed her body firmly against her partner's. She rested her head against Ryan's back. "I hope we're staying in tonight."

"Nope. We're going out, but we'll be able to kiss and hug to our hearts' content."

"We can do that here." Jamie's arms were still wrapped snugly around Ryan's waist, reluctant to release her captive.

"I know we can, but given how you're acting and how I'm feeling, I think being in a public place is a good idea. My self-control is a little wobbly tonight."

"Whew," Jamie said as she released her hold and shook her head. "I don't think I have any tonight, so that's probably a good idea. But I need to go change so I look like we belong together." She glanced down at her polo shirt and khakis. "I look like I'm going to play golf and you look like you're going to … well, I don't know what it is you look like you're going to do, but I want to be there to do it with you."

Ryan cooled her heels in the parlor while Jamie went upstairs to change. Ten minutes later she came back down, having performed admirably in the matching outfit competition. To Ryan's extreme pleasure, she had taken the tough theme and tweaked it to match her own style. In a surprise twist, she was wearing a dress. Ryan was generally very appreciative of Jamie's dress selection, and she had tried to banish lascivious thoughts from her mind on several occasions when her companion had worn one. But now that they were lovers, lascivious thoughts were not only allowed, they were welcomed.

Tonight's ensemble was sky high on the lascivious chart, and Ryan realized that they had better head out immediately or they would never be able to leave.

Jamie's mother had once told her that her clothing was a little juvenile, but her mother had obviously never seen the outfit she had on tonight. The dress was sleek, black, tight, shiny … and leather. Ryan wasn't sure what this style of dress was called—other than mouth-wateringly hot. The strapless top fit like a black leather long line bra—also a good fashion choice in Ryan's mind. But the dress continued down Jamie's body, caressing every one of her many womanly curves. It ended about four inches above her knee, and Ryan spent a moment wondering how Jamie was going to walk, much less dance, in the skintight outfit. But she decided that some sacrifices had to be made for fashion, and Jamie was just the one to make them.

As Ryan stood and gazed at her, Jamie smirked at her slack-jawed expression. She remained on the last step to equalize their heights and crooked her index finger to summon her lover. Ryan trotted over like a compliant pet and placed her hands on her partner's waist. As Jamie dipped her head to reward Ryan's obedience, their mouths merged in a sweet kiss that gradually heated up until it became nearly incendiary. A small growl escaped from deep in Ryan's chest as her hands strayed from her partner's waist and found the bikinis she was used to were missing. She couldn't help but trace the outlines of the tiny thong that she found in their place, and against her better judgment she ventured to ask with a weak voice, "What color is it?"

"It's black and it's lace," she whispered as her warm breath glided past Ryan's ear and sent chills up and down her spine.

"That's not fair," Ryan moaned. "I think the Geneva Convention covers this under cruel and unusual punishment."

"Ha! What do you think that little tank top does to me, Ms. Gorgeous Braless Breasts?"

"So … are you discovering that you're a breast woman?"

Jamie's deep blush was a clear enough answer, but she fought through her embarrassment to admit, "I didn't know that I was, but I must be. I get chills when you wrap me in your arms and I feel those hard little nipples rubbing against mine. Maybe that's why I had a hard time feeling much desire for men, huh?" She smiled wryly and wrinkled her nose in amusement at her amazing powers of denial.

Ryan chuckled and took her hand. "That could be a factor. I assume we'll drive your car?"

"Are we going far?"

"Nope."

"Then let's ride."

"In that dress?"

"Yep." She playfully tapped Ryan's nose as she enunciated each word. "I want to drive you crazy."

Jamie went to the hall closet and pulled out a black leather trench coat slightly longer than her dress. The coat had deep slits on each side that gave her some flexibility. When they reached the bike, she hiked her dress up a good foot and climbed on the back, tucking the leather coat around her legs to create a modest appearance. But Ryan knew what little was between them and that knowledge did indeed drive her nuts on the short drive.

As they pulled up near the lesbian bar on Telegraph, Ryan quickly turned around and instructed, "Let me get off first." Jamie obeyed and waited patiently as her partner climbed off. Ryan stood next to the big bike and placed her hands around Jamie's waist and easily lifted her from the seat.

Jamie shimmied around to pull her dress down to its normal length. "Why'd you do that? Just showing off?"

"Nope. You'd be the one showing off. I don't want that crowd of women to see your hidden assets before I do." She pointed at the group of women standing on the sidewalk smoking cigarettes. "Even you can't gracefully get off a motorcycle in a skirt that short."

Ryan paid the five-dollar cover for each of them and guided Jamie up to the bar after placing her coat on the handy rack. Jamie smiled to herself when she remembered the first time she had spent the evening with Ryan and how she had noticed her unconscious habit of guiding her by the small of her back.

Sandy, the bartender, was in her normal place and she greeted Ryan like the old friend that she was. "I haven't seen you two in here since ... I think it was your birthday," she said as she smiled at Jamie.

"That's right. Good memory. I've been keeping Ryan too busy to come back."

Sandy returned her smile and said to Ryan, "It's nice to see you're finally getting some sense into that beautiful head. I've been telling you for years you should get a steady girl. I'm glad you've finally listened to reason."

"Oh, this one's not steady," Ryan said. She slung her arm loosely around Jamie's shoulders as she added, "She's permanent."

"Excellent! That merits one on the house. What'll it be, ladies?"

"White wine spritzer," Jamie said. Ryan thought for minute and decided to throw her normal abstemiousness to the wayside, "Harp lager."

They had their stools very close together so that they could lean against each other in order to be heard. Ryan had an arm loosely draped around Jamie's waist with her other elbow on the bar. She held her chin in her hand and stared at her date with undisguised interest. Ryan's stare was so intent that after a while Jamie started to feel uncomfortable. "You look like you're planning on having me for dinner," she finally teased to lighten the mood.

But instead of lightening the mood, her comment served to intensify it. Ryan leaned even closer and let that deep voice rumble up from her chest. Her warm breath slid past Jamie's flushed cheek as she replied, "Mmm, now that would be a meal to remember. I don't think I'd be able to control my gluttony." She leaned over just enough to capture a pink earlobe and take a good nibble as an example.

The image that flashed through her mind caused Jamie's breathing to quicken slightly as the heat in the room seemed to rise a few degrees. "I think we'd better dance," she mumbled, hoping that her legs would hold her.

She thought that she had seen Ryan dance before, but what they had done before was a pale imitation of dancing compared to the way she moved tonight. Ryan slid her body against Jamie's so seamlessly and fluidly that it actually felt like making love standing up. She had removed her jeans jacket because of the heat in the room, but Jamie's temperature rose as the jacket fell. Those incredibly soft mounds of flesh moved slightly beneath her tank top, completely capturing Jamie's mind and imagination. It was all she could do not to grab both of the tempting breasts and explore them to her heart's content. It was clear that Ryan was taunting her and attempting to escalate her desire since she continually brushed her erect nipples teasingly against Jamie's aching breasts.

Even though Ryan seemed to enjoy teasing her, it was fairly obvious she was much more interested in Jamie's choice of underwear for her own growing arousal. She would come in close and wrap her arms around her partner, letting her hands drop dangerously low on her back, obviously trying to feel the outline of her undergarments. The teasing and taunting went back and forth until both women were completely and thoroughly aroused. A sexy, slow number came on and as Ryan drew her close, Jamie's head tilted up just enough to have her tender lips captured by her partner's seeking mouth. They were in the darkest corner of the dance floor, barely moving their feet, but their mouths were far from inactive. Their deep kisses continued to escalate in intensity as the song continued its driving, pulsing, Latin beat. By the time the last chords faded away, Jamie was nearly hanging from Ryan's neck, weak with desire.

Ryan gently guided her to a stool in the darkest corner of the bar and quickly lifted her up to seat her before leaning in to capture her swollen lips again. Jamie's heart was pounding so violently in her chest that she could feel the beat through every fiber of her being. She knew her resistance was fragile at best, and Ryan's seemed dangerously low as well, so she pulled herself away and gasped, "I have to … go …" She got to her feet and stumbled into the line for the bathroom, thankful for the respite from the overpowering aura of lust that was rolling off Ryan. When she finally reached her goal, a good ten minutes had passed and she spent another two or three splashing cold water on her face to cool down a bit.

Refreshed, she made her way back to her companion feeling much more in control. But faster than she could have imagined possible, all of her control vanished as she gazed at the dark beauty waiting for her in the corner. In her ever-expanding list of things she was learning about herself, Jamie had discovered that she was very aroused by Ryan's tough girl look. Her partner didn't affect the look often, but Jamie had already decided she could live with a steady diet of it.

The vision that greeted her return was more appealing than Jamie thought possible. Ryan stood next to the stool, one shiny black-booted foot casually resting on the lowest rungs. A sweating bottle of cold beer was dangling from her left hand, resting right at the apex of her thighs. Her right hand held her jeans jacket over her right shoulder in a very relaxed pose, and her hips moved sensually to the bass beat of the spine-numbing music. Jamie didn't know many things at that moment, but one thing was perfectly clear—no other human had ever aroused her so immediately or so thoroughly.

Ryan caught the gleam in her eye and immediately responded by lifting her onto the stool once again. She pounced on her lips with a wild ferocity as Jamie shivered uncontrollably. They both knew the scene was escalating too rapidly, but it was Ryan who pulled back, moments before their passions spiraled out of control.

She took in a breath so deep and heavy that Jamie was able to hear it over the thundering bass. Dropping her head onto Jamie's shoulder, she spent a few minutes trying to collect herself, breathing deeply the entire time. Jamie's hands ran up and down Ryan's damp back, silently thanking her partner for pulling them back from the brink.

"This is too much," Ryan murmured into her ear. "It's … it's too hard, Jamie. I … I can't …"

"I know, honey," she soothed, feeling completely overwhelmed herself. "Let's go home." Sliding off the stool she grasped Ryan's hand, noticing the slight tremor as she did. She led her through the crowd, dodging the women on the dance floor as they threaded their way toward the door. A quick detour to retrieve Jamie's coat, and they burst through the throng that was trying to enter. As soon as they cleared the crowd, they threw back their heads and sucked in the cool, moist air.

"We need a new plan," Ryan grumbled as she took Jamie's hand to lead her to the motorcycle.

"Let's walk," Jamie suggested as they neared the bike.

"Walk? Really?"

"Yeah," she insisted, pulling her along. "We both need to cool off, and the bike might not be the best place to do that."

"Good point," Ryan agreed with a tiny smirk as she gazed once again at the mouth-wateringly hot dress that covered her partner's body.

The night had cooled appreciably, and Ryan shivered as the damp air met her wet tank top. She shrugged into her jeans jacket and helped Jamie into her coat, and then draped her arm around her partner's shoulders as they began the short walk. "This isn't going too well, is it," Ryan said, more a statement than a question.

"The whole thing?"

"No," she soothed. "Just the arousal thing." After several more steps she asked, "What do you think we should do about it?"

Only the sound of Ryan's boots clicking on the pavement filled the air for several minutes as Jamie considered their options. "I think we can go one of two ways. We either jump in or pull back … a lot!"

Ryan gave her a gentle squeeze as a small smile curled the edge of her lips, "Which option do you pick?"

"It's not me who decides that. It takes two to tango … as well as other things."

"Are you leaning one way over the other?" Ryan asked carefully, her tone betraying nothing.

"I sure was a few minutes ago," she reminded her, her eyes comically wide. "I was leaning so far I almost fell over. I guess I need some time to think about it."

"Okay. Take your time." As they kept a slow, companionable pace, Ryan smiled down at her partner. Jamie was deep in thought, her brow wrinkled a tiny bit in concentration. Ryan absolutely loved to watch her think, but she was wary of revealing her interest. She knew that Jamie would want to know exactly what she liked about watching her. To be honest, she would have to reveal that she most loved the fact her partner looked considerably younger when she was deep in thought. She looked like a little kid trying to solve a puzzle that was too advanced for her. Sometimes the tip of her tongue even stuck out of the side of her mouth, adding to her juvenile appearance. But since Jamie was already sensitive about looking so young, Ryan didn't think it best to bring it up. Resisting the urge to pinch her cheek, she merely gave her shoulders a gentle squeeze and tried to hide her grin.

They walked the remaining distance in silence, holding hands in the cool evening breeze. When they arrived, Ryan paused at the door and said, "I think maybe I should go home."

"Home?" Jamie asked, her face immediately clouded with disappointment. "Don't you want to sleep with me? Mia and Cassie are both gone and I—"

"Of course I do," Ryan soothed as she took her in her arms. The warm golden glow of the porch light gave Jamie's hair such beautiful highlights that Ryan had to close her eyes to concentrate. "If I had my wish, I'd never be apart from you another night."

"Then why do you want to leave?"

Ryan pulled back to look her partner right in the eyes. "I think we both need some time to figure out what we want. We almost got carried away tonight, and that's not how I want it to be with us. I want our lovemaking to be slow and intentional and deliberate. I want our last 'first time' to be a time we always remember."

"Our last first time?"

"Yeah," she grinned. "It'll be our first time, and it's the last first time we're ever gonna have. I've already got our first real kiss burned into my brain. Now I'm gonna partition my mental hard drive to make sure I have room to archive our first time. Cause it's gonna eat up memory, big time!"

"That was the sweetest, nerdiest thing you've ever said to me." Jamie smiled as she stood on tiptoe for some tender kisses. As she settled back onto her feet, she left her hands lightly clasped behind Ryan's neck. "We could discuss how we feel … while you stay over." She had intentionally placed a deceptively innocent look on her face, but Ryan wasn't fooled.

"Do you promise you'll behave during this discussion?"

"Depends," Jamie replied as she wrinkled up her nose. "What do you have to sleep in?"

"Duh, I forgot to bring anything," Ryan groaned as she closed her eyes tightly and smacked herself on the forehead.

"I've still got some of Jack's sweats here. I'd like it if you stayed and I promise I'll behave. Scout's honor," she vowed as she held up all four fingers of her right hand.

"You weren't a scout, were you?" Ryan chastised as she bent the little finger of Jamie's raised hand down and brought the thumb up to trap it. "You don't even know the pledge!"

"No, I wasn't. We were gone most weekends, and that's when they did all the fun stuff. I always wanted to join though. Camping out sounded like so much fun."

She had a wistful, childlike expression on her face and as Ryan bent to give her a light kiss she said, "You'll get all the camping you can stomach on the AIDS Ride. Now let's get inside and warm up." As they walked in together Ryan thought for the thousandth time, *don't ever ask her parents for advice on childrearing!*

As they paused in the foyer Jamie asked, "Drink?"

"Yeah, I'll take whatever you've got. That dancing is dehydrating."

"The way you do it, it is," Jamie teased as she slipped into the kitchen. Popping out a moment later she questioningly held up a beer and a Pepsi.

"Ahh, let's go with the beer. 'Tis as well to hang for a sheep as for a lamb."

"Irish saying?" Jamie asked over her shoulder as she went back into the kitchen to grab one for herself.

"Yep."

Handing Ryan her bottle and adding a kiss she decided, "I like it ... a lot."

"Mighty!" Ryan replied with a gleam in her eye, leaning down for another kiss.

"Don't wear it out, O'Flaherty," she warned with a mock scowl as she slipped her hand around Ryan's arm to lead her upstairs.

Kicking off her shoes, Jamie flopped down onto the loveseat and tried to cross her legs. Ryan stood, hands on hips, as she pointedly gazed at the tight leather dress. "Now you know why cows don't cross their legs. Skin's too tight."

"Very funny," Jamie scowled. "I'll put my pajamas on."

"If you want this discussion to be rational, I'd highly recommend it." But she quickly added, "Unless your pajamas are hotter than that dress."

Heading to the dresser Jamie pulled a sedate pair of black-watch plaid flannel pajamas out for herself and then rifled through the bottom drawer, finally extracting a pair of gray sweatpants and a bright red T-shirt. "Put these on ... for your own safety," she warned her grinning partner with a wink.

Minutes later they were both in their nightclothes and they sat on the loveseat to discuss their situation. For a change they weren't sitting particularly close, and even more remarkably, they weren't touching. Each wanted to make some headway on the issue, and both knew that distractions were easy to come by so they silently agreed to keep a polite distance.

"Mind if I lay out the problem as I see it?" Ryan asked when they were both settled.

"Please," Jamie agreed, always appreciative of Ryan's analytic mind.

"First we have the big issue—do we let go and have sex when we can find a private space, or do we make a firm decision to wait until we're both sure we're ready."

"Okay," Jamie started to interrupt but Ryan held her hand up, asking for patience.

"Once we decide on that, we need to find ways to implement the decision and make sure we stick with it. That's the harder part."

Jamie grinned shyly as she amended, "If we decide to go ahead, I don't think we'll have a problem sticking with it."

"Good point," Ryan smiled in return. "One fewer issue. So, how do you want to attack this?"

Slumping down further on the cushions, Jamie let her head rest upon the back of the loveseat and moaned, "I don't know! I'm so confused." Raising her head a few inches to be able to make eye contact, she plaintively asked, "Do you know what I mean?"

Gently patting her thigh, Ryan murmured, "Sure I do. There are a lot of issues to consider no matter what we do."

"Well, let's get those out first. Then we can make a rational decision."

"Okay," Ryan said, ticking off the points on her fingers. "If we decide to have sex, we need a place where we can be alone. But you don't want your roommates to know we're together yet, so I guess it has to be somewhere that we could use for a few hours, but not stay overnight."

"Gee, that sounds great! Why don't we go to one of those nice places in the Tenderloin?"

"Jamie, we won't be reduced to going to skid row," Ryan gently rebuked her. "Come on, stay open-minded."

"I'm sorry, I promised to behave," she said with a guilty grin.

"That's better," Ryan said as she patted her leg absently. "Okay, I got ahead of myself here. First we need to decide if we're each ready to have sex. If we had a place, are you feeling comfortable enough to take that leap?"

"Uhm," Jamie mumbled. "I uhm … I'm … well, it depends …"

"I'll take that as a no," Ryan said patiently. "Look, this is really about your comfort level. If you're not sure you're ready, you're not ready. It's that simple."

"But I am sometimes. Like tonight. If we had the opportunity, I'd have had you right there in the bar!"

"Honey, that's not making a decision. That's letting your vulva replace your brain."

"Ooo, now that's a pretty image," she giggled, shaking her head at the thought.

"You know perfectly well what I mean. We need to be adults about this. I've sworn off sex in cars—I can't go back to that. This is too important to me to be cavalier about." Her deep blue eyes glittered as the warm lamplight hit them, and

Jamie was moved by how sincere her partner was about protecting their nascent relationship.

"I'm sorry," she whispered. "It's important to me, too. Really it is."

"My take on this is that if you're not sure—all the time—then you're not ready. I think we should wait until we both agree on the when and the where."

Much as she hated to agree, Jamie nodded her head slowly. "That makes sense. I … uhm … I think I might be trying to avoid responsibility for the decision. Anna thinks that's kind of a pattern."

"Do *you* think it is?"

"Yeah, it is. Especially around sex. This is just what I did with Jack, and it's probably why we waited so long to have sex. I was waiting to be swept away with the emotion, but that's not fair—to you or to me."

"I agree," Ryan said. "So let's move to making sure we can implement our decision … and stick to it."

"That'll be the hard part," Jamie agreed. "Any ideas?"

"Yeah, but I don't like 'em."

"Tell me," Jamie urged.

"The easiest way is if we see each other less. Fewer opportunities will keep us safer."

"That sucks. What else ya got?"

"We see each other the same amount, but we spend less time kissing."

"Sucky idea number two. Anything else?"

"No showers?" she asked with a hopeful grin.

"No."

"Eat lots of garlic?"

"No. I can't even smell garlic on you. One more example of your perfection," Jamie teased as she tweaked her nose.

"Chaperones?"

"Now there's a good one. How about Cassie?"

"I'd rather skip showers," Ryan said crossing her arms over her chest.

"Hmm, I guess the only thing that makes sense is to kiss less and make sure it doesn't get too hot. But that's kinda counterproductive for me."

"Counterproductive? How?"

"This is really different for me. It's a good difference, but a difference nonetheless. Kissing you and touching you gets me really, really turned on and that's something that didn't happen much with men. I guess I'm allowing myself to get used to that feeling."

"And not having sex with you allows me to experience what it's like to be turned on and not be satisfied immediately," Ryan said. "And as frustrating as that is, I think it's good for me."

"Really?" Jamie asked shyly. "You really think you're learning something from this?"

Ryan grasped her hand and brought it to her lips. She kissed it gently on the palm and held it to her cheek for a moment. "I am, Jamie. I'm learning what it is that I want from sex."

"Tell me."

"I've learned that sex becomes lovemaking when we touch each other not just with out bodies, but with our souls. It's lovemaking when I welcome you to touch me in ways no one else ever has or ever will. It's lovemaking when I show you the essence of myself, stripped of pretense and façade. Lovemaking is sharing souls, Jamie. It's profound and poetic, intimate and intense. Nothing less will do when we're together." She trailed her fingers through Jamie's soft blonde hair and smiled as her partner snuggled close. "I've been with many, many, women, but I swear I've never made love before. When we share that experience, it's going to be a first for both of us."

"That was so beautiful," Jamie whispered as she lifted her head for several achingly tender kisses. "God, you take my breath away." She dropped her head onto Ryan's chest and nuzzled contentedly for a few minutes. "It's gonna be wonderful between us." Lifting her head she gazed right into Ryan's eyes. "I love you, Ryan."

"And I love you, Jamie." They cuddled together on the loveseat for a few minutes, nuzzling one another, until Jamie sat up and sneezed.

"I'm at a disadvantage here," she complained as she grasped a handful of Ryan's long hair.

Ryan immediately scrambled to get up. "Hand me a scissors."

"You goof! Sit right back down here and tell me how we're going to control ourselves."

Collapsing against the loveseat, Ryan said, "That isn't the easiest task I've ever been assigned." She sat for a few moments, then nodded decisively. "Okay, I've got a plan. I don't like it, but it's a plan."

"What is it?"

She looked slightly ill, but she swallowed and said, "I volunteer to keep us on the straight and narrow."

"Oh, honey, I can't ask you to do that!"

"You didn't ask. It was my idea. It's hazardous duty, but I think it's only fair that I volunteer."

"Fair? Why?"

Ryan shifted a little bit and traced her thumb down the baby-soft cheek as she cradled her partner's face in her hand. "This is brand-spanking new for you. Even ignoring the same-sex aspect, you haven't had much experience in playing with your libido. I want to give you that gift. I promise to do my very best to keep a lid on while you feel free to explore."

Jamie sat immobile for a moment, stunned by the overly generous offer. "I ... I don't think I can accept."

"Why? I really think this is the best way."

"It's too unequal. I don't want you to be responsible for both of us."

Ryan leaned forward and brushed Jamie's forehead with her lips. "I've been unleashing my rabid libido on innocent young women for six years," she said with a touch of hyperbole. "I think it'll be good for me to learn a little restraint. Please, let me do this … for us."

Jamie sat quietly for a moment, considering the offer carefully. "Are you really certain you won't resent me?"

"I'm positive. This is entirely my idea. I'll do my best to let you explore, but if it gets too hard I'll let you know. You just have to promise to pull back if I tell you to."

"Hmm, that might be tough," Jamie said, laughing. "But if you can offer nearly a mile I can go the last few feet."

"Deal." Ryan got up and walked over to the bed, flopping down on the surface as she spread her arms and legs wide. "Whenever you're ready," she offered, lifting her head to make eye contact.

"Get back over here, goofball," Jamie laughed. "We're not done."

"Boy, you sure do know how to take the fun out of an offer." She got up and settled herself on the loveseat once again. "What else?"

"I'm sure this isn't an open ended offer. I mean, you wouldn't want to do this for a year would you?"

"Aah, no," Ryan said immediately. "I'd be ready for the asylum."

"So we need to make some progress on our end-date."

Leaning forward, Ryan puckered up for a quick kiss. "You mean our beginning date."

"Precisely. Tell me your thoughts."

"I think I could muster some enthusiasm for just about any date you might pick," Ryan said thoughtfully. "How about you?"

Jamie pursed her lips and sat quietly while she considered the request. "I guess I'm pretty close right now. I'm still nervous and all, but I think you could help me through that."

Ryan smiled brightly and took Jamie's hand. "Okay! Let's do it!"

Pulling the giggling woman back down, Jamie said, "Slow down, hot stuff. I want to wait until we can make it special. I've promised myself that, and I don't want to go back on that promise."

Ryan draped her arm around her partner and pulled her close. "I want that too. Tell me about your dreams."

"Well, I have this … uhm … fantasy … about the first time we really make love." Her cheeks turned a little pink as she continued, "We're in a special place and we spend hours touching and kissing and touching some more. I want to touch and kiss every little part of you, one inch at a time. That's what lovemaking feels like to me."

"That's what it feels like to me too. That's exactly what I want. I'd be very happy if we waited until we had a place to focus on each other."

"It's more than the place. I need time, too … unstructured time, with no interruptions. I want you and your beautiful body to be the only thing on my mind."

"We can do this, I swear we can. But I think we've gotta wait until finals are over, no matter what. If we don't, I'm gonna see chemical formulas imprinted on your beautiful little body!"

"Okay," Jamie chuckled. "We'll revisit the issue after finals."

"Deal," Ryan said, extending her hand.

Jamie shook it firmly, pronouncing, "We make a good team, Ms. O'Flaherty."

"The best, Ms. Evans."

"Bed?" Jamie asked with a smile as she got up she extended a hand to her partner. "I left a new toothbrush out for you."

"Excellent. Be back in a minute."

After Ryan spent her normal five minutes brushing and flossing every surface of enamel, she went back into the room, pleased to see Jamie in bed already. "Boy, you look good in a horizontal position," she said with a grin. "What a wonderful sight to look forward to for the rest of my life."

"I bet you say that to all the girls," she said, blushing at the compliment.

"Unh-uh," Ryan said with a completely serious expression as she sat on the edge of the bed. "I've never told anyone that I wanted to see her every night for the rest of the month, much less my life. I don't tease about the commitment I'm making to you."

"Oh, I'm sorry," Jamie said, cupping Ryan's chin in her hand. "I'll be more careful. I know you're sensitive about this."

"It's okay," she said quickly. "I know you didn't mean anything by it."

"Come here and let me apologize more convincingly," Jamie beckoned, jerking her head towards Ryan's side of the bed.

Ryan dashed around to the other side and hopped in. They fidgeted around for a minute trying to get settled. "How do you like to sleep? Side, back, tummy?"

"I'm very versatile," Jamie said. "I can sleep about any way I fall, but I tend to wake up most often on my side. How about you?"

"When I sleep alone I curl up in the fetal position," Ryan said with a laugh. "I take up about a quarter of my bed at home. But when I sleep with someone, I'm usually on my back or side. I think the only time I've slept on my tummy was when you gave me that great massage on St. Patrick's Day."

"Why do you sleep differently with people?"

"I'm usually the larger person and women tend to cuddle up to me. It's apparently one of the perks of having a big girlfriend. And it's pretty comfortable to have someone snuggle up against my side with her head on my shoulder or chest."

"Like this?" Jamie asked as she nestled up tight against her side.

"Exactly. Feels good, doesn't it?"

"Yeah," she said softly.

"Hey, we didn't discuss which side of the bed you want. Any preference?"

"I don't think so. You?"

"No, not really. Which side did Jack sleep on?"

"My left," Jamie said immediately. "Always my left."

"Excellent," Ryan said, already in the correct position. "New administration. New side."

"As long as we're trying new things, why don't I lie on my back and you put your head on me?"

"Okey dokey," Ryan replied, knowing this experiment would be short-lived. She snuggled up against her smaller partner's right side and gently laid her head just above her breast.

"Ohh, this feels nice," Jamie said, happy that she had suggested the arrangement. She could run her fingers through the dark hair, and Ryan's fresh clean smell wafted up to fill her senses. "You've been hogging the good position," she gently chided.

"I like it down here," Ryan happily agreed. "I feel all safe and warm, like I'm in a snug little cocoon. I've been missing a lot up there."

They were quiet for a few moments and Ryan was nearly asleep when she heard the soft voice say, "Uhm … my arm's falling asleep."

"Okay, I'll move further in." Now her head was nearly on Jamie's sternum, but that obviously wasn't going to work as she heard her labored breathing. Finally she rolled onto her back and held her arm open, smiling to herself as her grateful partner climbed into her embrace.

"Remind me to start following your advice to begin with," Jamie said sleepily as she tossed both an arm and a leg across Ryan's body.

"Mmm, trapped like a rat. Just like I like it."

Chapter Four

Finals were three weeks away, and another few days of trying to spend every minute together was making both women nervous and a little irritable. Neither had ever fallen behind in her schoolwork, and it made each uncomfortable to do it now, so they decided to try to learn how to study together. On Wednesday, after a quick dinner, they headed over to the Biosciences Library for a couple of hours of concentrated effort.

The night started out promising enough, but within twenty minutes or so, Jamie looked up to find her companion staring at her with a vacant, lovesick expression. Jamie gave her a playful scowl and point firmly at her books. Another twenty or thirty minutes later, however, found the same goofy look coming her way, and she nodded indulgently and followed Ryan for a break.

The Biosciences Library was a very large building, five stories tall and usually jammed with people. But since Ryan spent so much time in the place, she knew where the quietest nook was. She led Jamie to the most distant part of the stacks and pounced on her with abandon. The spot wasn't ideal—the dusty, old, little-used books in this section could have brought on an allergy attack and there was no place to sit. But it was quiet and that was all that they cared about. They spent five minutes or so gently kissing and hugging, with Jamie putting every bit of effort into making sure that the kisses were loving enough to satisfy her partner, but innocent enough to allow Ryan to go back and study.

Even with these little intimacy breaks, by nine o'clock Ryan's gaze locked onto her and she refused to be dissuaded. So they packed up their books and walked back to the bike then jumped on for a quick trip to friendly territory. "Wanna head over to the bar?" Ryan asked.

"Uhm ... probably not a good idea. We could combust."

"How about the bookstore? I know Babs keeps a lot of fire extinguishers."

"You're on."

They had to endure a little teasing from Babs until Ryan revealed that they had no place else to go. Taking pity on her friend, Babs turned off the lamps flanking a low velvet loveseat and guided the women over. "It's nice and dark now girls, have fun!"

They dropped down into the sofa and spent a nice half hour languidly exploring each other's mouths. That night, and each night thereafter, Jamie made it a point to buy coffee or cocoa and some little snacks, telling Ryan, "If we're gonna take up this much space we've gotta eat something."

By Friday night, they were both much more comfortable with the way things were working out. Ryan was comfortable being turned on most of the night since Jamie seemed to be relaxing quite a bit. And she was able to release her pent-up frustrations as soon as she got home.

Early Saturday morning, Ryan answered the phone to hear a very chipper-sounding girlfriend. "I had a scathingly brilliant idea."

"Do tell."

"Remember my father's city apartment?"

"Yeah, you've mentioned it."

"I've got keys," she stated rather dramatically.

"But doesn't he use it sometimes?"

"Yeah, but usually only on a weekday, like if he has a real late meeting in the city. It saves him having to drive home and then come right back the next morning."

"So your plan involves what? Sleeping over?"

"Uhm, that's a little adventurous," Jamie said. "But a nice long afternoon of studying in bed and smooching sounds pretty good to me. How about you?"

A deep winsome sigh was sufficient response.

Ryan was sitting on the deck—anxiously awaiting her date when Jamie pulled up at two o'clock. She was grinning like a two-year-old as she ran down the stairs and Jamie had to spend a moment taking her in when she hopped into the car. "You are so incredibly beautiful today," she said as her eyes ran up and down Ryan's long body.

The day was clear and warm and Ryan had taken advantage of the temperature. She wore a v-necked, red knit, short-sleeved shirt with small horizontal lines in shades of blue. It was quite tight, hugging her voluptuous form firmly, and it ended a good two inches above her navel. Her long legs were covered by dark blue stretch chinos. The pants didn't have pockets, but if they had, Jamie would have been able to call heads or tails on the change she carried. Jamie hungrily observed that her girlfriend looked like she was about to burst forth from her tight clothes, and she hoped fervently that a poor quality thread had been used on the seams.

Ryan laughed at her dumbstruck expression and removed the band from her wrist to pull her hair back in a ponytail for the windy ride. "Yet another generous compliment," she said lightly as she patted Jamie on the thigh.

"Wow!" she mumbled as she leaned over and kissed her roughly, right in plain view of the neighbors.

Ryan had to struggle to focus after that scorcher and she privately mused that she would need to be on her guard all day.

The drive to Telegraph Hill was quick and pleasant on this lovely Saturday. They pulled into the subterranean garage and left the Porsche in the tandem space marked 'Evans'.

Never having been in a building with personalized parking spots, as they waited for the garage elevator, Ryan said, "Nice place."

"Thanks," Jamie replied, even though she had no real connection to the place.

Moments after entering the brass-toned elevator, they were deposited on the first floor of the lavishly decorated building. Jamie immediately steered Ryan towards the uniformed man sitting at a large circular workstation. Ryan held back, letting her partner do her thing.

Jamie's habitual need to engage every member of the service industry in a private conversation had become a little joke between them, and when Jamie returned she smiled at Ryan and reminded her, "Doormen need love too."

As they walked across the polished granite floor, Jamie cast a narrow eyed glance at her partner's squeaky running shoes, and as expected, Ryan just had to scuff her feet a tiny bit more in response. The little pink tongue that stuck out of those luscious mauve lips was a surprise, but most definitely a welcome one.

The generous lift whisked them to the top floor in seconds as Ryan fought with her ears to keep them open against the pressure. "They should supply gum in the lobby," she grumbled as she followed her partner along the sumptuous beige and maroon paisley carpet. The key slid into the lock and opened with a click, allowing Ryan to follow Jamie into the apartment that screamed 'a man lives here'.

"Wow," Ryan said as she looked around the obviously expensive, but equally obviously masculine apartment. "My father would die to live in a place like this."

"Wanna take a look around?"

"Sure. I love to see how people who have taste furnish their homes," she said with a smile.

"Mother furnished the place of course," Jamie said as she pointed out the two generous bedrooms, each with its own bath. Next was the sunny dining room with the very modern brushed aluminum glass-topped table and deep maroon Ultrasuede covered chairs with frames that matched the table base. Modern impressionistic art lined the walls, and Ryan noted that every print had been signed by the artist and numbered. Tiny slatted aluminum mini-blinds covered the generous windows, and with a smirk Ryan slid her finger across one of the slats to illustrate that they were dust-free.

"Does your father have a staff just for the blinds?"

"No, but he's a neat freak, so I'd guess he has them cleaned every week," Jamie admitted.

Next, she led Ryan to the living room and its matching black leather sofas, on the edge of the cranberry and slate gray tweed area rug. Small, modern chairs in a shiny, gray material filled out the living room perfectly. Ryan turned to her partner and said, "There's more sitting space in here than we have in our whole house." But her tone was matter-of-fact, so Jamie merely agreed rather than trying to discern if that fact bothered her.

The kitchen was last on the tour, but Ryan decided she like it most of all. It was even more modern than the rest of the apartment, but there was a lot more color in the small, windowless room. Bright, wild modern art filled the stark white walls, making the room look bigger and more interesting. The cabinets and the appliances were uniformly stainless steel, but the counters were black granite. The floor was a dark gray stone of some sort, and Ryan found that she liked the hard surface even though she mused it would be hard to stand on for long periods of time. But she needn't have worried about that fact. The kitchen actually looked as though it had never been used. Opening the Sub-Zero refrigerator, Ryan nodded to herself, commenting, "Wine, beer, sparkling water, Pepsi, orange juice, oh … there it is," she declared, emerging with a jar of salsa in her hand. "Food!"

"Hey, he's a guy," Jamie shrugged as she went back into the living room.

"Is this just your dad's place?" Ryan asked as she joined her on the black sofa.

"Yeah, I'd say so. My parents stay here together occasionally, but I don't think mother has ever been here alone. He uses it as a quick place to shower or take a nap if he has an important meeting in the evening. A lot of his time is spent wooing international clients, so he sometimes has a teleconference at midnight or even three or four in the morning. When he has those, it makes sense to stay here rather than drive down to Hillsborough."

"Yeah, that makes sense. So both of our fathers have to sleep away for work sometimes, huh?"

"After a fashion," Jamie agreed as she snuggled up to her partner. They nuzzled against each other for a few minutes trying to keep things light. But the mere thought of all of those luscious curves in those skin-tight clothes compelled Jamie to begin running her hands all over Ryan's body. "You are so delectable looking in this outfit."

"Glad you like it," Ryan's deep voice rumbled back. "You don't think this shirt is too tight do you?" she asked in a faux innocent tone.

Jamie blew out a laugh as she sat up and smirked at her partner. "I'd like you in Caitlin's clothes, you silly goose!"

"Hmm, she has a hot, little, yellow terry cloth number I might borrow. Would I look good with little embroidered ducks dancing across my chest?"

"I don't know about ducks," Jamie whispered, "but I'd like to take a turn across that dance floor."

"My, my, Ms. Evans, you are the little minx today," Ryan teased as she tried to lighten the mood again. "Hey, is it just me, or is it hot in here? I'm dying of thirst."

"Oh-oh, my bad," Jamie replied as she hopped up and headed for the kitchen. On the way she made a stop at the thermostat to turn on the air conditioning in the seldom-used unit, joining her partner moments later with a sheepish grin and two large bottles of mineral water. "Sorry about that," she chuckled as she handed one over to her sweating lover.

"To tell you the truth, I didn't notice until about two minutes ago," Ryan laughed. They managed to gulp down most of the liter bottles without pause, trying to hydrate themselves.

"Wanna go to bed and cuddle while we do a little studying?" Jamie asked.

"Sure. Although I doubt we'll get much done." Ryan gamely picked up her book bag. They chose the guest room and together removed the bedspread and blanket before they kicked off their shoes and made themselves comfortable.

Several minutes later they were busy studying—but not their books. Jamie was intent on trying to examine Ryan's skin through her clothes and, even though she wasn't very successful, neither was complaining. Ryan was surprisingly in control since she had been expecting a full frontal attack. She was about to call a halt to the proceedings when they both froze in wild-eyed shock.

"Jamie?" boomed a voice from the entryway.

"My father!" she mouthed as she scrambled to her feet. "Get in the closet!" Before Ryan could utter a sound, her partner was dashing out the door and running down the hallway to meet her father.

Get in the closet! Not for you or any other woman on earth! But her love for the gentle woman she had held in her arms moments earlier got the better of her, and she silently put her shoes back on and climbed under the king-sized bed. *Never the closet,* she righteously declared.

The minutes ticked away, and with each sweep of the second hand Ryan felt her temper rise. She wasn't angry that Jamie was unwilling to reveal the nature of their relationship to her parents. Her years of experience with friends and kids on the teen talk line had given her ample evidence of how difficult that step was. But she was still nearly speechless that Jamie had denied her very existence. There were at least one hundred ways to handle this situation, and she honestly thought her partner had chosen the worst one. And as each scenario flashed through her mind, she grew more and more agitated.

"Daddy!" Jamie nearly shouted when she reached the living room. She had managed to straighten her hair into a reasonable facsimile of its usual order, and she offered up a silent prayer of thanks that she was not dating a lipstick lesbian.

"You're the last person I'd expect to find here, Jamie," he said. "But it's a very nice surprise."

"I was over here … uhm … in the city … uhm … working out," her mind rapidly constructed a reasonable lie. "And I've got plans in the city later tonight so I stopped by here for a little nap."

"Oh, I didn't wake you did I, cupcake?"

"No, not at all, I was already awake. I've been here for a while."

He walked into the living room and noticed the two water bottles on the coffee table. "My, you must have been working out," he laughed. "That's an enormous amount of water for one girl to drink. What were you doing that was so energetic?"

"Uhm," she fumbled, *all of my saliva's in Ryan's mouth* didn't seem like a good answer, so she opted for a lie. "I was on a long ride. Guess I got dehydrated."

"I didn't see your bicycle on your car. Is it up here?" he asked, looking around quizzically.

"Oh, no, I rode with a friend and left it at their house." *God, I'm already using 'their' as a substitute for 'her' and I don't even know the secret handshake.*

"Well, I must say I'm proud of the effort you're putting into this ride. I didn't know you had this kind of determination."

"Thanks," she said weakly, trying to figure out how to get out of the house. "Why are you here, Daddy?"

"I played golf with some clients at the club and I've got a charity dinner to attend tonight. I thought I could catch a nap before I have to get into my tuxedo."

"Well don't let me stop you," she urged. "I was about to get going anyway."

"I'd rather spend the afternoon with my daughter any time," he said. "But if you're ready, I'll walk you down to your car."

"No! No, really, that's not necessary. You go on and lie down."

"Jamie, I'm only forty-five," he chided. "And besides, I had to park behind you in the tandem spot. Let's go down together."

"'Kay," she said weakly. "Uhm … I left something in the bedroom. Be right back." She scampered into the room, closing the door almost in his face. Silently padding over to the closet, she opened the louvered doors and practically fainted when she saw that it was empty. But when she turned, she saw a dark head peeking out from under the tailored bed skirt. Dropping to her knees, she whispered, "He wants to walk me to the car. Then he's going to take a nap. Wait ten minutes after you hear him get back and then come down to the lobby. I'll drive around until you get there, okay?" Her eyes were wild with fright, so Ryan swallowed her displeasure at the rude treatment she'd been subjected to. She merely nodded and slid back under the bed.

Ryan lay on her back waiting for the door to open again. It took much longer than she expected, but she finally heard it open and close quietly. She set the timer on her watch, since her sense of time was obviously off, and settled back down to wait. But no more than two minutes had passed before she heard a gentle knock on the front door. *That must be Jamie coming back for something.* She pricked up her ears, listening intently for information. *That better not be Jamie,* she thought with horror as a woman's shrieking, giggling voice wafted to her ears. *Please let that be her mother,* she prayed, but she had a pretty good idea that the voice was not, in fact, Mrs. Evans.

"Oh! Stop that! I said stop that!" the young-sounding woman cried. "Oooh! Put me down!" Luckily, her cries were playful as Ryan thought about what she would do if she sounded serious. *That would be quite the introduction; Mr. Evans, unhand that woman! Who am I? Never mind who I am, just release that innocent young thing, you beast!*

The playful cries continued into the master bedroom, where Ryan heard a loud thump as he obviously granted the woman's wish to put her down. Now, loud giggles replaced the screams, and moments later she heard the woman dart down the hallway, with the heavier footsteps of Mr. Evans right behind her. "Come back here," he cried as he obviously chased her around the apartment. *Please, oh please don't let her run in here,* Ryan begged as she heard them dart down the hall again.

The chase continued back and forth between the bedroom and the living room. She hoped that he would finally catch her in the living room, since it was on the far end of the apartment, farthest both from the bedroom she was in and the front door. After a good ten minutes of shrieks and laughter, the chase seemed to stop. Now, she heard only an occasional cry. *Hmm, if they're going at it in the living room I could get out. I think I'll sneak over to the door and crack it open for more information.*

When she did, she actually blushed to hear the woman's voice echo through the apartment in a rough moan, "Oh, God! Yes! Do it, baby! Ooh, God, you're so big!"

Do they really believe that line? she marveled as she grabbed her book bag and tip-toed out the door only to stop in shock when she turned to find Jamie's dad, pants around his knees, humping a woman right on the elegant carpet runner, not ten feet from her. She had never felt so totally stunned, and her first instinct was to crawl back under the bed and wait until Mr. Evans left for his dinner. But she had a small glimmer of hope, since they were facing away from her. Even though a part of her wanted to poke her own eyes out after seeing Mr. Evans' bare ass, the position of the lovers guaranteed that either Mr. Evans would have to turn around or his 'date' would have to sit up—and neither prospect seemed likely. So she swallowed her fears and crept soundlessly across the hall. But to her horror, the very young, curly-haired redhead struggled into a semi-upright position, bracing her torso on her locked arms. Ryan was exactly halfway across the hall, but since it was as far to retreat as to move on she continued. Opening the door an inch at a time she slid out without detection. "Whew! That was close," she mumbled aloud. But her relief was short-lived when she realized that she had to use all of her acting talents to appear normal when she faced her girlfriend in a few minutes.

"Where in the hell have you been?" Jamie demanded when Ryan slid into the Porsche moments later.

"He was running around the apartment forever! I couldn't leave until I knew he was … occupied."

"Jesus!" Jamie moaned as her head dropped onto the steering wheel. "My entire life flashed before my eyes when I heard him come in."

"Because …" Ryan said, her ire beginning to rise again.

"He might have seen you … I mean us."

"That would have been tragic," Ryan snapped. Grabbing the door handle, she flung it open as Jamie was slowing for a stop sign. Before Jamie could even blink, Ryan was walking briskly down the street, a determined set to her shoulders.

Stuck on Lombard Street on Telegraph Hill, penniless, no change for the phone, and mightily pissed off were the best descriptions of Ryan's state. *How dare she! How dare she! She's actually ashamed of me!*

She was striding down the street, nearly oblivious to her surroundings. Her internal homing device was leading her in the right direction, but she was clearly not paying conscious attention. Telegraph Hill was probably the most distant point from her house in the whole city, and she knew she had a couple of hours of walking over the hills before she reached home. She decided there was only one good thing about her situation. It would give her a chance to cool down and reflect a bit on the whole terrible afternoon.

As soon as Ryan fled, Jamie pulled the Boxster up to the curb and sat numbly for a few minutes, trying to figure out what had happened and what she should do next. *What in the hell is she so upset about? She knows I'm not ready to tell my father. And to have him find us together in the bedroom would be a horrible way for him to find out.* She felt her head hit the steering wheel as she tried her best to open her mind and try to see the incident from Ryan's perspective, but she was having a devil of a time getting past her own hurt. Without warning it hit her—Ryan wouldn't have acted that way if she hadn't been deeply wounded. Going over and over the scene, she realized how terrible it must have felt for such a proud, self-assured woman to have to sneak out of an apartment so her lover's father wouldn't find out about her. *Jesus!* she cried as she thumped her head against the wheel repeatedly. *How could you have done that to her?*

As the minutes passed, she was yanked from her reverie when she was struck by the thought that Ryan couldn't have had any money. *She didn't have any pockets in those pants. And her book bag is right here. Oh shit! I let her get out on Telegraph Hill to walk all the way to Noe. That's criminal!* Throwing the car into gear, she pulled into traffic, nearly getting sideswiped by a passing car. *Shit!* she continued in her rant, ignoring the close call. *She had loafers on too, so she couldn't run even if she wanted to.* Making up her mind immediately, she started to slowly prowl up and down the streets that would lead Ryan to Market, the obvious choice to cross the city. She crept down Sansome, Montgomery and Geary, looking at every pedestrian she passed. Knowing that Ryan could have been walking very fast, she decided to proceed to Market and patrol it until her peripatetic lover appeared.

It didn't take long to get over to Market in the light Saturday afternoon traffic, but the street itself was a mess as it was at almost any time of day. The MUNI buses stopped constantly, blocked traffic fully, and were a general nuisance. The constant stream of tourists—who also drove the street—made it a nightmare much of the time, and this day the added issue of street repair made the trip even worse than normal.

After a few blocks, Jamie spotted her partner's dark head bobbing down the crowded street. She missed her for a few blocks since Ryan was moving faster than traffic, but finally pulled up at the corner that she would cross in a few feet. "Ryan!" she cried, but either the street noise blocked her out, or her lover was intentionally ignoring her. "RYAN!" she tried again, but the pedestrians had a walk light and the tall woman strode off again.

They played this cat-and-mouse game for another few blocks with the same result. Her patience was starting to fray as she came to believe Ryan was intentionally ignoring her. She cut around a pack of slow cars, nearly going into opposing traffic. But she finally got well in front of the dark haired form she could see approaching in the distance. Just when it seemed like she would intercept her, Ryan crossed to the other side of the street, neatly avoiding her once again. "*God damn it!*" Jamie shouted to no one in particular.

Now she had to turn across traffic, try to get ahead on a side street and then double back. But this task was much harder than it sounded, and it took her almost fifteen minutes to execute it. Just when she was about to yell Ryan's name again, a MUNI bus pulled up to the curb, obscuring her view and preventing Ryan from seeing her even if she wanted to. Now frustrated beyond good sense, she pulled up to the first spot she could fit in and parked. It was clearly not a legal space, and she knew she would get a ticket at best, but she was not going to be ignored like this when she was doing her best to apologize. She started running in the proper direction, but now she had lost her even though there was really only one way to go. "*Ryan!*" she cried as she stared up at the heavens in supplication. She scanned the street in both directions and caught sight of the top of her head—once again—across the street. "I'll kill her!" she yelled as she raced back to her car.

The officer who was writing the ticket was pleasant enough, and he informed her that she was a very lucky woman since he was about to call a tow truck. She tersely thanked him for the $105 present and once again took off, now madder than a hornet. This time she took no chances. She raced ahead of traffic, flaunting several sections of the vehicle code, but she got a good two blocks ahead of Ryan. This was a less-populated section of the busy street, and she pulled up next to a bona fide parking meter. Finding quarters in her wallet was another stroke of luck, and she fed the meter before taking off running back toward her lover. Playing it safe, she watched both sides of the street, but didn't spot Ryan until she was nearly even with her—on the other side of the street, of course. "Oh, no you don't!" she declared as she darted across the street—against traffic. She dashed a few feet, neatly bobbing and weaving to avoid the thankfully slow-moving glut of cars, then ran the rest of the way, narrowly escaping another close call with a Yellow Cab. Her heart was racing from excitement and anger when she finally caught up with the brunette. Without thinking, she impetuously grabbed her shoulder and hauled her around forcefully, forgetting for a moment who she was approaching so aggressively.

Ryan later swore that she hadn't known that Jamie had been following her. She vowed that she'd had no idea it was a friendly hand that was roughly grabbing her on the noisy, rather seedy street. And she pledged that she was truly, truly sorry for grabbing the startled woman by the throat and slamming her up against the plate glass window of a Subway sandwich shop so hard that her teeth rattled and her eyes rolled up in her head.

"Jamie!" she cried in horror when she realized the frightened face that looked up at her was not the armed attacker her body had prepared her for, but the normally gentle visage of her lover. "Oh my God!" Jamie sank to the ground in slow motion, Ryan too stunned to even attempt to catch her. A crowd gathered, mumbling among themselves about the big woman hitting the smaller one for no reason at all.

Jamie was conscious but stunned as she sat on the filthy concrete and tried to gather her senses. "I'm so sorry, I'm so sorry!" Ryan gasped, running her hands all over her lover's face and shoulders, trying to determine if she was seriously injured.

A few rough shakes of her head allowed Jamie's mind to clear enough to finally make eye contact. She leveled her gaze and asked the most hurtful question that had ever reached Ryan's ears. "Did you know it was me?"

The looks of shock, horror and astonishment that crossed her partner's face were enough to reassure her, but Ryan cried again and again, "No! God, no! I would never, never, ever hurt you! Don't you know that? My God, what do you think I am?" Now the tears started to flow as Ryan collapsed on the ground right next to the still-shaken woman. She cried disconsolately, attracting stares from everyone within ten feet, many of whom were witnesses to the whole scene. Jamie shakily got to her knees and wrapped her arms around her lover, murmuring comforting words to her as the sobs shook her body. It took a long while to calm the emotionally devastated woman, but finally they were both able to walk. Several of the witnesses made snide remarks about what had caused the lover's tiff, but both women ignored them, trying to maintain what small amount of dignity they still had.

The car was only about a block away, and they made the trip in silence. They were both fully aware that each had hurt the other grievously, but neither was exactly sure what she had done. Both were sure they were relatively blameless in the big scheme of things, but again, they didn't want to make a terrible situation worse, so they both held their tongues. When they reached the car, Ryan insisted that she be allowed to drive. Jamie allowed her to take the keys and didn't protest when they went to the O'Flaherty house.

Ryan pulled in front of the garage and got out to help her shaky friend into the house. Regrettably, Martin, Conor, and Brendan were all present, although all were speechless when they saw their faces. Ryan shook her head in reply to their silent questions, leading Jamie straight down to her room. Once she got Jamie settled on the loveseat, she dashed back up stairs for an ice bag. Three sets of anxious eyes were waiting for her. "Nothing serious," she said. "We had a fight and I got out of the car. I was walking and she grabbed me unexpectedly from behind and I threw her against a window. She's got a bump on the head, but nothing major."

Now, all three mouths dropped open to match the wide eyes. Ryan had to admit that the truth was pretty bad, but she didn't like to withhold information from her family, even if the information made her look like an asshole. "I've got to go back down," she said as she filled a big, plastic bag with ice. "Give us some time to work this out, okay?" Three heads nodded gravely as she ran back down stairs.

"How could any day that started off so nice end up so horribly?" Jamie asked plaintively when her lover returned, ice bag in hand.

"I don't know." Ryan sat next to her and gently applied the ice to the sizeable knot forming on the back of Jamie's skull. Ryan was inordinately glad they were at least speaking now, but she was loath to go into all of the issues that had made the afternoon so tumultuous.

"Can we not talk about it all?" Jamie asked timidly. Ryan nodded her complete agreement, looking rather uncomfortable as she sat on the edge of the piece. "But I'd love it if you'd hold me."

Ryan rushed to comply with the request. She sat very close and put the ice on her shoulder, urging Jamie to sit back and rest her head up against the bag.

After ten minutes or so, a small voice said, "The cold is giving me a headache. Can you take it away for a while?"

"Sure," Ryan said. "Wanna lie down on the bed and cuddle?"

"Yeah." Ryan helped her up then climbed up on the right side of the bed and waited for her lover to get in. They were both fully clothed, but had kicked off their shoes. After a few minor adjustments, they were as comfortable as they were going to get and within minutes both were sound asleep, the excitement, anger and hurt combining to drain each of them physically as well as emotionally.

Seconds after they had nodded off, Ryan jerked into a sitting position, scaring Jamie half out of her wits. "What's wrong?" Jamie panted, her heart racing.

"It's dangerous to sleep with a head injury!"

"It's okay," Jamie assured her. "I didn't lose consciousness you know. It's just a bump ... really."

Ryan slowly sank back down onto the mattress. "You're sure?" she mumbled through a yawn.

"Positive," Jamie said as she started to lightly rub her partner's back.

It was nearly eight o'clock when Ryan slowly woke—hungry, groggy and stiff from the uncomfortable position they were in. During the nap, Jamie had migrated closer and closer until she was sprawled across Ryan's body. The weight prohibited Ryan from moving at all, and her body was unhappy about the two-hour-long confinement. But stiff as she was, she was unwilling to wake Jamie. They had an awful lot of issues to work out, and many wounds to heal, and she wasn't in a hurry to get to any of them. *There was a certain simple beauty to casual sex*, she mused. *I didn't get my emotional needs met very often, but I also didn't ever get stomped on.* She knew in her heart that being with Jamie was worth any amount of pain, but she had to admit that today's pain would require an awful lot of pleasure to equalize it.

Jamie woke a few minutes later. "Mmm, what time is it?" she croaked out in a sleep-roughened voice.

"Little past eight. You wanna get up?"

"Yeah, I'm kinda hungry." She rolled off and let out a sigh. "Kinda stiff too." After a moment to recall that she'd been sleeping on another human being, she turned to her lover. "You must be stiff too with me draped across you all evening."

"Little bit," she agreed, uncommunicative and wary.

"Hungry?"

"Yeah."

"Feel like talking?"

"No. Not really."

"Feel like being with your family?"

"Unh-uh."

"Want me to go home?"

"Only if you want to."

"Will you talk if I stay?"

"Not sure."

Jamie got to her feet and padded into the bath. She spent a moment ordering her hair and washing her face with Ryan's nice-smelling soap. When she went back into the bedroom, she said, "I'm willing to hang out if you'll at least try to talk with me. But I don't want to bang my head against the …" She stopped abruptly when she saw the hurt, pain-filled eyes before her. "Ryan," she said gently as she squatted in front of the bed to maintain eye contact, "we need to talk."

"I'll try," was the terse answer as her gaze flitted everywhere but Jamie's face.

"That's all I ask." She held her hand out, and Ryan grasped it, getting to her feet and performing a few stretches to work out the kinks. Ryan spent a moment putting on a pair of socks and her running shoes, made a trip to the bathroom and was ready to go. Jamie said, "Let's walk over to 24th Street for some dinner, okay?"

A reserved nod was Ryan's only reply, and Jamie mused that her efforts to talk were less than overwhelming. But she decided to be patient and allow a conversation to develop over time. A very brief explanation to an anxious looking Martin, and they were walking downhill to the business district of the Noe Valley. Ryan didn't say a word on the walk, but when they reached their destination she asked, "What are you in the mood for?"

"Uhm, something kinda bland. My tummy's kind of upset."

"How about Peasant Pies?"

"I've never heard of 'em. What are they?"

"It's a little shop that sells home-made pot pies. They're really good," she said with her first smile of the evening.

Ahh, that's the key, Jamie thought as they walked along, *she can never maintain a bad mood when food's involved.* But to her surprise and displeasure, Ryan was able to maintain her bad mood all through their delicious dinner. She wasn't openly hostile and would answer direct questions, but she was guarding her emotions very carefully and Jamie wondered if it wouldn't be better to go home and just let her be.

After dinner, Ryan suggested they head over to The Dubliner for a pint. *Maybe alcohol is the key,* Jamie hoped as she quickly agreed.

A pint of Harp Lager seemed to be the solution. They grabbed a tiny table in the rear of the bar, and as soon as Ryan took a sip of her beer she was verbal. "I think we each have some things to say and I have a feeling that some of them won't be pleasant to hear. So I think we should each give our laundry list of why we're upset. I promise not to comment on or dispute anything you say if you'll grant me the same courtesy." She was staring at Jamie with an open, unwavering gaze.

"Okay," she replied, thinking that Ryan had never sounded more like a prosecutor. "I'll do my best. Do you want to start?"

A quick shake of her dark head was the answer. "I'd prefer if you do."

"All right," Jamie said slowly as she took in a deep breath and tried to order her thoughts. "My biggest issue is that I'm angry that you jumped out of the car with no money. I really wanted to go home and think about what happened, but I couldn't leave you once I realized that you didn't have any way to get home. If I hadn't had to chase you, I wouldn't have gotten this knot on my head," she said with a grimace as she reached up to gently touch the lump. Ryan was still silent, completely passive. "While I was following you, I believed you were intentionally avoiding me. I thought you heard me and were just in a funk and refused to stop for me. That's why I asked you if you knew it was me when you tossed me against the wall. I'd been chasing you since Montgomery Street, Ryan. I parked the car once and got a $105 ticket for being in a bus stop. I had been practically driving on the sidewalk to get your attention, and since I believed that you were intentionally avoiding me I was a little rough with you when I finally caught you. I know it hurt you that I asked if you knew it was me, and I want you to understand why I said that." She reached over and grasped the tanned hand that lay on the table, the dim candlelight dancing in faint patterns against her skin. Pulling the hand to her face she gently kissed the palm before placing it back down onto the table. "I love you, Ryan, and I know how much you love me. In my rational mind, I know you would never hurt me. But I was out of my mind with frustration." Grasping and cradling the warm hand again, she said, "I'm very sorry I hurt you and I hope you can forgive me."

After a few moments Ryan's gaze gentled, and she asked, "Finished?" At Jamie's small nod, she asked, "Do you mind if I kiss you?"

"In here?" She looked around at the very heterosexual crowd.

Ryan nodded with a small smile on her face. "This is Noe Valley," she reminded her.

"And?"

"Noe Valley has the biggest lesbian neighborhood in the city. People are very used to lesbians here. It's very common to see women being affectionate."

"I didn't know that! I swear you've never told me that."

"Is that a yes?" she asked, blue eyes twinkling in the low flame.

"Of course," Jamie said. "You never need permission for that."

Ryan smiled down at her as she rose in her seat and leaned over the table, capturing Jamie's lips for one chaste, gentle kiss. "Thanks for the apology." She smiled as she lowered herself back into her chair. "My turn?"

Jamie nodded silently and steeled herself for the blow she feared was coming. "I felt like you were ashamed of me," Ryan said quietly. "When your dad came in there were a number of options you could have chosen, but you picked the one that was the most humiliating for me. I'm proud of my love for you and I'm proud that you've chosen me to love. It hurt me deeply that the first time you had the opportunity to introduce me to your family, you not only didn't, you tried to make me disappear." She paused to let her complaint sink in and then continued. "I'm sorry I left you so abruptly. But I was hurt, and I didn't think I could hide my feelings so I thought it best to go. In retrospect, that wasn't a kind thing to do. I should have let you drive me home. I'm sorry for that, Jamie."

Her partner reached for her hand again and gave it a gentle squeeze.

Ryan brought her small hand up and gave it a kiss. "Thanks," she said, acknowledging the forgiveness. "My only other issue is how hurt I was when you asked if I knew it was you who grabbed me. That really hurt, Jamie, but I accept your apology, and I think I understand why you said it. And just for the record," she said as she squeezed her hand and stared right into her eyes, "I had no idea you were following me. I was in a real fog—I almost got lost getting to Market."

"Finished?" Jamie asked. At Ryan's nod, she leaned over the table and puckered up. "Thanks," she said softly as Ryan rose to kiss her lightly. "Now what?"

"Well," Ryan said as she reflected on the points they'd each made, "now we talk. But I need a fresh pint to relax. You?" she asked as she held up her empty glass.

"Not yet."

Ryan hopped up and carried on a few minutes of banter with the bartender, a woman that Jamie remembered from St. Patrick's Day. She made a show of refusing Ryan's money, demanding a kiss as payment. Ryan willingly complied, giving her a friendly kiss on the lips. Jamie was quite glad to find that the casual touch didn't make her jealous in the least.

Ryan sat back down, took a deep breath and said, "The only open issue is how you felt when your father came in."

"I know," Jamie nodded, taking a bit sip of her beer. "I admit that I freaked. And I couldn't be sorrier that I didn't use my rational mind and introduce you. But I'm not ready to come out to everyone yet. Please don't think I'm a wimp, Ryan, but I'm not ready. I have to feel comfortable first and I think that'll still take a while. Do you understand?"

Leaning over, Ryan gently kissed Jamie's cheek and nodded slightly. "I understand. I mean, I had a very supportive family and I lived in a lesbian neighborhood and it was hard for me. I don't want to rush you, Jamie, but I want you to promise that you'll work toward being open with everyone."

"I promise, Ryan," she said as she reached over and took a big gulp of Ryan's beer. "Does that cover your feeling that I was ashamed of you?"

"A little," she said, taking a matching gulp. "I guess it would have made me feel better to have you at least introduce me as your friend. Being told to get in the closet was really harsh. I wouldn't have played that game for any other woman."

"I know, I know," she muttered, dropping her head into her hands. "It was just a panicked reaction. There's no one on this earth whom I could be more proud of. You're an extraordinary woman, and I promise you'll be sick of me singing your praises to everyone I know. But right now this fear is about me—just me."

"Okay," Ryan agreed, draining her glass. "Another?"

"I'll buy this one," she said with a grin. "One kiss a night from other women is your new limit, hot stuff." With that, she sauntered over to the bar and ordered another Harp, this time from the other bartender, who gladly accepted her money.

When she sat back down, Ryan said, "I promise I'll give you as much time as you need to be open about our relationship. Just let me know if you need my help."

"Constantly," she said as she rested her head on Ryan's shoulder. "I've got to say, Ms. O'Flaherty, that if I'm gonna fight with someone, you'd be the one I'd choose. If I could've had a discussion like this with Jack, we'd still be together."

"Good thing for me he couldn't manage it!"

"It wasn't just him," Jamie said, smiling. "I was no better than he was at talking things through. You're so emotionally evolved. It's like you're a member of some super race of highly evolved creatures sent here to educate the lower animals."

Ryan picked up her glass and inspected it. "You've had enough," she decreed.

Around eleven o'clock, Brendan popped his head into the bar. He made eye contact with the bartender and gave her a quizzical look. She smiled back and pointed to the rear corner of the place. When his gaze followed hers, he stuck his head back outside. "Conor!" he called down the street. "They're in here!" His brother loped down the block from the bar he had been investigating. When he arrived, Brendan asked, "Should we go in or go home and tell Da they're okay?"

"Let's go in. I got thirsty looking all over the neighborhood."

They entered the dark space, but stopped almost immediately when they caught sight of the couple. Neither man had seen Jamie since Ryan's announcement, and they were both uncomfortable with this new dimension to their relationship. Neither was unhappy with the development, but it was a major change and they were each skittish. The young lovers were at the rearmost table, in the darkest part of the bar. Their chairs were shoved close, and Jamie was cuddled up to their sister's side, her blonde head resting on Ryan's broad chest. Ryan was obviously speaking to her, her breath slightly ruffling her hair. A sweet slow smile bloomed across Jamie's coral-tinted lips and she laughed a bit at something Ryan said. They were oblivious to every other patron and when the boys walked up, Ryan looked up at them like they were the last people she expected to see. "Uhm … hi, guys," she finally got out.

Jamie shot up, embarrassment evident on her flushed face. "Hi," she squeaked out.

Ryan noticed the change in her mood and tried to normalize the situation. "Have a seat, boys. The least you can do is buy your new sister-in-law a beer."

Both men grinned in response and went to the bar to buy a round. When they returned, each kissed Jamie on the cheek and toasted her. "Welcome to the family," Brendan said, gracing her with the patented O'Flaherty high wattage smile. "I couldn't be happier for you both."

Conor chimed in gallantly, "If I can't have you, Ryan's the one I'd pick."

"Thank you both," Jamie said, now at ease. "I'm sorry about earlier today, guys. We had a terrible afternoon, but everything's fine now."

"How's your head?" Brendan delicately asked.

"Head?" she asked, rather confusedly. "Oh! My head." She hoisted her glass. "Enough of these little babies can obviously soothe a silly little bump."

"Well, I'm glad you're okay," he said. "Da's worried about you both, you know. But I assume he'll figure we found you if we're gone long enough."

"Call him," Jamie urged, handing Brendan her cell phone.

He accepted the device and made the call, assuring Martin that all was well. "Okay, Da, I'll tell her," he said as he hung up. Handing the phone back to Jamie he announced, "Da says you're to stay over tonight. Rory's out of town on a gig and his room is being prepared even as we speak."

"No argument from me," she said as she tried to stifle a yawn. "Last thing I need is a DUI. A $105 ticket is enough for one day."

"What in the heck happened to you two?" Conor finally demanded, tired of being discreet.

Ryan laughed at his usual directness. "We had a fight when we were down around Telegraph Hill this afternoon," she said, skimping on the details. "I got mad and pulled my usual."

Both boys supplied, "You took off."

"Yeah," she said with a blush. Turning to Jamie she related, "It's kind of a habit. Anyway, Jamie knew I didn't have any money, so she tried to track me down. She thought I knew she was on my tail, and when she finally caught me she grabbed me from behind. But I didn't know she was looking for me and when I felt a stranger grab me …" She let them imagine the end to the story.

"God, Jamie," Conor said with wide eyes. "You're lucky she only tossed you against a wall. She could have easily broken your nose or your jaw. You should never, ever surprise her like that."

"Now you tell me," she laughed. "I mean, I know she's trained in the martial arts … I guess it didn't dawn on me."

"It's not a joke," Brendan said. "She can hurt you badly before she even knows what she's doing. Years of training like she's had just don't go away."

"I'll remember," she said with a smile as she grasped Ryan's hand. "I knew she was lethal with women. I just didn't know it would be me."

Ryan leaned over and kissed her gently. "I'm going to do my best to take myself off high alert status. You're too precious to ever take a risk with."

It was after midnight when they climbed the short hill to the O'Flaherty home. Brendan kissed the girls goodnight and continued on up the street to his own apartment just a few blocks away. When they entered the house, Martin was already in bed, but there was a note in the kitchen that welcomed Jamie and stated Rory's room was ready for her. "Oh yeah, like you'll use it," Conor teased, regarding the one hundred and ten pound appendage that his sister had grown.

"Oh, yes she will," Ryan said. "Da doesn't want us to sleep together so we won't."

Jamie had been remarkably quiet during this discussion, and when Conor made eye contact with her he noticed that her conviction seemed quite a bit weaker than his sister's. He'd heard the girls kissing all the way back to the house, and he'd had to stop himself from laughing when he'd heard his sister squeal a few times and beg Jamie to behave herself. "We'll see," he smirked as he gave each of them a kiss goodnight. "Have fun, lovebirds."

Ryan shot him a glare as she escorted her partner downstairs to find some acceptable pajamas. She rooted through her drawers and chose the same outfit they had shared before. A T-shirt and flannel pants for herself and the matching flannel shirt for Jamie. Turning to hand the shirt to the suddenly quiet woman, she was rather shocked to see her peeling off her sweater. Ryan didn't mind the display, in fact she welcomed it, but since it wasn't in character, she assumed it was because of the drink. So she tossed her the shirt and scampered into the bath to change, hoping Jamie would be clothed when she returned.

Her wish was granted, and when she opened the door Jamie was lying across her bed—outside of the covers that had been neatly turned back. "Can I tuck you in?" Her voice was lower than normal, and her eyes burned with seduction. It was the most frankly sexual look Ryan had seen on Jamie's face, and even though she was delighted that it was part of her new lover's repertoire, it was a few weeks too early to put it to much use.

"Why don't you let me take you upstairs?"

"Unh-uh," Jamie demurred. "I don't want Conor to hear us."

"Uhm … how noisy is it to tuck someone in?"

"Wait and see," she purred as she patted the mattress. "Come on." She was crooking a finger to lure her in, and Ryan tried to steel herself in the war being waged between her conscience and her libido.

She didn't want to reject Jamie out of hand, but she knew how thin the ice she was treading on was. Tentatively, she approached and sat down on the edge of the bed rather gingerly. The alcohol was working very well at loosening Jamie's inhibitions, but it did nothing to dull her reflexes. She lunged for Ryan and tumbled her onto the bed, kissing her with a wild fury.

Jamie draped a leg over Ryan's pelvis then began to slide across her until she was sitting on her hips. Her arms were locked possessively around Ryan's neck, kissing her without a hint of her normal gentleness. Even though Ryan usually loved the tender, sweet way that Jamie kissed her, the aggression of tonight's attack appealed to a moistening, swelling part of her body. Jamie's breasts were firm with arousal, and her nipples were so hard that Ryan could feel their outline through her T-shirt.

As Jamie's tongue probed her mouth she begin to shift her hips, grinding herself against Ryan's belly. This was too much for even Ryan's prodigious self-control, and she struggled to think of a way to honor their agreement. While she still had a shred of self-control she flipped her partner onto her side and spooned up against her back. While her hands glided up and down Jamie's writhing body she whispered, "I want you to slide your hand down and touch yourself, baby. Think of how you'd like me to touch you, of how you want me to kiss you, to love you. I'll be right upstairs, touching myself, wishing you were in my bed loving me." She smiled to herself when she felt goose bumps rise on Jamie's neck. "I love you, Jamie. We don't have to fantasize for long. Soon we'll naked, wrapped around each other, making love all night long."

"I love you too, Ryan," she murmured, turning to kiss her on the lips. "I miss you already." Her mouth was turned down in an adorable pout, but she seemed content to let Ryan control both of their sex drives for the evening.

Ryan quietly exited and walked to Rory's room, legs shaking so badly she could hardly stand. Holding up her hand, she smirked and informed it, "You've got your work cut out for you, Lefty. You'll never be able to recreate how it felt to have that beautiful woman just begging to be touched."

Not so early the next morning, Ryan sauntered downstairs in her pajamas. Her father was busy making his traditional after-Mass breakfast and he greeted her warmly when she appeared in the doorway. "Good morning, darlin'," he said. "Did you have a good rest?"

"Just fine, Da. Any word from Jamie?"

"No, not a peep. Breakfast will be ready soon though. Would you like to go wake her?"

"Sure. Do I have time for a shower?"

"No, not if you want your breakfast hot. Get on with ya," he ordered.

She obediently followed his command, walking downstairs and peeking in the door. As she paused in the doorway to watch her girlfriend sleep, she reflected on the sweet-looking woman's recent behavior.

She knew that discovering their lesbian identity was a very difficult thing for many women, and she sensed that Jamie was still suffering a bit from her very recent breakup with Jack. Given that she had so little sexual experience, it also made sense that she would be unsure of her desires. Even so, it was a complete shock to have her deny Ryan's very existence as she had yesterday. Ryan, though willing to cut her a good deal of slack, was still a bit hurt from being denied so rudely. But regarding her partner as she slept made her concerns seem very small and insignificant.

When the sweet face was in repose, Ryan had the chance to study her in a way she wasn't often able to do. She smiled to herself as she gazed at the tousled hair, so childlike as it draped over her eyes. And the smooth planes of her completely unlined face made her look so innocent and young—much younger than her twenty-one years. It was her eyes that made her look her age. Those clear, sharp, perceptive eyes that sometimes seemed to gaze right into Ryan's soul. But when the eyes were concealed, the face could have belonged to a sixteen-year-old. *A sixteen- year-old with a drop-dead gorgeous body*, she smirked to herself. *They didn't have sixteen-year-olds like that when I was in high school.*

Walking over to the bed, she sat on the edge and softly brushed the golden blonde hair from Jamie's eyes. Seconds later, the surprisingly awake green orbs blinked at her and gentled into a sweet smile. "Hi," she squeaked as she tossed her arms above her head and stretched like a happy cat. "Time to get up?"

"Yeah, if you want a hot breakfast. Da's about ready for us."

"Okay," she agreed, but Ryan placed a hand on her chest, stopping her progress abruptly.

She trailed her fingers along Jamie's cheek. "Are we okay?"

"We're fine." Grasping Ryan's hand she kissed the curved fingers gently. She pulled the hand back a bit to gaze at it carefully. "Is this my competition?" she asked with a chuckle.

Ryan gave her a slightly puzzled look, but caught on quickly. "Nope, this is," she said, holding up her left hand. "Righty gets involved too, but Lefty's indispensable." Raising an eyebrow, she twitched her head in the direction of Jamie's hands. "How about you?"

One hand shot up as she revealed, "Right hand only. And I'm guessing that yours has a lot more miles on it."

"Yeah," she said, blowing on the fingers. "The odometer's about to turn over on mine. Yours got a workout last night though, didn't it?"

"Not much of one," Jamie said with a wry laugh. "I think I was finished by the time you hit the stairs."

Ryan smiled back at her and gently grasped her right hand. Bringing it close to her face, she waved it back and forth in front of her nose a few times. "Smells delicious," she intoned with a sexy smile. "I can't wait to taste for myself." Leaning over she placed a gentle kiss on the shocked face and informed her, "Let's get moving. Breakfast calls!"

Jamie stared after her, feeling unable to move as the thought of her lover tasting her flooded her brain. *I wonder if she'll always make my knees weak?*

Even though she knew her breakfast would get cold, Jamie couldn't go upstairs in her abbreviated pajamas. She took a lightening quick shower and got back into yesterday's clothes, but in lieu of her own sweater she added one of Ryan's discarded T-shirts, as much to smell her fragrance as anything else.

Running upstairs, she was pleased to see that Brendan had joined the group. All of the men greeted her warmly, but Martin got up and wrapped his arms around her for a lingering hug. "I'm so happy you've chosen my little one," he murmured into her ear. "I couldn't wish a better partner for her."

She was shocked at this display of sentiment, but very grateful. She was especially pleased by the way he had phrased it—as if she had done Ryan a favor just by choosing her. Blushing furiously, she sat next to her lover at the table. "You've been officially given Conor's place at the table, Jamie. First change we've had in seventeen years," Ryan said.

Now her blush grew even more furious as she took in the four smiling faces gazing at her. "Thank you, Conor," she got out as Ryan leaned over to kiss her.

"Oh, I like this arrangement much better," her lover commented with a wide grin. "Finally some kissing at breakfast!"

After breakfast, they cleaned the kitchen in a much more cursory way than dinner called for. The women went onto the deck to soak up the remarkably bright sunshine, accompanied by a very happy Duffy. The big dog had taken to Jamie more than they had ever seen him do with anyone else. He followed her around the house as though he were her dog, causing all of the men to compliment his good taste. As soon as Jamie chose a chair, he tried to share the cushion with her, so today she anticipated his needs and chose the chaise lounge. Once she was settled, she patted the cushion and Duffy hopped up, lovingly nuzzling against her thigh for long minutes. "He obviously doesn't acknowledge that you prefer women," Ryan scoffed as she smiled at his antics. Leaning over to pet him as she grabbed a chair, she whispered, "I know how you feel, Duff. I fell for her the first time I saw her too."

"I'm going to become an ego-maniac if I hang out here too much. All I get are compliments!"

"That's all you deserve," Ryan said, somewhat seriously.

To deflect the focus from herself, Jamie said, "I'd better put some sunblock on. Do you need any?"

"Hnh-uh. It's in my medicine cabinet."

Jamie returned moments later, rubbing her SPF fifteen in as she walked. "I guess your tan lets you stay out as long as you want, huh?"

"I don't really have a tan," Ryan said. "And I do use sunblock. I usually put it on my face, neck and arms as soon as I get out of the shower. Then I don't have to worry about it all day."

"But you're very tan."

"No, I'm not," Ryan insisted. "Check it out." She pulled her T-shirt up with one hand while the other pushed her flannel pants down past her hip. Although there was about one shade of color difference between her tummy and her hip, Jamie had to agree that the untanned skin was pretty darned tan.

"But ... I assumed that because you're outside so much ..."

"Nope. I'm just dark-skinned. All of us are except Rory. He got my mother's coloring."

"But I thought the Irish were fair-skinned."

"Most are, but the O'Flaherty's are what they sometimes call 'Black Irish'. I'm not sure if it's a compliment or not though. It's not much of a thing now, but people used to look down a bit on the darker-skinned people. They used to say that they weren't pure Irish. I'd always heard that the coloring came from the sailors in the Spanish armada who came to Ireland in the 1400's. But I read an interesting web site not long ago that said that couldn't have happened. So I don't know where it comes from, but I like it."

"I like it, too," Jamie agreed. "Especially for California. Again, I believe it's part of your super-evolved genes. Your family moved to a sunny climate and your skin immediately adapted."

"Good theory, but it doesn't explain why my great grandfather was known as 'Black Jack O'Flaherty, the Terror of Tralee'." This last was said with one raised eyebrow and a rakish grin on the dark face.

"The 'Terror of Tralee'! What was he, the czar or something?"

Ryan laughed and replied, "No, just a local bare-knuckle fighter who packed a wallop."

"Wow! Do you know a lot about your family in Ireland?"

"Some," she agreed. "I only go back to Black Jack's father on my father's side, but I know of five generations on my mother's side, all from the same tiny town. They were as far from nomads as you can get!"

"What do you know about this Black Jack character?"

"Not a lot. Only that his reputation was so fierce it filtered down to my father's generation. They didn't go to Tralee much, but when they did people cut a wide swath to avoid offending any of the boys."

"Wow, that is a fierce reputation. Was he a professional?"

"Of sorts," she admitted. "It certainly wasn't like it is here, with governing bodies who watched over boxing, but it was how he made his living—such as it was."

"So ... he wasn't successful?"

"Oh, he was very successful at boxing, but much of every purse went straight to his liver. I assume he also used his skills on his wife and children, too. Not a nice man, from all reports."

"God, that sounds horrible."

"Ahh, different time, different culture. The Church and the husband ruled with an iron fist. I doubt that their lives were much different from many in their town," she said with a resigned shrug of her broad shoulders.

"But that's so sad," Jamie insisted. "To drink and abuse your family."

"Sure it's sad. I'm just saying it wasn't uncommon."

Her face had grown even darker, and Jamie sensed that she was finished with the discussion for the moment. To move to lighter topics, she asked, "Your skin does get darker in the summer doesn't it? I seem to remember my first thought of you being how white your teeth looked against your tanned face."

"Yeah, it does," she admitted. "I use block every day, but I'm outside so much that I darken up in the summer. I almost got the lead in 'West Side Story' because of my skin color," she said with a laugh.

"No!"

"Yep. My senior year the drama department was casting Maria. My music teacher begged me and begged me and I finally agreed to audition. We had a decent number of Latinas, but none of the women who could sing wanted to do the play. The drama teacher loved my audition, and I probably would have done it, but word was out about my lesbianism and the principal not so tactfully suggested that they should go with another girl."

"They wouldn't let you be in the play because you were a lesbian?" she cried loud enough to wake Duffy and cause him to start licking her face.

"Uhm, not just because I was, but it was a factor. There was a lot of controversy about me, and a lot of the girls were uncomfortable with me, I think she thought it was easier to avoid the mess."

"Easier for her!"

"I didn't care that much," Ryan fibbed. "And just after that, things started to go down that made that little slight seem like a day at the beach." Now her face had become a dark mask, and Jamie scolded herself for her unerring ability to find a topic that would depress her lover.

"Well, you would have been fabulous. And I bet you still know some of the songs, don't you?"

"A few," Ryan replied with a smirk. "I'll serenade you some night."

"Some night soon," she soothed as she wrapped her arms around Ryan's neck and pulled her over almost into the chaise. "When we're in bed, just after we've made love. I want to see you all sweaty with a satisfied grin on that beautiful face, singing to me as we fall asleep." The luminous grin and dancing eyes that greeted this wish made her reassess her ability to improve her lover's mood. *Not bad*, she smirked. *Not bad at all.*

Chapter Five

Even though the temptation was strong, Jamie refused Ryan's offer to join the family for dinner that evening. "I've got to make some progress on my big paper. It's got to be at least fifty pages long, and I don't even have a good outline yet."

"I understand," Ryan assured her, even though she was inordinately depressed by her partner's decision. "God knows, I've got enough to keep me busy."

"Yeah, we should spend the evening getting caught up so we're less stressed this week."

"You're right ... as usual," Ryan smiled as she walked her to her car. After a few minutes of giving the neighbors a free R-rated show, Ryan climbed the stairs to the front door and spent a few moments on the deck, watching Jamie's car descend Noe. *Could I be any more lovesick?*

Dinner would be ready in forty-five minutes, which wasn't enough time to really make much progress on her studies. Instead, she decided to take care of some housekeeping issues. Grabbing the phone from the living room, she took it onto the deck and plugged it into the outside hookup. She then started to make a few phone calls that were a little overdue.

She started with Ally, but her old friend wasn't home, so she left a brief message. "Hi, Ally, it's Ryan. Good news. Jamie and I have finally hooked up and I'm in L-O-V-E. Call me some time if you want to work out together. I've been slacking off in the weight room—other things on my mind. I hope things are going well for you. Bye."

Next on the list was Alisa Guerra, the assistant district attorney she'd last seen on the Mt. Tam mountain bike ride. As she dialed the memorized number, she spent a moment reflecting on the relationship they had.

Alisa was almost ten years older than she. Physically, she was one of the most attractive women Ryan had ever dated, with her long wavy black hair and deep brown eyes. But those eyes had seen a lot that had hardened Alisa, and Ryan knew from the start they could never make it as a couple. Alisa's perspective on life was always jaded and sometimes cynical, and after a while that attitude wore on Ryan. Even though Alisa could find the dark cloud around every silver lining, Ryan secretly thought there was a hidden optimist buried behind that tough shell of sarcasm. Alisa didn't seem to want a partner to help her release that lighter side, though. She actually seemed rather happy being a cynic, so Ryan took what she had to offer and was thankful for it.

They had been seeing each other for just over three years, with most of their liaisons coming after an exuberant mountain bike ride. They had drifted in and out of each other's lives, but Ryan felt close to Alisa in many ways and she knew she had to tell her about Jamie before she found out through the lesbian grapevine.

"Alisa?" she asked when a sleepy-sounding voice answered.

"Yeah," the voice croaked out. "Who the hell is it?"

"Ahh, wrong number?" Ryan tried, but her friend had recognized her voice by this time.

"O'Flaherty," she said with pleasure. "Where the hell have you been? I could really use a fill up, baby. My tank is dangerously low." Her lightly accented, honey smooth voice dropped into its lowest, sexiest register as she spoke, and Ryan felt the slightest stirrings of desire trickle down her spine.

"Ahh, that's kinda why I wanted to call, Alisa ..." she began, but the sexy voice cut her off.

"I'm already in bed, Querida, come on over and remind me why I love to see you."

"Uhm," Ryan gulped. "You see Alisa ... it's ahh ... well, I can't come over any more ..."

"What?" she snapped sharply. "Why can't you come over?"

Ryan shook her head slightly as she recalled why she had always thought Alisa would be a good trial attorney. She had an uncanny knack for lulling someone into an unguarded moment, but in an instant could pounce on her like a panther. "Because I've fallen in love," she said clearly. "I'm in a monogamous relationship."

"You?" Alisa cried, sending Ryan's teeth on edge. "You, of all people, are monogamous?"

"Yes, I am," Ryan said with her own voice taking on an uncharacteristically sharp tone. "I thought I owed you a phone call, Alisa, so I'll see you around ..."

"No, no, don't hang up, mí hija. I'm sorry I've offended you. I didn't think you had any interest in that type of thing. You always said you wanted to wait until you were through with school to find a lover."

Ryan felt her temper abate as Alisa tried to placate her. "That was my plan, but you don't always have control over your heart."

"So ... tell me, Dulcita, tell me about your lover." Alisa's voice had grown warm and comforting again, and Ryan found herself spilling everything about Jamie—her engagement and her confusion about her sexual orientation, her family's wealth, and her well-known and powerful father. To her surprise, she even told the attorney about Jamie's attempt at reconciliation with Jack. She didn't tell her Jamie's last name, even though she knew Alisa wouldn't know Jim. The worlds of civil and criminal lawyers rarely intersected, and, since Jim's firm never took on a criminal defendant, he'd be out of Alisa's world. Nonetheless, Ryan felt the need to protect Jamie's privacy while still being able to vent some of her feelings.

Alisa asked few questions, but she gently encouraged Ryan to continue until the whole story was out. It had taken quite a while to tell the tale and as she was finishing, Conor poked his head out to tell her that dinner was ready.

"I've got to go, Alisa," she explained. "Dinner's ready."

"Come see me after dinner. We have more to talk about."

"But Alisa—" she began, but once again the older woman insisted.

"I won't touch your perfect little body, Ryan. I don't want to change your mind … I just want to talk to you."

She took in a deep breath and let it out slowly as she considered the invitation. "Just talk?" she asked suspiciously.

"I promise. Just talk."

"Okay. I'll be over about … seven," she decided as she checked her watch.

"I'll be waiting."

On the way over to Alisa's apartment in Bernal Heights, Ryan mused that she probably should have told Jamie where she was going. She really didn't have a good read on Jamie's feelings about her past lovers, though, so she decided to tell her after the discussion was over, rather than have her worry about it.

She wedged her bike into a semi-legal space between two cars that looked like they were in for the night and approached Alisa's apartment with some trepidation. She knew nothing Alisa could offer could compromise her fidelity to Jamie, but she wasn't entirely sure her friend wouldn't try to tempt her. Alisa loved to play … and she was very good at most of the games she chose. Even though Ryan knew she could take anything her friend could dish out, she was not interested in having a scene.

Alisa's roommate Mike answered the door, and he gave Ryan a hug as she entered. "Hey, Ryan," he said. "Long time no see."

"Yeah, I've been pretty busy." Mike was also an attorney in the D.A.'s office. He was straight and Ryan had met many of his girlfriends, but they never seemed to stay around for long. As she entered the living room, she saw who she assumed was the girlfriend of the week, and Mike confirmed this fact as he introduced her.

"Ryan, this is Ellen. Ellen … Ryan." The women shook hands as Mike said, "Alisa's in her room. Go on back."

"Good to meet you, Ellen," Ryan said as she continued on through the apartment. She wasn't too happy to be consigned to Alisa's room, but she didn't have much choice at that point. Knocking lightly, Alisa's warm voice bade her to enter. "Hi," Ryan said as she breathed a sigh of relief that her friend was fully dressed and sitting on the neatly made bed.

"Hi, yourself," she said as she scampered off the bed and wrapped her arms around Ryan's waist. "Can I kiss you, or are your sweet lips off limits?"

Ryan gave her a smirk and a friendly kiss, adding a little squeeze for good measure. "I'm not really sure what the rules are, to tell you the truth," she admitted as she sat on Alisa's desk chair. "I've never had a steady girl before."

"I know, Querida," she said softly as she ran her fingers through Ryan's hair in an almost maternal gesture. "That's why I wanted to talk to you. Let me get us a glass of wine, okay?"

"Okay," Ryan said. "I'm not going to study tonight anyway."

Alisa's laugh floated over her shoulder as she left the room for the kitchen. "You could pass every class without opening a book and you know it. That struggling student act doesn't work with me."

Ryan laughed at her friend's teasing, admitting the truth of her statement. She knew Alisa had also done exceptionally well in school, earning a full scholarship to Stanford undergrad as well as a free ride at Harvard Law. The gorgeous, poised woman could have had her choice of any law firm in the city, and Ryan thought that Alisa must have been courted by Jamie's father's firm. But she had political aspirations and she thought the D.A.'s office was the best way to move up in the public eye.

Alisa had done very well for herself as a prosecutor. She had been promoted three times in her seven years and was now prosecuting high-profile death penalty cases. Ryan knew that Alisa was very committed to working for the Latino community, and she had every confidence that someday her friend would make it in politics if she continued on that path. But she also knew that Alisa would probably never have a permanent lover as long as she sought that goal. Lesbianism was no longer an insurmountable barrier in San Francisco politics, but such was not the case in the Latino community. Alisa had told Ryan on many occasions that her own father would disown her if she ever admitted to her lesbianism, and she firmly believed her political aspirations would be foiled if her private life was revealed. So she dated a lot, but kept the relationships mostly sexual. Ryan had a lot of empathy for her friend's dilemma, but she privately thought that perhaps Alisa used her reasons as a shield so she didn't have to risk being in a more intimate relationship. She wasn't going to figure that out tonight, though, so she brushed the thoughts away as her friend returned with two glasses of red wine. "Cabernet okay?"

"Perfect," Ryan agreed as she accepted the glass.

Alisa clinked the rims together and toasted, "To happy endings." She leaned over and placed another very gentle kiss on Ryan's lips and pulled back to lightly stroke her face. "I wish you every happiness, Ryan. You deserve only the best."

"Thank you, Alisa," she said softly. "That means a lot." They resumed their previous seats with Ryan astride the wooden-backed desk chair and Alisa sitting cross-legged on the bed. "So what did you want to talk about?" she asked after she took a sip of the tannin-rich wine.

"I'm concerned about you," Alisa admitted. "I don't want you to get hurt and I'm afraid that you're setting yourself up to do just that."

"Because ..." Ryan drawled.

"You know why. Straight girls are the kiss of death, Querida. And I don't want her to break your sweet little heart when she goes back to men. She will, Ryan. They always do."

Ryan knew her friend was speaking from painful personal experience. She and Alisa had spent the better part of a weekend once eating carryout and drinking wine while they tearfully confessed their broken hearts. Alisa's wounds were just as deep as Ryan's, and even though the stories had different results, they were equally painful.

Alisa had fallen in love for the first time in college. The object of her affection was a teaching assistant in the political science department at Stanford when Alisa was an undergraduate. Linda had equally strong feelings for Alisa, but she steadfastly refused to be open about their relationship. The end came rather violently when an acquaintance had greeted them on campus one day by asking Alisa if Linda was the mysterious girlfriend that none of her friends had met. Linda had been polite as she denied their involvement to the woman, but as soon as they were alone she told Alisa she couldn't see her any longer. All of Alisa's attempts to contact her were rebuffed, and less than six months later Linda married a professor in the Spanish language department. Linda had gone on to earn her doctorate, and the last Alisa had heard, she was on the faculty at Stanford and had just published a book on the increasing political clout of Latinos in California politics.

"I know that's a possibility," Ryan said. "But there are risks with any lover. Anyone can break your heart."

"Not like a straight girl," she said bitterly. "That is the worst. To love you and be pleasured by you and then to run back to their safe little world when things get difficult ... it is ... it is horrible," she concluded, her shoulders now slumped in defeat. "It is different for us, Ryan. We have no choice ... we either love women or we don't love at all. But a straight girl can always choose the other way ... and she will."

"Jamie won't," Ryan said firmly, full of confidence.

"Ryan, sweetheart, you already told me that she tried to go back once. What made her do that? Did she have a bad experience when she told someone about you?"

Ryan had to take in a calming breath before she could answer. She knew the truth was strong evidence for Alisa's point, but she had no interest in being less than forthright with her old friend. "She hasn't told anyone yet. To be honest, she tried to reconcile with her fiancé just because she was afraid of committing to being gay."

Alisa tried to jump in, but Ryan held up a hand, asking for a moment to complete her thought. "She worked that through. She really regrets that she tried to take the easy way out and she's spent a lot of time in therapy trying to get comfortable."

"She's told no one?" Alisa asked quietly, her eyes locked upon Ryan's.

"No. No one."

"Not even her close friends from college, or a brother or sister?"

"No. No one," Ryan admitted as she stared at the ground. Alisa crawled off the bed and squatted down in front of Ryan. She gently pushed the hair from her eyes and whispered, "Are you sure you can trust her, Cariña?"

Ryan closed her eyes and nodded almost imperceptibly. As her eyes fluttered open, a smile graced her face as she said, "With my heart … with my life … with my soul."

By the time the bottle of wine was finished, it was eleven o'clock and Ryan knew she was too drunk to drive, so she called home and asked for a ride. Rory was chosen to go since he had shoes on, and fifteen minutes later he buzzed the doorbell. Ryan bid goodbye to Alisa with a sweet, but chaste kiss as she thanked her for her concern and her companionship for the past three years.

"For your sake, I hope we never share a bed again, Querida, even though it will break my heart to lose you."

"I truly believe I'll be with Jamie for the rest of my days, but if I'm wrong you're the woman I'd choose to help mend my broken heart," Ryan murmured as she wrapped her in a warm hug. "Keep in touch, Alisa," she said as she scampered down the stairs, wobbling slightly.

"What happened to you?" Rory asked as she climbed into his truck. "And why are you over here anyway?"

"Old flame," Ryan said briefly. "Tried to warn me to expect a broken heart from Jamie."

"And she got you drunk?" he asked, unused to seeing his sister inebriated.

"A little," she admitted. "It's kinda upsetting to think about. I guess I let the wine take the edge off."

The O'Flaherty brothers had all been discussing their sister's new commitment, and after several discussions Rory was chosen as the spokesperson for their position. He knew he had won only because he was the youngest of the three and he always got the dirty jobs, but he agreed anyway. He had been trying all week to find a good moment to bring up their concerns. And now seemed just about perfect—Ryan was open, vulnerable, reflective and drunk. Rory could count on the fingers of one hand the number of times his little sister had actually heeded his advice, but he reasoned that her weakened state gave him a leg up.

"Uhm … what was your friend trying to warn you about?" he asked as casually as possible, hoping the liquor had dulled Ryan's always sharp mind.

"Oh, the usual lesbian stuff," she said lazily as her head dropped back against the seat. "Straight women are evil … blah, blah, blah."

"Is that a lesbian thing?" Rory asked, surprised that it would be. "I know it's a straight guy thing."

"Huh? What do you mean?" she asked as she turned her head in his direction.

"If a guy dates a woman who's ever been with another woman, everybody assumes she'll go back the first time he acts like an ass. Which usually doesn't take long," he added with a chuckle.

"Hmm," she said thoughtfully. "It's the same thing, but reversed. I guess everybody's leery of people who can go either way."

"What about you?" he asked with forced nonchalance.

"I don't think I'm going to give guys a try," she smirked. "I've got my hands full with Jamie."

"That's not what I meant, and you know it. Are you worried about Jamie?"

"Ooh," she drawled, "did you win the honor of talking to me about this?"

"Can't we ever get away with anything?" he grumbled. "Even drunk you're ahead of me."

"No I'm not, Bro. I'm not surprised that you guys are worried. Is Da among your group?"

"No! God, no! None of us would have the nerve to question anything about Jamie to him ... or to Duffy," he laughed. "Those two are her biggest supporters."

"Nope. I am," Ryan said seriously. "Look Ror, I know you all care about me and I know you only want to protect me. But I'm confident about Jamie's decision. I know her a lot better than you guys do and I know we're gonna be together for life. So get used to her, 'cause she's gonna be the mother of at least one of your nieces or nephews."

He turned as much as he was able and shot her one of the patented O'Flaherty dazzlers. "Nothing would make me happier. And if you need any genetic material ..."

"I know where to look," she laughed. "And since the lot of you doesn't seem to want to use it for anything constructive ..."

"Hey ... hey ... now watch it," he warned. "Don't go throwing stones at a lad's hobbies!"

Ryan spent their walk on Monday morning explaining to her partner the long talk with Alisa and her shorter one with Rory. Jamie was perturbed that she would be considered unstable just because she had recently been with a man, but she had to admit they had some valid concerns. "Are you worried about me going back?" she asked, realizing that only one opinion mattered to her.

"No, I'm not. I don't believe you'd hurt me like that, no matter how strong the pressure was."

"You do know me well, don't you?" she teased as she gave Ryan a small kiss right in front of the Applied Science Building.

"Apparently not!" Ryan gasped as she tried to reconcile this new boldness.

"I like to keep you on your toes," she purred as she added another kiss and scampered away to class.

Chapter Six

After a fairly productive study session on Thursday night, they decided to skip their make-out session at the coffeehouse and have a snack at their favorite coffee shop. Jamie smiled up at Ryan as she placed the cocoas and scones on the table. "You were quite the good little girl tonight. You barely looked up until nine-fifteen."

"I think my anxiety is beginning to overtake my lust. I've been slacking off ever since you told me you might be interested in me, and since you've changed that to a definite, it's gotten much worse. I think I'm gonna have to start studying during our lunch hours."

"I can get you some extra hours. Both Mia and I can use a break from weight training. Why don't you use our time to study?"

"Okay, if you think she wouldn't mind. Two hours extra on Monday, Wednesday and Friday would help a lot, and if I skipped our lunch, that's an extra eleven hours a week."

"Are you okay with losing that money?"

"Yeah, I'm fine, but thanks for asking."

"I love you, Ryan," Jamie replied as she cupped her cheek with her hand. "It's important to me that you're comfortable in every area of your life." Ryan sat and gazed at her lovingly for a few moments. Jamie was shyly smiling at her, and the energy that radiated from them was nearly palpable. It wasn't a sexual energy tonight, but even a casual observer would have noticed the loving gazes and gentle touches that passed between them. And when that observer was one very interested Cassie Martin, the little tableau became positively mesmerizing.

Cassie had wandered in to pick up a coffee on her way home from the library. She had placed her order and was standing around waiting when she caught sight of Jamie and Ryan in her peripheral vision.

Ryan had purchased both a chocolate chip and a strawberry scone. Jamie made a show of eating the chocolate chip one all by herself, but Ryan continually begged for a bite. "Okay, you can have a bite," she relented, "but I get to have portion control. Your bites are as big as my meals!"

"Okay, Ms. Stingy. Break me off a piece."

Jamie tore off a small piece and instructed, "Open up."

Through her wide smile, Ryan opened just wide enough for Jamie to pop the morsel into her mouth. But her reflexes were way too quick for her partner, and she caught Jamie's thumb between her teeth before she could extract it. She sat there grinning like a Cheshire Cat, holding the thumb gently between her white, even teeth.

"Release," Jamie ordered, repeating the command Ryan gave Duffy when he picked up a bit of trash from the street. She patted Ryan's pink cheek and added, "Good girl."

The game was too much fun for Ryan to let it go, so she held up her scone with an inquisitive look. Jamie nodded slightly and opened her mouth. But instead of biting, she chose the more loving path of firmly sucking Ryan's finger into her warm mouth. They both closed their eyes at the sensual contact and as Ryan pulled her finger out, she turned her hand and held Jamie's chin in her fingers for a few loving moments.

To avoid fainting or screaming, Cassie turned and ran out the door, leaving her coffee unclaimed.

Jamie strolled back into the house at around ten. Her hair was mussed from Ryan's fingers running through it, but her clothing was straight and she looked completely normal—unlike some nights when she looked like she'd just crawled out of bed. She noticed the light in the kitchen, and she walked over to turn it off before heading up to bed. When she swung the door open, she was surprised to find both of her roommates huddling at the table with anxious looks on their faces.

"What's up?" she asked with trepidation, afraid that something tragic had happened.

"We need to talk to you," Cassie said.

"W ... what about?" A twinge of panic began to form in her stomach.

"Sit down," Cassie ordered. Jamie glanced at Mia and saw that her friend looked concerned, but much less angry than Cassie. With growing anxiety, she pulled out a chair with nearly numb fingers and sat down, waiting for them to begin.

"We want to know what's going on with you," Cassie began. "You've been gone nearly every minute of the day. You were gone over a couple of weekends when you weren't at your parents', and there's something ... different about you."

"Nothing's going on," she lied, feeling trapped and very defensive. "I've been really busy."

"Who are you spending your time with?" Cassie persisted. "Are you dating someone?"

"No, I'm not," she lied again, feeling worse by the minute.

"Then where were you two weekends ago? Or last Saturday? We were worried about you when you didn't come home."

"I went to Muir Beach two weeks ago," she said, at least telling the truth about one part of her life. "And I stayed in the city last week because I had too much to drink. I didn't realize I had to check in. Are you gonna start calling to tell us when you're staying at your boyfriend's?"

"That's an entirely different thing," Cassie said. "When I'm not here, you know I'm with Chris. But when you're gone, we have no idea where you are. You could be hurt or injured, and we wouldn't even know where to start looking for you!"

Jamie looked from Cassie to Mia and back again. "Do you normally spend your evenings discussing where I am? I thought my days of captivity were over once I broke up with Jack."

"He broke up with you," Cassie sweetly reminded her. "And no, we don't normally discuss your social life, but we're both worried about you. We both believe that friend of yours is a very dangerous influence on you, and we want you to be safe."

"What are you talking about? Ryan hasn't been over here for weeks!"

"Jamie," Cassie said as she gentled her voice and placed her hand upon Jamie's arm, "it's obvious you're spending all of your time with her. We're concerned about you. People are going to start believing you're like her."

"I wish I were like her!" she screamed in frustration and anger. "If I were half as nice or half as sweet or half as thoughtful, I'd be the happiest person in the whole fucking world!" She leapt to her feet and started to turn for the door, when Cassie's cold, flat voice knocked her back into the chair.

"I saw you, Jamie. I saw you with her tonight. I, along with every other person at the coffee shop, think you *are* just like her."

Mia rushed to try and help out. She put her hand on Jamie's and said, "Tell us what's going on. We want to help. If you're confused or unsure about your feelings, maybe we can help you work through them."

Rebuffing Mia's soothing words, she turned to Cassie with fire in her eyes and demanded, "Tell me what you saw. Lay out your overwhelming evidence of my perversion!"

Cassie blinked a couple of times and looked unsure, but she rallied. "I saw you feeding each other," she said with a hint of disgust.

"You most certainly did not! You saw us giving each other bites of our scones. We were just fooling around." She turned to Mia and said, "You know how playful Ryan is. She was acting like she was going to eat my hand when I gave her a bite."

Mia looked terribly uncomfortable, but she replied, "Uhm … when I give a girl a bite of my food, I tend to just hand it to her. I don't normally put it in her mouth."

"I had a gooey chocolate chip scone! As a polite gesture, I popped it into my friend's mouth to save her from getting chocolate on her hands. She playfully bit my fingers because she's a very playful person. Doing that makes me what … a lesbian?"

"Yeah, that would probably be enough," Cassie decided. "Given how you were looking at each other, that would probably be enough."

"Doesn't lesbianism have something to do with sex? I've only taken one class, but I was sure they said something about vaginas. And Ryan has neither seen nor touched mine. But if giving my friend an affectionate look makes me a lesbian ... then you must be right. You're spending a suspicious amount of time thinking about my sexuality, but you must be right."

"I only think about your sexuality when you're flirting your asses off with each other," she said coldly. "When you fed her, it could have been play. But when she fed you ..." she shook her head slowly, a sour look on her otherwise attractive face.

"She did not feed me!"

"She certainly *did* feed you. And you sucked her fingers into your mouth like they'd been there, and lots of other places on your body, hundreds of times."

"That's a lie!" she growled as she jumped to her feet and leaned over Cassie with a menacing stare. "I've never had her fingers in my mouth or anywhere else on my body. I resent every nasty implication of your fevered imagination. Lesbians are not predators. Not all lesbians have to force unwilling straight women to sleep with them. And not all people who claim to be your friends really are!" She turned so forcefully that her chair fell against the floor and skidded a few feet before sliding to a stop. Kicking it out of her way, she stormed out of the kitchen, leaving both women to stare after her in shock.

Her body ached to call Ryan, but she knew they'd be up for hours discussing the issue, and she didn't have the heart to take that much sleep from her poor partner. An insistent little voice reminded her of the other reason for her reticence. *You completely betrayed her, Jamie*, she repeated over and over again. *You made it sound like she was just a friend, and you denied every shred of your love. How do you think that'll make her feel?*

A soft knock startled her out of her musings, and she tried to gather herself for another onslaught, muttering, "Come in."

Mia poked her head in and asked, "Really? Is it okay?"

She nodded her head, and scooted up on the bed to give her friend some room. But Mia chose to pull the desk chair over and sit facing the back of the chair as she leaned it over on the back legs. "I'm so sorry that all came out like that, Jamie. Cassie dragged me down to the kitchen not ten minutes before you got home. She was in the midst of explaining what she saw when you came in. I never would have agreed to gang up on you like that."

Jamie nodded. "Thanks. It really did make it worse to think you two were both against me."

"I'm not against you at all, Jamie," she said as she forced eye contact. "And I like Ryan, too ..."

"But ..." Jamie supplied.

"But I have a hard time thinking Cassie made that all up. "

"Oh, Jesus, I thought you were on my side!"

"I *am* on your side. I really am. But if you're going through some big changes, I want to be there to help you. I'm your friend, and I promise I won't judge you. Please be honest with me. I swear I won't tell anyone—especially Cassie."

Jamie took a deep breath and regarded her friend carefully. They'd been friends since they were freshmen in high school, and she knew things about Mia that would remain with her to the grave. They had always been close, but they had become even closer since they'd come to Cal nearly three years before. She tried to allow all of these reassuring thoughts to affect her answer, but almost to her own shock, she heard herself say, "She's wrong. Cassie has an irrational hatred of Ryan that makes her see things that aren't there."

Mia looked truly sad as she stood and returned the chair to its proper place. "Okay, I believe you. Sorry for everything that happened tonight." She bent over and kissed her friend on the forehead, ruffling her short hair affectionately as she stood.

"Mia," Jamie said, stopping her in her tracks.

"Yeah?"

"Would you mind if Ryan took a couple of weeks off from training? She's having a tough time keeping up this term, and she really needs time to study."

"No, that's okay," she said in an uncharacteristically flat tone. "I should study more too. Should I call her?"

"I can tell her. We uhm … see each other a lot since our classes are close to each other in the morning."

"Okay. 'Night, Jamie," she said as she closed the door behind her.

Jamie flopped down on the bed and began to berate herself for compounding her betrayal of one friend by lying to another. But using one of the tricks she had perfected through years of dating Jack, she closed her mind to all of the internal dialogue and forced herself into a deep, dreamless sleep.

Ryan was pacing around on the corner when Jamie came barreling out of the house at quarter past seven the next morning. "Are you okay?" Ryan asked with evident concern.

"Yeah, yeah, just running late. I didn't hear the alarm this morning."

They took off, needing to walk quickly to make it to class on time. Jamie felt guilty that Ryan wouldn't get breakfast, so as they passed the long line at the coffee shop she ran inside, waved a ten-dollar bill and pulled three scones from the covered tray on the counter. The clerk gave her a puzzled look, but she merely replied, "Tip," as she ran back to her companion.

Ryan shook her head as she accepted the scones. "What did these cost you?"

"Ten bucks. You're worth it," she said. "I have to make sure you have enough fuel to get you through your … what development class?"

"Neuronal development."

"Right. You must need extra fuel to study something I can hardly pronounce." She knew that her affect was off today, so she compensated by being overly cheery. But she knew that every moment with her hyper-alert partner would lead her one step closer to exposure. Obviously, she had to tell Ryan what had happened, but she needed some time to get a handle on her betrayal before she would be able to withstand the look that was sure to form on Ryan's sweet face.

As she munched on the first of her scones, Ryan said, "So we finally get a couple of days off. How do you want to spend them? Hey, I know, why don't you come stay the weekend? We can't sleep together, but we could have lots of uninterrupted kissing time." Ryan waggled her eyebrows in an exaggerated fashion while pasting a hopeful smile on her face.

Jamie hadn't planned on making the statement that came from her mouth, but she heard someone say, "I think I'll go down to Hillsborough for the weekend. My mother is leaving for Europe in two weeks, and she'll be gone most of the summer. I feel like I owe them a little bit of my time."

"Okay," Ryan said, trying to hide her disappointment. "Do you want me to come down for our ride on Sunday? We could do some of the long trails."

"No, I think I'll study in the afternoon, and I'm sure my dad will want to play golf in the morning. If I'm going to go, I should give all of my time to them."

"Oh … all right," Ryan said a little uneasily. "What about tonight? You won't want to get stuck in traffic will you?"

"It's not really that bad. I think I'll leave right after I see Anna so I can beat the rush."

"Oh, so you don't want to work out?" she asked, now even more tentatively.

"No, I'd better get going. Oh, and I talked to Mia, and she said she didn't mind skipping for a couple of weeks. Actually she'll be leaving for L.A. as soon as finals are over, so you can just pick up in the fall."

"All right," Ryan replied with a very concerned look on her face. "Uhm … Jamie," she began, but they were right in front of Jamie's classroom building.

Jamie gave her a gentle hug and whispered, "I'll miss you, Ryan. I love you very, very much."

"I love you too," she got out, but before she could utter another word, Jamie was scampering up the steps.

I don't know what she's hiding, but it must be a doozy, she thought as she shook her head and continued on her way.

She sat in Anna's office, head in hands as she berated herself for all of her betrayals. "I denied her, Anna," she moaned. "I claim to be so much in love with her, and the first time anyone questions me, I deny her completely."

"Jamie, Jamie," she soothed. "Being angry with yourself is just going to make the feelings last longer. Try to pull back to feel some compassion for yourself."

"Why do I deserve compassion?" she demanded as her head shot up and she leveled a withering glare at Anna. "It's Ryan that deserves compassion. She's the one who was betrayed!"

"Jamie, you did not betray her. You just refused to be baited by a person who has proven that she's not your friend. Once you made that choice, you felt trapped and you didn't want to be honest with Mia either. But you didn't harm Ryan."

"I harmed our love. I denied it even existed. I acted like being a lesbian was a bad thing."

"You don't think your love is resilient enough to withstand a lie to a woman who only wants to intrude on your business? Come on, Jamie, you can't really think that, can you?"

"No, I guess not," she admitted. "But Ryan is so precious to me, and she's so fragile sometimes. She was hurt so badly by the first woman she fell in love with, and I feel like I've done the same thing."

"What happened to Ryan?"

"She was in love with a classmate and she thought her feelings were returned. She made some overtures, which she thought were accepted, but in fact, the woman told her mother and other people at school and they all turned on Ryan. They nearly destroyed her self-confidence, and they ruined some of her plans for the future."

"And you equate telling Cassie that you aren't lovers with that type of betrayal? Do you think you might be being just a tiny bit hard on yourself?"

"I guess maybe I am being hard on myself, but Ryan deserves someone who'll shout her love from the rooftops, not a coward like me."

"I think Ryan gets to choose the type of lover she wants, and I'm pretty sure she's chosen you. Why don't you share what happened with her? I bet she'll be a lot more understanding than you think she'll be."

"I will tell her, but I need to spend some time examining my motivations for lying in the first place. I'll do that this weekend. Let's talk about this some more on Monday, and then I'll talk to her on Monday night."

She stopped by her house to grab some books and ran into Cassie coming down the stairs. They regarded each other warily, like natural enemies in the wild. Cassie backed down the stairs and said, "Now that Mia's not here, I really think you ought to come clean. I know you don't believe me, and I've got to admit that it really hurts, but I only want to help you get through this ... crush or whatever it is. I've known you since grammar school. We've grown up together, and I know you're not gay."

Jamie descended the stairs also and looked at her for a minute. "Then what's the problem?"

"Even though I know you're not really gay, I saw you with Ryan last night and I know what I saw. You were acting like lovers, and if you haven't slept with her, it's only a matter of time. You can still get out, Jamie. You don't have to ruin your entire reputation over her."

"Being friends with Ryan can only help my reputation," she said confidently. "Anything of her that rubs off on me can only make me a better person."

"Look, Jamie, I really feel for you. I know you don't have much experience with sex. She's such an operator that she's convinced you that she loves you, but she only loves what you can do for her. Can't you see that?"

"So, only people who want my money or my family connections would be stupid enough to want me?" she snapped.

"Of course not, but why would a slut like her waste her time trying to get you? There're thousands of women like her, and she certainly doesn't seem to have any trouble picking them up. She has to want something from you. The people who care about you can all see this," she insisted. "I spoke to Jack this afternoon, and he feels the same way that I—"

Her voice was cut off by one hundred and ten pounds propelled against her body in a wild fury. Jamie grabbed her blouse with both hands and shook her violently as she cried, "You bitch! You god damned bitch!"

Cassie was nearly too shocked to move, but her self-preservation instincts took over as she used her superior size and weight to push Jamie away from her roughly. "Listen to me," she said with cold rage marring her attractive face, "you can do whatever you want with that dyke. But you keep her out of my house! I won't have her fouling the air that I breathe."

"No, you listen to me. This is *my* house, and *I* decide who visits here. Ryan is welcome here. If you don't like it, you'll be the one who leaves, not her!"

"You mean to look me in the eye and tell me you choose that whore over our friendship?"

Jamie edged as close as she could get and glared at her, locking eyes as she enunciated, "If I had to make that choice one hundred times, she'd win every time."

Her hands were shaking so badly that she knew she shouldn't risk being on the road. She hadn't yet told her parents she was coming down, and now she began to doubt whether it was a good idea after all. She had nothing to talk about except Ryan and the AIDS Ride, and neither topic would be welcome at her parents' home. But she did have a lot of studying to do, and if she took the weekend off from seeing Ryan, they could both get caught up. The jumble of ideas rolled around in her head as she sank down onto her bed and promptly fell into a depressed sleep.

After her last client, Ryan ran by a favorite cheap and cheerful restaurant and got some dinner. She pored over one of her ever-present books while she ate and then decided spending the night at the library would be a better idea than fighting traffic on the way home.

The library was open late in preparation for finals, and she climbed into a carrel and didn't move until the lights flashed, signaling the close. *My God*, she thought in amazement. *I can't believe six hours flew by like that. At least I got my concentration back for an evening.*

She trudged all the way back to Jamie's with her heavy book bag, knowing that the ride home would keep her awake. As she passed by her lover's house, she was hit with a stab of shock when she saw that Jamie's car was still in the driveway. No lights were on in her room, and the living room was dark, as well. *God damn it, Jamie. You don't have to lie to me. You're still a free woman, and you can spend your evenings however you want to, but lying to me is unacceptable!*

She rode home in a funk and glumly welcomed Duffy into her bed. "And they call you a dog," she murmured as she snuggled up to him.

As soon as Jamie woke, she felt much more in control of her feelings. It was just after six, but she knew Ryan would be up and running. She quickly paged her and sat by the phone waiting for it to ring. After fifteen minutes, she gave up and got in the shower. She was slightly concerned, but not really worried since Ryan didn't normally take her pager when she ran. After her shower, she got dressed and took a novel she had to read and walked over to the coffee shop. She didn't want to be in the house since Cassie was home, and she thought she could get more done without the threat of running into her.

It was nearly eight o'clock, and her anxiety had been growing for an hour when her phone finally rang. "Where were you?" she quickly asked.

"I was asleep. I had the pager on vibrate." Ryan's voice was completely businesslike. She had answered the question, but no more information was forthcoming.

"Did you just wake up?"

"No. I got up about an hour ago. I had breakfast, then I called you back."

"Uhm … you knew I paged you two hours ago?"

"Yeah. Why does that bother you?" she asked bitterly. "Does it hurt you the way I felt last night when I came by your house at midnight and saw that you were home?"

For some reason, even though Ryan had every right to be mad, the tone and the assumption rubbed Jamie the wrong way. "I'm sorry if I disturbed you. I'm also sorry I didn't update you on my plans. I'll remember to go to the store and buy a Global Positioning System tracking device today." She clicked off her phone and didn't turn it back on, as she fumed over the rest of her coffee.

At ten, she went to the Biosciences Library. She'd never heard any of her friends mention using this library, and she guessed that Ryan would stay home to study, so she reasoned she could hide out and finish her novel. She felt really bad about the fight she had with Ryan, and she knew that, due to her own guilt, she was more sensitive than usual. But the bottom line was that she wouldn't allow Ryan to supervise her, no matter how much she loved her.

At eleven o'clock, she called home to check for messages and was stricken with guilt when she heard the plaintive messages from her partner. She had left four, each one more contrite than the last. She was in the process of dialing Ryan's pager when a dark head peeked around her study carrel.

With her flushed, damp face, Ryan looked like she'd been running laps. Her eyes were sunken and bloodshot, and she looked like she'd been up all night. When she made eye contact, Jamie was afraid her partner was going to burst into tears. She looked so sad and lost that Jamie immediately pulled her into the little carrel and cradled her on her lap. "I'll squish you," Ryan murmured against her ear.

"There's no one I'd rather be squished by," she said as she increased the strength of her embrace.

She heard the person in the carrel behind hers utter an exaggerated sigh, so she patted Ryan's butt and got up to lead her from the library.

They went through the south doors and immediately sat down on the wide granite balustrade that flanked the entrance. Even though this side of the building was less trafficked, they were quite exposed; nevertheless, Jamie ignored her normal hesitancy and sat right on Ryan's lap, wrapping her arms around her neck for additional comfort. "I'm sorry. I shouldn't have snapped at you."

"It's okay. I shouldn't have implied that I was supervising you. But I wasn't at all, really, Jamie. I don't do that!"

"Well, you never have before, and it was wrong of me to assume you were doing it now."

"I was worried about you," she murmured. "You weren't acting right yesterday morning, and I really felt like you were trying to avoid me. Then when I went to get my bike, I saw your car and I felt like you were lying to me. I was really hurt," she said with tears in her eyes. "I couldn't sleep at all last night, and I ... and I ..." Her voice trailed off as she tried to compose herself. She didn't like to cry in public, and she still felt odd crying in front of Jamie, so she pursed her lips and took a few deep breaths.

"I'm so sorry, Ryan. I'm so sorry," she soothed. "It's all my fault, honey. It's all my fault."

"B ... B ... But why?" Ryan's shaky voice asked.

Jamie took in a deep breath and closed her eyes for a moment. "Something happened between Cassie and Mia and me on Thursday night. It really upset me, but I didn't want to talk about it until I had some things resolved in my mind. And I know this is hard to hear, but sometimes your connectedness makes me feel overwhelmed."

"What do you mean?" she asked in a quavering voice as she looked up at Jamie with her red-rimmed eyes. She looked so fragile and young that it broke Jamie's heart to tell her, but she felt like she had to.

"You know me so well, and you're so attuned to my every mood that sometimes I start to feel swallowed. I love the way you know me, but sometimes it's a lot."

"But I know you because I love you," she murmured.

"I know, Ryan. I want you to know me that well, but no one else ever has. You know me ten times better than anyone else has ever tried to. And I normally think that's a tremendous gift, and I'm normally terrifically grateful you care enough to know me that well. But some times it feels like I can't tell where I stop and you start. Then it scares me, and I need to withdraw."

"And that's why you lied to me?" she asked softly. "So you could have some peace?"

"No, Ryan, no. I didn't lie to you. I *was* going home, and I *was* going to leave right after Anna. But I had another go around with Cassie when I went to get my stuff, and I was so upset afterwards that I went upstairs and fell asleep in my clothes. I woke up this morning at six and called you right away."

"But you *were* going to your parent's to get some peace, right?"

"No, that's not how I'd put it. I didn't feel ready to talk about what had happened, and I knew you'd know something was wrong, so to avoid having to explain myself, I tried to hide."

"But Jamie, there's such an easy way to deal with this."

"What's that?"

"When I ask you what's wrong, just acknowledge that something is wrong, but tell me you're not ready to talk about it. Isn't that easier?"

She nodded her head slowly, lightly rubbing her cheek against Ryan's dark head. "I'll try," she promised.

Ryan lifted her face and asked, "Is anything bothering you, Jamie?"

"Yes, Ryan, something is bothering me, but I'm not ready to talk about it right now. When I am, I'll tell you, okay?"

"Okay," she said and let her lips curl into the most amazing smile that Jamie had ever seen. She absolutely couldn't resist the need to lean down and kiss that beautiful mouth again and again. They were so involved that neither of them saw Mia jerk to a halt not twenty feet away, but she most definitely saw them.

"How much sleep did you get last night?" Jamie asked as they both stood.

"Uhm ... I got home about one and I tossed and turned until three. Then I woke up in a panic at five, thinking that maybe you were sick or hurt or mad at me. I went back to sleep until seven, but Duffy woke me then and I finally got up."

"What did you do after we talked?"

"I called you a bunch of times at home then I practically wore the numbers off the phone dialing your cell. I got dressed and came over here at nine, but I didn't have the nerve to go to your house. I went to all of your favorite coffee places and restaurants, and then I started hitting the libraries I know you like. I started in

Moffitt and searched every square inch, but then I thought you might come here. I'm not sure where I would have gone next," she said as she shook her head with a forlorn look.

"You poor, poor thing. It must have taken you an hour to search that huge building!"

Ryan nodded.

"I really thought you could catch up this weekend if we weren't together, and now look what I've done to you."

"It's okay. I'll go home and take a nap, and then I can study there."

"Come to my house," she urged. "I want to see if I can study with you near me. We're going to have to get used to that sooner or later, you know."

"Okay, but is that a good idea? I'm guessing any fight you had with your roommates had me somewhere in it."

"It's fine. I don't think Cassie could be any angrier than she already is and Mia likes you, so it's okay." They walked back across campus, hand in hand. When they reached the house, Cassie was in the kitchen and she opened the door a bit to see who was home. Her face soured immediately upon seeing Ryan. As they entered Jamie's room, Ryan asked, "How could such a pretty face look so ugly, so often?"

"You should see her mother. She always looks like there's a bad smell somewhere. It must be hereditary."

Jamie hopped onto the center of the bed and patted the side next to her in an inviting fashion. "Come on, get in."

"But I've got to study," Ryan complained weakly.

"Unh-uh, no dice. You come right here and lay your pretty head right on my lap. I'm going to put myself to the ultimate test. I'm going to read a boring novel by Henry James while I put you to sleep. This is a scientific inquiry and I need pristine conditions, so work with me here."

Ryan gave her a sweet smile as she kicked off her shoes and started to climb in. Instead, she detoured to the door and locked it, then stripped off her jeans. She left on her bright yellow T-shirt and as she crawled across the bed Jamie patted her butt and said, "You look like a bumble bee with those black shorts and yellow shirt."

"Well, if you're doing a scientific inquiry, you need to account for all of the variables. Having my pants off just makes your task a little bit harder."

"I'll say," she agreed as she ran a hand across the smoothly muscled rear. "Now put your head right here," she instructed as she indicated the spot where her thighs met her pelvis.

Ryan raised one eyebrow, but quickly complied, settling down comfortably with a minimum of adjustments. Jamie ran her fingers through her hair for a few minutes, smiling to herself when she heard the rhythmic breathing begin almost immediately.

By one o'clock Ryan had shifted her position so that she was curled up in a little ball on the left side of the bed. Jamie had been plowing through her novel, but she found that she was sinking lower and lower as the afternoon wore on. To combat her weariness and to satisfy her growling stomach, she decided to go downstairs to make lunch. She slipped out of bed and stood still for a few minutes to make sure Ryan didn't wake. *She must be a deep sleeper like me*, she thought as she watched her chest rise and fall in a slow cadence.

Even though she'd been doing well in keeping her pantry stocked, she found nothing that appealed to her for lunch, so she hopped in the car and drove to the market to do a little shopping. When she returned, she made two Italian cold cut sandwiches and grabbed two bottles of water before returning to her room. It was nearly two, but Ryan still hadn't moved a muscle. She sat on the loveseat and read while she ate, whiling away another hour. At three o'clock she heard a small noise and looked up to notice movement from her companion. She climbed in bed behind her and gently rubbed her body, smiling at the catlike way she stretched and twisted to wake. Cute little moans and tiny growls were the only sounds to come from the slowly waking woman. When Jamie was sure that her partner was fully awake, she started to nibble on her tender ear. "Want some lunch, sleeping beauty?"

"Yeah," a voice that sounded like five-year-old girl replied. "If my tummy hadn't been growling so much I'd still be asleep, but you know the beast can't be denied."

"Well sit up and I'll get your sandwich."

"What do I get?" she asked happily.

"You get ham and salami and prosciutto and provolone with mayo and a few pepperoncinis."

"Uhm, my favorite!"

"Do you make sandwiches like this?"

"No, but I can tell it's going to be my new favorite."

Jamie hopped back into bed and started to read again. Ryan gulped the sandwich down in record time, pronouncing it her most favorite sandwich ever. She snuggled up against Jamie, laying her head back in her lap, and was asleep within ten minutes. *Jeez, how little sleep did she get last night? I've never known her to sleep in the daytime at all, much less for hours at a time.*

By the time she finished her novel, she had an overpowering desire to snuggle down and join Ryan for a long nap, but since it was nearly six, she didn't think that was wise. She started to move a tiny bit, and Ryan quickly opened her eyes and sat straight up. "Time to get up?" she asked, sounding fully alert.

"Are you a heavy sleeper or not?" Jamie asked confusedly. "That one time you took a nap on my couch, you said you were a really light sleeper, but this afternoon you were nearly comatose."

"I'm generally a light sleeper, and I usually wake up pretty alert, but I was so relaxed and peaceful this afternoon that I just zonked. I've been fantasizing about sleeping with you a lot, but in my dreams we were never really sleeping," she said with a leer. "I've got to admit that actually sleeping when you're near me is one of the most pleasurable experiences I've ever had. This is the kind of thing I've missed out on, you know. I've never felt comfortable enough with the women I've been with to collapse like I did today."

"That's so sweet," Jamie said as she leaned over and hugged her. "I love hearing about the things that make our being together special for you."

Ryan was now lying on her back, and she pulled her companion down to rest against her side. "I felt warm and peaceful this afternoon. It felt like I must have felt lying in my mother's arms," she said softly. "I knew I was safe and that you'd protect me."

"You'll always be safe with me, Ryan," she vowed as she tilted her head just a bit to capture warm, full lips. They exchanged sweet soft kisses for a few lazy minutes, relishing the warmth and safety of their bond.

Ryan was beginning to stretch again, and she rolled onto her stomach to get the kinks out of her back. She stretched her arms straight out against the mattress and pulled her knees up until she was crouched down like a cat. She pushed first one arm, then the other as far as she could get them, stretching all of the muscles of her back and waist as she did. The display that she put on was entertaining enough, but the adorable little yawns and sighs made Jamie's eyes light up.

"You are so cute sometimes that I can't get over it."

Still in the middle of her routine, Ryan turned her now-red face to her lover. "What's cute?"

"You are," she insisted. "The dichotomy between how you are in public and how you behave in private is so adorable. I never would have seen your cute little baby side if we weren't together. That would have been such a loss!"

"Am I really that different?"

"Yeah, you are. Outside you seem bright and mature and thoughtful and patient. You seem really calm and forthright about things. But when we're alone, you're so playful and childlike. It's just so cute!"

Ryan tumbled over onto her back and regarded Jamie with a peaceful smile. "I'm not like this with many people. And I've rarely been this relaxed with a lover. I showed most of them my predator side."

"Did you really have a different way of being with your past lovers?"

"Yep. But I don't think that side has to stay in my repertoire any longer. The predator can be put out to pasture."

"Uhm, I don't know," Jamie said. "It might be fun to bring it out some day when things get dull."

As she swung her legs around to sit upright, Ryan grasped her lover around the waist for a firm hug. "I don't think things will ever get dull when you're around."

Jamie stood and did a little stretch of her own. "Hey, don't you have any studying to do?"

"Yeah, I do. I guess I should get going."

"Why don't you study here? I did very well on my half of the experiment, but we still don't know if you can study with me around."

"Okay. I'm game."

"Let's go walk around to get our blood flowing and grab dinner. Then we can come back here and work."

"Let me call home and tell them I'll be late."

"Tell them you'll be home tomorrow," Jamie corrected with an impish grin.

Ryan paused in mid step to turn and stare. "Are you sure about that? Isn't Cassie going to be home tonight?"

"Don't know. Don't care. She's so mad at me that I really don't think anything I do at this point will make matters worse, so I may as well please myself."

"I'm all for pleasing you when it involves sleeping together," Ryan said.

Cassie was still at home, judging from her closed bedroom door. "Just my luck to have her stay home to study this weekend," Jamie muttered as they descended the front staircase.

"We'll just stay out of her way. I'm happy to get up and leave before she wakes up in the morning."

"I don't feel comfortable asking you to do that," Jamie said. "I need to stand up for myself and do what I think is right. And I know that loving you is right," she added as she lightly gripped Ryan's hand.

During the rest of their walk, Ryan serenaded her appreciative friend with a soulful rendition of *If loving you is wrong, (I don't want to be right)*. The song was unfamiliar to Jamie, but Ryan explained it was a cheesy song from the '70s. Her knowledge of music never ceased to amaze, but what Jamie really appreciated was how catholic Ryan's tastes were. She could sing songs from every era, and she seemed to have an inexhaustible supply of appropriate songs with their lyrics stored up in her pretty little head, ready to be retrieved when the situation warranted.

As they walked along, Jamie began to wish they were walking to Oakland, rather than the few blocks they had planned. Ryan's natural flair for performing was out in full force tonight, and Jamie was as pleased by that fact as she was amazed. They were on a fairly well traveled street with occasional pedestrians and a constant trickle of cars passing by, but Ryan was belting out the song with every bit of her considerable charm. A chill ran down Jamie's spine and she actually shivered a bit as she considered the immense self-confidence her lover possessed. Even though her own voice wasn't bad, she had never had the nerve to sing for Ryan in private. But here was this gorgeous creature, singing a soulful song at full voice, complete with tiny hip gyrations, on a busy street in the middle of the evening. *I don't think it'll be humanly possible to ever tire of this woman*, she thought with a self-satisfied smile as she squeezed her hand tightly.

As they walked down Telegraph, Jamie spied one of her favorite vintage clothing stores and decided to go in. Ryan froze just a bit, and tried to decide whether to follow her in or not. Trying to avoid a potentially uncomfortable situation, she said, "You go on in. I want to look at some CDs."

"Come with me," Jamie urged. "I need your approval before I buy any new clothes, don't I?"

"The last thing you need is clothes," Ryan teased. "You've got more clothes than I have uhm … cousins."

"I don't have nearly that many," she laughed. "Come on. I want some dykier clothes for going to the bar with you."

"You don't have to butch it up, Jamie. You look wonderful no matter what you wear," she insisted as she tried to guide her past the store.

But the little bulldog was not to be deterred. She looked up at Ryan with a suspicious glance and asked, "Why don't you want me to go in there?"

Ryan's shoulders dropped and she adopted a hangdog expression. "It's not you, it's me. I kinda know the owner, and I don't want to make her or you uncomfortable."

"Did you have a bad parting?"

"No, but I think she … oh, I don't know. It's silly to speculate what she might have thought."

"Are you being intentionally obtuse?"

"No, it's inadvertent," she said, laughing at herself.

"Look, Romeo, given how many women you've known, we're going to run into this problem every once in a while. I'll just have to learn how to cope with your past."

"Okay," she agreed. "She might not even remember me."

"Yeah," Jamie nodded. "That's pretty likely."

The woman was sitting right behind the counter just as she had been the last time Ryan visited the store. She didn't really look up from her book when they entered, and shortly thereafter another customer took a number of items up to the counter, effectively distracting her. "That her?" Jamie asked quietly.

Ryan nodded and tried to look inconspicuous. After twenty minutes, Ryan was practically hanging from one of the overstuffed racks, reminding herself how much she hated shopping. Jamie was trying to decide from among five different blouses, and Ryan finally decided there was only one way to get her to move. She walked over and stood next to the counter, waiting patiently while the woman lowered her book. "Can I help you w —" she started to ask, but swallowed the end of her sentence when she saw Ryan looming in front of her. A smirk crossed her face as she said, "Took you long enough! A woman could get a complex waiting for you."

"It's not because I was an unhappy customer," Ryan purred in her old predator voice.

"She's been otherwise occupied," Jamie piped up, having appeared out of thin air to possessively slip her arm around Ryan's waist.

The woman blushed deeply and Jamie immediately took pity on her and apologized, "Sorry I'm so overprotective. She's just …"

"Yeah, she is," the woman said appreciatively, sneaking a quick look at Ryan. "Well, congratulations, anyway."

"Thanks," Jamie said as she piled all of the shirts on the counter.

A few minutes later, Ryan teased her partner for her inability to make up her mind. "I didn't really want all of them," she lamented. "But I wasn't going to let you talk to her all alone!"

"And you say I smother you!"

"Well, you're a very valuable asset. I'm just protecting my goods. Say, how long did you go out with her?"

"Not very long."

"What's her name?"

"Uhm, not sure."

"That's funny, you're usually very good with names," she said as she tried to fish for information.

Exasperated, Ryan gave up. "I can't remember them if I don't know them. I spent a total of one hour with the woman, and yes, we did have sex. Happy?"

Jamie stopped in the middle of the sidewalk and asked just one question. "Why?"

"Why what?" Ryan asked, looking cornered and a bit irritated.

"Why did you have sex with her?"

"Because I could," she spat as she shoved her hands in her pockets and strode off down the street.

But Jamie wasn't going to be tossed aside so easily. She ran down the street and grabbed Ryan by the back of her waistband. "Wait please," she begged. With a deep sigh the brunette stopped, but her eyes were flat and cold when she turned to face her lover. "Let's stop for some dinner to cool off, okay?"

She shrugged her broad shoulders, but didn't otherwise refuse, so Jamie took her hand and led her to a little sidewalk café where they could order some nice salads. After their order was taken, Jamie grasped her hand across the table and softly said, "I don't believe you."

"Pardon?" Ryan replied archly, still angry.

"I don't believe that's why you had sex with her. That's not who you are."

"That *is* who I am. That's exactly who I am. I used women to fill myself up. It makes me sick to think of you eventually meeting more and more of them, because I know what you're thinking."

"One—that's not who you are, two—you don't know what I'm thinking. Which point do you want to talk about first?"

Ryan had to laugh at her approach. "Number one, I guess."

"Okay, do you remember your encounter with her?"

"Yeah, of course I do. I wasn't drunk or anything."

"Okay. Tell me how it happened."

Ryan sighed heavily as she related the tale. "I was in there trying on clothes and she came up and started to flirt. I flirted back and she just kept coming on, so I eventually asked her if she wanted to go get coffee. She couldn't leave, so I suggested we use her office for a little love. She didn't protest, so we did. It took less than an hour, including the time it took me to try on clothes."

"How did you feel?"

"I felt good. It made me feel sexy and powerful. I liked that I could talk her into doing something hot right in the middle of the day with a total stranger."

Jamie didn't really like that answer. She hated to see Ryan in such a brutal light, but she decided that she needed to know her lover fully, even when it was painful. "Was she good? Did she please you?"

"Uhm, she was very responsive. I think she would have been a good lover."

"But you don't know? Why?"

"Uhm … I kept my clothes on."

Jamie's expression was one of total puzzlement. "You kept your clothes on to have sex?"

"I had sex with her. She didn't have sex with me." She rolled her eyes and asked, "Do you want me to be more explicit?"

"No, that's not important. But I still wanna know why."

"Jesus, could you ask broader questions?" she asked in frustration.

"Please think about this, Ryan. It's important to me."

"All right," she said as she took in a deep breath. She closed her eyes and concentrated for a few minutes before she said, "It just … I don't know … it was too intimate."

"So you didn't do it for sexual release?"

"I suppose not. At least not directly."

"But you wanted to touch her. It was your idea, right?"

"Right. I definitely wanted to touch her."

"Why?" she asked again.

"Because she was cute and she looked like fun and I was horny. Why else would I do it?"

"Well, when I'm horny, I'm interested in being touched. Doesn't that make sense?"

"Yeah, I guess, but I'm not like that all of the time. I like touching."

"Not at the bar the other night," she reminded her. "You wanted to be touched. Quite a lot, if my memory serves."

"But that's different. I know you and I want to be your lover. You really excite me."

"Granted. But why'd you want to touch her? What did you get out of it? Let yourself feel how you felt when you decided to bring it up."

Ryan closed her eyes again and furrowed her brow. When she looked up, she looked very young and very fragile. "I … I was lonely," she admitted. "This happened just before school started this year. I'd had kind of a tough summer, and I hadn't been out very much. I needed to connect with someone, but I was feeling vulnerable and I didn't want to open myself up too much. So I touched her and gave her some pleasure, and I felt better."

"Ryan, honey," Jamie said as she took her hand. "You didn't have sex because you could. You had sex because you needed to."

Scowling, Ryan asked, "What's the difference?"

"I think there's a big difference. You need a lot of touch. Your good looks and your charm have allowed you to get that without having to risk too much. You were just trying to fill yourself up."

"It's still completely self-centered, Jamie. That's not a very admirable trait."

"Well, it's not like feeding the starving or clothing the poor, but it's not a bad thing. You weren't just making another notch on your belt. You're not *like* that. You didn't have sex with her to show how powerful you were. You were trying to fill your need in the only way you felt comfortable."

"Do you really believe that?" she asked with her trusting deep blue eyes wide open.

"Yes, I do. You weren't using people to satisfy your sexual urges. They were actually using you. You gave sex to get connection and touch. I think you would have been as happy to stand in that store and hug for a few minutes."

"No, you're wrong there. I really enjoyed touching the women I was with. Hugging wouldn't have been enough. I loved trying to please them sexually. It filled me up to watch a woman throw her head back and have a great orgasm because of the way I touched her. It made me feel ... whole." She shook her head. "I can't think of a better word. It made me feel whole."

"Maybe you programmed yourself to feel that way," Jamie theorized.

"I might be a nerd, but I don't program myself."

Jamie squeezed her hand. "You know what I mean. I think your early sexual experiences were much more about touch than sex, but once you realized you were good at it, I think you used it as a way to get what you needed without having to reveal too much of yourself."

"Why would I do that? Why not ask for what I wanted if I just wanted touch. I'm sure I could have found some nice Mormon woman who wanted to cuddle if I promised never to touch her fun spots."

"Yeah," Jamie said, smiling. "Those women use the personals in *SF Weekly* all the time."

"Well, they could," Ryan said, wrinkling her nose.

"Don't try to get me off topic. I think you used a false intimacy as a way to avoid real intimacy."

"False intimacy is fucking strangers?"

"Yeah. Nice turn of phrase," Jamie said, rolling her eyes admonishingly.

But Ryan wasn't willing to settle down and let Jamie's words in. "What's real intimacy? Fucking someone you know? 'Cause I did a lot of that too."

"No, smarty-pants. It's easy for you to be physically intimate with strangers or women you know, but much harder for you to be emotionally connected. And for me, I can have emotional connections easier than physical ones."

Ryan nodded, a little furrow between her brows as she gazed at Jamie soberly. "So we both have some work to do, huh?"

"Yep. But there's no one I'd rather work with than you."

"I'd love to practice being intimate with you tonight," Ryan murmured as she lowered her eyes to lock onto Jamie's.

"And I'd love to practice being physical with you," she replied with a sexy growl. Ryan's hand dropped under the table to run up and down Jamie's leg as she continued to hold her gaze.

Jamie swallowed audibly as she dug into her pocket for twenty dollars. She tossed it on the table and grabbed Ryan's hand, brushing past their startled server. "Feed the homeless," Ryan instructed as the server placed their meal at the now empty table.

It was fairly obvious that studying was the furthest thing from Jamie's mind as she tore up the stairs to her bedroom. Ryan followed along obediently, relieved that neither roommate seemed to spot her. When they were safely locked inside, Jamie turned her stereo on to the classical station to provide some background noise and pounced on Ryan like a hungry dog on a bone. "Be gentle," she begged as Jamie tossed her to the bed and climbed aboard her body.

"Is that how you like to be touched?" Jamie whispered as she leaned down and hovered over her partner's flushed face, her warm breath tickling Ryan's face. "Do you like to be touched gently?"

Trying to summon enough saliva to speak, Ryan went for the easier means of communication and just nodded her head.

"I'd like to touch you gently," Jamie whispered, her eyes fluttering closed at the mere thought of how she wanted to touch her lovely body.

"Kiss me," Ryan begged, involuntarily closing her own eyes as her lips parted sensually.

Jamie immediately complied with her wishes, closing the inch distance with a tiny movement of her head. "Mmm," she murmured. "You taste divine."

Ryan was too intent on the gentle assault to acknowledge the compliment. Her mouth opened slowly as she sucked lightly, drawing Jamie's silky smooth tongue into her mouth. She felt her hips jerk as the sensation slammed into her central nervous system, and she heard a small moan rumble deep in her chest.

Just when she thought she was as hot as she could get, Jamie pulled away and shyly asked, "Can I touch you more … intimately? I wanna feel your skin under my hands."

"Okay," she replied in a voice that sounded an octave higher than usual. "I'd … like that."

Jamie got up and turned off the overhead lights. She lit two big candles and placed one on the bedside table and the other on her desk. Then she started to remove her clothing, but realized that she had her eyes locked on Ryan's so intently she was losing track of what she was doing. So she turned her back and pulled her T-shirt from her jeans, slipped her arms from the sleeves and quickly removed her bra. She put the shirt back on properly, unzipped her jeans and let them fall. As she stepped out of them, she turned to find Ryan gazing at her so intently that she seemed transfixed.

She crossed back to the bed and held her hand out to her stunned looking lover. As she got to her feet, Jamie placed her hands lightly on her waist and met her gaze as she said, "I'm going to undress you, okay?"

Ryan nodded her head vacantly, privately wondering what mastermind was dreaming up this exquisite torture. Maintaining eye contact, she placed her hands on Jamie's shoulders for support. Jamie slipped her hand under the bright yellow T-shirt and dipped the fingers of her left hand into Ryan's waistband. A tiny chill started at the base of Ryan's skull as the dexterous fingers touched the warm skin of her belly. Jamie sucked in a breath as she gently pulled the waistband tight to unbutton each of the little silver buttons. When she was finished, she pushed the pants down and urged Ryan to step out of them.

Now Ryan stood in her bright yellow T-shirt and tight knit black boxers. Jamie didn't quite know where to start to get what she needed. She wanted more skin contact, but knew they were treading on dangerous ground. So instead she wrapped her arms around Ryan and slid her hands up her back to remove her bra. She handled the closure pretty well, given her lack of experience from this angle, and as soon as the garment was loose, she ran a hand up each sleeve to pull it from her shoulders. Her hand snaked up the front of the shirt and quickly whisked the lacy black item away.

Okay, she thought to herself, *I've got her nearly undressed, now what do I do with her?*

Ryan obviously sensed her indecision and tried to offer a reassuring gesture. She sat on the edge of the bed and gently wrapped her arms around Jamie's waist. The long, tender hug they shared seemed to relax Jamie a bit, and she soon began to rub Ryan's back through her T-shirt. The last thing on Ryan's mind was her back, as Jamie's perfect breasts rubbed against her face. She fought with every ounce of her self-control to stop herself from sucking one of the tender mounds right into her mouth, satisfying herself by inhaling Jamie's sweet scent as deeply into her lungs as she could manage.

Without conscious thought, Ryan's hands had dropped to rest on Jamie's sculpted backside, and she began to knead the firm flesh with a slow, throbbing intensity. Jamie was very conscious of the massage, and knew they were headed right for a cliff.

Gathering her wits, she leaned over gently and placed a wet kiss on Ryan's lips. Holding her face in both of her hands she whispered, "We have to stop. It's too much."

"I know." Ryan nodded weakly. "We stop now—or a week from now."

"Yeah," she said as she gave her partner another kiss. "But I really want to keep going. This feels so right." She gently lobbed a grenade at her lover as she pulled the pin. "Should we?"

Of the millions of neurons firing in Ryan's brain at that second, nearly every one thought Jamie's hesitant suggestion was the best one they had ever heard. But one tiny holdout reminded her that she had made a promise to hold back. She knew breaking that promise would be pleasurable, but that the pleasure would have lasting repercussions. So she looked up at Jamie's hopeful face and spoke the hardest single syllable she had ever been forced to say. "No." Looking directly into her partner's eyes, she reiterated, "It's a very bad idea."

"Are you sure?" she asked again, running her fingers up and down Ryan's sensitive face. "I feel … okay about it."

All of Ryan's early religious training flew into her mind, and she mused that this must truly be the voice of the devil. The nuns used to tell her that temptation didn't come from a scary-looking horned creature; it came from normal-looking people who tried to convince you to abandon your principles and your morals for physical pleasure. She fought back the only way she knew how. She imagined that this was a contest, and she hated to lose no matter what the contest consisted of. Strangely enough, the image worked, and she gently pushed her partner away and stood up.

"I'm completely sure. I made you a promise, and I'm not gonna break it. Now I'm gonna get ready for bed." She brought her hand to Jamie's damp forehead and brushed the hair away with her fingertips. "When you're ready, I swear we'll make such wonderful love that you'll be glad we waited." With that, she stepped into the bathroom and turned on the shower.

When Ryan emerged twenty minutes later, Jamie had changed into some loose-fitting cotton pajamas. She was lying on her back with the sheet and blanket shoved down by her feet. The window was open and a cool breeze flowed through the room as Ryan crossed over to the dresser and once again pulled Jack's sweats out. She had a big towel wrapped around her body and she shot a tentative glance at Jamie as she passed.

She was greeted with a warm, tired-looking smile from her lover's still-flushed face. "Hurry up and get in here," she demanded. "It's lonely without you."

Ryan ducked back into the bath and quickly put on the now-familiar clothes. As she closed and locked the door to the bath, she hopped in next to her lover. "Nice hand-held shower massage," she intimated with a chuckle.

There was no response for a minute, and as she leaned over her partner, Jamie's timid voice carried back to her. "Mad at me?"

Ryan leaned over at far as she could in order to make eye contact. "Of course not. Why would I be mad at you?"

"'Cause I tried to manipulate you into breaking our agreement?"

Ryan laughed gently as she settled back down behind Jamie's warm body. "Well, I did have a flash of you as the devil incarnate, which helped my resolve," she admitted with a laugh. "I just hope I didn't hurt your self-confidence by saying no."

"No, I could tell it wasn't from lack of interest. You looked like you were gonna explode. I was really a little worried about your blood pressure."

"I have honestly never been more interested in anything in my life," she conceded. "But we're in this for life, and I want to make our first time special. Having to be quiet and worrying about Cassie being in the next room wouldn't create the kind of atmosphere that I know you and I both want."

"I completely forgot she was even there!" Jamie moaned, slapping herself on the forehead.

"That's why you have me," Ryan said as she nuzzled against the back of her neck. "I'm the voice of reason."

"You are. I'd give you a solid A minus for your performance tonight."

"A minus! You've gotta be kidding!"

"We wouldn't have gotten that out of control if a certain pair of big, strong hands hadn't started massaging my butt in the most erotic fashion I've ever experienced," she chided as she pulled one of the hands in question to her mouth for a kiss.

"A minus seems generous, now that you mention it," Ryan murmured as she gathered Jamie even closer to her body and drifted off into a satisfied sleep.

The next morning, they stayed in bed cuddling much later than either was accustomed to. It was nearly eight when Ryan heard the shower start, signaling that Cassie was both up and occupied. "I'm going to sneak out while she's in the shower," she said as she dragged herself to the side of the bed. Jamie was still clutching her tightly, and she was dragged along right behind her. "Gosh I feel so heavy and lethargic today," she teased as the playful blonde refused to release her. A quick tickle to her exposed waist did the trick, and Ryan jumped to her feet with a laugh. "You're so easy!"

"Someday I'll find all of your ticklish spots."

"That will be my pleasure. Especially since all of them are well hidden under my clothes."

"Do you really have to go?" Jamie asked as she rolled onto her back and dropped her head off the edge of the bed. "You know, you're even cuter upside down."

"Thanks, maybe I'll have to start walking on my hands. And yes, I do have to go, since I did exactly nothing yesterday, thanks to you."

"Can you really?"

"Can I really what?"

"Walk on your hands?"

Ryan placed her hands on her hips and regarded her sternly. "Don't you trust me?"

"Of course I do. I just can't imagine that you can do that."

Ryan began to grumble under her breath, but compliantly went to the wall and executed a perfect handstand. When she was sure of her balance, she took a few steps and paused right next to Jamie's still upturned head. "Scoot over," she ordered. As soon as Jamie did, she flexed her arms and propelled herself onto the bed, landing on her face right next to her startled friend. "I never exaggerate," she said as she rolled onto her side.

"Not at all?" Jamie asked.

"Nope. Not at all."

"Then tell me how you rate as a lover," she purred as she rolled Ryan over onto her back and climbed on top.

"Well, I'm also fairly modest, so keep that in mind," she warned.

"I'm waiting."

Ryan grabbed her by the hips and bench-pressed her into the air, much to the giggling woman's delight. She pressed her into the air and lowered her for a wet kiss as she spoke each word. "I'm ... absolutely ... positively ... stupendous," she promised as she released her grip and welcomed Jamie back into her arms.

She gulped audibly. "Then I'm in deep, deep trouble."

"You have no idea," Ryan purred. As she watched the goose bumps roll down Jamie's body, she patted her on the cheek and said, "The shower stopped. I'm really gonna have to make a run for it."

"Just stay in my room all day. I'll keep you as my little captive."

"I'm gonna be your little captive who flunks out of school if I don't get busy. And, may I say, you have officially proven yourself to be the world's worst study partner." She grabbed her clothes and made a small circle with her index finger. "Turn around," she said with a cute grin.

Jamie made an exaggerated display of turning her head while Ryan pulled her jeans back on. "You don't happen to have any of Jack's underwear lying around do you?"

"No, but why ... oh!" she said as she remembered the way the evening ended. "Sorry," she said as she wrinkled up her nose in a grin.

"You should be. I hate riding my bike with jeans and no underwear. I'm gonna have to keep some spares here for emergencies." She was fully dressed now, and she came back to the bed for a few tender kisses. "I'll miss you," she whispered as she placed one final gentle kiss on Jamie's sweet lips.

"See you tomorrow bright and early?"

"Without question," Ryan promised, blowing one final kiss as she snuck out the door.

Chapter Seven

O n the way home from school the next day, Jamie stopped to do a little shopping. She found some new Ralph Lauren boxers that were even longer than Ryan's current Calvin's. So she got her two pair in white, two in gray and two in black, as well as the matching ribbed knit tank tops and a few close fitting T-shirts in the same colors and material as the shorts. Then, just as a tease, she bought one pair of panties that would have had to grow a bit to even be considered a thong. *I know she won't like to wear these out, but I could explore her body a lot better if she were wearing these. Actually I could explore her body from across the room in these.*

Ryan wasn't due for another hour, and she had just laid the gifts out on the kitchen table when the doorbell rang. She waited for a second, but when she didn't hear anyone else come downstairs, she realized she was alone in the house. She spotted a blonde head through the leaded glass window of the front door, but it took a moment for the realization to actually hit her brain. "Mother!" she nearly gasped when she opened the door.

Although Jamie lived only forty-five minutes away from her parents' home, her mother had not once paid a visit to the Berkeley house in the three years she had lived there. She and Laura Martin had furnished the place before the girls moved in, but once they were firmly ensconced, Catherine made herself scarce.

"Hello, Jamie," she said softly as she lifted her head to kiss both of her cheeks. Catherine Evans was one of the few people who actually had to stretch to reach Jamie's lips, a fact that had pleased Jamie to no end when she was fourteen and finally surpassed her mother's height.

"W ... What's wrong, Mother?"

A flash of pain raced across the smaller woman's face, but she hid it quickly and asked, "Is it that odd to have me visit?"

Jamie didn't want to say the truth so she quickly replied, "Of course not. I'm just surprised to see you, especially without warning."

"Warning?" she asked quietly as another hurt look passed over her patrician features.

"I mean notice," she amended, but quickly decided that wasn't much better. "It's a long trip to make, and I'm home so little during the day."

"That's all right, dear," her mother reassured her, sensing her discomfort. "I suppose I can't blame you for being surprised when I visit so infrequently."

Yeah, never is pretty infrequent, she thought. "So why visit today?" Jamie asked. She was getting a very strange vibe from her mother, but since she couldn't read her emotions very well, she had a hard time guessing what the issue was.

"I just came by to chat for a while," she said, rather mysteriously. Her impeccable manners kicked in and she asked, "I'm not interrupting you, am I?"

"No, not at all. Would you like something to drink? I have some bottled water."

"That would be nice," Catherine agreed. "I like your kitchen quite a lot. Could we sit in there and chat?"

"Sure, Mother," she agreed, her feeling of unease growing.

Jamie went to the refrigerator as her mother pulled up a chair at the table. "Been shopping, dear?" she asked rather absently as she held up a pair of the boxer shorts. It was obvious that the large shorts would fall off Jamie, and the T-shirts were labeled extra-large. She picked up the tiny black panties that were also clearly labeled large, though they were anything but, and stared at her daughter with a puzzled expression on her face.

"Uhm ... yeah. Just shopping for a friend," she explained as she gathered up the clothing and shoved it back in the bag.

Catherine didn't comment, but her expression grew troubled as she took a deep breath and asked the question that had been burning in her brain since the previous day. "Jamie, I know we haven't been as close as I wish we could be, and I know I've not been your confidant. But I have to ask you a question that's deeply personal. If you choose not to share the answer with me, I'll understand. I merely ask that you not lie to me."

Jamie knew that all of the color had drained from her face, and she felt that familiar clenching in her stomach. *Oh, please, oh, please*, she begged as she braced herself for the inevitable.

"Laura Martin called me yesterday. She says that Cassie called her in a frantic state over a dispute you two had."

Jamie merely nodded, hoping against hope that Cassie had the decency to only speak of the fight and not the underlying reason. Her hopes were dashed when Catherine continued. "Cassie claims you're involved in a lesbian affair." She locked her big brown eyes on her daughter's and gently asked, "Is that true?"

Jamie sucked in a few deep breaths, trying to regain her composure without making it too obvious that she was panicking. "I know that one thing is totally true, Mother. Cassie Martin is no friend. She's developed an intense, almost irrational, hatred of my friend Ryan, who *is* a lesbian. She's tried to convince me not to hang around with her merely because of her sexual orientation, and when I refused, she obviously made up a ridiculous story about us."

"Jamie, the things Laura said were really quite specific. She said you were feeding each other and kissing and sucking on each other's fingers." Catherine looked embarrassed to even relate this tale, but she had such a worried, pained expression on her face that Jamie felt compassion for her.

"Mother, you know from listening to Daddy talk about trials that the easiest thing in the world is to take things out of context and use them to impeach someone. That's what Cassie does."

"But how …"

"Look, Ryan and I were kidding around in a very public place. I'm not the kind of person who'd be kissing and sucking on anyone's fingers in public. I gave her a bite of my food, and she acted like she was going to bite my fingers. It was totally innocent, and anyone else would have come up to the table and either teased me about it or at least said hello. But she went home and got Mia involved and then jumped all over me when I came home. She wouldn't listen to any of my explanations, and we finally had a very big fight. I basically told her that I chose Ryan's friendship over hers, and now she's running to her mother just to get back at me. She's a very small-minded, mean-spirited person, Mother, and I feel like I'm well rid of her!"

"But what about living together next year?"

"I've had it with her. I refuse to allow her back in next year."

"Oh, Jamie, is that really wise? You've known each other since you were children!"

"I can't feel comfortable having her in my house if she's going to go behind my back to try to create trouble for me."

"But Jamie, Laura claims that she's concerned about you. I didn't get the impression she was trying to cause trouble."

"Mother, if you were concerned about one of your friends would you run to her husband or her children with the problem? Of course not. You'd work it out with her alone, if you really cared for her. Cassie telling her mother was a sure fire way to get you upset. That was her goal. I'm certain of it."

"So you're telling me, unequivocally, you aren't involved in a relationship with this woman?" Her deep brown eyes were still intently focused on her daughter's, and Jamie knew that she would be betraying her trust for the first time in her life if she was not honest with her now.

"I'm most definitely in a relationship with her, Mother. She's my very close friend, she's my training partner for the AIDS Ride, and she's my personal trainer. But I do not have sex with her." She honestly couldn't decide what felt worse—lying to her mother so blatantly, or once again denying her love and her passion for Ryan. Part of her actually felt the lie to her mother was the more egregious wrong, since her main reason for lying was that she didn't trust enough to tell her the truth, but she acknowledged she felt worse about the denial of her love for Ryan.

Catherine looked at her carefully for a moment and finally raised her hand to cup her daughter's flushed pink cheek. "I'm sorry if all this upset you. I know you feel betrayed, but please give it some more thought before you do anything rash."

"I will. And thanks for your concern."

"Jamie, no matter what you think of me as a mother, I hope you know that your happiness has always been paramount for me. I really regret the distance that has built up between us and I'd do anything to close that gap." She reached across the table with her elegant, perfectly manicured hand and lightly grasped Jamie's hand. Gazing into her eyes with a winsome look on her face, she explained, "That's the biggest reason I wanted you to go to Italy with me this summer. I miss the time we used to spend together when you were younger. It just seems like we have so little time before you'll be involved in a career or married. Will you work with me to try to regain some of our connection?"

"Of course I will. I miss those times too," she admitted truthfully.

"Remember how we used to try out all the new restaurants in the Peninsula and the South Bay?" She smiled softly at the memory. "That was fun, wasn't it?" The fragile, pained expression on her mother's face made Jamie want to take her in her arms and comfort her like a child. But physical expression of their love was something they had never done, and she didn't feel comfortable starting now.

"They *were* fun. We've had lots of fun together, and there's no reason not to have more in the future. We need to work on making more time for each other."

"Thank you, dear," she said as she patted her cheek. "Your father and I are so lucky to have you as our child. You make us both very proud of you."

Jamie fought back a tear as she grasped her mother's hand. "Thanks. That means a lot to me."

"Well, I'd better get going if I want to beat traffic," she said as she stood. "How are things going with your preparation for your ride?"

"They're going well. Very well. I'm really excited about it."

"Will you call me when you get back? I'll be worried about you the whole week, you know," she said with a small smile.

"I promise I'll call."

"So what will you do the rest of the summer?"

"I actually had a favor to ask concerning the rest of the summer," she said. "Would you mind if I took Ryan down to the weekend house for a little rest after we get back?"

"No, of course not. You're welcome to bring any of your friends at any time, dear. Just let the maid know if you want daily cleaning service. And call ahead to have them stock the refrigerator if you wish."

"Thank you, Mother. I really appreciate your generosity."

"Jamie, you're my only child. I'd do anything for you," she said as her voice caught a tiny bit. She gave her daughter a firm hug and turned to leave. As she reached the door, she said, "Please be careful, dear. You're very important to me."

Wow, what was that all about? Jamie thought as she stared after her. *She seemed so ... interested.*

Perhaps betraying her lover on a regular basis was making the task easier, but for whatever reason, Jamie didn't feel all that bad when Ryan showed up at six. She decided to hold off on the presentation of the new underwear, and grabbed her book bag for the walk to Telegraph. As they were descending the stairs, Mia came walking up the sidewalk. "Hi guys," she said when she caught sight of them.

"Hi," both women replied. "We're going to grab some dinner and then go study. Wanna join us?" Jamie asked.

Mia looked uncomfortable, and she stumbled over her words as she obviously tried to come up with a reason to demur. "Ahh, no I don't think I can. I've got to, you know, uhm … study, and I might go out later, so …"

"That's okay," Jamie said. "Some other time."

"Yeah, okay," she said as she dashed into the house without another word.

As they walked down the street, Ryan said, "Was she acting funny or is that normal?"

"She's acting funny. I think she might be having an attack of homophobia."

"Really? She's never seemed uncomfortable with me before."

"It's not you," she said quietly. "It's me."

Ryan stopped abruptly and gazed at her partner carefully. "Did you tell her?"

"No. This is what I was hiding from you on Friday. Cassie was at the coffee shop on Thursday night and she saw us feeding each other."

Ryan closed her eyes and allowed her head to drop back against her shoulders. She shook it slowly a few times, long dark hair twitching against her back. "Oh, Jamie, I'm so sorry. I … I forget what it's like to not want others to know. I really apologize for being so obvious."

"It's not your fault. I just need to get over it."

"Jamie," she said quietly as she took her hand. "This is a big change for you. I want you to have the time and the space to go as fast as you're comfortable with. I've been encouraging you to be more open than you're probably ready for, and I truly apologize for that."

"No, I'm the one that needs to apologize," she insisted as she blinked her eyes and tried to summon her courage.

"Why?"

"Because I told her she was wrong," she said in a voice so small Ryan had to bend over to hear her.

"Why on earth would that make you feel the need to apologize?" Ryan asked, clearly puzzled.

She stopped in her tracks and stared at her companion. "Because I denied our love. I didn't have the courage to face her and admit the truth."

"Jamie, Jamie, Jamie," Ryan murmured as she slid an arm around her shoulders. "That wouldn't have been a courageous thing to do. That would have been self-defeating. You're not ready to tell everyone about us yet. Telling Cassie would have been like putting an ad in the Chronicle. I thought you understood how I felt about this after that incident with your father. It's perfectly okay with me if it takes you a long time to be open about us. Please don't worry about my feelings."

"How can you even say that? Your opinion of me means everything!"

"I know. And I'll admit I'm really invested in having you be honest with everyone about us. That's something that I think we both need to do in order to feel like our relationship is something we're proud of. I just meant that I don't want you to worry about my feelings about this right now. You need time to work on this on your own without worrying about me."

"But ... I don't understand why you're not upset about this, given how you felt at my dad's apartment."

"It's simple, babe. You denied *me* that time. It felt like you didn't want him to know that I was even your friend. This time it's about you. This is all about your relationship with Mia. My feelings about it shouldn't matter."

"Thanks," she said as she gave her a gentle hug. "I think I get it. But now I have another person to worry about. Cassie told her mother."

"How do you know that?"

"Because I got a visit from *my* mother this afternoon. Actually, it was the first time she's visited since we moved in three years ago, just to show you the level of distress this created."

Ryan was nearly speechless as she blinked her eyes slowly. The Evans family was a breed she was unfamiliar with, but this was too much even for them. To have their only daughter live forty-five minutes away and never visit her was so alien to Ryan that she had to force herself to not comment, lest she say what was really running through her mind. "What happened?" she asked instead.

"I lied to her too. I said that we were just playing and Cassie misinterpreted. I ... I've never lied like that before, Ryan. I'm ... beginning to doubt who I even am anymore."

"Did you consider just telling her that you didn't want to talk about it?" Ryan asked gently.

"That's the funny thing. She wasn't angry or confrontational at all. She gave me a perfect out, but I didn't take it. That's what puzzles me. Why did I feel the need to lie?"

"Only you can answer that for sure, but I have a theory."

"Besides that I'm a spineless slug who's never going to be trustworthy again?" she asked with a bitter laugh.

"Yeah, besides that," Ryan said as she squeezed her hand. "I think you were put into a really tough place by Cassie. I assume she didn't approach you in a gentle fashion and ask if you were ready to talk about this?"

"No. She and Mia were sitting at the kitchen table, and she jumped on me like a district attorney. I thought Mia felt the same way, and I felt overwhelmed and trapped."

"So, once you lied to both of them, you were in a bit of a bind. I assume your main reason for not confirming our relationship to Cassie was because you're not ready to tell your parents?"

"Yeah, basically that's true."

"So telling Cassie is the same as telling them since you know what a gossip she is. Then when your mother asks, it only makes sense to keep up the lie since she was the reason you lied in the first place. It all fits, Jamie, and it's all understandable. I'm just concerned about how you feel about yourself for lying."

Jamie stopped and took in a few deep breaths, trying to stem the tears that were trying to get out. With her lower lip quivering, she closed her eyes and grasped Ryan in a tight embrace. "I can't believe how sweet you are to care more about my feelings than your own. I thought you'd be badly hurt by my betrayal and that's why I was afraid to tell you. I was so ashamed."

"Did you tell any of them that I was a big scary dyke who was trying to seduce you?"

She jerked noticeably and stared at Ryan in shock. "Of course not! I said you were my closest friend, and I told everyone how fond I was of you."

"Then why would I be hurt? Jamie, this is about you and your relationship with these people. What you tell them about us is purely your decision. I only care about how these things affect you, don't you see that?"

"As usual, Anna was right," she said with a little laugh. "She said you'd be understanding and reassuring."

"She sounds like she knows me pretty well. Maybe you'd better describe her. We might have gone out!"

Jamie chased her laughing friend down the street, not stopping until she ran her into her favorite restaurant for a quick dinner.

After dinner, they walked to the library and studied until ten, with only one short kissing break. Ryan was pretty frantic about her studies, and Jamie didn't even mention going to the coffeehouse or bar. On the walk home they talked about the other victim of Jamie's lies. "I feel dreadful about lying to Mia," she admitted. "I really feel like I need to come clean with her, but she's been acting so funny toward me since it happened that now I'm afraid to."

"It might lighten things up if you told her the truth. You trust her, don't you?"

"Yeah, at least I always have. But if she's gonna be weird about it, I'd rather wait until I'm more comfortable."

"Why don't you spend a little time thinking about it? You'll know when you're comfortable."

"I will," she promised. They were nearly at Jamie's house by this time and they both locked eyes when they noticed the house was dark. "Come on," Jamie urged as she tugged at Ryan's hand. "Let me give you a real good-night kiss."

"But don't you have to be more careful than normal? I don't want this to get worse for you."

"I've got yet another fiendishly brilliant idea," she said with eyes dancing.

Ryan let herself be dragged along the sidewalk, and they quickly dashed inside. Instead of going upstairs, Jamie led her to the lovely redwood-paneled library just off the parlor. She had seen the room when Jamie took her on a tour of the house, but she'd never seen anyone use it. The room was accessed through pocket doors that silently glided along tracks to disappear into the wall. Jamie slid one of the pair open and led Ryan inside. After she closed and locked the door, she tugged Ryan towards the dark brown leather sofa that rested underneath the leaded glass windows at the front of the house.

Moments after they entered the room, they heard one of the roommates enter the house. Ryan's sensitive hearing picked up that the person was in the living room.

They heard her dial the phone on the entryway table and after a few seconds Cassie's voice drifted through the room clearly. "Hi, Mom, it's me," she said. Jamie rolled her eyes and gripped her stomach as if she was going to vomit. Ryan just smirked at her and motioned for her to be quiet, then carefully got up from the sofa to avoid having the leather squeak. She sat on a straight-backed wooden chair, and Jamie quickly straddled her lap. They started to kiss softly, but neither could ignore the conversation going on in the other room.

"What do you mean she believed her? Oh, come on, Mom. I saw them nearly making out. What is she, delusional?"

After a moment, she barked out a laugh and agreed, "Yeah, she probably *was* drunk. What time was it?" Another pause. "Yeah, three o'clock is plenty of time for her to get hammered."

Ryan badly wished she wasn't there to listen to the spiteful woman's slurs, since they were clearly embarrassing Jamie.

"Well, she can deny it all she wants, but sooner or later I'm going to catch her red-handed. No," she added after a pause. "I'm not surprised. I've suspected ever since she brought her over here in September. I'm not sure what it was, but there was just something between them from the start."

Jamie's mood lightened at that comment. She patted her lover's face and smiled sweetly as she nodded her head in complete agreement.

"Yeah, I suppose she's pretty." Now, Ryan gave her a smirk and an eyebrow wiggle. "But in a really mannish way." Ryan's eyes shot open and her shocked expression caused her mouth to form a circle. Jamie had to bury her head in Ryan's chest to stifle the laugh that tried to burst from her. "No, I don't think it's anything but a conquest for her. I mean, not to be cruel, but would you choose Jamie if you were just interested in sex?" she said with a snicker. Ryan had to grab her feisty partner by the shoulders to hold her down and stop her from running into the living room to pummel her roommate at that comment. "She's so, I don't know, reserved," she finally decided. "She just looks like she'd be a cold fish." Partly to prove Cassie wrong, Jamie started to work on Ryan's mouth with a fiery intensity. They quickly lost track of Cassie's conversation, but they did hear Mia come tromping in a few minutes later.

Cassie was just hanging up. "Hi," Mia said.

"Your mail's over there, and here're your phone messages," Cassie said.

"Jamie home?"

"No. I assume she's out with the whore of Babylon," she replied drolly, as Ryan pursed her lips and scowled.

"Knock it off," Mia snapped.

"What?"

"I said, knock it off!" she replied at higher volume. "I like Ryan and I love Jamie. She's been our friend for years, and no matter what you think of her sexual orientation, you owe her at least a little civility!"

"You heard how she was with me last week. Would you call that civil?"

"Look," Mia said in a calmer tone. "If she is having an affair, I agree she hasn't been very honest with us. But it might be too hard for her to talk about it. Maybe she just doesn't trust us."

"But we're the only ones she *can* trust," Cassie fumed. "Ryan certainly can't be trusted. She's the one who got her in to this!"

"I don't think that's true. But what if you're right? What if Ryan did seduce her? That's no reason to be mad at Jamie. No matter what, she's been a good friend and a great roommate for both of us. We have to cut her a little slack while she tries to figure out what's going on in her life. I'm just really sad she isn't being honest with me. I thought she trusted me."

Jamie looked physically ill at this revelation. Ryan wrapped her arms around her tighter to comfort her as Cassie snapped, "Jamie might have been a friend before, but she's made sure that's no longer true for me. She's basically told me to leave if I don't want Ryan in the house. She's made me look foolish by denying that they were making out together, and I don't tolerate that type of treatment. I'm going to catch her, and when I do the whole campus will know about it. Then her stupid alcoholic mother won't be able to dispute the truth."

"What? You told her mother?"

"I told *my* mother. What she did with the information is her business."

"You are really a piece of work," Mia said with disgust as she stomped up the stairs.

"If you're really her friend, you'll help me catch her, Mia," she called after her. "She needs to have someone help her before she gets into this too deep. It's going to be all over campus soon."

"With friends like you ..." Mia snarled before she slammed her bedroom door.

The inhabitants of the library stared at each other in shocked silence for a few moments. Jamie was outrageously pleased that Mia had defended her so staunchly, but now she felt even worse about lying to her. She couldn't get much angrier with Cassie, but she was irate about the comments concerning her mother. Although her mother did drink too much for her comfort, she thought it both rude and mean-spirited to characterize her as an alcoholic. But she realistically didn't for a minute doubt her roommate's vow to catch them in the act.

Even though she was confident that loving Ryan was exactly the right thing to do, Jamie was not at all ready to talk to her parents about her feelings. She rested her head against Ryan's broad shoulder for a few minutes, feeling overwhelmed with the weight of keeping their love a secret. Ryan patted and rubbed her back as she rocked a tiny bit in the chair. To their dismay, Cassie immediately got on the phone again. She obviously called her mother again to start slamming Mia this time. Ryan couldn't stand to listen to another minute of this drivel, but she knew they were stuck until Cassie went upstairs. The call lasted for almost fifteen minutes, during which time Jamie nearly fell asleep on Ryan's lap. Deciding that she needed to go home herself, Ryan finally motioned for her lover to get up. She tiptoed to the window and saw that she could easily climb out and drop to the ground without harming herself. She whispered her plan in Jamie's ear, and after checking out the drop herself, Jamie kissed her goodbye and watched her go.

Jamie now had two options. She could lie down on the couch and sleep until Cassie went upstairs, or she could walk right by her. The debate lasted less than two seconds as she took out one of her texts from her book bag and strolled right past a startled Cassie while she was hanging up the phone. As Jamie hit the stairs, she turned to her and sweetly said, "Busy sharpening your knives, Brutus?"

While Jamie was brushing her teeth the next morning Cassie came barging into the bathroom. "That was really cheap of you to eavesdrop on me last night."

"I was studying. I believe I am allowed to use all of the rooms of my house, aren't I?"

"Any decent person would have let us know she was there!"

"Any decent person? What on earth do you know about decency?" Jamie asked as she rinsed her mouth and walked back into her room. Cassie started to follow, but Jamie stopped her with a withering glare. "We have nothing more to discuss. When you leave for New York, take your things with you."

Cassie glared back for a full minute. Her face was screwed up into a very unflattering grimace as she turned and stomped back into her own room.

Mia made herself so scarce over the next few days that Jamie began to doubt that she was even sleeping at the house. She accidentally ran into her on campus on Friday morning, but Mia was late for a class and didn't have time to stop. As she scampered away, she called, "I'm going to L.A. for the weekend. See you Monday!"

That night over dinner, Ryan asked, "Busy tomorrow?"

"Well, I should study, but I'm sure you could talk me out of it. What do you have in mind?"

"Two things. First, I'm going to play rugby in the afternoon, and I thought you might like to come watch—"

"You play rugby?"

"Sure. We've played as a family since I was in high school."

"You play with your … family?"

"Yeah. Why do you look surprised?"

"Uhm … couple of reasons. One—you're the only girl."

"I am?" she asked in mock horror.

"Come on, Ryan," Jamie laughed as she pinched her playfully. "Is this a girls' team or a boys' team?"

"You're gonna have to come to find out. Interested?"

"Absolutely."

"What's your other reason for being surprised?"

"Because I've kept a very tight watch over you in the last few months, missy. And I'd know if you were doing something like this on a regular basis. So what gives?"

"We're not together every night, Jamie," she reminded her.

"No … that's true. But I always ask you what you did on the nights we're not together, and I'm certain I'd recall you saying that you were going to play rugby."

"Well, it sounds like your questions have been too broad then, doesn't it?" Ryan asked playfully, blue eyes twinkling with mischief.

"Oh, so I should say, 'What did you do last night, Ryan? Play any rugby?'"

"Well, that would be the best way," she said as she tapped her chin thoughtfully with her index finger.

"Ryan! You've got to be kidding!"

"Nope. I'll tell you anything you want to know, babe. But I don't give up my secrets easily. Ya gotta work for 'em."

"Sheesh!" Jamie shook her head roughly and asked with some trepidation, "What's the other thing you wanted to ask me? Although now I'm afraid to find out."

"Oh, Rory's leaving for the entire summer on Sunday morning. So we're having a big goodbye party for him tomorrow night. You have to come to that, so I don't even know why I'm asking."

"Speaking of asking, how long ago did you know about these events?"

"Uhm … a while."

"You're already starting to take me for granted!"

"Never," Ryan insisted. "I just forget that you don't know every thought in my head. You're such an integral part of me, I forget I have to actually tell you things." She had the most innocent, angelic look on her face that Jamie had ever seen on an adult human.

"Good recovery," she said with a smirk as she patted her cheek.

"Years of practice," Ryan agreed as she ducked her pinch.

After three solid hours of studying, they headed back to Jamie's. The house was dark, and since Mia was gone, she knew they would be totally alone if Cassie was with her boyfriend. Jamie talked Ryan into chancing it and they once again went to the library since that offered the most inconspicuous escape route. After a quick detour up to her room, she handed Ryan the little gifts she had purchased for her and grinned shyly as she opened the bag.

"You bought me a present?" Ryan asked in a delighted voice. "This is the first present you've bought for me since we've … you know." She opened the bag and said in surprise, "Underwear?"

"Yep. Although it your case it's underwear/pajamas. Do you like them?"

"Yeah, they look cool, but I have lots of underwear."

"Not here, you don't. You need to leave some here, and I chose these because they're a couple of inches longer than your Calvin's. Since you hate to have them ride up, I thought these might be even better for you."

"I like them a lot," she said as she pulled all of them out. "But you didn't have to buy so many."

"You seem to run through them pretty quickly when you stay overnight," Jamie teased as she blushed a tiny bit.

"Good point," Ryan agreed. "I'll let you know if they fit well."

Jamie looked uncomfortable as she said, "I, uhm … thought you might try them on for me … now."

"Are you sure?" Ryan asked, worried about Cassie coming home.

"Yeah. I'd really like it, if you don't mind," she quickly added.

"No, I'm happy to drop my drawers for you," the grinning brunette said as she began to unbutton her fly.

Jamie immediately turned her head even though she really, really wanted to watch. She heard Ryan's shoes being kicked off, and then the rustle of fabric as her jeans hit the floor. "Color choice?" the deep voice asked.

"White," said Jamie decisively.

She heard the fabric sliding up Ryan's legs, and her resolve almost left her but she waited until Ryan said, "What do you think?" to turn around.

Jamie was very disappointed to find that Ryan had put her jeans back on over the new shorts. "I can't tell how they look with your pants on."

"I know that," Ryan purred. "So why don't you come over here and take them off me."

She had to smack her lips together to make the saliva return to her mouth. Ryan had a way of knowing exactly what would turn her on, and she had yet to be wrong. Jamie walked over, returning Ryan's sexy grin. When she got right next to her, she pulled her tall lover down with one hand while the other grabbed her butt. Once their mouths were firmly attached, she dropped her other hand and felt every inch of those thighs and that firm butt. They both let out a little gasp when she started to unbutton the fly, then her hand slid in. After a dizzying minute of kisses and cautious explorations, she shoved the jeans down and stood back to take in the view.

Ryan looked hotter than she had ever seen her, and she had seen her look pretty darn hot. But there was something so totally sexy about her confident, relaxed posture as she stood there in her sky blue polo shirt, tight white boxers and a pair of jeans pooled around her ankles that Jamie was nearly faint with arousal. Ryan lowered her eyes just a touch and let her deep sexy voice rumble up from her belly, "Don't you want to check the fit?"

Jamie had never heard such a brilliant idea in her whole life. She stood so close she could feel Ryan's breath flutter across her face. She sucked in a deep breath to imprint Ryan's sweet smell on her brain, smiling to herself as she considered how important smell had become to her in the few weeks they had been intimate. She had noticed Jack's scent when they were together, but it hadn't seemed to play a big role in her arousal. With Ryan, however, she felt like she needed to smell that body to start the chain reaction of sexual response. Part of the attraction was that Ryan was an absolute scent junkie, and Jamie could imagine her nose twitching with pleasure as they shared the sensation.

Her hands could no longer behave themselves and almost of their own accord began to roam all over Ryan's body. But as much as she needed to smell and feel her, she also needed to see how those sculpted legs looked in the new garment. She sank to her knees and took in another deep breath as she saw Ryan's body shudder at her closeness.

The shorts clung snugly around her lover's thighs, and Jamie realized that she had been holding her breath. Shaking her head to order her thoughts, she lifted the long polo shirt just enough to see the entire fit. She smirked a bit noticing that Ryan could probably fit into a medium if they stopped at the traditional spot, but those thighs definitely demanded a large.

She ran her hands up and down each rock hard leg, delighting in the way the muscles twitched under her touch. The fabric bagged from waist to pubic bone in the front but there wasn't an extra centimeter in the back. Ryan's round ass filled the shorts out so perfectly that Jamie's heart actually skipped a beat as her hands cupped the firm flesh.

Jamie rested her cheek on the concave belly as her hands continued to stroke and palm that lovely rear. As she continued to excite her lover, she noticed that Ryan's scent began to change from sweet and clean to musky and spicily exotic. Her heart began to thump loudly in her chest as she acknowledged that she was the cause of Ryan's arousal, and that she controlled the expression of her desire. The feeling was both heady and frightening, and she trembled slightly as she considered it. Ryan noticed her apprehension and began to run her fingers lightly through her hair in a reassuring gesture. The gentle touch effectively stilled her fears, and she rubbed her face against the white fabric in grateful acknowledgement.

Emboldened by her newly discovered power she pushed the shirt up. Ryan reached down and tugged it off to provide her lover full access to her body. She was wearing a white sports bra that hid her assets quite well, much to Jamie's relief and disappointment. But seeing all of that smooth skin so close made her a bit more daring than she normally would have been. She stretched as tall as she could and began to kiss Ryan's adorable midriff.

She could tell her kisses were having a powerful effect on her partner, but she was getting so much enjoyment from the intimate contact that she started to lose track of Ryan's responses and to concentrate only on her own pleasure.

She grasped the waistband of the shorts and pulled them down a few inches. Placing delicate little kisses around Ryan's navel, she finally poked her tongue right into the little depression. Next she began to kiss down the centerline of Ryan's belly, pushing the waistband lower and lower, when her nearly frantic lover abruptly gripped her head. "I can't," Ryan moaned, shivering with unquenched desire. "I'm sorry, baby, but I can't!"

Jamie immediately regained her senses and realized what she was doing to the poor woman. She looked up at Ryan and saw the lines of stress creasing her beautiful face. "Oh, honey, I'm sorry," she gasped as she got to her feet. "I'm so sorry for torturing you."

"S'okay," Ryan mumbled, her legs feeling a bit rubbery. "I'll just ahh … get dressed and ahh … get going."

"You're in no shape to ride home. Can't you stay here tonight? I really need to feel your warm body next to mine."

They were startled out of their musings by the sound of Cassie coming home. She wasn't alone, and Jamie recognized her boyfriend Chris's voice as they spoke softly in the living room. They both sounded a little drunk, and it sounded like Chris definitely had love on his mind as he urged her to follow him upstairs. Cassie quietly complied, and moments later they heard two sets of feet climb the stairs.

Ryan asked, "Is it safe to go upstairs together?"

"No, I don't think so. Would you be willing to stay right here? You could leave before they got up in the morning."

"I'd love to stay with you. Even sleeping on the floor would be just fine if we were together. Let me call home and tell them not to expect me," she said as she bent to pick up her pants.

"You call home and I'll go to the bathroom. Be right back," she whispered as she slid the door open and snuck out.

Ryan left a message since no one was home, and by the time she was done Jamie was back. "Why don't you go freshen up a bit," she suggested. "Use the bath by the kitchen," she said as she handed Ryan a clean pair of underwear and a T-shirt. "See what I mean about how fast you run through clothes?"

When Ryan returned, her grinning lover was lying on her side in her panties and Ryan's polo shirt. "You don't mind sharing do you?"

"No," she said with a big smile. "That's a really nice color on you, as a matter of fact." She walked towards the sofa after carefully locking the door again.

"Wait right there," Jamie instructed. "That's a completely different look." She gazed up at her lover and signaled for her to turn around. "The black shirt with the gray shorts gives you a very dangerous aura," she said. "I actually think you look sexier in those."

"Ahh, maybe I should go home after all," Ryan said, a trifle nervously.

"Do I frighten you?" Jamie asked with a sexy leer. "Come here little girl," she urged as she crooked her finger.

Ryan returned her smile and joined her on the sofa. "You're not going to drive me out of my mind again are you?"

"No, I just want to hold you." She patted the deep leather cushions of the sofa and eased her arm around Ryan's back when she joined her.

"I have a little proposal for you," Jamie murmured as she snuggled up. "How would you like to take a little vacation with me once the ride is over?"

"Vacation? Uhm … I guess I'd like that. I mean, of course I'd like it, but I don't know if I can afford it."

"What if I could arrange for us to stay at a little getaway where we could enjoy each other in complete privacy at absolutely no charge?"

"How could you do that?"

"We have a weekend house down in Pebble Beach. Mother said we could use it for a week after the ride. I think it'd be wonderful to just relax and get our strength back don't you?" she asked as she drew little patterns on Ryan's belly.

"Well, I've never had a more tempting offer, but knowing you I'll come home twice as tired as I was after the ride!"

"We'll just have to pace ourselves."

"Do you think you'll be ready to enjoy each other … thoroughly by then?" Ryan asked, eyebrows waggling wildly.

"I'm ready now," she moaned. "If we had somewhere to go, I'm sure I'd be ready. But I've been thinking of what we spoke about before, and I know that once we start I won't want to stop. I think it'd be too frustrating to spend every evening trying to find a place to be together. It'd really take the special feeling out of the experience."

"I want it to be a time we'll both remember for the rest of our lives, Jamie. Going to Pebble Beach sounds perfect. I'll arrange to take a second week off."

"Are you tired yet? I could probably sneak upstairs and get us a pillow and a blanket."

"I'm beat," Ryan conceded. "But I don't want Cassie to hear you. The arm of the sofa looks perfect for my head. Would you mind using my chest for a pillow?"

"Let's give it a try." Ryan scooted up until her head rested on the soft, low, wide arm of the leather sofa. Jamie cuddled up against her side and rested her head just above her breast. "Uhm, I think I'm going to throw my pillow away permanently," she murmured. "I love it here. I can feel your heart beat and hear your steady breathing … it's perfect."

"You won't be cold will you?"

"Not with your hot body next to me. I think I can throw my blankets away, too."

"That's premature. We can't sleep together every night you know."

"How about tomorrow?" Jamie asked with a grin.

"Tomorrow would work fine. We'll figure out some place to put you. Our game starts at two, so come over by one-thirty. Don't forget your toothbrush."

"I'll bring my books on the off chance we might do any studying on Sunday."

She could feel Ryan stiffen perceptibly. "Jamie, I have to study on Sunday. Finals are in one week!"

"Okay, I promise I'll behave. I won't kiss you, I won't even touch you if you don't want me to."

"Hey, you don't have to be a lunatic about it," she teased. "But I've got at least ten hours of work to get through this weekend, and I'll start stressing if I don't finish it."

"I promise I'll put your needs ahead of my desires," she promised. "But I can play with you tomorrow night, can't I?"

"My body is yours to do with as you will. But at midnight, I'm reclaiming it."

"It's a deal, Cinderella," she promised as she kissed her one last time and snuggled up contentedly.

Ryan woke a little after three with an insistent pain in her bladder. As she struggled into consciousness, she realized that the pain came less from fluid consumption and more from Jamie's knee pressing firmly into her abdomen. She gazed down at her still face, so open and guileless in sleep, and brought her hand up to lightly touch her cheek. A strong burst of emotion welled up in her chest as she regarded the woman she loved. Jamie looked so childlike and trusting as she clung to her body, that Ryan was reminded once again how vulnerable each of them was now.

Ryan trusted her family as much as she trusted herself. That confidence had been with her since birth, and even though they fought like any other family, she knew none of them would ever hurt her intentionally or betray her. But she had always been very leery of allowing an outsider to get close enough to risk being hurt. Jamie was the first to ever really get inside, and even though Ryan would lay down her life for her lover, she had to admit the unfamiliar vulnerability sometimes frightened her. Just the few minor spats they had already gone through had hurt her in a way she hadn't considered possible. Jamie's opinion of her meant everything now, and she realized that for the rest of her life she would have to consider Jamie's view on every major decision that she made.

Even though the exposure and vulnerability would take time to get used to, she honestly felt that choosing to be with Jamie was the best decision she had ever made. No one had ever excited her as much as the small woman who now cuddled up against her side, but the overpowering sexual attraction was one of the least compelling reasons for her commitment. It was Jamie's soul that was the most beautiful part of her. Her kindnesses, her empathy for others, and her deep moral convictions were the qualities that attracted Ryan so powerfully.

Jamie shifted a little in her sleep, causing Ryan to smile down at her as her mouth worked slightly. A stirring in her groin reminded her of how powerful her attraction was, and she smiled contentedly as she thought of spending a whole week with her sometimes unpredictable, but always frisky partner. She could no longer resist the lure of those sweet pouty lips, and she allowed herself the guilty pleasure of lightly kissing them. Luckily, Jamie could sleep through anything, and she didn't stir at all. Ryan closed her eyes and let herself dream of their upcoming trip, unable to keep the broad smile from her face.

Chapter Eight

O n Saturday morning Jamie got up extra early to make sure she had plenty of time to attend the rugby game. Her studies went better than she expected, and she found that she completely lost track of time. She had to rush to get to Noe Valley by one-thirty and was disappointed to learn that all of the players had already left. Martin and Caitlin met her at the door and both welcomed her enthusiastically. Tommy was playing and Annie was working, so Martin had agreed to handle babysitting duty while Maeve prepared the post-match picnic at her home. "We'd best get moving, Jamie," Martin suggested. "They like to start on time."

He was driving Maeve's car since the car seat was already in place, and they all piled in for the short drive to the Driscoll house. Martin ran in to help his sister-in-law carry the enormous basket, which was loaded to the brim with snacks for the players. During the trip to Kezar Stadium in Golden Gate Park, Martin explained the overall objective of the sport, which seemed easy enough, but he started to get bogged down with the details of the innumerable rules. Maeve stepped in to help.

"Here are the simple facts, dear," Maeve explained patiently. "Each side tries to run or kick the ball over the goal line. The other side tries to tackle them and steal the ball. It's such a jumble that it's almost impossible to tell who even has the ball most of the time. It just seems like an organized street fight to me, and I've been watching matches my whole life. I spend half of my time praying they all come out of the match in one piece, and the other half filling up water bottles for them."

"Do you enjoy watching them?"

"Well, I must say I enjoy watching more when my sons and nephews aren't on the field. Oh, I should say niece and nephews," she amended with a laugh.

"That's all right, Maeve," Martin reassured her. "After fifteen minutes, you can't tell the men from the women anyway when the field is wet like it is today."

They arrived at the well-tended field just before two o'clock. Martin told Jamie that they were in a city league that played throughout the winter and spring. The field was lighted for night play and most of their games this spring had been on weeknights. This Saturday afternoon game was a rarity and was also their final game of the season. Martin proudly explained that today's game was for the championship of their division.

Their team consisted of all of the boys in the family, plus Ryan, and a few family friends to insure they always had the required fifteen healthy players. As the spectators approached the field, they saw 'Team O'Flaherty' performing some easy stretches to get ready for play, and Jamie had to really concentrate to spot Ryan amidst the crowd. However, as they got closer it was almost as if the tall, rangy woman could sense Jamie's presence. That dark head turned and locked eyes with Jamie as a brilliant smile lit up her lovely face. Jamie returned the smile and added a wink for good measure as Ryan ran over.

Jamie was carrying Caitlin, and both blondes happily greeted Ryan when she approached. Maeve came over and gave her niece a gentle hug as she asked, "Now what's this secret you promised to reveal today?"

Ryan slipped her arm around her aunt's shoulders, led her about five feet away, and replied. "This is kind of a secret," she said quietly. "I want you to keep your eyes open for a very special woman today, Aunt Maeve."

"And who might that be?"

"Against all odds, I've finally convinced the most wonderful woman in the world to fall in love with me," she said with a wide smile. "She might come to see us play, so I want you to keep an eye out for her. She's shy and I don't want her to be overwhelmed with all of the family, but I know you'll be discreet."

"Ryan, sweetheart, that's wonderful!" she cried. "But how will I notice her?"

"You can't miss her, Aunt Maeve. She's easily the most beautiful creature you'll ever hope to see." She gave her aunt a kiss on the cheek and ran right by her smirking lover, calling out a casual, "Glad you could come, Jamie."

The blonde just shook her head as the chuckling woman ran back to her mates. As Ryan jogged away, Jamie mused that the view she was now afforded was well worth the effort she had expended getting to the match on time. The whole team wore what Maeve informed her were the jerseys of the Irish national squad. The long-sleeved garment was a bright kelly green with a white collar and a white badge with three shamrocks embroidered over the breast. Very brief, wide-legged white cotton shorts and knee-length kelly green socks completed the uniform, and Jamie wished she had brought Mia or some of her other straight friends to see how the O'Flaherty boys filled out the little shorts.

Still, no matter how many gorgeous hunks of O'Flaherty thigh flashed before her eyes, she truly noticed only one body in the crowd. Ryan looked as cute as she had ever seen her in her outfit, and the energy flowed from her body as she jumped around trying to stay loose in the damp, foggy wind. The black-shirted referees ran onto the field then a whistle blew to begin the game. From the opening moment until the end of the first half, more than forty-five minutes later, Ryan never stopped.

She was a complete blur most of the time, running all over the one hundred and ten yard-long field with absolutely no regard for her body. Jamie winced and grimaced every time she was tackled, and it seemed that she was tackled more than anyone else. Martin assured her that it was just because her lover was the fastest player and carried the ball more often than the others, but she hated it nonetheless.

To Jamie's amazement, Martin said there were no time outs during play, but the clock did stop when there was a penalty or after a "try," which he likened to a touchdown in football. Every time there was a break in the action, Ryan would run by and give her aunt a questioning glance. Jamie noticed that each glance was met with a shrug of Maeve's small shoulders. After one such exchange, Ryan came close and said, "She has the most adorable smile you've ever seen. Her eyes crinkle up and sometimes she gets a little wrinkle across the bridge of her nose. Think gorgeous!" she added, as she ran back to the game.

Jamie knew Ryan was toying with her, and that the game included somehow duping Maeve, but she wasn't exactly sure what the game was. Her curiosity finally got the better of her, and she sidled over to Maeve asking, "What's that about?"

"Oh, ah, I suppose Ryan wouldn't mind if I mentioned this to you," she said quietly. "She says she's fallen in love, and she's expecting her young lady to come to the game. She wants me to keep an eye out for her."

"Really?" Jamie asked with a smile.

"Do you know her, Jamie? Can you point her out to me?"

"Can't help you there, Maeve. You know how secretive Ryan can be. By the way, how did she describe her?"

"Oh, you know Ryan. She said she was the most beautiful woman I would ever see," she laughed.

"Well, Ryan does tend to exaggerate," she modestly agreed.

Play began again, and by half time the players were all caked in mud and dirt and grass. Ryan had her hair tied back in a tight braid but even it was covered in mud. During the break, the players lounged on the ground while they gulped sports drink and relaxed a bit. Jamie had no idea what the score was. There was no official scoreboard, so she was surprised when Martin informed her the O'Flaherty's were leading by twenty-one points. "How can you tell?"

"You have to pay attention," he said as he cocked his head just a bit. "Haven't you been watching, darlin'?" Jamie nodded her head as he laughed at her puzzlement. "The game takes a little while to get used to."

When Ryan got up to hit the field, she gave her aunt another set of attributes. "She has a great body, very athletic and fit. Beautiful hair, almost the color of the sun, with perfect, golden-toned skin."

Play began again and the frantic pace never abated. Jamie paid rapt attention this time and began to figure out the scoring system. She proudly called out the score to Martin after every point scored, and he praised her effusively. But, in yet another quirk of the unfamiliar game, no one except the referees knew how much time remained, and the game ended rather abruptly for Jamie's taste. The teams graciously shook hands, then the O'Flaherty's came back to their side to celebrate.

They wiped off as much muck as they could, but they were still disgusting, sweaty messes.

Ryan plopped down near Jamie and her aunt, allowing Caitlin to climb all over her. Maeve crouched down next to her and said, "I'm sorry, dear, but I couldn't find your friend."

Ryan adopted a deeply dejected look as she said, "Maybe I was wrong. Maybe she doesn't love me." She looked up at Jamie, who was trying to hide a smile, and asked, "What do you think, Jamie?"

"Well, a person would have to love you an awful lot to want to get near you right now," she agreed as she scrunched her nose in distaste.

"That's true," Ryan conceded. "If a woman could stand to kiss me now, that'd be an irrefutable sign of her love."

Jamie gave her an indulgent smirk and sank to her knees right in front of the whole flock of O'Flahertys. Ignoring the shocked glances from each and every one, she tossed her arms around Ryan's filthy neck and dipped her head to plant a scorcher on the dirt-flecked lips. Ryan gathered her into her arms and pulled her down into her lap, tickling her unmercifully as Jamie giggled wildly.

"It's true," Ryan cried loudly for all to hear, squirming under Jamie's return tickle, "this unreasonably gorgeous creature has fallen in love with me."

Jamie laughed along with her partner as all of the cousins teased Ryan about snatching away the only straight girl she had ever brought home. But Maeve didn't find the development funny in the least. She crouched down next to the women and gave each of them fervent hugs as she wiped the tears from her eyes. "I'm so happy for you both," she said with a catch in her voice.

Martin came over to the group and patted Maeve on the back as he agreed. "Could you wish for a better mate for our Siobhán?"

"This is all together the best news I've heard in an age, Martin," she said. "Although I didn't expect Ryan to be the second one of the group to give her heart away. Let's get moving, the lot of you!" she exhorted the assembled men, who let out a collective groan.

The party moved from the field back to the house after everyone stopped at their respective homes for showers. By six o'clock, the barbeques were going, and the house was packed to the gills with O'Flaherty cousins, aunts and uncles. The boys verbally replayed the match for the uncles and aunts who had been unable to attend, and Jamie was thrilled to notice that every reprise included generous praise for her lover. She found it totally charming that the men appreciated their only female cousin and let her play on their obviously important team. Rory set her straight on her misperception when he explained that not only was Ryan welcome, she was the vital link to their success.

"Ryan plays the 'fly back' or the number ten position," he explained. "The ten is a bit like the quarterback in football. She makes all of the tactical decisions concerning whether the ball will be kicked or run and, since she's easily the fastest player, she advances the ball better than anyone on the team. When you add in the fact that she's absolutely fearless, you get an accurate picture of what she means to us."

"I guess I just assumed that you let her play because she was fast and agile," Jamie admitted.

"No, Jamie," he said with a big smile. "You'll soon learn there's not much our Ryan does where she's not the best. Believe me, it was tough having your little sister beat you at everything you tried to do. Luckily for the rest of us, she acts so darned matter-of-fact about everything that you don't feel as humiliated as you would if she lorded it over you."

Jamie reached up and gave him a friendly hug as she said, "You know, Rory, one of the things that most attracted me to her was seeing how crazy all of you were about her. No one knows her as well as you guys do, and if you were all wild about her, I figured I had to get to know her better."

He looked at her soberly for a moment and wrinkled up his brow before he leaned over and softly said, "She's precious to all of us. We all made a vow to our mother that we'd love and protect her for the rest of her life. I can tell how much you love her, but I'm not sure that you realize how fragile she can be."

She looked up at him and cocked her head quizzically, urging him to go on. "I'm not even sure that she realizes it sometimes," he said. "She acts as though she's been too busy or otherwise occupied," here he blushed at the obvious reason for her preoccupation, "to fall in love. But it's only because she's so afraid of having her heart broken. I think you're a wonderful choice for her, but if there's any doubt in your mind about your commitment to her, please don't lead her on. I don't think she could bear another broken heart." He looked down at Jamie with nothing but love and concern on his handsome face. A tiny part of her thought she should be insulted by his meddling in their business, but her more mature side took over almost immediately. She stood on her tiptoes and wrapped her arms around his neck, placing a gentle kiss on his now deeply blushing cheek.

"I swear, Rory, if I weren't wildly attracted to your sister I'd want to be with each of you boys. I really appreciate your concern for Ryan, and I want you to know that I've made the same vow that you have. I've promised her that I'll love and protect her for the rest of my life, and I don't renege on my promises."

He was still blushing as he said, "I guess I'm just concerned because I know you were recently engaged to a man and I uhm ..."

"It's okay, Rory," she reassured him. "I made a mistake. I was deeply attracted to your sister, but I didn't have the nerve to tell her. It took me a while, but I'm not going to turn back now. I'm like a loyal little dog. Once I follow you home, you have to take me to another county and throw me out of the car to get rid of me."

He placed his large arm around her shoulders and tilted his head until it lightly rested upon hers. "Believe me, if Ryan tried to toss you aside, the lot of us would knock some sense back into her straightaway!"

With her unfailing ability to sense where her lover was at all times, Ryan zeroed in on her and sidled over to remove her brother's arm from Jamie's shoulders. "This is why I never brought a woman home before," she informed Jamie while she shot a broad smile at her brother.

"You can't blame a lad for trying," Rory said, smiling back at her.

"Well, lucky for me I have the whole summer to cement my position in her heart. When you come back in the fall, she'll be firmly under my spell."

"Pretty confident, aren't you?" Jamie asked as she snuggled up against her side.

"Yep. I'm going to devote every bit of my energies to making you the happiest woman in the Bay Area."

"You're gonna have to aim higher than that," Jamie teased as she tilted her face up for a kiss, "since I'm already the happiest woman in the world."

As Ryan slid her arms around her and placed several warm kisses on her pink lips, Rory rolled his eyes and walked away, unnoticed by the cuddling twosome.

By ten-thirty, the party showed no obvious signs of slowing down except for Caitlin, who was removed by Tommy from Ryan's protective embrace and taken home to her own bed. Ryan glanced around for her lover and found her once again in the corner, this time with Kevin. As Ryan approached, Jamie gave her the tiniest of headshakes, and she immediately rerouted and went into the kitchen to help her aunts with the clean up. Jamie came in as they were finishing and slipped her hand into Ryan's, leading her discreetly away from the crowd and down the stairs.

"Every time I look up you're in the corner with one of the boys!" Ryan groused. "What gives?"

"I've been welcomed and warned by every male member of your family except for Duffy!"

"Welcomed and warned?" Ryan asked with a confused look.

"Yes. 'Welcome to the family, Jamie. You're a wonderful girl and we're very happy that Ryan chose you, but if you hurt her, we'll track you down and kill you.'"

"They didn't!" she gasped as she dropped to her bed.

"Oh, yes, they did," Jamie assured her as she sat across Ryan's knees and kissed her cheek. "Oh, they were more tactful than that, but the message was the same."

"I'm so sorry," she murmured.

"Sorry? You have nothing to be sorry for. I think it's adorable that all of them care for you so much. It's reassuring to know that you have over a dozen people watching out for you when I can't be on the job."

"You know, every day you give me another reason why I made such a good decision in choosing you. Most women would be intimidated or insulted by that, but you take it as a reassuring gesture. That's really wonderful."

"That's all true, except for one small detail."

"What's that?"

"*I* chose *you!*"

Ryan nodded her head agreeably as she conceded, "I suppose you're right on that point. So let's say I made a wise decision in accepting your proposal."

"I just want to keep the record straight," she said as she pushed her taller lover down and covered her body with her own.

When Cassie Martin returned from her date that Saturday night, she stared at the small note lying on the hall table.

> *I'm staying at my parents' tonight. I'll be home late Sunday,*
> *Jamie*

We'll just see about that, she thought as she dialed the phone. "Hello, Mrs. Evans?" she asked sweetly when the phone was answered.

"Yes," replied the cultured voice, just a trifle thick from her usual evening pastime.

"It's Cassie, Mrs. Evans," she said as she thought, *I hope she's not too drunk to have noticed if Jamie's there or not.*

But Catherine was only a bit inebriated since it was only nine o'clock. Her voice snapped to attention and became sharper as she asked, "What is it, Cassie? Is anything wrong?"

"No, not at all," she said. "I just need to ask Jamie something. Is she there?"

"No, she's not here," Catherine replied, sounding confused. "Why do you think she is?"

"She left a note saying she was going to your house, Mrs. Evans," she said slowly. "Oh, I hope I didn't cause any trouble by calling you."

Even though Catherine had consumed quite a few drinks, her quick mind homed in on a critical point. "Why didn't you call Jamie on her cell phone, Cassie? That's always the best way to reach her."

"Oh, that's right. Silly me," she said. "I call her so rarely that I forgot about her cell phone. I certainly hope I haven't caused you any alarm, Mrs. Evans."

"Actually you have, Cassie," she said rather sharply. "I'll call Jamie to make sure she's all right. And then, of course, I'll ask her to call you back. Are you at home?"

"Uhm … yes, I'm at home, but it's really not necessary, Mrs. Evans."

"Nonsense. If it was important enough for you to call here, it's important enough for Jamie to return your call. Goodnight, Cassie."

Catherine slumped back into her chair and tried to gather her thoughts. She didn't want to get involved in any adolescent squabbles between her daughter and Cassie, but there was a glimmer of a chance that Jamie had been on her way home and had gotten into an accident. So she hit the speed dial and waited for six rings before her daughter's happy-sounding voice answered. To her own surprise, she immediately hung up. She sat in her chair and stared at the receiver, which she still held in her small hand, and considered her actions. She realized she didn't have any interest in checking up on Jamie, she just wanted to know that she was safe. Once she was assured of that, she really had nothing to say. *Although I suppose Cassie will be waiting for a return call from Jamie,* she thought absently. A sly smile curled up the corner of her mouth as she rose to pour herself another vodka. *Let her wait.*

As the last of the relatives left the house, Rory bade everyone goodbye. Brendan had offered to take him to the airport in the morning, so he decided to sleep at his brother's apartment and allow Ryan to use his room for the night. Jamie gave him a big hug and a kiss and quietly promised to watch over Ryan in his absence. She left the rest of the family to say their goodbyes and went downstairs to get ready for bed.

Twenty minutes later, Ryan came down, red eyed and glum. "Are you all sad that Rory's leaving?" Jamie asked as she wrapped her arms around her.

Ryan just nodded, her lips pursed together tightly.

"You poor little thing," she soothed as she led her to the loveseat for a little comfort. Jamie sat back in the corner against the cushions and urged her lover to rest her head in her lap. Running her fingers lightly through her hair, she gave her the physical comfort she obviously needed. She didn't think there was much to actually talk about since it was clear that Ryan had a hard time being away from any member of her family for a significant time period. She thought about her own family and realized that she often couldn't remember if her mother was even in the country, and her father traveled so often for business that it wasn't odd for him to be away for weeks at a time. She reflected that she and Jack had planned on being apart for a whole year while he clerked for a federal judge, and was struck with the realization that things would be very different with Ryan. *There's no way in the world I'd let her be away from me for a whole year,* she thought with amazement. *Why didn't it seem odd to me at the time? I thought it was perfectly natural to see my fiancé only on weekends and to plan to have him be gone for a year. God, I can hardly stand to be apart from Ryan overnight.*

As if she read her thoughts, Ryan murmured, "Don't wanna go upstairs," in her adorable child voice.

"I know, sweetie. I don't want you to go either, but we're still close. I'll just be downstairs if you get lonely."

Ryan struggled to her feet and went into the bath to get ready for bed. Jamie heard her muttering to herself the whole way, and she was once again charmed by her companion's complete vulnerability with her. When Ryan came out, Jamie offered to take her to bed and tuck her in. She accepted with a dropped chin and a shy little grin that peeked out via her sparkling blue eyes. On the way upstairs, they stopped in Martin's room for their goodnight kisses. He gave Jamie a curious glance while he hugged his daughter, and she mouthed that she'd stop in on her way back down.

The next stop was Conor's room. He was just leaving the bathroom he and Rory shared, and he likewise gave both women a hug and a kiss. He looked very tired, and as soon as he entered his room the lights went out. Jamie led Ryan to Rory's bed, and sat on the edge ruffling her hair through her fingers. "I love you, Ryan," she said softly as she leaned over for a tender kiss.

"I love you too, Jamie," she said sadly. As Jamie got up to leave, she turned for one last look and felt her heart nearly break at the wide-eyed, childlike expression on her lover's face. She blew her a kiss and started to close the door, but Ryan instructed, "Leave it open, please. I want Duffy to be able to come in and cuddle."

On the way back downstairs, Jamie stopped in Martin's room and quietly closed the door to be able to speak without her keen-eared lover noticing. "What's with the Princess?" he asked with a furrowed brow.

"She's very sad that Rory's leaving," she confided. "She seems really fragile tonight, and I think she needs some comforting."

"But you're honoring my rule about not sleeping together, correct?"

"Of course, Martin. We wouldn't dream of going against your wishes."

"Well, you know, Jamie," he said as he slid an arm around her shoulders, "the rule was designed solely to maintain family harmony. But the only member of the family who would notice is Conor. If you could manage to be a bit stealthy, there's no reason for him to find out."

"So you really wouldn't mind?"

"How can I put this delicately?" he said. "I feel uncomfortable having my children acting like married people before they're willing to make a public commitment. But it sounds like you're asking to give Siobhán some comfort rather than ..."

"Absolutely, Martin," she said as her blush rivaled his. "Besides, given Ryan's mental age tonight, the last thing on her mind is ..." she said with a wink.

After another good night kiss, she crept up the stairs, being careful to avoid the third step, which had a definite squeak to it. Quietly entering the room, she slowly closed the door as she heard Ryan give a start. "It's me," she whispered.

Ryan quickly sat up and gazed at her with a puzzled look. "What ..." she began, but Jamie quickly silenced her with a gentle kiss as she slid into the full-sized bed.

"Your father said we could sleep together as long as all we did was sleep," she teased as she snuggled up next to her.

"You asked?" Ryan's expression was so amazed that Jamie had to laugh.

"No, no, honey, I just said you needed some comfort tonight. He actually made the suggestion. He loves you very much, and he wants you to feel better."

Ryan sniffled at the thought of Jamie and her father trying to find a way to care for her. Jamie scooted up on the bed and drew Ryan in close so that her dark head rested against her soft breasts. Ryan sighed so deeply it was nearly comical, but she immediately nestled snugly in Jamie's tender embrace, so that there wasn't a millimeter of space between them. Moments after settling down, her deep, even breathing lulled Jamie into a sweet, dream-filled slumber.

She woke long before the sunrise, but it took her a moment to get her bearings. The feel of Ryan's body against hers was still unfamiliar, and it took her a second for her brain to get the message that she wasn't wrapped around Jack. But when she allowed her senses to really open up, there wasn't a doubt in her mind who shared her bed. The first thing that caught her attention was the alluring aroma that emanated from Ryan's body. The scent was almost indescribable, but she was sure she could pick it out given a thousand choices. There was something so Ryan-like about the scent: it was sweet and spicy, complex and simple, sexy and innocent.

But even without her scent, the way Ryan's body felt was so different from Jack's that it continually surprised her that she could mistake one for the other. Where Jack was hard and strong, Ryan was soft and supple. He carried much of his weight in his broad shoulders and chest, and the dense muscles felt heavy and oppressive when he lay against her. But Ryan's softness molded against her so perfectly that she felt more like a comfortable extension than a separate person.

Jack was an athlete too, and his breathing pattern was very similar to Ryan's. They each drew long, slow, deep breaths with a surprisingly long pause between each one. As she tilted her head just enough to rest her ear against Ryan's chest, she noticed that their heartbeats were also similar, steady, slow and strong. Even though Jamie had enjoyed resting her head on Jack's chest, the sensation of doing so on Ryan was a much richer one. Lying on Ryan's chest was like being enveloped in a warm maternal embrace. There was something so soft and warm and reassuring about hearing that strong heartbeat, and having those amazingly supple breasts just inches from her face, that it nearly made Jamie swoon with pleasure.

Jamie knew she had only slept for about five hours, but it felt so wonderful to have Ryan wrapped around her, she actually hated to go back to sleep. There was something so unspeakably delicious about feeling Ryan's warm body caressing her that her overwhelming urge was to remain awake and luxuriate in the sensation. Ultimately, the warmth and the comfort that flowed from their tender connection pulled her back down into slumber, despite her best efforts to remain alert.

For the next two hours, they repeated the cycle over and over again. One would awaken and change position to make their connection even more airtight. The other would quickly wake, and they would spend a few minutes in a deeply sensual dance, moving slowly and tenderly against each other until sleep reclaimed them. Neither had any inclination to actually break the spell, but when Ryan heard Conor start the shower she finally spoke the first words of the day. "I hate to say it, but you should probably go back downstairs. Once Conor's out of the shower, it'll be hard to sneak away."

"Mmm," Jamie's deep morning voice rumbled. "Don't wanna leave."

"I don't want to either." Ryan let Jamie's kisses weaken her determination. After ten minutes of increasingly sensual touching, she realized they were much more able to comply with her father's wishes when they were actually asleep. "I've got to get up," she mumbled as she pried herself away from her frisky lover. "Way, way too tempting." She sat on the edge of the bed and shook her head quickly to order her thoughts. "You can stay in bed for awhile; I'll go have breakfast with Conor and Da."

"No, no," Jamie insisted. "If you get up, I can get up." She started to struggle to her feet, but she was still so tired that she leaned heavily against Ryan as soon as she was vertical.

"Go back to sleep," Ryan insisted. "There's no rush."

"But I want to be with you," she mumbled into the fabric that covered Ryan's chest. "I like you."

A very amused chuckle greeted that remark. "I like you, too. But you can still go back to sleep."

"Unh-uh," she insisted as she shook her fair head.

Ryan started to back out of the room, but Jamie clung to her like a drowning woman. Her hands were clasped firmly around Ryan's neck, and she let herself be dragged along as Ryan continued to move. "Jamie," she soothed. "Your bed is calling you …"

"Unh-uh. Only your mouth calls to me." With that she tightened her grip and plastered herself against Ryan's body. They were now in the upstairs hallway, just outside of Rory's room. Ryan stumbled and was stopped abruptly by the railing. Giving in to the warm, sensuous kiss, she sat on the railing and enjoyed Jamie's mouth for several seconds. They were so involved that they almost didn't hear the muffled thump and sharp gasp that echoed up from the living room. Ryan tore her mouth away and looked over her shoulder to see her father gathering up the laundry he had been carrying. She turned and gave her partner a dramatic eyebrow lift as she calmly drawled, "Morning, Da."

"Ahh, good morning girls. I didn't see you up there," he said nervously, not making eye contact. "Ready for some breakfast?" He was busily trying to refold the neat piles he had been carrying, but it was obvious that he was flustered at seeing them in the rather passionate embrace.

"Sure," Ryan said smoothly. "Be right down."

Jamie's hands had dropped to her sides as soon as they saw Martin, and she now gave Ryan a very guilty look. Her partner just pushed her gently into the bedroom and said, "I think that made him uncomfortable. Let me go smooth things over, okay?"

"I'm sorry I did that." Jamie looked contrite, but Ryan was having none of it.

"Nonsense. We weren't doing anything wrong. He's just got to get used to it. It's an adjustment for him, too."

"You sure?" Jamie asked, obviously hoping to be reassured.

"Positive. Now will you go back to bed?"

"Yep," Jamie agreed as she hopped back in. "I'm staying in bed until he goes to work!"

Ryan strolled into the kitchen and grabbed a piece of crisp bacon that her father had just prepared. She placed a kiss on his cheek and climbed aboard a tall stool, staring at him thoughtfully the whole time. Martin was concentrating on his cooking as though it was mesmerizing, but he looked up quickly when Ryan asked, "Want to talk about it?"

"It?" he said absently.

"Uh-huh. The big 'it' that's making that pancake batter so utterly fascinating."

He uttered a small, nervous laugh as he turned to face her. "I hate to be so transparent," he grumbled.

"It's okay, Da. This has got to be hard for you. It's completely understandable."

He smiled at her with a look of utter relief on his handsome face. "Is it really, darlin'? I've been worried that maybe I'm not as open-minded as I like to think I am."

That admission took Ryan aback, and she blinked slowly as she tried to comprehend exactly what he meant. "Do you think it bothers you because I'm with a woman?" she asked slowly, as she tried to keep the hurt from her voice.

He looked very uncomfortable as he pursed his lips and said, "I … I'm not sure, Siobhán. I've just had a bit of a hard time adjusting … I … I'm not sure."

Conor's heavy tread echoed through the dining room, and father and daughter paused as he entered the kitchen. Taking one look at their faces and sensing the tension in the room, he turned and marched right back out. Martin smiled at his son's retreating form and said, "The lad has an aversion to serious talks, doesn't he?"

"Yeah, he's the smart one," Ryan grumbled, now wishing she hadn't brought the topic up at all.

Seeing that he had upset his daughter, Martin wiped his hands and pulled up another stool right next to hers. He sat down and waited until she made eye contact to say, "I'm sure this is temporary, sweetheart. But you might have to have a little patience with your old father."

Ryan gave him a small smile and nodded her head. "I can be patient," she said. "I just don't understand why it would bother you. It certainly isn't a surprise that I'm a lesbian."

"No, of course it isn't. I've known that you were … you know … with women … for years now, but Tracy was the only woman you've ever brought home."

"Did it bother you to think of Tracy and me … together?"

He blushed as he conceded, "Yes, it did a bit."

"I could have reassured you on that one, Da, we didn't have sex."

"You didn't?" he asked, slightly stunned. "Why not?"

"For the same reason I haven't had sex with Jamie," she explained. "I was trying to find out if Tracy was right for me, and I wanted to concentrate on building a relationship before I muddled the issue with my raging hormones." She looked at him with a very serious expression as she said, "About five years ago, you told me that sex was much more special if you waited for the person that you loved. I obviously didn't heed your advice then, but I'm giving it a go now. I'll let you know how it works out," she said with a charming grin.

"So how do I get over feeling odd about you two?"

"I don't know," she said honestly. "I guess we just see how it goes."

Jamie snuck her head into the room and asked, "Is this a private conversation, or can I join in?"

Ryan opened her arms as she gave her a wide smile. Jamie walked over and snuggled into her embrace as she sat on the tiny edge of the stool that Ryan left for her. "You're welcome to join us," she said as she rested her chin on Jamie's shoulder.

"I was just telling Siobhán how happy I am that she's found you, Jamie. You're the best addition to the family that I could ever dream of." He bent to kiss her cheek. As he stood, he gave his daughter a reassuring smile and a kiss.

Jamie blushed a bit at the praise and turned her head to Ryan as she said, "That's one of the nicest morning greetings I've had in a long while."

"They're only going to get better," Ryan's deep voice burred against the back of her neck, sending a good-morning shiver down her spine.

After breakfast, Jamie decided to go to church to see her grandfather, but Ryan couldn't spare the time. She grabbed a liter of water and went downstairs with Duffy to get to work. She was completely amazed to feel a soft kiss on her neck after what seemed to be just minutes later, but Jamie assured her it was nearly noon. Pulling her lover onto her lap, they spent a few minutes kissing before Ryan patted her butt and sent her on her way. After changing into khaki shorts and a sky blue tank top, Jamie went upstairs to make lunch, coming back a few minutes later with two sandwiches and one happy dog. They spent a few minutes sharing their lunch while Jamie related the message of the sermon and gained a promise that they could spend some time with her grandfather after finals. After their meal was finished, Jamie said, "When I was upstairs with your father, he acted just like he always does. How did your talk go this morning?"

"It went okay," Ryan said, thinking about the whole exchange. "But he is a little uncomfortable with us. I think he needs some time to let the change sink in."

"Is he uncomfortable with it because we're women? Or just because we were being too affectionate?"

"Not sure," Ryan said. "I don't think he knows, either. But he's willing to talk about it, so I'm sure it'll be okay eventually."

"Hmm, has he ever seen you kiss anyone before me?"

Ryan thought about that for a minute, eventually smiling up at her partner. "You know, I don't think he has. God, that's gotta be kinda rough on a parent. I mean, he knows I've been having sex for a long time, but it must be weird to actually see evidence of the way I feel about you."

"Yeah," Jamie said with a chuckle. "Your intentions were pretty clear this morning, too. That kiss was way friendly."

Ryan laughed as she reminded her, "You started it, smarty-pants. I'm just a slave to your desires."

"We're both prone to losing control," Jamie agreed. "But to be fair to your father, I think we should tone it down in front of him. It's kinda rude."

"You're right, as usual. I don't wanna have to avoid showing affection, but we shouldn't go much past that."

"You know," Jamie said thoughtfully. "I wonder if that's the real reason behind the 'no overnight dates' rule. I bet your brothers wouldn't mind having dates around."

Ryan laughed quietly as she nodded her head. "You know, I've never considered that. But I know Conor would love to have another woman in the house even if she was in my bed! And Rory's so casual about things that he wouldn't bat an eye. I think we may have stumbled upon one of Da's weaknesses."

"Well, let's make sure we don't exploit it," Jamie declared as she patted Ryan on the cheek and released her to resume her studies.

Ryan got up from her chair at three and lay down on the floor. After performing an elaborate series of stretching moves, she was right back at it. Jamie loved watching her concentrate, and Ryan's trance was so deep that, for a change, she didn't even notice she was being observed. She was wearing her little wire-rimmed computer glasses as she sat in front of her monitor, fingers flying over the keys. Jamie was fairly computer literate, having had her own system since she was in grammar school, but Ryan acted like her computer was an extension of her brain. She could find the most obscure site on the Internet in a matter of moments, and Jamie suspected that she could make a good living in the software business if she chose that path. Still, even though she was a prodigy with computers, she didn't seem to love them with the same passion she held for science and math. She actually never looked more content than when she was sitting in front of her computer working on a particularly difficult problem. The look of joy and excitement that graced her beautiful face when she solved whatever issue was vexing her was truly a thing to behold, and Jamie smiled when she thought of spending the whole next year watching her plow through her studies. There was just a tiny part of her that felt left out, since she had absolutely no idea what Ryan was talking about when she tried to share her discoveries, but she was happy to witness her delight even if she didn't understand it.

Since Ryan was so engrossed, Jamie had no choice but to get caught up on her own work, and they were both surprised when Martin called them for dinner. "Dinner?" Ryan said as she lifted her head. "Did we have lunch?"

"Yes, dear," Jamie said as she tried to roll her away from the screen by tugging on her chair.

Ryan dug her heels in and said, "I've almost got this figured out. I need a few more minutes," and turned her laser-like concentration back to her computer.

Shaking her head, Jamie climbed the stairs with Duffy and informed Martin of Ryan's statement. "I've heard that excuse a thousand times or so," he said. He was busily arranging the repast on a pair of platters, but he stopped for a moment and reflected. "You know, she's been like this since she was a tiny little thing. I used to wonder at the mothers at the park complaining about their children never paying attention to their schoolwork. It was all I could do to get her to stop for dinner when she was working on her little math problems."

"I don't remember doing much math homework when I was small," she said.

"Ha! She wasn't doing homework," he laughed. "She could easily handle her homework at school and keep one ear open to pay attention to the teacher. She's always been able to devote her attention to two or even three things at once. No, she was working her way through her brothers' math books by the time she could read. I'll never forget her explaining some difficult concept to Brendan when he was studying for the SAT's. He was nearly seventeen and she was eleven, sitting on his lap in the dining room, patiently explaining whatever was stumping him. She's truly a prodigy, you know."

"I … I really had no idea," she said with a stunned expression on her face. "I just assumed she liked math and was good at it."

"No, I don't think math is something she likes," he said reflectively as he gazed into space for a moment. "It's more than that for her. I don't pretend to understand it, but I know it's much more than a simple affinity." He furrowed his brow for a moment, trying to explain his idea. "We started noticing that she was different when she was just learning to talk. She was very slow to talk, the slowest of all of the children. Fionnuala was actually quite worried about her, but the doctor assured us that she was perfectly fine. She just had three older brothers who did whatever she wanted as long as she pointed. Anyway, Conor was in first grade when she was just turning two. She was usually on his lap or being carried around by the lad, and it seemed that she was learning his school lessons right along with him. One evening Fionnuala was working with Conor on his math homework. She asked him what two plus two plus one was. He fumbled around for a bit, but couldn't figure it out. Fi noticed that Siobhán was getting frustrated, and before you know it she cries out, 'Five, Cono! Five!'"

Jamie's eyes had grown wide and her mouth dropped open in amazement.

Martin laughed and informed her, "That's just the look Fionnuala had on her face when she came into the living room carrying the little scamp. Her first sentence turns out to be a math solution!"

"That's truly amazing."

"Oh yes. She amazed the teachers in school. After kindergarten, they wanted to jump her ahead a year or two since she was so advanced. But Fi was so sick," he said, his eyes taking on a sadness Jamie had rarely seen in him. "We both knew she had very little time left, and it seemed unwise to cause any more disruption in the children's lives. It would have been very hard for Rory to have his little sister in his class and, aside from math, she was perfectly suited for first grade."

"What did you do?" Jamie asked. "How did you keep her interested in school?"

"Well, she was lucky to have a wonderful teacher in first grade."

"Sister Kevin?" she asked, remembering the teacher who helped Ryan pick her new name.

"The same," he said with a fond smile. "She obtained some teaching materials for fourth and fifth graders and let Siobhán work on them on her own when the others were having their math instruction. It worked out very well and it let her figure things out on her own, and that probably helped her in the end. Sister Kevin spoke to each of Siobhán's subsequent teachers, and they each followed her advice. It worked out brilliantly."

"Wow, that really was smart."

"Yes, but we had another go-around when she was in high school."

"How so?"

"Did you know she earned a perfect score on the SAT's in math?" he asked, knowing that his daughter wouldn't impart this type of information voluntarily.

Conor came in while they were talking and added, "Tell her the amazing part, Da." Unable to wait, he turned to Jamie and said, "She took the SAT's when she was a freshman in high school as part of a program to identify kids who could benefit from entering college early. She sucked at the verbal part," he laughed as his father cuffed him on the head for that comment and continued, "but when she got an 800 on math, they went nuts!"

"She did not ... suck," Martin said with a sour look on his face. "Her verbal score was in line with that of a fourteen-year-old year old. Nonetheless, they tried to talk me into letting her skip the rest of high school and go on to college, but there was no way she was ready for that emotionally. I thought she'd be a much happier adult if she stayed with her own class."

"Plus, she sucked in every course that wasn't math or science," Conor had to add as he dashed from the room to avoid another pop.

"Did she want to go?" Jamie asked as Martin shook his head at his mischievous son.

"I don't think she had any interest, really," he admitted. "She loved sports as much as she loved studying, and she knew she wouldn't be allowed to compete in college when she was fourteen-years-old—even though she probably could have!" he laughed. "I'm sure she'd have a doctorate or two by now if I'd let them rush her through, but she's got plenty of time to make her contributions to the world. It was more important to me that she have an environment where she could mature at her own pace. Although after her senior year, I certainly did regret my decision. She would have been well served to have left that place a year earlier."

A thought dawned on Jamie and she asked, "Why didn't Ryan have academic scholarships to college?"

Martin shook his dark head again at that question. "She could have gone to any school in the country, Jamie. M.I.T., Cal Tech, the Ivy League, North Carolina, they all wanted her. The people from Stanford would have given their eyeteeth to get her. Their soccer coach courted her like a lovesick suitor, but she wanted Cal and she wanted the athletic scholarship. I'm not sure why it meant so much to her, but it truly did. When she decided to attend USF, they were more than happy to find some money for her, but she didn't think that was fair. She felt that accepting money at that late date would take a scholarship away from someone else, and she just couldn't do that. Personally, I think she set things up the way she did to punish herself for all of the troubles that befell her. I think she still accepts all of the blame for the whole incident."

"But what does she have to feel guilty for?"

"I think she feels like she should have known better than to be vulnerable with that girl," he said, unable to even speak Sara's name.

"But that doesn't make any sense!"

"Jamie, one thing you'll learn about my little one. Once she makes up her mind about something, it's nearly impossible to change it, no matter the evidence."

Jamie nodded slowly, having figured that trait out already. But she was determined to one day make Ryan see that the troubles she experienced in high school were the result of vindictive, small-minded kids, and that she was truly blameless.

After dinner the boys insisted that they would clean up so that the students could get back to work. They went back downstairs and hit the books until nine o'clock, when Jamie realized she was getting too tired to continue. "I'm gonna head home," she said through a yawn.

Ryan looked up as though she had forgotten her lover was even there. "I'm sorry I haven't paid more attention to you. Are you sorry that you spent the day here?"

Jamie came over and straddled her lap, facing her squarely. "Of course not. I had a really nice day. I had to study anyway, and it was so nice to look up and see you every time I took a break. You're the best view in town, you know."

"Why don't you stay over again? Your roommates think you're at your parents, don't they?"

"Yeah, but I'd normally come home on Sunday night. Besides, I don't have any clean underwear for tomorrow."

"Well, I want you to do what you want, but I have some tiny little underwear that's too small for me. I bet it would fit you just fine."

"Okay," she grinned. "I'll go sleep in Rory's room so you can use your computer."

"Great," said Ryan. "Then we can drive to school together in the morning."

"Will you wake me up? I don't have an alarm on my watch."

"I'll get you up an hour before we have to leave. Then we can have breakfast."

She knew how serious her partner was about her studies when she was seemingly content to receive a single kiss goodnight. But before she left, Jamie had to lean over and kiss the dark head that held so many secrets that she was looking forward to discovering.

Chapter Nine

On Monday evening, Jamie and Ryan had dinner together, but Ryan insisted that she had to study at home. Since her bike was in the city, after a brief argument Ryan agreed to take the Boxster. Jamie kissed her goodbye and, standing on her front porch, watched her drive away until the taillights were just tiny red dots.

When Jamie went into the house, she distractedly walked up the stairs, reaching her door just as Mia was leaving her room. "Are you staying home tonight?"

Mia regarded her friend's pink face, disordered hair and agitated demeanor and carefully said, "Yeah, why?"

"I need to talk to you, if you have time."

"Sure, I have time," she said. "It's too late to start studying at this point in the term."

Jamie gave her a smile and said, "Let me change, and I'll be right down."

Five minutes later, Jamie came back downstairs. She had changed into an extra large, yellow T-shirt and a pair of green, blue and yellow plaid, flannel boxer shorts. The shorts were way too big for her, so she had rolled the waistband over three times to snug up the fit. With her tousled hair, oversized clothes, and still flushed face, she looked like a young child who was wearing an older sibling's clothes. The childlike image was shattered when she said, "I need a drink. Join me?"

"Uhm ... sure," Mia said, reasoning that since she wasn't going to study anyway, she might as well have fun. "Do we have any of that beer that has tequila in it?"

Jamie poked her head into the refrigerator and found a new six-pack. She pulled out two bottles and set them on the kitchen table as they each pulled out a chair.

She took a long pull on her beer and shook her head as she made a face. "You like this stuff?" she gasped, convulsively smacking her lips.

"Yeah, it's got a kick to it," Mia laughed.

"That it does," Jamie replied, pushing the bottle away. Without the beer, she had nothing to occupy her shaking hands, and she could feel Mia's eyes assess her critically. Grabbing the bottle again, she took a very deep breath to gather her courage, but couldn't seem to make any words come out. She closed her eyes to try again, but soon felt Mia's warm hand cover hers. "Jamie," her roommate said softly, "I know."

Jamie's eyes flew open as her head jerked up abruptly. She tried to make her mouth work, but the look of total compassion and understanding on Mia's face dissolved whatever composure she still had, and she burst into tears. Her head dropped to the table, and great sobs wracked her body as she shook and gasped for air. Deciding that this conversation would likely be a long one, Mia gently took one of Jamie's arms and urged her up from her seat. Firmly wrapping her arm around her, she took her into the library, where she deposited her on the leather sofa. Mia sat down right beside her and pulled her sobbing friend's head against her chest. She tenderly patted Jamie's back and smoothed her hair, murmuring reassuring words the whole while. Jamie clung desperately to her friend, letting all of her pent-up feelings flow through her body unabated.

It took a long time, but she finally had enough self-control to try to express herself. She murmured into Mia's chest, "I'm so sorry."

"Jamie," Mia soothed, "You don't have anything to apologize for. If this is who you are, you need to accept it. It'll be okay."

She shot up and stared at her friend with wide eyes. "No, God, no! I'm not sorry about Ryan. I'm sorry that I lied to you."

Mia breathed a deep sigh of relief as she said, "Thank goodness! God, you frightened me there for a minute. I thought you were unhappy that you'd fallen for her."

"No! Not at all." After a moment, she gazed up at her friend and timidly asked, "So you're not mad at me?"

"About which part?"

"Well, either."

"Your sexual inclinations don't mean a thing to me. Straight ... gay ... other. No big deal. No surprise. But I am hurt about being lied to."

"I don't blame you," Jamie said softly. "I feel worse about that than anything that's happened so far. It's not really a very good excuse, but I was so taken aback by Cassie jumping on me that night that I just didn't know what to do. When you came upstairs, I knew that I should level with you, but I just couldn't, Mia. I felt so overwhelmed by her that I couldn't open it all up right then."

Mia draped her arm around her friend's shoulders and said, "I understand that you didn't want to get into it, but it would have hurt a lot less if you'd just said you didn't want to talk about it. It's the outright lie that hurts, James."

"I think I get that now. I think I learned a valuable lesson, though. This lying stuff is a lot harder than it looks!"

"Well, I could have told you that," she laughed. "It's a skill, like anything else, James—you shouldn't try to just jump in with the pros!"

Jamie snuggled up against her friend and rested her head on her shoulder. "I really am sorry, Mia. I knew in my heart that you'd be supportive, but I chickened out. Forgive me?"

"You've got to do a lot worse than tell a lie to get rid of me, girlfriend," she said as she gave her a firm squeeze. "I want to be in your life for a long, long while."

"There's nothing I'd like better. I want to know your grandchildren." Her forehead a bit as she considered Mia's first statement. "What did you mean when you said you weren't surprised about my relationship with Ryan?"

"I started suspecting the first time you told me about her," she admitted. "You were too interested in her for her to be just be a classmate. I've known you for a long time, James, but I swear I've never seen your eyes sparkle like they did when you talked about her."

"But that wasn't enough to make you sure about it, was it?"

"No, but I've been pretty sure ever since I started working out with her. And that night around Thanksgiving when we went out to dinner together made it totally obvious," she said as she rolled her eyes.

"But how can that be?" Jamie cried. "I didn't even know until a little over a month ago. Ryan didn't know then, either. Right after that she started dating someone seriously."

"I don't know, James. You've been acting like a lovesick puppy for a long time. And that night at dinner, you both acted like lovers."

"But we aren't ... I mean we weren't ..." she said as she blushed a deep shade of pink.

"What's going on?" Mia asked suspiciously. "Are you lovers, or not?"

"Well, yeah, we are. I mean, we almost are in some ways, and we really are in others." She looked up and laughed at herself. "Wasn't that clear?"

"Crystal," agreed Mia as she playfully ruffled her hair.

"Okay, I'll give you the whole sordid story." Jamie took a breath to organize her thoughts and began, "The night in February that Jack broke up with me, I went over to her house. I was a wreck, as you might imagine," she laughed wryly. "But she held me in her arms and rocked me and sang me a lullaby to put me to sleep." She blushed again at revealing this tender intimacy, but Mia smiled reassuringly and urged her to continue. "The next day she had the woman over that she was trying to be serious with, and I was so irrationally jealous. *I* wanted to be her girlfriend, and I swear that's the first time I knew."

"So what did you do between February and now?"

"I immediately found a therapist. What else? This is California, after all," she said, laughing at the stereotype.

"Wow, I had no idea you were in therapy. You've always seemed so well adjusted."

"Well, I am ... kinda. But this was really hard for me, not to mention the fact that I was having a tough time adjusting to having Jack break up with me."

"That makes sense. But I want you to hurry up and get to the good parts."

"Okay, okay. Remember that Jack popped back into the picture for a short while? Well, that was just my inability to face the facts about Ryan. After being in therapy for about two months, I started to believe that this was right for me. I mean, I'm still not sure if I'd be with women other than Ryan, but I know she's the person for me."

"Good parts?"

"Okay. I knew I was going to tell her the day we went on a long bike ride to Marin. At the end of the day, we decided it was too late to come home on the ferry, so I found us a room at the Pelican Inn. We were up on the top of Mt. Tam, sitting on a big boulder, and watching the sunset. I gathered up my courage and told her that I loved her." She smiled broadly at the memory, feeling a chill chase down her spine even now. "To my amazement, she told me that she loved me too."

"So then you went to the inn, and you did it until you passed out!" Mia exclaimed.

"No. Not quite."

"Why not? She's so hot looking I know I couldn't keep my hands off her," she said with a leer.

Jamie gave her a startled look, but finally just shook her head at her friend's sexual hyperbole. "Far be it from me to argue that point, but I'm just getting comfortable with this. This is a very big change for me, you know."

"I know it is, Jamie. But don't you think you'd get comfortable faster if you just did it a whole lot?"

Jamie laughed and patted her cheek fondly. "I think you and I have different ways of dealing with things. My way is to feel comfortable first, have sex later."

"Not to slight you, but I'm amazed she's willing to wait. I mean some of the stuff I've heard about her …"

"Hey, watch who you're talking about," Jamie said defensively. "That's the woman I love."

"I just mean that I've heard she really gets around. A lot of women at the gym talk about her, and they've said that she has a lot of sex with a lot of women. It sure sounds like she's not used to being celibate."

"Well, to be honest, she's not used to being celibate. She has a very active libido. But she loves me, Mia. She wants me to be happy and secure. I don't think you've seen that side of her."

"So … you do nothing for her? I mean, how do you decide how far to go?"

"I do things for her," she said defensively. "Well … okay, to be honest, I drive her crazy," she admitted with a laugh. "We … I guess we make out. Sounds pretty juvenile, but that's what's working for us."

"So how is it for you? Are you more interested in sex than you were with Jack?"

"Whew!" she said as she blew out a breath that fluttered her bangs. "No comparison. She makes me hotter than I ever thought possible. It's … well, I don't have anything to compare it to. It's just more than I ever dreamed of."

"You get so hot that you don't have sex," Mia said, laughing.

"Right. But that'll change soon. We're making progress."

The front door opened at that point, and Cassie glared across the library at them. They were sharing a single seat cushion, and Mia still had her arm around Jamie, who was snuggling up against her side. "Oh great," she growled, "now both of you are turning!"

Mia looked over at her with a placid expression, but Jamie could see the impish look in her eyes. "Hey, Cassie, would you do me a favor?"

When Cassie tilted her head questioningly, Mia sweetly asked, "Go fuck yourself, will you?"

Jamie's eyes nearly popped out of her head, and Cassie looked like she might storm over and pop Mia one, but the outraged woman merely threw her books to the floor with a thud and stalked off to her room.

"Mia," Jamie squealed. "Why'd you do that?"

"Because she's a big pain in the ass, and I'm sick of her."

"But ..." Jamie began, but Mia cut her off.

"I wasn't going to tell you this, but you'll find out anyway. On Saturday night she called your parents' house because she didn't believe that you went down there. Which I might add, you did not," she said as she wiggled her eyebrows.

"I was with Ryan at her family's house," Jamie meekly admitted.

"Geez! You sleep with her and still don't have sex with her? That's beyond cruel!"

"But she likes to sleep with me."

"Of course she does!" Mia cried. "She thinks she's gonna catch you at a weak moment and have you in the ready position."

"Mia! She's not like that. Now tell me what happened with Cassie."

"She spoke to your mom. Apparently your mom wasn't very happy with her calling the house rather than your cell phone, and that really pissed Cassie off," she said with a smirk. "But your mom said she'd call you and have you call Cassie back. So what happened? Did she call you?"

"No ... oh, wait, someone did call me on Saturday night, but they hung up when I answered."

"Has anyone else called you since then?"

"No, I don't think so. Why?"

"Go get your phone," she instructed. Jamie went to the entry table and fetched the device. Mia picked it up and dialed *69 and handed it back.

Seconds later, Jamie said, "Hi Marta, this is Jamie, is my mother home?"

After a pause she continued, "No, that's okay, I'll call tomorrow. I just want to say goodbye before she leaves for her trip. Goodnight, Marta," she said as she clicked off. She looked at Mia rather dumbfounded and asked, "Why would she call me and hang up? That doesn't make any sense."

"I think she might know more than she's letting on."

"You don't know the half of it," she grumbled as she rolled her eyes dramatically. For the next fifteen minutes, she explained Cassie's other little tricks and related her own lies to her mother. They weren't able to resolve much, but they both agreed that they were well rid of Cassie.

They walked back into the kitchen, and Jamie poured their now warm beers down the sink, running the water for a while to remove the sharp odor of the tequila. They went up to bed with their arms loosely draped around each other's waists, their friendship once again on solid footing.

Chapter Ten

When Jamie called her mother on Tuesday, neither woman mentioned the incident with Cassie. Catherine asked about the ride and quizzed her daughter a little bit on her preparations, but she seemed perfectly normal, and their interaction was the same as always. The incident still puzzled Jamie, but she finally chalked it up as unexplainable and got back to her studying.

When she got home from her last class, the keys to her car were lying on the floor under the mail slot. A sealed note explained that Ryan was working on an important problem for her biology class and, since she needed her computer to do some computations, they wouldn't be able to meet at all that evening.

Jamie was unreasonably depressed to not even be allowed to kiss Ryan's sweet lips and she spent more time than she should have moping in her room. At eight o'clock her phone rang, and a smile graced her face when she heard the familiar voice. "I miss you."

"I miss you too. It seems like forever since I've kissed you."

"It almost *is* forever. It was a whole twenty-four hours ago."

"If you'd let me, I'd drive over to your house for a good night kiss."

Ryan paused for a long minute but finally said, "I don't think that's a good idea, as tempting as it is, Jamie. I'm really having a hard time concentrating. It worked well when you were with me on Sunday, but seeing you for a little bit and getting all worked up isn't working for me."

"I understand. I don't like it, but I understand."

"Uhm … I don't really need to come back to Berkeley this week since my last class was today and my first test isn't until Monday. Would it be too terrible for you if we didn't see each other this week?"

Jamie was stunned that Ryan would even ask such a thing. She tried to force herself to be mature and sensitive to her lover's needs, but she was wounded that Ryan could even make the suggestion. As the silence stretched on for a while, Ryan realized she wasn't taking well to the idea. "Jamie," she said softly. "I'm sorry if that hurt your feelings. But I don't know what else to do. I want to see you and touch you so bad my teeth ache, but after we touch for a while you're all I can think about."

"Oh, honey, I know things are hard for you right now, but I don't think I can concentrate if I don't see you at all. Isn't there some other way?"

"Well, you could stay over here until finals are over. We'd at least be in the same house."

"But we couldn't sleep together."

"No, I don't think Da would like that. Saturday was an exception, but I don't think he'd want us to continue that."

"Why don't you come sleep with me?"

"You know there's no way to avoid Cassie and Mia."

"I have some good news on that front," she said brightly. "I told Mia last night, and she took it really well. She wouldn't mind if you came over, and after we talked she really insulted Cassie, so I doubt that she'll come home."

Ryan was quiet for a few minutes, so quiet that Jamie finally asked, "Tell me what's going through your mind."

A deep sigh began the reply. "I … I just don't feel right sneaking into your house," she said softly. "I mean, I guess it shouldn't bother me, since I've done it so many times before, but something about it really gets to me."

Jamie's return sigh was just as deep. "I think I know what it is," she said softly. "You told me that you never want me to feel ashamed of our love. And even though I think you know that I'm not ashamed, a little part of you is still hurt by having to hide."

"I guess you're right. It's just such a joyous time for me that it really hurts to have to sneak around. It puts a bad taste in my mouth. I'm sorry, Jamie, I really am," she said, "but it's really starting to get to me."

"Let me think for a minute," Jamie said, rather brusquely. "I'll call you back."

Ryan started to protest, since it was obvious that she had hurt her lover's feelings, but the phone had gone dead before she could utter a word.

Almost fifteen minutes passed before the phone rang. Ryan had actually been pacing across the living room floor for ten of those minutes, driving Conor and her father slightly mad. Both men were watching the Giants play the Dodgers, but the incessant pacing was diverting their attention. "Who says love is bliss?" Conor muttered just loudly enough for his father to hear.

All three O'Flaherty's were relieved when Jamie's happy-sounding voice came through the phone. "You have twenty minutes to pack," Jamie said. "Bring everything you need for the week—including your computer."

"What? Jamie, we don't have to do this. I know you're not ready to tell …"

"I'm not telling anyone anything. Now pack up and kiss your father goodbye. I'll be there soon."

Conor poked his head out of the bedroom door to see his sister standing in the middle of the room, receiver still in her hand, dial tone echoing loudly. "Uhm, Ryan?" he said softly, trying not to startle her. "You okay?"

She shook her head to clear it and gazed at him for a minute. "I'm gonna be gone for a few days," she mumbled as she started to walk to her room.

"Where are you going?" he asked her departing form, narrowing his eyes at her normal bedtime attire of an old T-shirt and baggy sweats.

"Don't know," she replied as she shrugged her shoulders.

Jamie was optimistic on her estimate—the drive actually took her thirty minutes. Ryan needed every minute—getting her clothes ready was not a problem, but she had a massive amount of books, notebooks, lab notes and floppy disks that she regularly used. She had recruited Conor to help her load everything into a big box and they were just finishing when Jamie came running down the stairs in an ebullient mood. Conor greeted her warmly and started up the stairs with the heavy box. "Be back for the computer," he called as he climbed the stairs.

"All set?" the perky blonde asked.

"I guess so," Ryan replied with a rather helpless look on her face. "Did Cassie move out or something?"

"Nope." Jamie started to carry Ryan's suitcase up the stairs, but she stopped and asked, "Did you pack your swimsuit?"

"Huh? No, of course not." Putting her hands on her hips she demanded, "Jamie, what's going on?"

"All in due time, my dear. Just stuff a suit in here and let's get shaking!"

The Boxster was filled to capacity once Conor got everything loaded into the very petite trunk. They had to remove Jamie's suitcase in order to squeeze in Ryan's books, but they finally got the trunk closed. Conor and Martin stood on the sidewalk in front of the house. "Goodbye, darlin'," Martin said as he kissed his youngest. "Have fun or study hard or, well, be safe," he finally said since he had no knowledge of her itinerary.

"Oh, I'll take very good care of her, Martin. I promise to return her on Friday well fed, well rested, and ready for her exams."

"I trust you, Jamie," he said fondly. "I know my precious one is in good hands." He kissed the smaller woman and hugged Ryan again. Then Conor did the same to both of them.

"See you soon, I guess," Ryan said, still looking shell-shocked. Conor hoisted Jamie's suitcase over the door through the open window and Ryan spent a moment maneuvering it into a comfortable place. When she was finished, she waved at her family, a nearly dumbstruck expression on her face.

As they drove off, Conor opined, "I've never ever seen her so compliant."

Martin laughed at that characterization, but he had to admit it was accurate. "You'll be the same some day, lad."

Jamie drove since Ryan had no idea where they were headed. It appeared they were going to Jamie's, but she took a different turn and went towards Oakland. A few minutes after they left the freeway, they pulled into the grounds of the Claremont Hotel. Ryan had seen the huge white edifice many times, but had never actually been on the property. Looking around excitedly, she asked, "Are we staying here?"

"Yep," Jamie said firmly. "We're staying here until Friday. I'm paying so don't even bother to argue. We're going to pamper ourselves outrageously."

"But …"

Jamie quickly cut off Ryan's protest, "I can't stand to be around Cassie for another minute, and I can't stay at your house and not sleep with you—it drives me crazy! So even if you don't want to join me, I decided to do this. I just want to study and have someone else take care of every need. Room service … maid service … swimming pool … Jacuzzi tub …"

"Sold!" Ryan agreed as they pulled up in front of the valet.

Exhibiting her typical take-charge attitude, Jamie hopped out and began instructing the bellman on how to unload the car. Their luggage looked odd, consisting of two computers, one printer and two small suitcases, but the young man took it in stride.

That attitude continued as Jamie dealt with the pleasant woman at the front desk. "We need the top floor," she instructed. "The quietest room you have. We're working on an important project and we need privacy."

"How many beds?" the woman asked, with a completely neutral expression.

"One king bed," she replied, obviously not afraid of coming out to strangers.

"Hmm," the clerk said as she considered her choices. "I'd say the quietest room we have is in the rear corner of the hotel, facing the hills. But that's a suite …"

"Fine," Jamie informed her briskly. "Four nights."

"Are you sure?" she asked, looking closely at the young woman in front of her, seemingly for the first time. The confident young woman met her gaze evenly. She wore a dark green, fleece-lined anorak, a gold turtleneck and a pair of jeans, and could have passed for a high school student. Ryan didn't help matters much, dressed as she was, in her hooded 'Cal' sweatshirt and jeans. Their luggage was on a cart right next to them, and they looked like what they were—students from Berkeley trying to have peace during finals. To avoid potential misunderstandings, the woman printed off a sheet that showed the charge for the room, the applicable tax and the parking fee and handed it to Jamie.

She cast a cursory glance, handed it back with a smile and her platinum American Express card and said, "I'll need two keys."

The bellman who escorted them chattered non-stop on the short elevator ride. He was about their age, and it was obvious he was intensely curious about the two young women he was escorting.

He started with Ryan. "So how long are you planning on being in the Bay Area?"

She replied with her normal habit of responding only to the question she was asked. "Mmm, I suppose the rest of my life. You're not planning on leaving, are you, Jamie?" she asked as she turned her gaze to her partner.

"Nope. I think we're lifers."

"Oh! You're locals?"

"Yep," Ryan replied, once again giving the barest response.

"Here for a convention?"

"Nope."

His brow was furrowed in concentration and frustration as he tried to find a way to pry information out of the enigmatic raven-haired woman. As usual Jamie couldn't stand the silence and she offered, "We're students at Cal. We just need a quiet place to study for a few days."

He gave her a look that implied he had heard better stories, but he quickly put on his polite face and said, "I hope you enjoy yourselves then." He walked ahead of them down the hall, and the smaller woman couldn't stop herself from pinching her tall partner as they walked after him.

"Brat!" she whispered.

Ryan gave her normal "who me?" look as the bellman opened the door and guided their things into the spacious room. "Here we are," he announced as he spent a few minutes showing them all of the amenities.

Jamie was satisfied with both the layout and the orientation of the lovely room. It faced the gently rolling Oakland hills, giving them a nice view of homes and young trees. A tragic fire had dramatically altered this view, but the homeowners had done their best to replant with varieties of trees that wouldn't explode in a fire the way the firs and eucalyptus had done. Since the new homes were so outrageously large, the landscape would never approach its former beauty, but it was still a lovely view. "I do need a modem line," she said. "Is there one?"

"Oh, yes," he replied. The jack was conveniently located right next to the small writing desk that she had already decided would be Ryan's.

"One more thing," she said, looking around quickly. "I need another desk chair. Can you help me out?"

"I'll arrange to have one sent up," he confidently replied. "Anything else, ma'am?"

"No that's fine," she said, handing him twenty dollars.

He left with a smile and a promise to have the chair sent up. Ryan gave her a curious look and asked, "Twenty dollars?"

"Yes, that seemed about right," she said thoughtfully. "He was with us for almost a half hour, the box of your books was really heavy, and he was very careful with the computer equipment. I usually give three dollars a bag and I think this stuff is the equivalent of about seven bags."

"I think that's sweet," Ryan said as she gave her a squeeze and a kiss on the forehead.

"What is?"

"That you really thought that out. You considered how heavy the stuff was and acknowledged that it was kind of hard to wrangle it all up here without dropping anything." She cocked her head a bit and added, "I really like the way you treat people in the service industry. You act like they're professionals too."

"Well, they are," she said. "You don't have to have a title to deserve respect for doing a good job."

"That's what I think is sweet," Ryan restated as she swooped her into her arms and flopped onto the bed. "You're very sweet and very tasty," she growled as she pinned her and started to nibble on her neck.

But Jamie placed her hands flat against her lover's chest and reminded her, "Study time, Tiger. Let's get organized and do a little work tonight."

"Party pooper," Ryan grumbled as she got to her feet and pulled her partner up with her.

It took a good twenty minutes to get organized, but when they were finished they were both satisfied that they could get their work done very nicely in the comfortable room. Jamie chose to work at the table near the window, and once her desk chair was delivered, it was perfect. Ryan took the writing table, and as soon as she was hooked up, she sat down at her chair and started working. Jamie needed more time to ease into studying, so she spent a little while unpacking their clothes and neatly arranging their things in the large dresser. In her rush, Ryan hadn't brought any toiletries and Jamie chuckled to herself that her partner would probably not even get up to shower if she weren't there to remind her to.

After she pulled a can of Diet Coke from the mini-bar, she sat cross-legged on the bed and started to organize her notes for the paper she had to write. The evening zoomed by, and the next thing she knew, it was eleven o'clock. After a few stretches, she walked over to her partner and started playing with her hair. "Hey," Ryan said absently. "Need something?"

"Yeah," she whispered into her ear, "I need you—in my bed."

That broke Ryan's concentration, and after a few more keystrokes she shut down her computer and stood to stretch for a few minutes. "I could work for a couple of more hours," she said as she checked her watch.

"I'm sure you could," Jamie replied as she reached for the hem of the dark blue sweatshirt and started to tug it over her partner's head. "But I promised your father I'd make sure you were rested. I know you'll be up by six, so I've got to put you to sleep early."

Ryan stood there in her jeans and a gray ribbed knit T-shirt that Jamie had recently bought for her. "You look nice in this," the blonde murmured as her hands glided up Ryan's smooth back. "And I love it when you don't wear a bra." As her hands slid down to unbutton the snug jeans, she asked, "What color are your shorts?"

"Not wearing shorts," Ryan whispered in her ear, as her own hands buttoned back up. "I was already in my jammies when you called, so I just threw on my jeans. I didn't think ahead to the ritual undressing," she said with one wiggling eyebrow.

"Are you gonna sleep in the nude?"

"Not for another four weeks," she replied with a look of regret. "I brought underwear. But since you seem to care, you can decide on color."

"Hmm," she said appraisingly as she squinted and tried to imagine the different combinations. "Let's go with white. The gray/white combo is a bit unconventional, but so are you," she added as she slapped her partner rather hard on the butt.

Ryan feared that they would spend half an hour wrestling with their desires and her self-control, but to her amazement, when Jamie got into bed she kissed her sweetly and whispered, "Goodnight, Ryan."

"That's it?" the stunned woman asked. "One kiss?"

"Yep. We're here to study. I have no interest in getting all hot and bothered and spending the night frustrated. Let's just be loving, rather than passionate toward each other for the next few days." Seeing the amazed look on her lover's face, she teased, "Think you can control yourself?"

"Uhm, yeah, I think I can," Ryan said. As she cuddled her partner against her body she whispered, "Thank you. It means a lot to me that you take me seriously when I say I have to work. And I love how you've found a solution that's gonna let each of us get our needs met."

"My main need is completely satisfied," she sighed as she contentedly cuddled even closer.

Six o'clock saw Jamie's prediction come to pass as Ryan slid from her limp embrace and stretched languidly for a few minutes. *Nice day*, she mused as she surveyed the sun peeking out of the slim band of clouds on the horizon. A delighted little grin graced her face when she considered that she could begin her day with a nice long swim, rather than her traditional run. Minutes later, she was wrapped in a thick terry cloth robe the hotel provided and padding down to the very large, heated pool.

She didn't swim any longer, but it wasn't for lack of interest. She hadn't really had a pool available to her except for the one at Cal. But she hated to go to class in the mornings with wet hair, and her evenings were completely occupied by a certain woman. Swimming was a pleasant change of pace from the pounding of jogging, and she had to admit that she felt more relaxed after a nice long swim. Since her anxiety was building about finals, this seemed like a perfect morning to indulge.

The water was cool, about eighty degrees, but she really appreciated the temperature. Since she swam hard, an overly warm pool was actually unpleasant for her. A few slow laps to warm up and she switched into high gear, grinding out the laps by doing ten each of crawl, back, breast and fly. When she completed a forty-lap set she started over, churning through the water unceasingly until she had completed two hundred laps. Her heart was really pumping, and she floated rather unsuccessfully for a few lazy laps of backstroke. After ten minutes in the spa to stay loose, she returned to their room, only to find her partner still sound asleep. She tugged last night's clothes on and ran across the street to one of her all-time favorite coffee spots. A nice little bakery next door yielded some delightful pastries, and she crept back into the room a little after seven-thirty, laden with goodies.

As she expected, her lover's cute little nose twitched a bit as the smell of the lattes and baked goods wafted over to her. Those adorable green eyes blinked open moments after Ryan had arranged everything on the table. "You went out to buy breakfast?" she mumbled as she tried to focus.

"Have you seen these prices?" Ryan asked with wide eyes as she held up the room service menu. "I'm going to the grocery later to buy snacks. No more mini-bar Cokes for you!"

"Yes, Mom," she said contritely as she held out her hand. "Do I get coffee?"

"In bed, no less," Ryan informed her as she brought the tray over to the bed. The cardboard carrier held not only the coffee, but also two flaky pastries for the hungry woman.

"You're the best," she moaned as she gulped down a mouthful of the strongly flavored coffee. "Wow," Jamie said as the full impact of the coffee hit her. "I forget how strong this is. Been out running?" she asked with a cock of her head at Ryan's sweatshirt and jeans.

"Nope. I swam for over an hour. It was bliss," she informed her with a big smile. "You know, I kinda like this lap of luxury stuff."

"It does have its advantages," Jamie had to agree. They ate their breakfast rather quickly, and by eight both were back at work, neither lifting her head until Ryan's stomach began to rumble at noon.

"We could set our watches by 'Old Faithful' there," Jamie observed as she stared at Ryan's tummy.

"Mmm," Ryan said, completely absorbed by her studies.

"I'm ordering lunch. Want me to choose for you?"

"Mmm."

"I'll take that as a yes."

When the tray was delivered twenty minutes later, Ryan swore she hadn't heard any of the conversation that led to the food's arrival, but she was pleased with Jamie's selections nonetheless. She ate with one hand while she typed with the other, completely absorbed again in a matter of seconds.

This routine was also followed at dinner, but Jamie heard a sharp intake of breath at around seven as Ryan stood up to go to the bathroom.

"What's wrong?"

"Stiff. Very stiff. I should get up every hour or so but I forget. I really enjoyed my swim, but it stresses muscles in a different way and I'm paying for it now."

"How much more work do you have to do tonight?" she asked, hatching a plan.

"Hmm, I'm actually doing great. An hour or so to finish something up and I could stop. Why?"

"Just asking ... no reason," she said innocently as Ryan closed the bathroom door.

At eight o'clock on the button, Jamie jumped up to open the door after the gentle knock attracted her attention. Ryan actually heard it, too, and she gave Jamie a very curious glance as a very large, very muscular man in a white polo shirt and white poplin slacks entered the room. "You ordered a massage?" he asked in a slight Slavic accent.

"There's the client," she informed him as she pointed at her partner.

"I'm Vlade," he said as he held out his massive hand to Ryan. She grasped it in reflex, and then shot Jamie a glare. Vlade went back to the door to pull his massage table in. As he was setting up, he asked Ryan, "What type of massage do you like?"

Deciding that she was stuck and might as well enjoy it, she said, "I like any kind as long as it's deep."

"Excellent!" he boomed. "I like to be able to use my muscles."

Ryan ducked into the bath to drape the pink sheet Vlade provided around her body. Moments later she was face down on the table moaning in delight as Vlade used every one of the muscles in his strong arms and hands to turn her into a quivering ball of mush.

As the first glimmer of dawn broke through the open curtains, Ryan stirred and stretched her body out, smiling at the response from her well-rested, well-massaged muscles. She was lying mostly on her stomach, an odd position for her, but the odder sensation was the sheet separating her from her clinging partner. *How did we get twisted up in this sheet?* she wondered for a moment. Once she started to investigate, she determined that she was under the sheet and Jamie was on top of it. She found a crucial clue when she realized that she was as naked as the day she was born. *God, I don't remember Vlade leaving, I don't remember getting into bed, and I certainly don't remember Jamie joining me,* she marveled. *That massage knocked me into another world.*

Deciding not to repeat her swim of the previous morning, she tugged on her running gear and silently exited the room, remembering to put twenty dollars in the pocket of her windbreaker for breakfast. When she returned to the room, Jamie was in the shower, so she stripped and dried her body with her T-shirt before slipping into her sweats from the previous day.

The morning passed in the same fashion as the day before, but this time Jamie had ordered her to set her watch timer for an hour. Every time the little beep sounded, Ryan dutifully got up and spent five minutes stretching on the floor. The break helped keep her body limber throughout the long day, and it helped keep Jamie's motor running as she studiously watched her lover twist and grunt.

For dinner, Jamie decided that she needed a pizza, and her wish became a requirement when Ryan informed her that she had never been to Jamie's favorite place. Ryan stayed to finish up her studies for the day, and when Jamie returned just after seven, she nearly grabbed the box from her hands. "I frankly don't care how good this is," she said with wide eyes as she yanked the top open. "I'm so hungry I could eat … well, I can't think of anything big enough," she finally conceded. "But I might have met my match here," she amended as she looked carefully at the food in her hands.

The scrumptious-looking deep-dish pie was stuffed with all of Ryan's favorites—sausage, pepperoni, mushrooms, red peppers, and black olives. Jamie's assessment of the quality was right on, and Ryan ate with her normal litany of moans, groans, whimpers and exclamations. "This is the best pizza I think I've ever had!" she cried during one small break. "The crust is soooo good. And the sauce is just the right combination of sweet and tart. I love the big pieces of tomato on the top!"

"Told ya," she smirked. "I can't believe that you, of all people, have never had one."

"Word obviously hasn't traveled over the Bay Bridge," she said. "But this pizza and I are going to become much better acquainted in the very near future."

To help digest their dinner, they went for a stroll around the grounds of the hotel. There were neat little gardens and tons of tennis courts, but Ryan noticed the fitness course they had set up. "I think I'll do this in the morning," she said. "I've been getting bored with running."

"Well, you know you're going to have to give up running soon anyway," Jamie informed her regretfully.

"What? Why do you say that?"

"'Cause I'm not going to let you out of bed," she growled right into her ear, sending chills down Ryan's suddenly warm body.

When Jamie came out of the bath after preparing for bed, Ryan was sitting on the bed, a large bottle of Jamie's body lotion in her hand. "Your turn tonight."

"Really?"

"Yep. Wrap that pretty little body up in a bath sheet and come get it."

Jamie didn't have to be told twice. She was jumping across the bed in a heartbeat, wrapped only in a big towel.

Ryan put on her usual professional attitude and got to work, expertly moving the towel as she labored, never leaving Jamie's body more exposed than it needed to be. Just to be prudent, Ryan avoided her buttocks and didn't go as high on her thighs as she would in a few weeks. Turning Jamie over onto her back, she took the same precautions, staying well away from any erogenous zones. It took a lot of willpower to avoid sneaking a few peeks, but she didn't really need any more temptation. Just touching Jamie's firm, toned body in this intimate way was more than enough to cause her to throb, and throb she did. When she was finished, Jamie was limp and nearly asleep. She returned the courtesy of the previous night and pulled the sheet up to her chin, gently removing the towel as she did. When she was ready for bed, she got between the sheet and the bedspread, finding the arrangement to be perfectly cozy, if a little sterile. As she cuddled up to her partner's warm, relaxed body, she felt all of the tensions, sexual and otherwise, leave her, and she sank into a peaceful sleep, dreaming of more intimate massages to come.

Ryan kept her promise and ran around the fitness layout the next morning. It was more fun than running, and she enjoyed it enough to run it three times. Once again she brought breakfast to her partner, again having to wake her to consume it.

"I hate to have you leave me in the morning, but I truly love waking up to a Danish and a steaming hot latte," she said gratefully as she took a big sip

"Tell the truth, sleeping beauty," Ryan playfully chided. "You don't really know I'm gone, do you?"

"Mmm," she batted her big green eyes seductively. "Not consciously, but my body misses you."

"Mine misses you too. It's gonna miss you tonight for sure," she added.

"I was going to bring that up," Jamie said, sitting up completely to order her thoughts. "Do you have to study all weekend?"

Ryan thought for a minute and slowly nodded her head. "I've got a good ten hours to slog through each day. Why?"

"Let's just stay here. This is working for you, isn't it?"

"Well, yeah," Ryan agreed. "It's been idyllic. I don't have to make meals for myself; I don't have to exercise Duffy. I'd say it's been the most productive studying I've done all year."

"Then why not stay?"

She pursed her lips and considered her reasons, finding that they were purely financial. "I hate to have you spend this kind of money. I know you say you'd do it anyway, but it still feels like you're doing it for me. I feel like I'm taking advantage of you."

Jamie carefully placed her coffee on the nightstand, and yanked the sheet from its moorings to wrap it around her bare body. She carefully scooted across the bed to climb onto Ryan's lap. "Why won't you let me spoil you once in a while?" she begged as she trailed her fingers down her partner's smooth, warm cheek. "I can easily afford it, it makes me happy, and it's allowed me to study without interruption. I've almost got my big paper done, and if we stayed, I could finish up everything by Sunday."

Ryan could feel her resolve weakening, as it so often did when Jamie was astride her lap. But she felt like she needed to hold out for at least some concession. "Could we go to my house for Sunday dinner?"

"I wouldn't miss it for the world," she promised as she bent to kiss her grinning mouth.

Jamie's businesslike mind couldn't rest until she called down to the front desk and asked to speak to the manager on duty. After a brief conversation, she hung up and smirked at her partner. "He cut the room fee by fifty percent if we stay for another week," she said with a waggling eyebrow. "That'll take us through finals for only the cost of the weekend!"

"That's amazing! Especially since we were already here."

"I think he took a peek at how much we've spent on room service and quickly decided that he could give us the room for free and still make a profit," she teased as she patted her partner's perennially empty stomach.

The weekend was spent in rapt concentration for both women, with an intense hour-long run through the hills on Sunday as the only break. By late Sunday afternoon, they both felt good about their upcoming finals. Jamie actually only had two tests now that she had finished her final papers, but Ryan had five finals in classes that Jamie could barely pronounce, and her two hardest ones were both on Thursday. The good news was that by Thursday evening, they would both be finished for the term.

They drove over to the O'Flaherty home, pleased to find that Maeve would be joining them. They related their adventure of the past few days, causing quite a few laughs when Jamie related how much they had spent on room service. Ryan, of course, got her back when she told of Jamie's negotiations with the manager.

They decided to take Duffy for a long walk in the neighborhood since he was nearly wild with excitement to finally have his mistress home. Ryan spent an extraordinarily long time letting him lick her thoroughly before they left, but it was obvious the intelligent dog knew his fate. "He knows we're leaving again, doesn't he?" Jamie asked as they bid the family goodbye.

"Oh yeah, he can definitely tell," she agreed, looking at his sad brown eyes. "He's gonna have a tough summer," she said wistfully, anticipating their absence for the AIDS Ride as well as Pebble Beach.

"He's just a love junkie like his mommy," Jamie whispered for Ryan's ears only.

"Look who's talking, cuddle junkie," Ryan laughed. "Let's get back to our hideout so you can get your jones."

"Mmm, I might be a junkie, but I can only get my fix from you."

Chapter Eleven

O n Thursday morning, they checked out of Chez Cram, as they had nicknamed their hideout. Since Ryan's first test was at eight in the morning, they left much earlier than Jamie would have preferred, but Ryan made it up to her by delivering coffee and Danish one last time. Jamie's last exam was from twelve-thirty to three-thirty, and since she had an easier time than she had expected, she was ebullient when she returned home at four.

Ryan had to work at the gym that night, since she had been forced to move a lot of her private clients around to accommodate the study period and her exams. It had been more than a little difficult for Jamie to hold her tongue at Ryan's decision to work that afternoon, but she realized that Ryan followed her own muse on such matters. It just seemed masochistic to Jamie for her partner to have two tough exams in subjects too obscure to pronounce and then to squeeze a couple of hours of work in. But Ryan had an iron will when it came to her obligations, and Jamie knew that she had to give her support, rather than advice. Even though she was sorely tempted to go to the gym just to watch her work, she thought better of it. *Give her a minute's peace. Remember life before Ryan? You actually had other friends.*

She was a bit surprised, but pleased, to find Mia at home when she arrived. A thread of guilt had been nagging her because of the pathetically small amount of time she'd been spending with her friend. People who gave up their friendships when they got into a new relationship had always annoyed her, and she decided that she had to stop being one of those people.

She jogged up the stairs and poked her head into Mia's chronically messy room. The curly haired woman was lying on her bed in her underwear reading a magazine, and she gave Jamie a big smile when she saw her. "Hey girlfriend! Long time no see! How did your week at the Claremont go?"

"Absolutely perfect," Jamie beamed. "Are you all finished with exams?"

"Yep. I had my last one this morning. How about you?"

"I'm done too. Wanna go out tonight to celebrate?" Mia sat up abruptly and tried to see around Jamie's shoulder. "What are you looking for?" Jamie asked as she turned around.

She laughed as she replied, "I was looking for Ryan. I haven't seen you two apart for months."

"I know, I know," Jamie replied guiltily. "I was just thinking about how much I miss spending time with you. I promise I'll be better next year."

"It's okay, sweetie. I want you to be happy; I just wish you'd save time for me. But I know what it's like to fall in love, so I've cut you some slack for this year."

"Well it's either love, or I've turned into a stalker," she groused. "I've never been this way about another human being. Sometimes it actually scares me. I used to pride myself on my independence. I really liked the fact that Jack lived almost an hour away, and I had my week to myself."

"And it's not that way with tall, dark and gorgeous, is it?"

"I swear I'd switch to MCB as a major if I had any idea what the hell she talks about when she tells me about her classes. I'm so hopelessly stuck on her it's pathetic."

"I still don't understand how anybody could major in molecular and cell biology," Mia said with her faced scrunched up into a grimace. "Did somebody make her do that?"

"No, silly, she just likes it. And to make you sicker, she's a double major in math and MCB."

"That's not human," Mia said, sitting up carefully. "Have you ever seen her bleed? Or sleep? I think she must be an alien of some sort."

"No … well, now that you mention it …" Jamie said, playing along for a while. "She does breathe under water …"

"Ah ha! Just as I thought!" Mia cried. "I saw a creature just like that on the X-Files!"

"I don't care if she is an alien," Jamie said dreamily. "I'd follow her to any planet in the universe."

"Is she as goofy about you?"

"In a way she is, but in another way she's so mature that I think she can turn it off easier than I can. Still, sometimes when we're studying together I see her staring at me like a lovesick sixteen-year-old. It's soooo adorable."

"You've definitely got it bad, girlfriend."

"Let's go to dinner and then go have a few drinks so I can bore you to death talking about her."

"Sounds great to me. We can go anywhere you want, since you're buying," Mia informed her with a laugh.

A few hours later, the roommates were sitting outside in the surprisingly warm night air, sipping rather potent apple martinis as they talked about the just-completed school year and their plans for the summer. Although Jamie did her very best not to talk about Ryan the whole time, Mia realized that she was intentionally not talking about her and after a while suggested, "Why don't you ask your beloved to come join us when she's off work?"

Jamie's eyes lit up immediately, but she said, "Are you sure you don't mind?"

"No, I like Ryan, and if we're all going to live together next year, I might as well get used to seeing you two together constantly."

"When did I say we were going to live together next year?"

"Well, aren't you?"

"Yeah, but I didn't say it," she laughed. "Ryan and I haven't even discussed it yet, but that sweet little thing is gonna be in my bed next year, no matter what!"

At nine-fifteen, Ryan roared up on her Harley, which she had brought over to the East Bay on Sunday night. She circled the bar three times before she reminded herself that there was no parking whatsoever at any time of day in Berkeley. Ryan had often thought that the cars in front of every meter were really just an elaborate art installation, even insisting to Jamie that they were all papier mâché.

Eventually, she gave up and wedged her bike into the tail end of a space occupied by a new, lime green Volkswagen. *Boy, the artist did a nice job on that one*, she smirked as she walked away. *Very realistic.* She was just beginning to cross the street in front of the bar when she heard a rather loud whistle coming from the outdoor dining area. She ignored the sound, but as she was about halfway across she heard it again. This time it was followed by a loud, "Hey, baby," in a familiar, but strange-sounding voice. She followed the voice and came upon two very drunk roommates, both ogling her. She stood with her hands on her hips and an amused smirk on her face. "What have you two been up to?"

"We were celebrating!" Jamie slurred. "School's out for a whole summer!" She finally seemed to focus on Ryan as she added, "C'mere and give me a big wet kiss, you gorgeous hunk of woman."

Ryan just shook her head and gracefully leapt over the small wrought iron fence that separated the diners from pedestrians. She pulled up a chair and picked up Jamie's glass, making a face as she sniffed it, then patiently asked, "How many of these little beauties did you girls have?"

"Four, I think," Jamie said. "Those nice men over there bought this last one for us." She turned in her chair to wave at three frat boys, "Thanks again, fellas!"

Jamie turned to Ryan and leaned in close as she asked, "Where's my kiss?"

"Yeah," Mia chimed in. "Give her a big one, Ryan."

"Come on, don't you love me anymore?" Jamie asked pathetically.

"Of course I love you," Ryan soothed. "But won't your new boyfriends get jealous if I kiss you?"

Jamie looked at her with a completely puzzled expression. "Boyfriends? We don't have no stinking boyfriends." She howled with laughter at this statement, for reasons that escaped Ryan completely.

"Then why did you let those guys buy you drinks?"

"I don't know," she said slowly. "Was that a bad thing to do?"

"Well, most of the time when you buy a woman a drink, you expect her to at least spend some time getting to know you. I assume they think you're cute, which you are, and they want to go out with you."

Jamie turned around immediately to straighten out the matter. "Hey, fellas! We don't wanna be your girlfriends. We're lesbians!" she said the last word in a loud stage whisper. "Well, she's not," she pointed at Mia. "But this one and me are," she said as she helpfully indicated Ryan.

Ryan took this opportunity to find the check and quickly settle the large bill. She guided both of them to their feet and tried to wrangle them out of the restaurant. "Did you drive or walk?"

"Drove!" Mia stated confidently. "Walked," Jamie declared, just as confidently.

"Well, whichever one it is, we're walking home," Ryan said.

She walked as best she could, standing between the tottering roommates. She had a strong hand around each woman's waist and was constantly grabbing one or the other of them by the waistband of their jeans to keep them on the path.

After an interminable time, they finally reached the house. She was relieved to find the Boxster still in the drive, but seeing Cassie's car caused her to roll her eyes heavenward in supplication.

She had to perform a thorough pat down to find the house keys, a procedure that was made more difficult by Jamie's intense ticklishness. She giggled and yelped and fought to keep Ryan from her pockets. Ryan persisted even when she was caught in the eye by a flying elbow.

She got the key in the door and pushed both of her charges through, spying Cassie in the kitchen as she did. Swallowing her ire, she forced herself to be as pleasant as possible and asked, "Cassie, could you come here for a minute?"

With a scowl, Cassie strode into the room, staring at the sight before her. Jamie was draped around the right side of Ryan's body and Mia held onto her just as tenaciously on the left. "Uhm, they got a little drunk, and I don't think I can get both of them upstairs. Will you take Mia?"

Cassie shook her head in disgust at the three of them. She started to remove Mia from Ryan's control, but Mia looked at Ryan with big brown bloodshot eyes and begged, "Can I have a kiss?"

Ryan was mortified, but she knew Mia would persist. So she leaned over and gave her a peck on the cheek.

"C'mon," Mia urged as she remained in her kissing pose. "You can do better than that! I've heard that you can ..."

Ryan stopped her story the only way she knew how. She leaned over and really let her have the kiss she sought. Cassie stared at her in horror, but Ryan figured Cassie's opinion of her couldn't go much lower, so she didn't have much to lose on that front. She was afraid Mia might start blabbing about her and Jamie, though, and that's why it was important to her to keep Mia's mouth occupied. If the kiss shocked Mia, she did an admirable job of hiding her feelings. Ryan was just about ready to release her when she felt Mia's tongue dart into her mouth and start exploring. Ryan couldn't pull away at that point and let Cassie and Jamie see Mia's tongue hanging out, so she stayed right where she was and let Mia investigate to her heart's content.

With a sexy little moan, Mia's tongue returned to its home, and Ryan quickly straightened up. Mia, however, stayed exactly where she was. Her lips were still puckered up and her eyes were tightly closed. She was swaying back and forth a bit and she clearly looked like she wanted more. Ryan stood her up and handed her over to Cassie, who fumed, "I will never, ever, understand the hold you have on women."

Ryan smirked at her departing form and then focused her attention on Jamie, who had a look of abject sorrow on her face. "Why did you kiss her, but you won't kiss me?" she asked as she began to wail plaintively.

Ryan stooped and picked her up gracefully, carrying her up the stairs and into her room. She performed her all-too-familiar ritual of undressing the relatively helpless woman, averting her eyes as much as possible.

Once she'd dressed Jamie in a long T-shirt, she guided her into the bathroom to brush her teeth. She got the toothbrush ready, but the blonde was not up to the task and, sitting on the edge of the tub, just opened her mouth and let Ryan perform the duty for her.

Then Ryan squatted down beside her and asked, "Do you have to pee?" Jamie nodded her head. "Do you want me to help you?" A shake that almost knocked her off the tub was the answer. "Okay, can you do it yourself?" Another violent shake. "Then I'll have to help you."

"No!" Jamie protested vehemently. "I don't like anybody to watch. It's private!"

"How about if I sit you down and then leave. Is that okay?"

"You won't watch?"

"I promise I won't watch," Ryan said as she crossed her heart.

"Okay," she replied warily. "But don't watch, 'kay?"

Ryan lowered her panties and got her situated. "I'll be right outside. Call me when you're done, okay?"

"Okay, I love you, honey bunch," she said sweetly, blowing her a big kiss.

Ryan blew a kiss back as she went outside and closed the door. She ran to the bedside table and quickly called home to tell Conor that she was staying over. Then she dashed back to wait by the door. Long, quiet minutes passed before she finally knocked. "Jamie?" No answer. "Jamie," louder this time, but still no answer. She opened the door to find her lover leaning against the back wall, sound asleep. Once again she stooped to pick her up, grunting with the effort. When she got her on the bed, she removed her panties to avoid the struggle of getting them back into place and slipped her under the covers.

Going to the dresser, she found the new underwear that Jamie had purchased for her, changed into them and got into bed behind her friend. Moments passed as she tried to relax when she was startled by a very insistent, very annoying snore.

Just before dawn Ryan woke from a deep sleep to the sound of a soft, low moan. She struggled to get her bearings, finding herself alone in bed. She got up and, following the sound, discovered that the bathroom door was open. She poked her head in to find Jamie sitting on the edge of the tub, holding her head in both hands. She walked over and sat down next to her, bending her head down to closely observe her face. "Don't feel so good, huh?" she asked softly.

The tousled blond head slowly lifted, revealing a pasty white complexion and red-streaked green eyes. "Very observant."

Ryan was taken aback by her partner's surliness, but she maintained her compassion. "Can I do anything to help?"

"If you don't have a revolver, you may as well go back to bed."

"I definitely don't want to shoot you, but I could get you some Tylenol and something to drink to help hydrate you."

"I don't think anything will help."

"Let's try anyway. I'll be right back." Ryan ran downstairs and found two bottles of ginger ale in the refrigerator. She filled two glasses with ice and brought them both back upstairs. Then she went into the bathroom and found a bottle of Tylenol. Quickly removing four tablets, she gave Jamie two as she filled the glass with the soda. "Shhh!" her friend warned. "That's too loud!"

As Jamie struggled to swallow the pills, Ryan filled the other glass and sneaked into Mia's room. She placed the soda and the pills on her bedside table and crept back out without disturbing her.

When she returned, Jamie was sitting on the bed, looking absolutely miserable. "I think you need some more sleep."

"You're just full of insight, aren't you?" she replied with a grimace, grasping her head in pain from the mere effort of speaking.

"Jamie, I love you even when you're cranky. But please don't be so sarcastic. I'm just trying to help you."

Ryan could actually see her teeth clench, realizing with a smile that the poor woman was really trying to control her sharp tongue, albeit with only partial success. "I'm sorry. I just want to go back to bed, but this headache is honestly about to kill me. I'll be nicer if I can get some sleep, I promise."

"I think I can help with that." Ryan slid in behind her partner then began to apply pressure to various points on Jamie's head and neck. At first the pain-wracked woman fought the intense pressure, but after a few minutes she began to relax and allow Ryan to work. After a while, she started to sigh deeply as her body grew heavy and sagged against her partner.

Sliding out from behind her and placing her on her stomach, Ryan started to slowly and firmly knead the muscles in her shoulders and neck. Contented grunts and small moans now greeted her ministrations. After a long while, she leaned over and kissed her head as she got out of bed. She got dressed in the previous evening's clothes and went back downstairs, feeling a little regret that she wouldn't be able to spend the day with Jamie. Walking over to Telegraph in the early morning light, she fetched her bike, removed the ticket that one of Berkeley's ever-thoughtful meter maids had left for her, and headed home.

Ryan decided she needed to blow off some steam, and her father gladly acquiesced to the loan of his truck—after securing a promise that it would be washed and vacuumed upon her return. She loaded Duffy and his bag of floating toys in the vehicle and took the wildly enthusiastic dog on a spirited run on the beach. After the run, and a half hour of retrieving his toys from the cold water, Duffy's exercise needs were taken care of for the day, and his mistress was in a much better mood. When the truck was once again spotless, she took a long shower and then decided to clean her room, having noticed quite a layer of dust gathering on her photos and books. After a good two hours, everything was in order and she was just putting her cleaning tools away when her pager went off.

She smiled at the familiar number as she went to dial the phone. "Hi," she said, wanting to test the waters before she said too much.

"Do you still love me?" was the shy plea.

"Of course I love you. It's gonna take more than a little grumpiness to get rid of me. Are you feeling any better?"

"Yeah, I feel a lot better. Thanks for taking care of me last night and today." After a pause she added, "We must have been a mess."

"Nah, you were actually kind of entertaining. I honestly didn't mind at all, Jamie. But I do think you should give some thought to how you deal with alcohol. You don't seem to tolerate it very well."

"That's an understatement," she agreed. "I think one is my new limit. And since I will never, ever drink another martini, I don't have to worry about them."

"So, do you want to rest today, or would you like to see me?"

Jamie's voice softened, and Ryan could almost see her smile. "I always want to see you. You're the best part of every day for me."

"Well, I've got to work from two until five, and then I'm free. Do you want to see me during the day or in the evening?"

"Yes," was the forceful reply.

Jamie showed up a little after eleven o'clock, looking much better, although still a touch pale. Ryan greeted her warmly, trying to give her the clear message that she wasn't angry with her. They stood in a warm embrace for a long while, with Jamie uttering a deep sigh occasionally. "I'm sorry I was so rude to you today," she said as she looked up with sad eyes.

"It's okay. Bad headaches can do that to anyone."

"Have you ever had a hangover?" she asked.

"I've had my share," Ryan admitted. "I have a pretty big capacity for alcohol, but as you know, I rarely drink anymore. When I was in my 'acting out' phase, I drank more than I should have, mostly to appear older and more experienced." She laughed at the memory. "I decided fairly quickly that hangovers were not for me."

"I couldn't agree with you more," Jamie agreed with a wry grin.

Ryan went downstairs to change as Jamie went to get a glass of water. She was still dehydrated, and Ryan had assured her that she'd feel better if she got a lot of fluid down. The day was warm and Jamie wore cuffed khaki shorts and a salmon polo shirt. Several moments later her mouth went dry when Ryan came back up wearing one of the outfits from Jamie's fantasies.

They had recently visited a sporting goods store, Ryan had purchased some of their baggy print shorts for Caitlin. Jamie had liked them so much that she'd gone back and bought several pair for Ryan. Today she had on a pair in sky blue, deep blue and salmon. She wore a tank top in the same deep blue; the colors making her eyes look an even darker blue than normal.

Jamie stood back and gazed at her partner lovingly. Her hair was back in a high ponytail and showed off the strong planes of her face. The tank top revealed her tanned broad shoulders and muscular biceps, and the shorts fit closely around her trim waist, but were quite roomy in the short legs. Jamie came up next to her and wrapped her arms around her. "Thank you," she whispered into Ryan's ear.

"What for?"

"Fulfilling another fantasy," she replied as she nibbled the pink ear. "But you can't wear your normal underwear with these. What do you have on under there?" she asked with a seductive tone.

"Why don't you find out for yourself?"

Jamie proceeded to do just that as she ran her hands down the sides and around the back of the shorts. She let her fingers tease the strong legs as they slid up and under the fabric. She was rewarded by the feel of a very tiny pair of bikinis that failed to cover all of the strong firm flesh. As she ran her hands over the surface again and again, Ryan dropped her head for a series of gentle kisses. She consciously kept the touch light, knowing Jamie's tendencies. When her partner's hands rose to pull her head down more firmly, she smiled through the kissing and shook her head as she murmured, "Unh-uh. I don't want your blood pressure to rise and make your headache worse."

Jamie released her head as she pushed her face into the broad chest and moaned, "Why do you do this to me?"

"Do what?"

"Look like this!" she groaned.

Ryan just patted her on the back soothingly. "In three weeks, you can handle the merchandise at will."

"I don't think I can wait three minutes. How can I wait three weeks?"

"If we start doing all the things I want to do to you, I guarantee you won't want to sit on a bike seat for 500 miles," she said with a smile that belied her seriousness.

Jamie gulped noticeably as she squeezed Ryan again in frustration.

After unloading all of her things from the Porsche, they spent a little while getting the computer up and running again. That done, they decided to go steal Caitlin and take her over to the Marina district to play in the park and watch the boats. The baby was with Maeve today, and after her self-imposed exile in Oakland, Ryan was anxious to see the little sprite.

When she greeted them at the door, Caitlin had on her own little pair of baggy shorts in greens and yellows and a yellow T-shirt. They laughed at her antics as she slapped the glass of the storm door, turning her head repeatedly to look for her grandmother while she waited for the barrier to her favorite playmates to be removed.

Maeve finally arrived and unlocked the door, laughing at the glee on the baby's face. Caitlin launched herself at Ryan's knees, and then raised her arms demanding, "Uh, Uh."

Ryan looked at her aunt in wonder as she lifted the joyous infant in her arms. "When did she learn that?"

"Today, I guess," she replied as she shook her head. "I can't keep up with her, Ryan. She learns a new way to express herself every day."

Caitlin leaned over precariously in Ryan's arms to offer a hug and a kiss to Jamie. She smiled sweetly at her second favorite playmate as she patted Jamie's face with her tiny hand. Jamie reached out and snatched her from Ryan as Caitlin giggled at the tussle. The baby threw her arms around Jamie's neck—she was happy to be with her pals once again.

The weather at the Marina was quite a bit cooler, but still warm enough that they were all comfortable. They all took off their shoes and played in the grass, along with the dozens of others soaking up the sun. Ryan had brought a kite, and she ran around wildly trying to control it in the stiff breeze. Jamie sat on their blanket with Caitlin on her lap and watched with a contented smile on her face. At one point, she watched with alarm as Ryan was seemingly headed right for a large trashcan. Ryan spotted it at the last minute, put on a burst of speed and jumped right over it. She slowed down then and trotted back over to the laughing pair. "Pretty cool, huh?" she asked proudly.

"You never cease to amaze me," Jamie replied fondly as she leaned over for a kiss. Caitlin wanted in on the fun, too, so she leaned over in the same way and puckered up. Ryan placed a sweet kiss on each set of lips, smiling broadly as she pulled back.

They let the baby practice walking, taking turns as her guide. She walked quite well so long as she held on to a pair of hands, and both women enjoyed helping her accomplish such an important milestone. After a while, Ryan ran a few blocks to buy sandwiches for them. When she returned, Jamie was feeding the baby some strange tan concoction. Ryan sat and watched them for a while with a fond smile on her face, finally commenting, "I can't wait until we have a baby of our own."

"Yow!" Jamie said with a shocked look. "You don't mean that, do you?"

Ryan's eyes grew wide as she stuttered, "I ... I ... I ...thought ... you wanted ..."

"Oh, honey, of course I want to have children with you. I was just shocked at the thought that you can't wait to do it. I don't think I'm ready for that yet."

"Whew!" Ryan cried, as she dramatically wiped her forehead with the back of her hand. "I thought you meant that you didn't want kids at all."

"Oh, no. I still remember the discussion we had at your birthday party. I know how you feel about kids, and I'm sure we'll have them, one way or the other."

"Thank God," Ryan said as she breathed a heavy sigh of relief. "It would be hard for me to give up that dream."

Jamie looked at the open, trusting look on her beautiful face. "This is really it for you, isn't it? I mean you believe we'll be together for life, don't you?"

"Yeah, don't you?" she asked, as her eyes once again grew wide with alarm.

"Yes, I do," she replied reassuringly, gently rubbing Ryan's thigh. "It's just surprising to me that you've never even had a girlfriend, and yet you slipped into this lifetime commitment so easily."

Ryan was leaning back against her locked arms, and she dropped her head back and let the warm sun caress her face as she considered her response. "Part of the reason I've never had a girlfriend is that I wasn't looking for one. I really didn't want the complication that a relationship would bring. But the other reason is that I didn't see the point of being in a relationship I wasn't sure about." She placed her hand on Jamie's knee as she stared deeply into her eyes. "I've known what I wanted in a lover for a long time. I'd just never met anyone who fulfilled all of my requirements until you."

"You are such a romantic, Ryan. I can't believe how often you take my breath away."

"I love you, Jamie. And I want to be with you for the rest of my life," she declared solemnly.

"I feel exactly the same way about you. And I can't wait to have a baby with you either." After a pause, she added, "But I'd like to have a good long time with you alone, to just be selfish and enjoy you without any competition."

"Agreed. Besides, I've got enough brothers and cousins to keep us stocked with babies for a long time, if they'd just get busy," she said with a laugh.

Chapter Twelve

Since Ryan had to work from two until five, Jamie decided to go home and pack up her things for the next four weeks. Even though they both knew the situation was less than optimal, they had decided to stay at Ryan's until the ride. Ryan wouldn't stand for Jamie paying for another night in a hotel, and Jamie couldn't stand the thought of being with Cassie for another moment, so it was the best option.

Upon arriving at her home, Jamie jogged up to the second floor and poked her head into Mia's room to see if she was there. Her friend was sitting in the middle of a chaotic jumble of clothes, shoes and suitcases. Her father had used some of his contacts to get her a summer job reading scripts for a small film company. Since her boyfriend was in L.A., she had been very excited about the job when she landed it, but now that things had cooled between them, she was ambivalent about the trip. The office was in Santa Monica, and on her last trip to L.A. she'd found a nice apartment to sublet for the summer, but her sadness at leaving the Bay Area—and all of her friends—was affecting her mood.

When Jamie came in, Mia looked up in dismay, "How can I possibly take all of this stuff with me?"

"Uhm … you can't?" Jamie replied helpfully.

"I just don't know what I'm going to need. I'm not sure how casually people dress at this place, and I don't want to look like a geek." As she gazed around the room, she added with a smirk, "I guess I could buy all new clothes after I figure out the dress code."

"That would go over big with your father."

"Do you think you'll have a few minutes to see me when you're in L.A.?"

"Yeah, I was going to invite you to the closing ceremonies. They're on the thirteenth in Century City, and I think you'd enjoy it."

"Are you coming back that same day?"

"We're not sure. One option is to take our bikes apart and fly back that night. But I think we'd enjoy it more if we could stay over one night just to relax."

"Why don't you stay with me? My sublet is two bedrooms, and I'd love to have you. You won't by any chance have Conor with you, will you?" Mia asked coyly as she batted her eyes.

"No. Just Ryan. You haven't spoken of Conor much. What do you think of him?"

"Because of school and everything, we've only gone out once. We've talked on the phone a couple of times, but it's clearly not a big deal between us. I like him a lot though," she said thoughtfully. "If I were going to be here this summer, I think I'd really concentrate on getting to know him better."

"Would I be prying if I asked if you have …"

"Yes, you would be prying," she teased. "But I have no secrets from you, James," she replied. "No, we haven't. But, if he's still available in the fall, I'd like to give it a try. I'm guessing I'll officially be single by the time I get back"

"Not much hope with Jason, huh?"

"I'd say our relationship is on life-support," she muttered. "It's gonna take some extraordinary measures to save it."

"Well, I'm sorry to hear that," Jamie said. "But you seem to have pulled back an awful lot anyway."

"Yeah, you're right. Jason's not right for me long term. Conor, on the other hand …"

"He's really a nice guy, Mia. He's a little sold on himself, but underneath that he's very sweet."

"It's not his sweetness that I'm attracted to," Mia said with a grin. "But I guess that's a nice side benefit."

"When do you leave for L.A.?"

"Monday afternoon," she said with a sigh. "I wish I were more excited about it, though. I'm not in the mood to have to make all new friends for the summer. And part of me wishes I could spend a little time finding out if there's any chemistry between me and Mr. Muscle."

"Hmm, I can't help on the first part, but maybe we could arrange for something for the weekend. If he's available, would you like to do something with us?"

"Like a double date?"

"Yeah," Jamie said with a smile. "A date would be cool. I've never been on a date with a girl." She had a cute grin on her face as she considered the prospect. "We haven't had time to actually go out since we've been together."

"Well, I've never been on a double date with two girls," Mia laughed. "I think it'd be fun. See what you can come up with."

"Will do. I've got to get packed, too. I've decided to stay with Ryan until the ride. Then we have our little vacation, so I've got to pack almost as much as you do!"

"Yeah, but for one of those weeks you probably won't be wearing clothes," Mia predicted with a wiggle of her brow.

The foursome decided to borrow Jamie's father's boat and go for a sail around the bay on Sunday. Just to make sure, she called her father in Italy and got his enthusiastic permission to go and enjoy.

Ryan and Jamie both had a tough time with the prospect of sleeping apart on Friday. They had become so dependent on feeling each other's warm bodies during the night that they knew it would be another big adjustment to forego that connection. Summoning their collective willpower, they managed to pry themselves apart after only a few minutes of passionate smooching. Once Jamie was ensconced in Rory's room, Ryan trotted back downstairs, running into her father. "This is hard for you, isn't it, darlin'?" he asked when he saw her flushed face.

"Yeah, it is," she admitted somewhat shyly. "But I'll get through it, Da. She's well worth the wait."

"She's a lovely girl, Siobhán," he heartily agreed. "And I'm very pleased that she's kept her word about sending you home rested and well fed. You actually look like you've put on a few pounds."

"Yeah, I think I have," she agreed. "I really like to add a few before the ride, but finals usually stress me out too much to eat right. Jamie really took care of me, though. She fed me, made me stretch every hour, and made sure I was in bed early every night."

"That's a good sight more than I was ever able to do."

"You never batted your big green eyes at me like she does," Ryan teased. "That's obviously the key!"

On Saturday morning, they got up early and went for a very long, very strenuous ride. They had decided they would do a big blowout that day, then cut way back for the next two weeks. This regime would allow them to work on their cardiovascular fitness and keep their legs strong, while giving their butts a thorough rest before the ride. On this cool, late spring day, they rode all the way to Half Moon Bay, following the route the actual ride would take, so they would feel less nervous on the day of the ride.

They slowly pedaled back up the hills of Noe Valley at around four o'clock. They once again blew through all the hot water as they tried to relieve some of the soreness from their muscles. After a couple of gentle massages, they were sound asleep in their respective beds.

Around six, Jamie tiptoed into Ryan's room and sat down on her desk chair to watch her lover sleep. She was unable to resist the siren call of her steady breathing and sweet, open expression, so she climbed into bed behind her, gently wrapping her in her arms. Ryan woke slowly, nestling back into her partner, trying to increase the contact of the embrace. "Dinner's going to be ready soon," Jamie whispered.

"Mmm, I'm starving," she replied as she began her normal series of stretches. After a minute of slow, feline moves, she lay on her back and slipped her arm around Jamie. They lay together, enjoying the contact until they heard Martin call them to dinner.

After dinner and the ensuing cleanup operation, they decided to go for a walk around the neighborhood, even though Jamie's legs were tired. She tried to hold firm when Ryan wanted to go to the Castro for ice cream, but since she could never resist those baby blues, a few minutes later they were climbing the hills towards their destination.

"Okay, Thunder Thighs," Jamie joked when they started off. "You promised a massage as payment for me trudging up these hills. How long will it last?"

"As long as you request, my queen," Ryan replied while performing a deep bow.

"No falling asleep?"

"Scout's honor," she replied seriously.

As they walked along, hand in hand, Jamie said, "I have such fond memories of the first time we took this walk."

"I had a great time that night too," Ryan said. "You were so helpful to me when I was trying to sort out my feelings for Tracy."

"Oh, don't remind me!" she moaned dramatically. "I wanted so much to tell you to drop her, but I knew I had to be neutral. It would have been unfair to try to influence you, but God, I wanted to."

Ryan stopped and stared at her for a long minute. "I guess I didn't put this time line together in my mind until now. I can't believe I was asking you for relationship advice when you'd decided that you were in love with me." She grasped both of Jamie's hands in hers, "I can't imagine how hard that must have been for you. I'm so sorry that I didn't know."

Jamie smiled up at her, "I'm not sorry at all, Ryan. Hearing you talk about what was important to you was very helpful for me. It actually made me even surer that I loved you. It was so gratifying that the exact same things were as important to you as they were to me." She stood on her tiptoes and kissed her softly. "I'm so happy that it all worked out."

They continued to walk up the tall hill, pausing every few minutes for a kiss. As they reached the crest, Jamie said, "You told me that night that one of the things you were concerned about with Tracy was that she wasn't close to her family." Ryan nodded as she turned to look at her. "How do you feel about my relationship with my family?"

Ryan thought about the question for a few minutes, her eyebrows knit together as she stared straight ahead at the sidewalk. "I'd prefer that you were close to your family," she admitted, "but I wish that for you, rather than for me. It hurts me to know that you've never known the unconditional love that I have. I truly wish I could go back in time and make your parents see how precious a gift you are." She faced Jamie and wrapped her arms around her. "You are so very precious," she whispered fervently.

After soaking up the warmth for a few minutes, Jamie pulled back to wipe the tears from her face, laughing as Ryan tried to help with the hem of her T-shirt. "It doesn't bother you that I haven't known that deep love? I mean, are you worried that I won't be able to love you without reservation?"

"No, I have no worries in that area. You've shown me such love in the months we've known each other, it's clear you know how to love. I'm absolutely confident that you love me totally. And I'm absolutely confident that you'll be a great parent, too." She wrapped an arm around her partner's shoulders as she continued, "Do you think Da is a good parent?"

"He's the best I've ever seen," she replied without hesitation.

"His family situation was pretty bleak. His mother was ill during much of his life, and she died when he was only thirteen. They hadn't gotten much mothering when she was alive because of her illnesses, and my grandfather was largely absent. My Uncle Francis and Da raised the two younger boys, basically without any guidance. My grandfather's drinking became worse and worse after my grandmother died. Da couldn't tolerate the way he treated my Uncles Pat and Malachy, so he and Francis worked their tails off to be able to afford airfare for all of them. They all came over in 1965, as soon as Malachy graduated from secondary school. Just three years later, my grandfather died of alcoholism," she said. "My point is that Da is a marvelous father, and I'm certain he was a wonderful husband. I don't know where he learned to be that loving, but I couldn't ask for anything more from him. You don't have to come from a lot of love to know how to love."

"Well, I'm surrounded by love now, and it's the nicest feeling I've ever experienced. I'm eternally grateful for this gift, Ryan."

Ryan gazed at her fondly as she held her hands, "Even though I've always been surrounded by love, there's a euphoria to being in love with you that I'd never imagined. The love I feel from my family is a nice, warm, safe feeling. With you it's … it's … joyous."

"Just for that, Ms. O'Flaherty, you get extra hot fudge," Jamie said as she enveloped her in a hug.

Ryan was very playful and lighthearted that evening, and it was obvious that she needed to release some energy. It was unlike her to remain indoors as much as she had the last two weeks, and she continually ran ahead of Jamie and sprinted back just to burn up some energy.

About halfway to the ice cream shop, she started to muse about their upcoming trip to Pebble Beach, and by the time they got there they both needed a little cooling off. They hadn't been very intimate for the last two weeks, and Jamie knew she was ready for some action. They sat in the small shop and stared at each other with desire-suffused faces. Jamie resigned herself to another night of self-pleasuring, but Ryan got a fiendish look on her face and asked, "Can I borrow your phone?"

After she dialed an obviously familiar number, she paused for a second and said, "Weight room, please." She looked up and made a cute face while she waited to be connected. "Hi, is Ally working tonight?" Her face lit up as she paused again and winked at Jamie. "Hey, it's Ryan," she said with a big smile on her face. "No, no, I'm keeping the faith, how about you?" Another pause while her friend spoke. "Excellent! I'm glad it's going well. I'm actually calling for a tremendous favor. Could I possibly use your apartment for an hour or so?" She blushed and said, "I know an hour isn't very long, but it's more than enough for what I have in mind." She nodded happily and said, "I'm just down the street. Can you leave the keys at the front desk?" She stood up and motioned Jamie to join her as she said, "Thanks a million, Ally. You're a pal."

Jamie grasped her hand as Ryan practically pulled her down the street. After the quick stop at Castro Fitness, they climbed back up the hill to Ally's neat little apartment. As soon as the door was closed, Ryan was on her partner like a tiger, locking their mouths together with a passionate fury as she pushed her against the nearest wall. "Hey, hey, slow down," Jamie soothed as she pushed Ryan away and tried to catch her breath.

Ryan looked chagrined as she blushed and said, "I'm sorry. Damn, that was ... rude."

"It's okay," she assured her as she absently patted her shoulder and looked around warily. "I just have to get my bearings. It feels odd to be in someone else's apartment. Especially somewhere that you've obviously been a lot," she added, getting to the real issue.

"Is this okay with you?" Ryan asked gently. "I guess I didn't consider that this might be uncomfortable for you."

"No, I'll be okay," she said as she looked around. She immediately noticed that the room was obsessively neat, but also that there were no books or any personal items to identify the owner. "This place is kind of cold."

Ryan looked around and had to agree with her lover, "I guess I never noticed."

"Have you been here often?" Jamie asked, trying to fish for information without being too obvious.

"I've told you about Ally," she patiently reminded her.

"You've told me some things, but not a lot. How often would you say you were together?"

"Uhm ... define together," Ryan hedged, not really in the mood to have this particular discussion.

"What is this, twenty questions?"

"No, but I've told you how it was with us. We saw each other for sex. So are you really asking how many times we had sex, or do you want to know something else?"

Jamie pursed her lips as she flopped down on the sofa. "I want to know what she meant to you," she asked softly as she met Ryan's gaze.

Ryan joined her on the sofa and tried to banish thoughts of how well used that piece of furniture had been in their sex play. "She meant a lot to me," she said. "I met her not long after the Sara debacle, and she really helped me a lot. If she'd been willing, I could have loved her, but she wasn't interested."

"Why not?" Jamie asked indignantly.

Ryan laughed at her defensive reaction. "Not everyone thinks I'm all that hot, Jamie."

"Oh don't be ridiculous. If she weren't attracted to you, why would she have had sex with you so often?"

"Okay, I admit that she liked me, she probably even cared for me, but she absolutely didn't want to have a relationship with me. I'm not sure why, to tell you the truth," Ryan said, even though she thought that Ally's molestation had a lot to do with it. "When we got too close or too intimate, she'd pull away and refuse to see me for a couple of months."

"Months!"

"Yeah. It was hard at first. I really felt kinda used. Over time, I came to accept that all she could give me was as much sex as I could handle, as long as it wasn't too emotionally charged. So I accepted her terms, and we had a nice sexual partnership for over five years."

"Five years!"

"Yeah, I said it was right after Sara. It was the end of the summer after my senior year. A month or two before my nineteenth birthday."

"And you've seen her consistently ever since then?"

"Yeah. I last slept with her the day I broke up with Tracy."

"Did you love her, Ryan?" she asked softly.

Giving the matter the serious consideration that it was due, Ryan sat quietly for several minutes. "I don't think so," she said reflectively. "I was infatuated with her, and I loved having sex with her. She had my number like no one else I'd ever been with. But I didn't really know her well enough to love her. We probably had five meals together outside of her house. We never even went to a movie together."

"It amazes me that you could have sex with her dozens of times and not form a deeper attachment."

"I took what she was able to offer. You don't always get to choose what someone can give you," she said. "If I wanted her in my life, I had to take her on her terms. And I'm glad that we were together. She was a good friend when I really needed one, and she really helped set me straight on safer sex. If not for her I'd probably have contracted a couple of dozen venereal diseases, if not worse."

"Is it painful to think of the time when you wanted more, but couldn't get it?"

"Not now. It was hard at the time, of course. I was still pretty raw after Sara and it hurt to think that Ally didn't think I was worth a chance. But I realized she liked me a lot. She just didn't want to be in a relationship. And over time, she helped me realize that sexual chemistry wasn't enough. I don't think we could have been a successful couple, and if we'd tried, we probably would have lost what we did have. So I think it worked out well in the end. She still means a lot to me, Jamie, and I plan on keeping her as a friend."

"I'd like to meet her. I should spend a few days with her and pick her brain," she added wryly. "I'd like to have your number too, you know."

"Oh, you've got my number. Believe me, you've got it," she promised as she placed a scorcher on Jamie's lips and unsteadily got to her feet.

"What are you doing?" Jamie asked in surprise.

"This wasn't a good idea," Ryan declared as she extended her hand. "I want the places we caress each other to be as special as the experience." Looking around with a smirk firmly attached to her face she added, "This place has far too many miles on it!"

On the way back home, Ryan broke the silence, "I have good news."

"Really, what is it?"

"I'm HIV negative, and I don't have any sexually transmitted diseases."

"That's really nice, Ryan," she said tentatively. "Are there any other diseases that you don't have?"

"Lots of them I hope," she laughed. "I had to go to the doctor to get my medical release for the ride, and as long as I was there I had him do an AIDS test and check me for STDs."

"Were you concerned that you had something?"

"No. Not really. I've been pretty careful with safer sex practices, thanks to Ally, but I absolutely refuse to take any chances with you, my little gem," she said as she pinched her cheek.

"That is so thoughtful of you, Ryan. Would you like me to do the same?"

"Well, you only have to worry about Jack, so it depends on how confident you are about his status."

"I'm very confident. I made him have a test before I'd sleep with him, and then I made him have another six months later. He wasn't very happy about it, but he did it."

"Did he also get checked for STDs?"

"Yep. All clear."

Ryan cleared her throat nervously as she brought up a sore subject. "What about when you … uhm … started to see him in April?"

"No problem," she said confidently. "No bodily fluids were exchanged." *Oops, I guess I should clarify that he got my bodily fluids that one day but I never got his. Mmm, that's not something she needs to know.*

Ryan looked surprised, but she didn't question Jamie any further. "Then I guess all systems are go."

"Pebble Beach can't come fast enough for me."

On Sunday morning at eight o'clock on the dot, the big, black Dodge Ram crew cab pulled up in front of Jamie's home. Much to her surprise, her curly-haired roommate came running down the stairs before she could even make a move to go fetch her.

"Hi, guys!" Mia said brightly, as she opened the front passenger door and climbed inside. "Oh, who's my best friend?" she gasped in delight as Jamie handed up a steaming hot latté.

"I am, and don't you forget it when you're gone all summer," Jamie warned as she leaned over the seat to give her a kiss.

"You're my goomba forever!" she declared, reverting to her mother's Italian slang. Turning to Conor, she asked, "Have you been sailing before?"

"Nope. Even though our relatives came from the coast, neither of us has been sailing. We've both been on more fishing boats and row boats than we can count, but we're sailboat virgins."

Mia shot him a look, guessing that was the only area in which he could make that claim. "Well, you're gonna love it," she promised. "Jamie's really a pro. Her dad loves it when she crews for him 'cause she's so good. And now that she's got those muscles, she's really gonna be in demand."

"Unh-uh," Jamie corrected. "I'm the captain today. I've got tons of O'Flaherty muscle here for the crew, and I'm gonna use it."

"I shoulda known you had an ulterior motive for choosing a strong girlfriend," Ryan chided her.

"Oh yeah, I had an ulterior motive all right," she agreed as she leaned over and took a little nibble of a soap-scented earlobe.

"Are we gonna have to watch you two smooch all day long?" Conor whined.

"Don't worry, Conor," Mia assured him as she patted his thigh in a friendly manner. "If they get too irritating, we can focus on something else."

He shot her a quick glance and was pleased to find a sultry gaze that belied her deceptively cherubic countenance.

"Looks like a great day for sailing," he decided, smiling brightly.

It was a short drive to the Berkeley marina where Jim Evans kept the boat. He'd begun sailing when he was dating Catherine, and took to it like a duck to water. Something about the freedom of the ocean and the inherent risk in the sport formed an attractive combination for him.

Catherine's father had been a sailor, and he had enjoyed having his young son-in-law crew for him on his yacht. It was a few years before Jim could afford his own boat, and it was an important sign of his independence for him to pay for his hobby with his own money. Eventually, he began to work his way up, trading in his small boats for progressively larger ones. He had owned a forty-five-foot Swan for about four years now, and he thought he would probably stick with it, not needing any more length or speed to feed his habit. This was just what he had always wanted—a large boat, built for speed, but with enough amenities to easily sleep six or eight people for overnight trips. It was far from luxurious, but that wasn't an issue for him; he wanted as little excess weight as possible so he could stay competitive in his frequent races, and the Swan fit the bill perfectly.

Normally, a boat as large and as nice as his would be berthed in one of the marinas in the city. But Catherine's father had kept his boat in Berkeley and when he died Jim had taken over his slip as a small tribute to the man who sparked his love for the hobby.

Jamie had been sailing with him since she was a tiny child—much too tiny for Catherine's more cautious nature. She loved the ocean as much as she loved being with her father and, up until this year, had never refused an invitation to crew. She knew he'd been disappointed when she had begged off several times this year because of training rides, but he seemed to understand.

The marina parking lot was nearly empty, as always, but the few prime spots were taken this morning so they had to walk quite a way with all of their gear. Jamie and Ryan had prepared a large, if not gourmet, lunch the night before, and Ryan now lugged the big bag they had packed it in. Conor carried a cooler filled with beer, wine and bottled water, while Jamie carried nothing but a large thermos of hot cocoa. Mia came up beside her on the walk and snaked an arm around her waist. "Thanks for arranging this, sweetie. I can't think of a better send-off."

"You're starting the flirting a little early, aren't you?" she teased, referring to Mia's earlier comments to Conor.

"Hey, I don't want him to get the wrong impression," she said rather defensively. "I've only got one day to make an impact!"

"Oh, I think you made an impact. He gave you the same look Ryan gives me before she jumps me!"

"He's following my evil plan perfectly then," she grinned mischievously.

The boat was docked near the edge of the marina with the other large vessels. The two strapping stevedores had no trouble climbing aboard, even with their loads, and within a few minutes they had everything stowed away and were ready to sail.

Mia had been sailing many times. It seemed most families on the Peninsula sailed, and she had frequently accepted invitations to spend a day on the ocean. While not nearly as competent as her friend, she had enough experience to make her a perfectly acceptable first mate.

The first order of business was a short lecture on the basic elements of sailing. Since both O'Flaherty's were practical people, with a good understanding of the natural world, they immediately grasped the basic concepts. "I've got it," Ryan said. "You can't sail directly into the wind, but you can sail directly with the wind. If you don't want to go the way the wind is blowing, you have to cut across it and use the sails and the rudder to provide lift and thrust."

"Uh, maybe you should give the lecture," Jamie mumbled.

"No, no, not at all. You just explain it very well," Ryan said with a grin. "It makes it obvious."

"Right," she drawled. "Anyway, let's cover some basic terms. The sails are pretty obvious, but the ropes that move them are called sheets."

"Shouldn't the sail be the sheet?" Conor asked, his forehead wrinkled in question. "It looks like a big sheet."

"Ahh, probably," she agreed. "But they're not. The big pole down the center of the boat is the mast. You put the mainsail up the mast via this rope called the mainsheet. A very important piece of equipment is the boom," she said as she slapped the heavy canvas-covered piece that stuck out at a right angle from the mast. "The term is important, because that's just what it feels like if it hits you."

"Why would it hit you?" Ryan asked.

"Well, remember how we have to tack across the wind?"

Two dark heads nodded.

"The boom moves from side to side, holding the sail out to catch the wind. You trim the sail by moving the boom using the sheets. The boom moves independently, and rather abruptly, if the wind changes unexpectedly. So it's best to never let your attention wander too much if you're in the path that it travels."

"Got it," Conor stated. "Don't get hit by the boom."

"A few more terms are mandatory. The front of the boat is the bow, but if you're going towards the bow you're also moving fore. Likewise the rear of the boat is the stern, but moving towards the stern is aft."

"Huh?" Ryan asked, actually scratching her dark head. "Why not just say bow and stern?"

"Uhm, think of fore and aft as signposts leading you to the destination of the bow and stern."

"If you insist," she replied, casting a dubious glance at her teacher.

"Two more must-knows. Port is the left of the boat when you face forward. And starboard is the right."

"What's the left of the boat when you face the stern?" Ryan asked, obviously trying hard to lock this information into her brain in some semblance of order.

"It's the starboard," Jamie said slowly, now casting a dubious glance at her student.

"Oh! I get it. You meant that each side has a fixed name no matter which way you're facing!"

"Well, yeah," she said slowly.

"She could have just said so," Conor muttered under his breath.

Jamie ignored his grumbling and started to discuss casting off, but was once again stopped by her partner. "What is the term for going towards the port or the starboard?"

"Uhm ... just port and starboard."

"Shouldn't they have signposts too?"

"Let go, Ryan, just let go," she said soothingly as she massaged her temples.

"All right," she agreed as she shrugged her broad shoulders. "Just trying to get some consistency here."

Jamie continued to instruct her small class for a few minutes. It wasn't important that they learn too much at first, since she really only needed them for one task. "Okay," she said as she handed each O'Flaherty a pair of leather-palmed gloves with shortened fingers. "Your main job is to be my grinders. You keep the sheets taut by sticking those big cranks in the winches here and grinding for all you're worth when I tell you to."

The bright blue eyes shared a glance and then fixed upon Jamie again. "So you and Mia do the fun stuff, and we work our asses off?" Ryan asked.

"Pretty much."

"Sounds good to me," Conor said.

"Me too," his little sister agreed.

Since they knew the drill, Jamie and Mia inspected each line, shackle, bolt, screw, winch and strap they could get their hands on. When they were certain the boat was shipshape, Jamie instructed Conor to stand on the dock and cast them off. After checking the fuel tanks, she started the surprisingly powerful inboard engines. Conor's eyes bugged out a bit as she motored the Swan out of the slip. "Wow, why learn all this sailing stuff if you can hit those babies hard and cruise around the bay?"

"They're just big enough to get us in and out of the slip and help us get in if we can't sail in. The fuel tanks aren't really that huge anyway, Conor," she called over the growling of the engines.

He released the lines, one at a time, and hopped back on just as she started to clear the dock. Mia showed them how to remove the small bumpers that protected the boat in the dock, but looked rather unsightly when under sail. When all of the gear was stowed away, they were clear of the marina and ready to rock.

"Okay, Buffy," Jamie called to her partner. "Ready to hoist the mainsail?"

"Aye, aye," her lover answered happily. Following the instructions Jamie had given earlier, Ryan did an admirable job of hoisting the huge piece of fabric up the very tall mast. The halyard that pulled the material up was engineered to make the work fairly easy, but she used most of her arm and shoulder muscles in the task. When the mainsail was secure, Conor got to work on the jib.

Mia helped him secure it properly, and then scampered aft to await instructions from the captain. "Okay, we're going to start off on a port tack. Mia, set the sails," she ordered. With a small salute, Mia quickly reminded Ryan how to trim the main, and sat next to Conor to help him with the jib. Just to keep them on their toes, Jamie executed a few little tacking drills, forcing them to grind almost constantly just to keep up.

"Hey! Make up your mind!" Conor called as he stopped to wipe the sweat from his brow.

"Just a little test," she called back, satisfied with the rigging. "Come on back, Ryan," she called.

Ryan walked back to the stern, grinning a bit when she paused a moment to take in her lover. The day was warm and dry on shore, but the always-brisk wind of the bay constantly required plenty of clothing. An orange nylon baseball cap, its closure pulled snug to keep it secure in the breeze, covered Jamie's head. A wind and waterproof navy blue anorak covered a bright yellow turtleneck, and under her matching navy blue pants, she wore a silk thermal union suit that Ryan had teased her about when they were getting dressed. She had never been too warm while on the bay, and she doubted this day would be any different. Her navy blue leather topsiders, which obviously had a lot of miles on them, covered two thin pairs of nylon socks.

To Ryan's appraising eye, she was the cutest thing on water, and her approving gaze told Jamie just that as she approached. "What's that look for?" Jamie asked, knowing full well what that look usually meant.

"Just thinking that the Sirens' song wouldn't mean a thing to me if I could just get one look at you," she said with a lovesick grin on her face.

"Come sit down and let me sit on your lap, you sweet thing."

Ryan did just that, happily nuzzling her lover's neck while Jamie expertly steered the boat, using the very large wheel. "Wanna take over?" Jamie's voice carried back to the human chair.

"Yeah! Can I?" she asked with all of the excitement of a seven-year-old at Christmas.

"Absolutely. Come stand in front of me, and I'll let you get a feel for the action." Ryan did, and after a few moments of resting her hands on top of Jamie's, she was given control of the big boat. Jamie would have given anything to have a camera at that moment. Her broadly grinning lover was standing comfortably on widely-spread legs, her proud face staring into the wind, dark hair streaming behind her. Surprisingly, she didn't wear a hat—and her hair was unrestrained. She wore a white turtleneck under the bright blue wool sweater that was a favorite of Jamie's. Her yellow nylon windbreaker covered both, but it was unzipped enough to show both of her sweaters. Her ever-present jeans and running shoes completed an outfit that didn't have Jamie's approval. She'd strongly suggested they buy proper sailing gear, but her proud lover wouldn't let her buy it and was reticent to buy it for herself until she was sure she would enjoy the sport. "I might be hanging over the side the whole time," she had joked the previous evening. Jamie let her win the round, but she was determined to have an outfit for her the next time they went out. She knew from experience that wet jeans were no fun when the brisk wind hit them, but she had decided to let Ryan find that out for herself.

As acting captain, Ryan, of course, had to make her brother jump from port to starboard several times to trim the sails, but she knew he would get her back at some point during the day. The wind was picking up, making the bay a little rough, but neither sibling seemed to mind. In fact, Ryan seemed to smile wider and wider every time they hit a depression, making the boat thump hard against the water. "Wanna do something really fun?" Jamie asked as the wind gained even more velocity.

"I'm in!" Ryan stated dramatically, hardly caring what the event was.

"Hey, Mia!" she called, interrupting her friend's flirting.

"Yo!"

"Show our guests how to ride the rail!" she called out over the howling wind. "Get them some foul weather gear and life jackets first," she added.

Mia went below and retrieved bright red rubberized overalls for Ryan and Conor. They both looked adorable in their matching gear, which covered them to mid-torso. Jamie turned the boat just a bit, causing the starboard side to lift off the water at a dramatic angle. Showing, rather than explaining, Mia sat on the deck and wedged her torso between the two rubber-covered safety lines that ringed the boat. Her butt was resting right on the toe rail, her feet dangling over the waves. It was a fairly dangerous move, given the conditions, but she seemed totally confident, so the O'Flahertys followed suit.

There was something so elemental and freeing about the experience that Ryan wished it could last for hours. The ride was jarring and rough and very wet, and she knew that she would be chilled to the bone in a short time, but she loved it. Looking at the smile on her brother's face, she knew that he felt the same. When she turned back to Jamie, they locked eyes for a moment—just long enough for Ryan to experience a stab of connection right in the pit of her stomach. Having Jamie understand what this felt like, and having her know that she would totally love it, was a very powerful experience. She wanted to wrap her arms around her partner and give her a big squeeze, but that would require climbing back up on the deck, and she was not ready to give up her perch.

Catching Mia's eye, Jamie signaled that she wanted to tack again. Mia informed the siblings, and they scrambled to trim the sails and jump to the port side to ride that rail.

They continued in a similar vein for almost half an hour. They looked like they were having a very good time, but Jamie was worried that they would freeze if she left them out there much longer. A small adjustment righted the boat, and the rail sitters slid from their positions and crawled along the now-slick deck to join Jamie at the helm.

"God, that rocked!" Ryan cried, tossing her arms around her lover. "I could stay out there all day!"

Conor echoed her sentiments, adding, "The only thing I still have to do is steer, and I'll be happy," as he gazed at Jamie with puppy dog eyes.

She smiled back and crooked a finger, beckoning him to join her. "Come on, Mia, you help out here, and I'll tend the sails with Buffy."

Conor did well at his task, carefully piloting the boat. Ryan had ditched her overalls—claiming they had more water in them than they had repelled—and judging from her now dark blue pants, Jamie thought she might be right.

Conor didn't really take advantage of his position, but they still had to scamper back and forth a few times to keep up with his tacking. They had just gotten the sheets set after one such tack when he began to turn in the opposite direction. Ryan jumped to her feet to help her partner, but she forgot the cardinal rule for one short moment. A moment was all it took for the boom to come flying at her so quickly that she only had time to grab on and let it yank her off her feet, her long body dangling precariously over the choppy water.

Jamie was well used to situations just like this one, and she didn't panic. She slowly began to pull on the sheet, reeling her partner in. She yelled as loudly as she could to Conor to maintain his position, but he obviously didn't hear her or couldn't make his body follow her instructions. He did what most beginners would do—he yanked the wheel in the opposite direction, thinking that would bring his baby sister back. Instead, it jerked the sail so abruptly that Ryan's tenuous grip failed, and she slid into the ocean with a small splash.

"*Jamie! Help!*" he cried, stunned and panicked.

She wanted to take the time to reassure him, but she couldn't waste a second. She grabbed the closest life preserver, tossed it in the general direction of her partner, and then ran back to the helm. "Drop the sails!" she ordered, Mia and Conor scrambling to obey her command. While they made a mess of the deck with yards of sail billowing around them, Jamie started the engines and quickly turned the boat around.

She knew that Ryan wouldn't drown, since she was wearing a buoyant life vest, but she was worried about her being in the frigid water for any length of time. The ocean was about 58 degrees during the spring, and she knew that hypothermia could set in quickly, especially with the cold wind that was still blowing fiercely.

When the unbearably cold water rushed over her head, Ryan thought for one panicked second that either her heart would stop or she would be unable to take a breath once she surfaced. To her eternal gratitude, neither happened, but the painful shock of the water nearly made her wish they had. Actually, it had taken a few seconds to be able to feel anything, but once her heart stopped beating double time, she was able to feel the terrible needle-like sting of the frigid water on every square inch of her body. Ryan had been in the ocean in May on many occasions, but had been wearing a full wet suit each time. This experience was unique, and she made a promise to herself that it would be a once-in-a-lifetime treat.

She could see the sails drop and a question formed in her mind, but when she saw the boat turn quickly she realized it was the only way for Jamie to come back into the wind. Faster than she would have imagined, she started to feel her mind disconnect from her body, which felt so heavy that she knew she would be useless in the rescue effort. *Thank God Conor's here*, she thought as the boat raced towards her.

She was aware of being pulled up to the hull by the long rope attached to her life ring, but she was unable to help as her anxious friends tried to haul her in. Conor finally leaned over the deck so far that Mia had to sit on his legs to stop him from going over as well. He used every ounce of his substantial strength to drag his limp sister onto the deck.

Adrenaline was still pumping through his system, giving him the strength to pick her up and carry her below decks with Jamie right on his heels. Mia stayed topside to tend the wheel as the threesome descended.

"What do we do?" Conor asked, his skin ashen from fear and shock.

"Get her clothes off and wrap her in blankets," Jamie said briskly. "She'll be fine once she's warm." Looking down at her partner, who shivered painfully, she asked, "Won't you, honey?"

Ryan nodded, but her entire body was shaking so hard that it was hard to tell what was nod and what was shake. Jamie looked up at Conor for the first time and saw how devastated he was. Summoning all of her composure, she took a deep breath and did her best to reassure the shaken man. "This happens all the time, Conor," she said soothingly. "I swear she'll be fine. Go in the forward cabin and change into some of my father's warm clothes," she commanded. "Then go get me the hot cocoa."

He obeyed her orders, but with a slight change. He ran up to get the cocoa first, handing the large mug to Jamie with shaking hands.

"Go change and then help Mia," Jamie repeated firmly.

"But ..."

"Go," she said firmly. "I can undress her just fine. I've been getting lots of practice you know," she added, trying to draw a smile from the poor man.

"Okay," he said softly, gently patting his sister on the leg as he departed.

As he left, Jamie leaned over and asked, "How are you, really?"

"G ... g ... gotta g ... g ... get out of these c ... c ... clothes," she stuttered, unable to hold her chin still to speak clearly.

"I'll do it. Drink some of this and try to relax." Jamie set about the normally fun task of undressing her partner that, in addition to not being fun this time, was damned difficult. Ryan was often weak with desire, but this was much more extensive. She was barely able to help at all, and the soaked garments were so ungainly that Jamie gave a quick thought to cutting them off of her. The life jacket came off easily, as did the wool sweater. The turtleneck was tougher, and as soon as she got it off she tucked a blanket around Ryan's shaking shoulders, not having the patience to deal with her sports bra just yet. With persistence and patience she finally had the shoes, jeans, and socks off, and she could feel Ryan's body start to relax a bit as the ice cold clothes were removed. Taking a break, she wrapped the second blanket around Ryan's shivering legs and gave in to her overwhelming need to wrap her in a fierce hug. "God, you scared me," she whispered.

"I scared me, too," she agreed, her voice sounding much more normal. "Do me a favor?"

"Anything," Jamie promised.

"Go tell Conor and Mia that I'm okay. I know he's worried."

"Okay. Be right back," she said with a wan smile.

"Jamie?"

"Yes?"

"I've heard the best thing for hypothermia is to snuggle with another warm body while you're both naked."

A fond smile greeted that suggestion. "You *are* feeling better."

They followed Ryan's suggestion, but their approach was more chaste than the purported life-saving prescription. Ryan had taken off her soaked undergarments while Jamie was topside and had quickly snuggled back into the blankets after turning them to their dry sides. When Jamie returned, she shucked her jacket and pants and climbed in with her.

It was an odd feeling, cuddling a stark-naked Ryan while in thermal underwear and a turtleneck, but Jamie quickly put aside her discomfort and snuggled closer, allowing her body heat to warm her partner.

"That was the oddest feeling," Ryan mumbled, her voice now completely normal, if a bit sleepy.

"It's happened to me several times," Jamie sympathized. "It's amazing how quickly you become helpless, isn't it?"

"Yeah, I felt like I'd been given a big dose of Novocain right into my central nervous system. I couldn't feel my hands at all and I couldn't pick my arms up to help you guys get me out."

"I know, honey," she soothed. "It's okay now, baby. Just close your eyes and feel safe for a little while. I've got you. Just relax." Her hands were slowly rubbing her partner through the blanket, comforting and relaxing her simultaneously.

"Can Mia handle the boat?" she asked, jerking awake abruptly.

"Yes, she's fine," she soothed. "The sails are down and we're motoring slowly. We've got plenty of fuel, and the wind is behind us, so we'll be fine."

"Okay," she muttered wearily as she fell asleep in Jamie's protective embrace.

When Jamie woke up a short time later, she was immediately aware of the stillness of the boat. The engines were clearly off, and she hoped it was because Mia had turned them off. She got her answer a minute later when Conor stuck his head into the cabin.

"Everything okay?" Jamie whispered.

"Fine. But Mia doesn't want to blow all the fuel, so she shut off the engines. She thinks it's safe to drift for a while. Is that okay?"

"Yeah, but you should at least raise the jib in case you need to get out of trouble," she said. "I want Ryan to sleep as long as she can, so go ahead and have lunch if you're hungry."

"That was my second question," he grinned.

Moments after he departed, Ryan started to wake. "Mmm, this is nice," she mumbled as she snuggled tighter against her lover's body.

"You feel okay?"

"Yeah," she replied as she stretched languidly. "I actually feel fine. I mean, I wasn't hurt or anything—just really cold."

"Well, you certainly feel warm now," Jamie whispered as she ran her hands up and down her partner's body through the blanket. "This is a delicious feeling, you know."

"Our attire is a little discordant," Ryan agreed with a chuckle.

"I wouldn't change a thing," she breathed right into her ear.

"I would," Ryan complained as she tried to snake her hand under her partner's clothes only to be stopped by her all-encompassing union suit.

"Everything *I* need is readily available," Jamie insisted as she turned Ryan onto her tummy and started to kiss her neck.

"N ... no," Ryan muttered into the pillow. "Too much emotion."

Clambering up to cuddle behind her, Jamie asked, "Are you all right, honey?"

"Yeah, I'm fine," she said. "Falling into the water freaked me out a bit. I don't feel like I'm in control."

And in that instant Jamie not only knew just what her lover meant, she agreed with her fully. "Let's just snuggle and try to get our equilibrium back, okay?"

Ryan nodded, and they spent the next fifteen minutes nuzzling and kissing lightly. Things were just starting to escalate when they heard an amused voice say, "Look who feels better!" Two heads jerked to attention to focus on the open door of the cabin. Mia stood with her arms folded across her chest, a wide grin plastered on her face. "Sorry girls, I just came down to check on you and use the head. I take it that moaning was not from pain?"

Her quick reflexes allowed her to dodge the pillow her roommate tossed at her, but the laughter of the two women assured her there were no hard feelings.

Luckily, Jim Evan's clothing was the perfect size to fit Ryan's large frame. She pulled on proper sailing gear, without complaint this time, even agreeing to the thin navy blue Polarfleece stocking cap that Jamie insisted she wear. She put it on in the same quirky style that Jamie had seen her adopt for other hats; rather than have the cap rest on the rear of her head, she pulled it straight down her forehead so that it rested an inch or so above her eyebrows. It was an odd affectation—and it would have looked stupid on Jamie—but Ryan pulled it off beautifully with her strongly planed face and square jaw line.

When they climbed up the few stairs to the deck, they both cleared their throats a few times to announce their presence. Conor tore his mouth from Mia's and gulped, blinking a few times to get his bearings. "How do you feel, Ryan?"

"Just fine. No harm done."

"You scared me half to death!" he said emphatically, as he pulled away from Mia's embrace and went to wrap his sister in a hug. "I'm so sorry I did that to you."

"It's okay, Con, really," she soothed as she gently patted his back. "Jamie says that happens all the time, even with really experienced crews."

"I've gone over three times," Jamie volunteered.

"Just once for me," Mia added. "The guys I was with were so drunk they almost couldn't turn the damn boat to come get me."

"See?" Ryan asked as she pulled away to get a good look at his eyes. "It's not a big deal."

"Okay," he conceded, nodding briefly. "You're never going sailing in jeans again. If you hadn't grabbed that ring and weren't wearing your life vest, you couldn't have tread water that long with those heavy pants on."

"But I did, and I was and you guys rescued me easily," she reminded him. "Let it go, Conor. It's really okay."

"Will you let me buy you sailing gear and call it even?" he asked, looking down at her with a smile.

"Deal!" she happily agreed. "Hey, I'll *jump* over for a nice set of golf clubs!"

"Don't press your luck, Sis," he warned as he playfully thumped her on her cap-covered head.

Jamie sat on Ryan's lap as the dark haired woman lovingly fed her bites of a delicious turkey sandwich. They were steering the boat together using only the jib. Not trying to get anyplace in particular, and not caring how long it took them to get there, they were enjoying the solitude of the now calm day. Their companions had gone below, ostensibly to use the head, but after fifteen minutes the girls assumed they were engaged in some sort of merger.

Much to their surprise, Conor's dark head popped out of the hatch, his face looking green around the edges. "I don't feel so hot," he muttered, looking at them pathetically.

"Come up here and breathe some fresh air," Jamie urged. He complied, climbing over the gear to sit right next to his sister.

"How could you stay down there so long?" he moaned, as he took several deep, cleansing breaths.

"Uhm, I hadn't just had lunch and," she leaned over to count the empties, "three beers."

"This fresh air makes you thirsty."

"Yeah, but going below after a few beers makes you sick," she reminded him. "So you can either be thirsty or frustrated. Take your pick."

"Shoulda picked thirsty," he grumbled as his sister and Jamie burst out laughing.

When Mia returned to the group a few minutes later, they decided to hoist the mainsail and prepare to return. It was about two o'clock, but the wind wasn't favorable, and Jamie predicted—accurately, as it turned out—it would take a while to get back; it took a full two hours to return to the marina. Conor offered to jump onto the dock to secure the boat, and they all had to stifle a laugh when it took him a moment to get his land legs. His stumbling gait only lasted a few steps, and he smoothly secured the big boat to Jamie's satisfaction.

It took much longer to put the boat to bed than it did to take it out, and by the time everything was perfectly ordered, it was after five. Mia still had a ton of things to do to get ready for her departure, so she declined their invitation to join them for dinner. Conor walked her to the door and stayed inside for several minutes, but he returned with Jamie's mail and a few phone messages, so he was forgiven.

Martin wasn't at home, so they were left to forage on their own. By the time the pizza arrived, they were all dozing on the big bed in Martin's room, Ryan across the bottom with Duffy curled up against her chest and Jamie and Conor in the traditional position.

Their lethargy was such that they barely finished a medium sized pizza. By nightfall, all three were snug in their separate beds, Duffy being the happiest of the group since he got his mistress all to himself.

Chapter Thirteen

Monday morning found them lounging around the dining room table, surveying their options for the week. Jamie was content to just lie around the house as long as Ryan was with her, but she knew her lover needed a lot of stimulation to keep her interested. She was also learning that Ryan needed at least a general idea of her schedule, or she became a little anxious.

Rather than switch clients around too much, Ryan had decided to work at the gym from three to six, her normal hours. Since Mia was leaving and Jamie no longer needed a formal session, Ryan had tinkered with her schedule to compress it into her preferred time period. The fifteen hours of full-fare clients gave her an income that far surpassed anything she had ever dreamed of, and gave her the financial security to take two weeks off without worry.

The only downside was that her work prevented them from ranging very far afield during the week. Jamie would have preferred spending a few days up in Napa or Mendocino, but Ryan's financial autonomy obviously meant a lot to her, and she decided not to challenge her strict work ethic.

"Okay," Jamie said, as she stood to clear the breakfast dishes. "We've got to be back by one for you to get to work. It's almost eight so we have five hours to play with. Since you didn't run today, I assume you want to spend the morning doing something energetic?"

"I've got a few suggestions," Ryan said, obviously having thought this through earlier. "I really enjoyed being at the Marina. Why don't we go back and do our workout there."

"Oh, like we did at the track that time?"

"Kinda," she said with a twinkle. "I think it's time you learned the rudiments of kickboxing, little girl," she added as she pinched her partner rather hard on the butt.

Jamie looked up to the heavens for assistance. "Why do I get the feeling that I'm going to wind up bruised?"

A short while later, they were warming up on the broad, grass-covered lawn that fronted the Marina. The day was bright and warm for May, and it seemed like every baby in town was out on the green with their mothers or their nannies. Ryan decided to teach Jamie the basics of the cardio-kick class she used to teach at Castro. She had a small boom-box resting on the ground, along with some lightweight padded gloves and a big blue padded mitt.

They followed their usual warm-up routine, and then Ryan gave her some instruction on proper kicking technique. Jamie was now muscular enough to brace herself on one sturdy leg while kicking out forcefully with the other, a required element for kickboxing. She took to the instruction very well, kicking the padded mitt with some force, and after just fifteen minutes Ryan pronounced her ready to begin.

She switched on the music and led the way, showing Jamie at half speed how to execute the series of kicks and jumps timed to the music. She added the punching moves that made the exercise a full-body workout, and then started the tape again.

This time they went through the moves at full speed, kicking, jumping and punching the air in a graceful series of moves—rather, Ryan was graceful, and Jamie struggled to keep up. But when they went through the series again and again, Jamie started to catch on. By the time she fully understood and could follow the signals, however, she was so tired she could hardly move.

Her arms felt like she had ten-pound weights attached to them and her legs were heavy and slow. "God! You really had weights in your hands, but I'm the one who's pooped!" she cried when she surveyed Ryan's calm, even breathing.

"I've been doing this a lot longer than you have."

"Oh please! That has nothing to do with it, and you know it, Buffy. You're just amazing, and I won't accept any other explanation!"

"Well," she drawled, "I guess I am rather remarkable." But she gave her partner such a goofy look when she made this statement that Jamie had to laugh at her good-natured teasing. "And that reminds me," Ryan said. "What's with this 'Buffy' stuff? Is that like Buffy the Vampire Slayer, or Buffy like Buffy and Muffy and those other rich girl names?"

"Neither, silly," she laughed. "You don't look even a little bit like Sara Michelle Gellar, and you could never pull off the preppy rich kid thing."

"So ... why do you call me that?"

"Because of these," Jamie said as she ran her hands down Ryan's arms, trailing her thumbs over the smooth dips and protrusions of muscle. "You're terribly buff, you know."

"Ahh, Buffy," Ryan nodded, fairly satisfied with the name now that she knew its origin.

"Buffy, indeed," Jamie nodded in concert, leaning in for a sweet kiss. "But right now, I've gotta find a bathroom. Is there one around here?"

"Yeah, but it's pretty far," Ryan warned, indicating the building in the distance. "Want me to pack up and go with you?"

"No, I like this spot. Why don't you sit by that tree and take it easy. I can tell you're really beat. You're just hiding it well."

"Good idea," Ryan agreed. "You always know best."

She watched Jamie jog, admiring the way her firm little butt looked in her navy blue Lycra shorts. Deep in concentration, she didn't hear the footsteps that approached her from behind. "Police officer," the rather deep, but decidedly female voice boomed. "Don't make any sudden moves … keep your hands right where they are."

Ryan's heart started beating so fast she could actually feel it in her chest. She knew she had done nothing wrong, but the thought of having a police officer call her out was alarming. "What's the problem, officer?" she asked, as calmly as possible.

"You answer the questions," the woman snapped. "I ask them." The rough tone and brusque treatment were not making Ryan feel one bit better. "Get on your knees and put your hands behind your back," she ordered.

Ryan had every intention of obeying the command, but she had a momentary flash of doubt that this really was a cop. "Let me see your badge," she said with more conviction than she really felt.

"Been in this situation a few times, huh, tough girl?" the officer growled. She produced a badge that she flashed right in front of Ryan's face. It certainly looked authentic, having the same general style as her father's Fire Department badge, but even though Ryan was reassured that this wasn't an imposter, she didn't feel a hell of a lot better with this confirmation.

She followed the officer's instructions to the letter, getting to her knees and docilely placing her hands behind her back. She hadn't heard handcuffs opened before, but she got a crash course in the distinctive sound when the cold steel was slapped first on one wrist and then the other. Ryan had been in many touchy situations in her young life and had gone up against some very tough guys, but she had rarely felt as powerless as she did at that moment. The fact that she couldn't defend herself, either physically or verbally was combining to make her absolutely panic-stricken.

A jumble of thoughts raced through Ryan's mind as she considered her options. As the daughter of a civil servant, she had been taught since she was a toddler that police officers were the guardians of the city. Her father had always stressed that if she was in trouble, she should never hesitate to ask an officer for help, and her personal experience with the police had been uniformly positive. But she also knew that members of the force were trained to demand complete obedience from suspects, and that when they didn't get it they sometimes reacted badly. She had no interest in being booked for resisting arrest, and even less interest in being goaded into assaulting an officer, since that would definitely land her in serious trouble. So she ignored every one of her instincts to defend herself, and tried to be as docile as a kitten.

"I don't want you to move one muscle," the officer growled, seemingly right into her ear. "One move, and I slap another pair on your ankles and hog-tie you."

Now Ryan's discomfort was turning into panic. Trying to keep her wits about her, she tried again, "What do you want with me?"

"Did I tell you to talk?" she spat. When Ryan meekly shook her head, she added, "Good girl. Following orders is the only way you're going to get out of this in one piece."

One piece? What in the fuck does she think I've done? Is there a lunatic murderer on the loose?

The officer grasped her around her upper arms and pulled her easily to her feet. "Lean your head against that tree," she stated as she pushed Ryan in the general direction. "And spread your legs shoulder width."

She managed the move, but it caused her to lean up against the tree in a very ungainly position. Even with her strong abs and thighs, she doubted that she could stand up again without assistance. The officer began a thorough pat-down, maintaining a cool professional attitude throughout. But another stab of panic shot through Ryan when the officer lingered longer than was necessary at her crotch.

Is this some renegade, lesbian cop rapist? she wondered as she was pulled into an upright position. "We're gonna go for a little walk now," the officer stated. "You're gonna move nice and slow and go just where I tell you."

Another docile nod was Ryan's only response. The cop placed a surprisingly small hand on the back of Ryan's neck and started to push her in the direction of the street. "My stuff," she weakly protested, not wanting anyone to wander off with her gear.

"We'll be right at the squad car," she declared, indicating a car parked next to a maintenance building. "Nobody will touch your stuff."

Ryan's panic was building, as they got closer to the car. It was parked in such a way that it was hidden from both the street, and the people on the green, by dense shrubbery. The thought hit her that it was just the way you would park the car if you didn't want anyone to see it.

When they were about ten feet from the car, Jamie was just drawing close enough to see her lover being led away by a police officer. *Oh shit! Now what?* she cried to herself, as she began running.

When the officer had Ryan right up against the car, she unlocked one cuff. Reaching around her, she quickly moved both arms to the front and cuffed her back up. "What are you doing to me?" Ryan finally cried in frustration.

A low laugh was the officer's response. She opened the rear door, pushed Ryan roughly and laughed again when the larger woman fell face first against the seat. In a flash, the officer jumped in, landed on top of her, and murmured in her normal, higher-pitched voice, "I always told you I'd be on top someday, Ryan."

"Carolyn?" Ryan squeaked as the front door flew open to reveal one hundred and ten pounds of outraged fury.

"Oh-oh," Carolyn mumbled, when Jamie began to yell at full volume.

"Yeah, oh-oh is right," Ryan fully agreed, to the not-so-fresh smelling vinyl seat that her face rested against.

"Who the fuck are you, and what are you doing to my girlfriend?" the little dynamo shrieked.

"Girlfriend? When did you get a girlfriend?" the chagrined officer demanded of the back of Ryan's head.

"Uhm, Jamie?" Ryan mumbled, unable to speak clearly because of her position. "This is my friend Carolyn." After a beat she added, "She's a police officer."

"You know each other?" Jamie stuttered as she turned around and sank into the passenger seat.

"Shit!" Carolyn muttered, "I'm so fucking sorry, Ryan!" She was frantically sticking her hands into her various pockets, looking for the elusive key to the handcuffs.

"Uhm, wouldn't that be easier if you got off me?" Ryan tactfully suggested.

"Oh, fuck," she cursed, as she crawled back out of the car, blushing furiously. "I don't have any idea what I'm doing right now." She quickly found the key and rolled Ryan onto her side to unlock the cuffs.

"Is anyone going to tell me what in the hell is going on here?" Jamie demanded.

"I don't know what's going on, so Carolyn's in charge of that one," Ryan said as she sat up, rubbing her wrists.

"Uhm … Jamie, is it?"

"Yes," she drawled, staring right into the small woman's shifting eyes.

"This was all a really big misunderstanding," she began.

"It better have been."

"Hey! I'm blameless in this!" Ryan protested.

"You're never blameless," Jamie corrected. "There's always some degree of culpability when you're involved."

"No fair!" Ryan cried. "I was just sitting by the tree minding my own business. Actually," she corrected, "I was busy watching your butt as you ran across the green. My attention was so focused I didn't even hear Carolyn approach."

"See, you were partly to blame," Jamie said rather pointedly.

"No, no, this was all my fault," Carolyn insisted. "Uhm … Ryan and I have been uhm … friends for a couple of years now," she said. "We don't see each other often or anything, and I didn't know she had a girlfriend."

"Is Carolyn one of your 'special friends', Ryan?" Jamie demanded.

"Yep. Carolyn is most decidedly special," she admitted, with a wolfish grin at her old friend.

"You know about her uhm … friends?" Carolyn asked, truly surprised that Ryan would tell her new girlfriend about her past.

"Yes," Jamie dryly informed her. "But I don't know how many there are. *Were*, and I stress the 'were,' you friends for long?" she asked hoping Carolyn wasn't another member of the five-year club.

"Uhm, yeah," she admitted. "But I had a steady girlfriend for a while, and we haven't seen each other since … when was it, Ryan?"

"No, that's okay," Jamie interjected by holding her hand up. "I'm going to question you separately. You tell me when it was, Carolyn."

"Ahh, I think it was uhm … some time in the fall. I'm not sure exactly when though."

"That's acceptable," Jamie pronounced. "I've only had dibs since April."

"Oh, it was lots longer than that," she assured her, with a look of obvious relief. "Anyway, I broke up with my girlfriend a couple of weeks ago and I was just about to get back into the dating scene. I finished my shift at ten and was driving home when I caught sight of Ryan here. I thought it would be fun to uhm … play a game with her."

"Have you played this little game before?" Jamie asked as she turned her attention to her blushing lover.

"I like a woman in a uniform," she squeaked, blushing furiously.

After Jamie assured Carolyn that she was mostly joking, they all said goodbye. "Now don't forget to lose her number," Jamie reminded the chagrined officer as they parted.

They stood together, watching the squad car depart. Ryan slid her arm around her partner and said, "Would you ever consider …?"

"In your dreams, Buffy," she said as she strode over to reclaim their gear with Ryan's amused chuckle just tickling her ears.

On the way back to the car, Jamie absently kicked a rock. "Why wasn't she on your list to call?" she asked Ryan.

"Huh?"

"You told me that you went over to Alisa's to tell her about us. You said you were telling your special friends that you were off limits."

"I started to," Ryan said, "but I didn't really enjoy having Alisa give me a hard time about dating a straight woman."

"So … you're gonna do what?" Jamie asked as she looked up at her partner. "Just wait until they call you … or jump on top of you?"

"Jamie," she began, but her obviously miffed partner just shook her head and moved ahead of her to walk to the car alone.

The short ride back to Noe Valley had never seemed so long to Ryan. An uncomfortable silence had descended upon the car as soon as they climbed in, and Jamie gave no signs that she was going to end it anytime soon.

Ryan had always prided herself on her ability to bide her time when she knew there was trouble brewing. She'd always thought that it was best to let the other person figure out what was bothering them, and then talk about it. But as with so many things, her budding relationship with Jamie was changing her attitude. She wanted nothing more than to jump right in and make her partner talk about it—ready or not. She was just about to blurt out her question when Jamie turned to her and said in a very quiet voice, "That scared me."

"Scared you?" she asked, totally caught unawares by the statement. "Because she was taking me away?"

"No," her partner replied quickly. "That was frightening for a moment, but that's not what scares me."

Ryan immediately picked up the change in tense. It was obvious that whatever had bothered Jamie was still bothering her. Pulling the car to the curb, she shut off the engine and turned in the seat as much as her long body would allow. "Tell me," she urged as she reached over and lightly grasped her hand.

It was clear that Jamie was embarrassed. Her mist green eyes refused to meet Ryan's, even though the dark haired woman tried to engage her. "I worry about pleasing you," she finally said in such a quiet voice that the gentle, muted sounds of the cars passing by almost obscured her words.

"Pleasing me?" Ryan asked, still confused—both by the direction the conversation was taking, and the tone of her partner's voice.

"Sexually," she clarified, looking embarrassed.

"But why ... what about Carolyn ... why now?"

The green eyes finally shifted and locked onto Ryan's, accompanied by one arched blonde eyebrow.

"Because of the way I teased you?"

"No, well, not entirely," she said. "Uhm, that's part of it, but not all of it."

"Come on, Jamie," Ryan gently urged. "This is important to me because it's obviously bothering you. Please tell me what's going through your mind."

"You've just done so much," she finally said in frustration. "I worry that I won't be able to please you like you're used to being pleased. I mean, I don't even really know what you're talking about when you implied that you wanted me to be in a uniform."

"Jamie," she said softly, obtaining and holding eye contact. "You're right about one thing. I know that you'll never please me like I'm used to."

The mix of hurt and shock that flew across Jamie's face was nearly heartbreaking, but Ryan had a point to make and she wanted to make sure it sank in. "I just wish I had some way of convincing you that I don't want to have sex the way I used to."

"What do you mean?" she asked, her lower lip trembling slightly.

"I probably had sex with Carolyn two dozen times," she said gently, still holding one small hand. "She's touched my vulva every way imaginable, and I've got to admit that she did a damn good job of it. But she never, not once, touched my heart. She never made my chest feel like it would burst with love. She never made my knees weak with emotion. My point is that it's really not that hard to make me come, Jamie. I'm ... easy." She shrugged her shoulders, an adorable smile gracing her face.

Her partner had to smile at that characterization.

"Yeah, you already guessed that, huh?"

"Kinda," Jamie admitted.

"If I let a woman touch my vulva, I'll eventually have an orgasm. Well, there have been exceptions, but not too darned many. Coming isn't that hard, so doing it isn't that big a deal. But I've almost never let a woman touch my soul. I've kept a very tight lock on my heart. I swear that you're the only woman who has that key." A tear had escaped from her lover's eye, and as she reached over to catch it, she pressed her lips against Jamie's, savoring the taste. "Sex between us is going to be so much more than manipulating genitals," she vowed, not moving her head an inch. "It's gonna be tender and sweet and passionate. Most of all it's going to be loving, Jamie—it will always come from love."

"Are you really sure that love can make up for inexperience?" she asked timidly, dearly wanting to believe Ryan, but having a difficult time of it.

"Really," Ryan vowed, placing a kiss on her smiling lips. "Truly," as she placed another. "Absolutely." The final kiss, punctuating her sentence, lasted longer than either had planned. The kiss got wetter and hotter and deeper, ratcheting up the desire between them until Ryan pulled away with a whimper. She shook her head so roughly that her bangs flew from side to side. "Jesus, Jamie, you make me hot just sitting in a car having a conversation!"

"Uhm ... sorry?" she said in a teasing tone.

"You've got nothing to be sorry for. It's all good. You know," Ryan murmured, continuing to speak softly right into Jamie's ear. "I really need to sleep with you tonight. Do you think we could sneak into your house?"

Jamie gazed at her in thoughtful silence for a few moments. Pursing her lips she replied, "I don't have any way to check on Cassie now that Mia's gone. I know she's not supposed to leave for New York until the middle of June, so there's a pretty good chance that she and Chris will stay at my place now that Mia's gone."

Ryan tried to hide her disappointment with a casual tone but was largely unsuccessful. "That's okay, maybe I can get my snuggle quotient before we go to bed."

"Uhm, if you really want to, we could go to my dad's apartment," she offered tentatively.

"That sounded significantly less than sincere," Ryan said with a furrow in her brow.

"Well, it would probably be okay, but the last time really bothered me. I guess I'm a little hesitant to stir up those feelings."

Ryan considered this for a moment, nodding her head briefly. The thought occurred to her that the woman Jim Evans had been with might have a key to the place, too, so even if he was gone, there was a tiny chance that she might show up. "That settles it," Ryan stated firmly, deciding not to risk either Jamie's comfort or her illusions about her father just to satisfy her own needs. "We'll be on the ride soon, and from·then on we're stuck together like glue—24/7."

"How about a hotel?" Jamie ventured, unwilling to let the issue die.

"No," Ryan said quickly, not even taking the time to consider the question. "It was hard enough for me to let you pay for the room during finals. I think it would bother me too much."

"*Duh!*" Jamie cried as she slapped her head with her open hand. "I've got just the place! Private, quiet, no roommates, free and convenient!"

"Where?"

"You just wait and see, baby. I'll pick you up from work at six."

Jamie was waiting for her partner at six on the dot. The sweaty, dark-haired woman came out, looking the worse for wear.

"Were you working out, too?"

"Kinda," she admitted. "My five o'clock is a new client, and she doesn't have a clue what I'm talking about. I have to show her every single exercise, and she still has trouble. I wound up doing as much as she did today." Shaking her head in exasperation, she added, "I've never had a client like that. It almost seemed like she just wanted to see me work out. Weird, huh?"

"Yeah, really weird," Jamie said with an internal smirk, having a very good idea why a woman would want to watch her buff lover work out. "Hey, good news," she cheerily announced. "I went to the house to get my mail and ran into my soon-to-be ex-roommate."

"That's good news?"

"No. The good news is that she was leaving for a movie. She won't be home for a couple of hours, so we can stop by there to get you showered."

"That is good news," Ryan agreed as she delicately sniffed under her raised arm.

As they were getting out of the car, Ryan looked on questioningly as her lover popped the trunk and pulled out a duffel bag. "What's that?"

"A change of clothes for you," she smiled. "You do have a tendency to ruin a perfectly clean outfit in a very short time, you know."

"Hey, why are we here anyway? Couldn't we go to our destination and get showered and changed?"

"Not really," the smaller woman replied. "This is much easier."

Ryan decided to take her partner at her word as she hoisted the heavy bag from her grip and toted it inside.

A few minutes later, when Ryan emerged from the shower, she smelled something delicious wafting up from the kitchen. Jamie had laid out a complete outfit for her so she put on the clothes, smiling to herself as she considered how butch her lover liked her to look. She shrugged into the shorts and faded jeans, then added the red hooded sweatshirt, smiling to herself that Jamie hadn't provided a bra. She then sat down to lace up the tan suede work boots. When she was finished, she slipped on the jeans jacket from which she'd removed the sleeves after she'd seriously ripped one of them while trying to leap a barbed wire fence during the AIDS Ride several years before. *I'm glad we're not going to a nice hotel*, she mused as she ran her fingers through her hair and grinned at her reflection.

Trotting down the stairs, she stood in puzzled silence as she watched her lover work at the sink. "So where we're going has no adequate shower, no adequate kitchen, and is casual enough for me to look like a big dyke?" she asked, as she stood in the doorway with arms crossed, nearly filling it with her size.

"That about sums it up," Jamie laughed as she turned her head just enough to take in her tough-looking lover. "Nice outfit, Buffy," she added with a definite leer.

"Just trying to keep the customer satisfied," Ryan joked as she crossed the room and leaned over to get a look at the dinner preparations, as well as nibble on a tempting neck.

The giggles that greeted her attack only served to increase the ferocity of her nibbles. "Mmm, let's skip dinner and just munch on each other."

"Oh, you are hot tonight," Jamie teased as she pushed her butt out just enough to rub it against her partner's thighs. "When you want to skip a meal, it's obviously a serious problem."

"Mmm, is that shrimp and mussels you're cleaning?"

"Yep."

"Then I can wait to nibble on you," Ryan decided with a small chuckle as she gave her partner a playful swat on the butt.

The frutti di mare over pasta was a thing of beauty. Once again, Ryan ate far more than was wise, finally leaning back in her chair and unbuttoning the top two buttons of her jeans.

"I've wondered why you always wear button-fly jeans," Jamie teased.

"Yep. It's hard to let a zipper down just a little. More than once, I've stood up after a meal only to have my pants stay seated when I had the zipper down."

"Well, in a few weeks, you're never going to have pants on while we're in the house, so it won't matter."

"That day can't come soon enough for me," Ryan said as she gazed at her partner with her best lovesick look.

It was almost nine o'clock when they arrived at their destination. "Uhm, isn't it a little late to go sailing?" Ryan wondered aloud, as the car pulled up right next to the entrance to the docks.

"Yep. But it's not too late to sleep on a nice private boat."

"You just keep thinking, Jamie. It's clearly what you do best."

It didn't take long to load their gear since all they had was a duffel with warm coats and a bottle of wine. The night was cool, but not really cold given the time of year. The fog hadn't yet come in, and the stars were clearly visible as Ryan stood on the deck and leaned her head back to gaze at them. "I hate to go below on a night like this," she said, as her partner walked up and snuggled against her side.

"We don't have to," Jamie said with a twinkle in her eye as she dashed down the stairs. A few minutes later she was back, lugging a very large cylindrical duffel. "As requested," she said with a flourish as she presented the bundle to her partner.

Ryan's quizzical expression turned into a delighted smile when she dumped the large, bright blue canvas hammock onto the deck. "Where do we hang it?" she asked excitedly.

"One end on the mast and the other goes on this standard my father had installed for just this purpose." She motioned for Ryan to hook up the mast end while she tugged her hook into place. "It's funny. He had this set up a couple of years ago, but I've never seen he and mother get into it," she said. "It might be one of those things that sounds better than it feels."

"One way to find out," Ryan said with a waggling eyebrow as she climbed in and patted the space next to her.

"I think I'd better get the wine and a blanket," Jamie said, "because I have the feeling we won't want to get out once we get in."

"I think you're psychic," Ryan smiled. "Let me help you."

They decided to go all the way and bring not only a blanket, but a couple of pillows also. Ryan carried the bedding and tossed it all on the deck right next to her feet. "I think we'd better get in first and get comfortable, then add the blanket and pillows," she decided. She sat down first, bouncing a little to get the feel of the contraption. "Nice."

"You lie down and then kinda hold it steady for me," Jamie instructed. Her partner did, managing to maintain the stability of the hammock even as she was getting elbowed and kneed in various sensitive places.

"Geez, you've got sharp elbows!" Ryan cried as her partner finally got settled.

"Give me that mouth, and I'll take your mind off your pain."

Only too happy to oblige, Ryan wrapped her arms around her lover and they spent quite a long time kissing and relaxing against one another. "I don't feel a thing anymore," she smiled when they broke their embrace.

"That's certainly not the reaction I was looking for," Jamie purred as she started to work on her neck.

"Oh, don't get me wrong," Ryan corrected as she leaned her head back sensuously as the nibbles and bites continued. "I feel plenty in all the right places. But I'm getting chilled. Blanket?"

"Sure."

Ryan leaned over farther than she had planned, causing the hammock to teeter on the edge of tossing them over. But she righted it with her arms and made another, more prudent attempt. Seconds later, they were wrapped in the thick, warm blanket, pillows behind their heads, and glasses of a rich, red Cabernet in their hands. "La dolce vita," Jamie murmured, as they began to slowly rock the hammock while they sipped at the wine.

"This is pretty fine," Ryan agreed. The hammock actually made them feel like they were being cuddled while they were cuddling each other. Ryan was mostly on her back with Jamie nestled up against her side, her head resting on Ryan's shoulder.

"Can we just stay here until the AIDS Ride?" Jamie asked, her voice so soft it was nearly a whisper. "I feel so perfectly content."

Ryan knew the question was mostly rhetorical, so she didn't point out all of the logical reasons why that was impractical. Rather, she indulged in the fantasy herself. "It would be nice to just rock in this hammock under the stars every night," she said. "Even though the city is right behind us, it feels like we're far away from everything."

"I'm close to the only thing that matters," Jamie murmured softly against her neck. "When we're together like this, I feel so perfectly safe and protected. Like nothing can ever hurt me."

"I'll do everything in my power to make that dream come true," Ryan pledged with a kiss to her smooth, unlined forehead.

They rocked for a long while, sipping contentedly on their wine. Neither spoke, each caught up in her own dreams. They could hear the water gently lapping at the hull of the boat, and the gentle wind caused various parts of the vessel to clang and thump, but the overwhelming sensation was of a deep, intense stillness. Nearly a half-hour passed, before Jamie broke the silence. "What are you thinking about?"

Ryan's low chuckle rumbled against her ear for a moment. "I was actually thinking about our honeymoon," she admitted. "Just kinda daydreaming about how it's gonna be between us."

"Anything in particular you were thinking about?" Jamie asked in a seductive tone as she snuck her warm hand under the red sweatshirt and began to tease the soft skin her fingers found.

"Uhm," Ryan said slowly, her lids fluttering a few times as she tried to maintain her focus. "I was just thinking about what a fantastic lover you're gonna be."

"Really?"

"Yeah," she murmured. "Mostly that."

"What else?" the lips situated next to her ear demanded.

"Well, uhm, I was thinking about things I'd love to do with you," Ryan said, her voice rising a bit as Jamie's hand crept beneath her waistband and snaked down her belly.

"Tell me," the smaller woman insisted. "Tell me what you'd like to do to me."

Ryan actually giggled a bit as she considered her answer. Even though she laughed loud and long and often, Jamie had almost never heard the girlish giggle that now tickled her ear. "It's funny," she explained. "I keep trying to picture us in bed together, but I can never get past being stunned into paralysis by your body. In my fantasies, we're both naked and you're lying on your stomach. I keep trying to kick-start my brain to make my body react, but I just sit on my heels, staring at you, and I always find that I'm too overwhelmed to do anything!"

"I think you're gonna be a bit disappointed in that area, Buffy," Jamie said with a chuckle. "My body's really nothing to go nuts over."

"Are you crazy?" Ryan cried, pulling up on one arm so abruptly they almost tumbled out again. "I've seen most of you, and I've got to tell you that your body just knocks me out! Even without seeing your hidden assets, my mouth goes dry sometimes when we work out together. And sometimes, the sight of you in a little black dress makes my knees week. You've got one smokin' hot body, girlfriend, and I can't wait until my mouth gets to taste every bit of that gorgeous skin."

Ryan couldn't see the color of her lover's skin, but she could feel the heat of her cheek where it rested against hers.

"Do you really feel that way?" she asked in a very quiet, almost childlike voice.

Ryan smiled to herself, relieved that her thoughts on the topic were completely sincere. She had complimented many women in the past and had always gone out of her way to praise body parts that really were not very attractive, if she sensed her partner was insecure about a particular area. But she could be completely honest about Jamie's body. She leaned over the edge of the hammock and placed her glass on the deck to free up her left hand. Raising it to grasp Jamie's chin, she turned her head and held it steady so she could look directly into her eyes. "Jamie, I'm going to tell you the complete and unvarnished truth about my feelings."

She noticed that her partner's eyes grew large, and she looked as though she was preparing for a blow to the face.

"I have looked at thousands of women, and I've touched … well, I've touched a lot," she said, overwhelmed when she even tried to guess the number. "And I've been very aroused by different parts of different women. I also have the ability to find something arousing about most women. It might just be her eyes or her legs … heck, I've gotten turned on by a woman's feet! But I've never been with a woman whose total package was so pleasing to me," she said softly as she gazed deeply into her lover's eyes. "I mean that sincerely," she insisted while leaning forward to gently kiss her lips. "I truly love your body, and I can hardly wait to explore all of the uncharted territory." Her waggling eyebrows caused her partner to laugh at her antics.

"You are so good at reassuring me about things," Jamie said with a note of amazement in her voice. "Will you always be able to do that?"

"I'll always try," Ryan vowed. "But I'm not just reassuring you. I meant every word that I said."

"I don't know why I'm so insecure," Jamie muttered. "I've got to admit that I feel beautiful when you look at me with that gleam in your eyes."

"This one?" Ryan asked, willing her eyes to take on their hungry, love-starved look.

"Oh, that's the one," her lover murmured as she leaned forward to kiss the rose-tinted lips.

Jamie began kissing her partner with a slow, gentle, emotion-filled touch. In a very short while they were moaning into each other's mouths, their hands roaming all over each other's bodies. Ryan felt her control slipping dangerously, and she had to force herself to finally pull back. "We've gotta slow down!" she gasped, panting a bit.

Her lover buried her head against her chest and squeezed her so hard she nearly broke a rib. "I don't wanna slow down. I want to touch you everywhere, Ryan. Jesus! This is getting too hard!"

"I know, honey," Ryan soothed. "It's really hard not to go further when we're in a nice quiet place like this." They rocked and held each other gently for a while, both of them throbbing with desire. "You haven't changed your mind, have you?"

"About waiting?"

"Yeah," Ryan said softly. "About waiting."

"It's tempting. So, so tempting. I mean, finals are over and we've got a few days before the ride. There's really no good reason to keep torturing ourselves."

Ryan didn't say a word; she just waited for Jamie to work the issue through.

"But ... there's something about going to Pebble Beach that I've really been looking forward to. It feels like we're waiting for a special occasion, and that means something to me." She turned to Ryan and asked, "What do you think?"

"Depends on which part of me you ask," Ryan said, laughing. "One part keeps trying to talk me into going for it."

"Is that right about here?" Jamie slid her hand down Ryan's belly, and she laughed when her partner grabbed her hand short of her goal.

"If you touch me there ... the question's been answered. And ... I don't think I want that," Ryan said. "I don't want this to be about scratching an itch. It's fun to dream about our honeymoon and if we start having sex now ... it'll lose some of its power."

Jamie sighed. "I ... agree. I'm a little worried that I'm building this up too much in my mind, but that's no reason to ruin it."

"Building it up?"

"Yeah. Like there might be too much pressure. This is really gonna be like a real old-fashioned honeymoon. Has anyone had one of those in this century?"

"Since we've both had sex, I don't think we can really say we're chaste," Ryan chuckled. "But I get what you mean."

"I wanna wait," Jamie said. "That's what we've planned, and that's what I'm looking forward to."

"Fine with me. But we've got to cut back a lot on the kissing and touching. It's getting too hard for both of us. I mean, I'm throbbing, and it doesn't feel so hot to just stay frustrated."

"Okay," Jamie agreed. "Let's try to keep it a little lighter between us. I still need to kiss you a lot, but after tonight, let's sleep apart until the ride and let's try not to get so carried away."

"Are you sure you're okay with that?" Ryan asked, making eye contact.

"Yeah," Jamie replied, nodding her head briefly as she closed her eyes. "Perfectly sure. Unhappy as hell, but perfectly sure," she added with a wry chuckle.

They went below to sleep in the big berth in the bow of the boat. It took a while for Ryan to adjust to the rocking motion, but she found that she enjoyed the sensation once she got accustomed to it. The nicest part for her was to be able to smell the salt water and feel the heaviness of the air in her lungs. It was almost like camping under the stars, but a lot more comfortable.

"I think my seafaring heritage is kicking in," Ryan murmured as they snuggled in the cozy berth. "This feels very, very comfortable for me ... sort of like it's something I've done thousands of times ... it feels a bit like home."

"Are both sides of your family connected to the ocean?" Jamie asked.

"Yeah, pretty much. My mother's father was a fisherman, and near as I can tell, that was the family profession for many, many years. Their little town is very close to the water, so it makes sense that would be the choice."

"What about your father?"

"Well, his people come from Tralee, which is a bit inland, but still close to the water. His great-grandfather was a fisherman, but his grandfather wanted nothing to do with it and that's why he became a fighter. Career options were pretty darned limited for people from the lower classes, but he must have really hated fishing to choose bare-knuckle brawling over it."

"What did your grandfather do?" Jamie asked, realizing that Ryan was in a loquacious mood, and that she had better make good use of it.

"As little as possible," the dark woman said briefly in a tone that let Jamie know the door was closed. "Sleepy?" she asked, making it even clearer.

"Yeah," her partner answered, knowing that pushing her lover was an exercise in futility.

"Come here," Ryan demanded, stretching her arm out for Jamie to curl into. When they got settled, the warm, soft tones of an old fishing song served as a gentle lullaby. Jamie wondered briefly if her lover had learned this song from her grandfather, but no more than five lines into the song she unconsciously lapsed into a very thick Irish accent. *I've never heard that one*, Jamie thought to herself with an internal chuckle. *Guess that answers my question.*

Chapter Fourteen

T hursday morning found them bundling Caitlin into a thick jacket for a walk to the playground. Annie was home, but she appreciated the little break and jumped at the chance to do some grocery shopping alone.

Rather than take the stroller, Ryan strapped the baby in a sturdy backpack for the six-block walk. Jamie entertained their passenger, walking behind her partner and making faces at the baby. The park was rather full despite the cold foggy morning, and Caitlin immediately found some likely looking playmates.

When Ryan was a child, the neighborhood was filled with working-class people and lots of stay-at-home moms, but the Internet boom had brought many young professionals and their families into the Noe Valley. Many of them hired babysitters or nannies—often Spanish speaking immigrants—to watch their children. Ryan mused about this phenomenon while she watched Caitlin make some tentative overtures to another baby about her age. *That's exactly how young Irish women started out in this country in the late 19th century—minding people's children and cleaning their houses. I wonder if Latinos will one day be as welcome here as the Irish are now?* There were ads in the local paper every week for agencies that promised au pairs from the British Isles, but she didn't see many young colleens from the Emerald Isle at the park this morning. A group of about six young Latina women chatted while they sipped cups of coffee and ate sweet rolls.

The kids at the park were all playing nicely, and everything was calm and peaceful in the cold morning. "That coffee looks delicious," Ryan said, looking longingly at the steam rising from the cups.

"You had your coffee, young lady," Jamie said pointedly.

"I can dream, can't I?" Ryan asked as she batted her eyes at her partner.

Her companion stood and held out a hand. "Gimme some money," she said with a mock scowl as she shook her head.

"You don't have to go," Ryan said unconvincingly.

"I don't mind, love. I can get a cocoa and pick up a biscotti for the baby. She's nuts for the almond ones."

"Well, if you're sure you don't mind ..."

"I'd do anything to please you, and you know it. You and the little blonde one both have me wrapped around your little fingers."

"You're just a sucker for the Irish lassies," Ryan chided. "I'm lucky I claimed you before some Kelly or O'Reilly or Shaunessy got her paws on you."

"Not a chance, babe. I'm a sucker for O'Flahertys only." A little kiss on the forehead and she was gone, leaving Ryan to her musings.

Ryan generally tried to hang back and let Caitlin play with the other kids when they went to the park. She knew it was the right thing to do, but she still felt left out when the baby would spend ten or fifteen minutes totally ignoring her. *Guess I'd better get used to that*, she considered. *Someday, she'll be a teenager and have no use whatsoever for her old cousin.*

While she was considering her cousin's adolescence, an older woman appeared with a baby about Caitlin's age. The baby was cranky and out of sorts, and the woman looked like she'd had more than her fill of the child for the day. She dumped her onto the sand right next to Caitlin and plopped down on a bench about ten feet away. Ryan observed both of the newcomers, paying particular attention to the babysitter. The woman seemingly had no connection to the child. She barely looked in her direction and just seemed glad to be a few feet away from the wailing infant. The baby looked like she was having a bad day, and she obviously was not bonded in any way with the woman. Ryan sat down in the sand and tried to comfort the baby. The sitter certainly didn't seem to mind Ryan's attempt, but it was largely unsuccessful also. The baby was crying so loudly that the other kids seemed bothered by it. The other nannies cast a disapproving glance at the woman, but she was not paying enough attention to even notice their stares.

Some of the other kids now started to cry and, one by one, the other nannies buckled their charges into their strollers and took off for quieter playgrounds. Only Ryan, the seemingly deaf babysitter, and the two babies were left at the park after the others departed, and Ryan would have left if she weren't waiting for Jamie. The crying baby, while probably about nine months old, didn't have the motor skills Caitlin had, and she kept falling over, getting sand in her face time and again. Ryan propped her up a few times, then finally held the baby on her lap. Still she cried, actually managing to increase the volume and the incessant sobs and gasps for breath.

After a while, she couldn't take it any more. Caitlin was getting annoyed and looked like she might cry at any minute. Actually, Ryan herself felt weepy, and she decided to ask the babysitter to take over. She carried the baby over to the woman and placed her on the bench next to her. "Maybe she needs a bottle or something," she lamely suggested.

The woman looked up at her with a look of total shock. "Pardon?" she asked in a clipped British accent, unaware that Ryan had even been holding the child.

"Your baby seems to be having a tough time today. Do you have anything that might calm her down?"

"Thank you for your concern," she said briefly, as she turned away from Ryan's gaze.

But the nanny made no move to provide comfort for the infant so Ryan persisted, "Don't you have a bottle for her? She seems hungry."

"Listen to me young lady," she said in a very sharp tone. "I'm trying to put this child on a schedule, and that schedule does not call for feeding at this time. Now if you have no further business with us, I'd prefer that you entertain your own child."

Ryan knew this was truly none of her business, but she had a hard time allowing this woman to treat the poor little girl with such rigid disregard. She began to make another point, but as she did, the baby started to teeter on the bench. Ryan made a grab for her, but the babysitter grabbed her first. She grasped her arm and yanked sharply, making the baby stop her crying for a few seconds. But when she started again, the sound that came out was unlike any Ryan had ever heard from an infant. She was hysterical in a matter of seconds, and Ryan quickly realized that this time she was crying from pain. The babysitter just sat and stared as she wrung her hands in a helpless gesture. So Ryan quickly unzipped the little jacket and immediately realized that the baby's arm had come out of the socket.

The two women seemed to understand the severity of the injury at exactly the same time. The nanny looked at Ryan with very wide, terror-filled eyes, got to her feet and started running, covering ground at a surprising clip for one her age. Ryan's mouth dropped as her eyes bugged, but the screaming quickly brought her back to focus on her task. She now had two babies, one with a dislocated arm, the other crying from lack of attention. "I'll be right there, Caitlin," she soothed as she tried to focus completely on the child in her arms.

"What in the hell?" she heard over her shoulder and almost cried with relief at the sound of her lover's voice.

"Can you get Caitlin?" Ryan cried over the shrieks.

Jamie hustled over and did just that, setting the drinks on the concrete surround of the sand pit. "What in the hell is going on?" she repeated, shouting to make herself heard.

"Long story," Ryan said in a more normal tone as Jamie carried Caitlin around to face Ryan. "Her arm is out of the socket." Ryan was bent over, carefully examining the little arm, seemingly determined to take some action on her own.

"What are you going to do?" Jamie asked, astounded that her partner would try such a thing.

"I'm gonna try to put it back into place," she muttered, not very happy to be interrupted.

"You can't do that!"

Ryan gave her one of her best no-nonsense looks and declared, "Of course I can. This is a pretty common injury for babies. I've read about it."

"Well I've read about heart transplants! I wouldn't try to do one!" Jamie had her cell phone out and was dialing a number which Ryan guessed was 9-1-1.

Ignoring her partner, Ryan placed her left hand on the baby's tiny chest, holding her firmly against the back of the bench. With her right, she grasped the little arm and slowly rotated it back and across the child's chest. She could feel a small pop as the bone slid back into place. The child's hysterical crying ceased immediately, though she still cried at a more moderate pace.

The dark head lifted, and dancing blue eyes blinked up at Jamie. "I think I did it."

Jamie let out the breath she didn't know she had been holding and flopped down next to her partner, snapping her cell phone shut as she did. "Do you mind filling me in here?" she asked weakly. "Who is she, and why do you have her?"

"Don't know who she is, and I have her because her sitter yanked her arm out of the socket, got scared and ran!" Ryan said, just now grasping the entirety of the events.

"She ran?"

"Yep. Like a sprinter," she muttered, turning her attention once again to the slightly quieter baby. "Wonder if she'd like half a biscotti."

"I bought more than one, you know," her partner said. "I knew there was a chance you'd steal Caitlin's."

"Ha, Ha," Ryan muttered. She offered each baby a cookie and within minutes they were both contentedly gnawing away. "Now what?" she asked. "I hate to take her to the police station, but we have to report this."

"Let's go to Annie's and see what she thinks."

They did just that, and luckily Annie was home from shopping. "I think we should call the Department of Children and Family Services," she advised. "The police will get them involved anyway, and if we go direct she might not have to spend time in the station house. Let me call someone at the hospital and see if we have any good contacts."

She made a few phone calls and finally got hold of a very nice social worker. When Annie identified herself, the woman said they could keep the baby while the paperwork was being written up. Ryan got on the phone and made a complete report, mentioning every detail she could remember. The social worker promised to call back after she had notified the local police station, since that was likely where the parents would begin their search.

When Ryan hung up, Annie said, "I've seen this baby at the park before. I think she lives really close." As she was talking, she sat down at the small desk they had wedged into the corner of the kitchen. She turned on her computer and printer and quickly drew up a notice stating that they had found a brown-haired, brown-eyed baby girl, about nine months old, at Douglas Playground. She listed the number of the police station and her contact at DCFS, and after playing around with the font size, she printed off thirty copies and sent Jamie to ring every doorbell on the two main streets near the park.

An hour later, the messenger returned. "I'm pretty sure she lives on Diamond, right by the park. A neighbor said there's a baby that fits that description there, and she thinks the mother went back to work a week or so ago. I handed the flyers out to everyone who was home and taped them to the doors of the houses where I didn't get an answer."

"Good girl," Ryan praised her as she bent to kiss her on the head. The babies were both in Caitlin's playpen, mostly ignoring each other—as babies that age tend to do. The visitor had stopped crying, however, and Ryan was happy about that.

By the time Ryan had to get ready for work, both babies were down for a nap. Jamie decided to stay and help Annie with them, and they promised to call Ryan with any news.

"If the parents don't want her we, could always keep her," she reminded Jamie as she batted her big blue eyes at her.

"First comes love, then comes marriage," Jamie teased in a singsong voice. "Then comes a long period of nothing but hot sex, *then* comes Ryan with a baby carriage," she added, spicing up the nursery rhyme a little bit.

"Spoilsport," Ryan mumbled as she walked down the street to pick up her motorcycle.

When Ryan returned from work, the baby's parents had just arrived to claim her after a trip to the police station to file charges against their erstwhile nanny. The mother, Michelle, told Jamie and Annie that she had just gone back to work after seven months of maternity leave. She claimed they had thoroughly checked the references of the nanny, but it was obvious that she was too distraught to discuss the matter at much length.

The baby, Taylor, was overjoyed at her mother's return, but everyone in the room knew the joy was short lived. Robert, the father, grasped the tiny child in a tight embrace and spoke softly to her while the women briefly discussed the immediate future. "What will you do until you find another nanny?" Annie asked.

Michelle lifted her hands and covered her face as she shook her head roughly a few times. A deep sigh preceded her answer. "I ... I guess I'll have to stay home."

Robert gave her an incredulous look as he said, "Honey, you have your first trial starting tomorrow. You can't miss that."

She looked at him with a face full of angst. "What else can we do? You have to go to L.A. for that meeting—they'll have your hide if you skip that."

"No family in the neighborhood?" Annie asked.

"None in the state," Robert informed her as he bounced the baby in his arms. "I work for Bank of America. We were transferred here from North Carolina right after Michelle graduated from the University of North Carolina Law School. She got a job with Lexington, Park and Greene, and things were going great, but we kind of unexpectedly got pregnant and they weren't very happy about it. She wants to be a litigator, and they put her on this important case with some senior attorneys. All she has to do is make the appearances just to get some experience, but if she isn't reliable, I'm afraid they'll pull her off."

"Let me watch her tomorrow," Annie volunteered. "I don't go to work until four in the afternoon."

"We couldn't do that!" Michelle cried, but it was obvious she wished that they could, judging from the hope in her eyes.

"Nonsense," Annie stated in her most nurse-like voice. "Two aren't much worse than one at this age and, since neither can walk, it won't be bad at all."

"We've got nothing planned tomorrow," Jamie piped up. "We'd love to help."

"Oh, I don't know," Michelle wavered.

"Look," Annie said. "We don't mind, it's no trouble, and you need the help. We're all neighbors here and we need to watch out for each other. Give it up, Michelle."

The small, thin, overly stressed woman gratefully agreed. "You're quite persuasive," she laughed. "Maybe you should be the lawyer."

"No, I'm an anesthetist at San Francisco General. I only convince people to go to sleep."

Martin had held dinner for the girls after Jamie called to tell him of their exciting day. When they arrived, he sat at the table with them as they recounted all of the events.

"I'm proud of the lot of you," he beamed with pride. "It's a rare thing to get involved in other people's troubles, and I'm very happy you three understand what it means to be neighbors."

"I feel so bad for little Taylor," Jamie said. "It's hard enough to have your mommy leave you all day long. But to hear Ryan tell it, that babysitter should be found and arrested!"

"Yeah, it wasn't so bad that she yanked on her arm like that, but her indifference was just astonishing! The dog walkers at the park are much more concerned about the pets they watch than she was. To get up and run after the baby was hurt was truly criminal. My guess is she's in the country illegally, and that's why she ran. She was probably afraid the authorities would get involved."

"Did the parents take the baby to the doctor?" Martin asked.

"Not yet. She really seemed fine, and her arm didn't seem to bother her at all. Annie said she'd take her with her to the hospital tomorrow and have one of the bone doctors look at it if she acted like it bothered her."

"Annie says it's a common thing for some kids. Their ligaments are very stretchy, and a sharp tug can easily yank the arm from the socket," Jamie said. "Ryan, of course, knew this," she added, sticking her tongue out at her partner.

"I wouldn't have done it if I didn't know it'd take an hour to get her to the hospital," Ryan said. "I figured it was worth the risk to save her an hour of terrible pain."

"Don't forget to tell your father that Annie said you did a perfect job when you popped it back in," Jamie said.

"She should know how!" Martin laughed. "She's dislocated her right arm twice and her left once. She's such a tough little thing that she watched the doctor when he put it back in every time!"

Sunday morning found Ryan standing in front of her closet, hands on hips, scowl firmly etched on her face. She was grumbling under her breath, but the tone was so low that Jamie had no idea of the content of her quiet diatribe. "Need some help?" she finally offered.

"Love some," Ryan said with a disgusted shrug, "but the department stores aren't open yet."

Jamie got up from her perch on the bed and went to stand behind her partner. "You have some perfectly nice things in there," she reminded her. Turning Ryan around, she captured her chin and tilted it until they were gazing into each other's eyes. "Maybe you're just nervous."

"A little," Ryan muttered softly as she rolled her eyes. "It's worse than meeting the in-laws for the first time."

"Why, honey? I'm certain my grandfather will love you!"

"Because you love *him* so much," Ryan explained. "I know his opinion means more to you than your parents' does, so it's even more important that he like me." She looked so fragile and unsure of herself that Jamie wanted to wrap her up in her arms and cradle her until she was her normal confident self. But she also knew that wasn't what Ryan needed at the moment. So she helped in the way she thought would be most effective.

"Let me help you pick out an outfit, okay?"

"Okay, but I'd really rather not wear that stupid skirt if I don't have to," she insisted with her lower lip sticking out like a five-year-old's.

"All right, love, no skirt," Jamie soothed as she started assessing the modest wardrobe. "You go brush your teeth, and I'll be ready for you when you're done." As Ryan compliantly walked away, Jamie re-thought her earlier assessment. It wasn't that Ryan didn't have a lot of clothes—she actually had more clothes than Jamie did. But ninety-five percent of them were shorts, T-shirts, Lycra leggings, and sweats—none of which were appropriate for mass at a conservative Episcopal church. Plus, since Jamie was wearing a dress, she knew Ryan would want to look like she was going to the same event. She quickly pulled out several perfectly acceptable selections and waited for Ryan to return.

"Hmm," her slightly grumpy partner said when she viewed her choices. "You'll look lots better than me."

"Not at all, babe. I want you to look like yourself. Your own personality and your style are part of what makes you unique. I want my grandfather to meet the real you, and these outfits reflect that."

"Oh, all right," Ryan agreed. "Pick one out. I really don't care."

Jamie had on a bright blue and beige cotton print dress that looked very summery and casual. So she chose khaki pants, a white knit shell and a light blue chambray shirt for her partner. Ryan raised an eyebrow, but started to drop her sweats and put on the outfit. Jamie studied the pictures on the bookshelves to distract herself, and a few moments later Ryan asked, "Okay?"

Turning around, Jamie gave her a very big smile and said, "Almost perfect." She went to the closet and added a black leather belt and a pair of shiny black loafers, which Ryan dutifully slipped on. Then, in one final touch, she rolled Ryan's sleeves up three turns, leaving them at mid-forearm.

"Really?" Ryan asked, doubtful that the casual look was appropriate.

"You always roll your sleeves up," she reminded her, aware of the fact that few blouses in Ryan's size had sleeves long enough for her arms.

"I know but ..." she muttered as she pursed her lips.

"But nothing. You don't have to put on a show for my grandfather. You'll feel more comfortable if you're dressed in a way that makes you feel like you."

"Aw, Jamie ..." she groused.

"Okay," she said quickly. "I'll tell you the real reason." She bent over and kissed each exposed forearm and traced the protuberant muscles with her index finger. "Your arms make me drool." As she tossed her arms around Ryan's neck, she caught the barest hint of a grin start to peek out of her grumpy face.

"Drool, huh?" she murmured into her nearby ear.

"Definitely drool," Jamie pronounced, thoroughly satisfied with another job well done. *Now I have three weapons to fight bad moods: talk about food, sex or her muscles.* A smile curled up the corners of her own mouth as she considered, *Why shouldn't that work with her? It works for me!*

The service on this last weekend of May was notable for two reasons. It was not only the first time Ryan would meet Rev. Evans; it was also the beginning of the priest's summer vacation.

Charles Evans spent every summer on some type of sabbatical, and this year was no exception. Instead of journeying to another country this year, he was taking an intensive course in Spanish at Cal. He was looking forward to the time away from tending to the needs of his congregation and equally happy to be able to sleep in his own bed while expanding his mind.

When the young women arrived at the small, but lavishly decorated church, they sat close to the aisle, but positioned themselves further back than the bulk of the other congregants. Jamie wanted to be able to offer commentary to her partner, and she wanted to be careful not to annoy any of the others.

When the service began, Ryan was able to pick out Rev. Evans immediately. It helped that he was the only man among the three priests, and his position at the rear of the procession certainly didn't hurt, but even in a crowd of similarly attired men she thought she would have been able to spot him. There was just something so 'Jamie-ish' about the man, even though Ryan couldn't quite put her finger on the resemblance as the procession moved down the center aisle. When the minister reached their pew he broke ranks and threw an arm around his only granddaughter and gave her a kiss on the cheek as well as a generous hug. Looking up at Ryan, he smiled and added a wink for her benefit as he released Jamie and scurried to catch up with the rest of his staff. "The apple doesn't fall far from the tree," Ryan whispered as she leaned over her partner. "He's as cute as you are!"

"I wish I were half as cute as he is," Jamie smiled, enormously pleased by the comparison.

Forty-five minutes later, they were walking down a stone path to the small house on the property that his position afforded him. "So, Ryan, what did you think?" he asked with a twinkle in his dancing green eyes.

"It was very nice, Rev. Evans," she said. "Very much like what I'm used to, but a little more formal in some areas like the music. Parts of the service were much more progressive than my church."

"Like what?" Jamie asked.

"Oh, like women priests, for one tiny thing," Ryan said with a smirk. "More subtle things too, like the entire congregation being welcomed to receive the Eucharist. That was really nice."

"They don't do that at Catholic church?" she asked, shocked by the news.

"Nope. Catholics only. It seems that Jesus was very specific in his instructions," she said, tongue in cheek. "He said 'Do this in remembrance of me if you're a Catholic. If not, convert before you're damned to hell.' Not many people know the whole story," she added with a wink.

Rev. Evans tossed his head back and laughed at that comment, causing Jamie to join him. "Isn't she cute?" Jamie asked as she grasped Ryan's arm and pulled her close for a hug.

"You both are," he replied with a fond smile at both young women.

Over a simple, but delicious lunch served by his housekeeper, Rev. Evans turned to Ryan and asked with mock seriousness, "So, Ryan, what are your intentions toward my granddaughter?"

"Poppa!" Jamie cried, amazed that he would even tease Ryan that way.

"It's okay, Jamie," Ryan said easily. "I know exactly what my intentions are, and I think your grandfather should know too." Jamie gave her a wide-eyed stare as she thought about Ryan's often felt, but not yet expressed intentions. Her partner merely reached across the table and lightly grasped her hand, gazing into her eyes with a somber look.

"My intention is to love, honor and cherish her for the rest of my life," Ryan said slowly, smiling at Jamie as she spoke. "I want to build a life with her, and have children with her, and grow old with her. I'll consider my life well lived if I can die in her arms," she concluded, her smile dimming as she let the words sink in.

"You are so incredibly sweet," Jamie murmured, her attention fully engaged.

Rev. Evans gazed at the two young lovers and thought to himself, *There's the spark that was always missing with Jack! This is exactly how a young couple should behave.* As the intense gaze continued, he added with an internal chuckle, *But that's also why I feel like excess baggage at the moment.*

The babysitting worked out so well that they offered to watch Taylor for the entire next week. Michelle set about interviewing every domestic agency in the city, but Annie stepped in and found an ideal situation for the baby. A lesbian couple at work had a baby just a little older than Taylor. The moms were both nurses, and they worked split shifts so that one was always at home. They were trying to move to a bigger apartment and some extra cash was badly needed. Annie vouched for both of them and assured Michelle that she couldn't do much better than to have a pediatric nurse and an emergency room specialist caring for her child.

Michelle and Robert were very excited about having Taylor spend the day with a slightly older child, and they quickly agreed to the arrangement.

The Friday before the ride was spent with two babies who seemed to enjoy each other's company quite a bit. They paid attention to each other in spurts, their temperaments were similar and they seemed to like to sleep at the same time. In a way it was easier to watch two of them, since they did entertain each other a little bit.

Tommy was at home and, even though he loved his child deeply, he was always happy to have someone take her for a day. Since they had Taylor's jogger stroller, they each put a baby in a stroller and took off for a long run/walk. Helping Annie and Tommy with the kids had actually proved fortuitous for Ryan and Jamie. They didn't want to ride their bikes this week, but running up and down the hills with their young charges gave them a cardiovascular workout that easily topped a long bike ride. They both felt like they had not only kept up their fitness level, but they had actually increased it a bit while saving their butts completely.

After almost two hours playing at the playground in the Castro, both babies were ready for their naps. Rather than take them home, though, they settled them into the joggers and rocked them while they rested against a big tree. Once the babies were quiet, Ryan ran over to Hot 'n Hunky for some nice sloppy cheeseburgers and malts. They decided to splurge on calories since they would expend so many in the next week, but Jamie had to laugh when she saw her lover carrying two huge bags of food with her. "What did you buy?" she gasped as Ryan started to pull the food from the bags.

"A single for you, a double for me, chili fries, and malts," she said in a matter-of-fact tone.

"How many malts are in that bag?"

"Uhm … three?"

"You're gonna have two malts?" she gasped.

"Well … I kinda thought I'd get two and a half," she admitted with a grin. "You never finish yours."

"You have the metabolism of a hummingbird!" Jamie laughed as her lover sat down to demolish the meal.

"Yep and in ten days I'm gonna have my beak in your nectar for hours at a time!"

"Gulp!" the smaller woman said as she audibly mimicked the word.

Chapter Fifteen

Saturday at seven in the morning found Jamie and Ryan packing up their bikes in Conor's truck for the trip to Fort Mason. They had checked and double-checked that they had all of the necessary papers and forms, and when they were confident all was in order, they took off.

Jamie was once again thankful that Ryan had done the ride so many times. She knew all of the shortcuts and all of the little tricks that would make the experience more enjoyable. Today, for instance, she parked a good half-mile away from the Pavilion at Fort Mason. Since they had their bikes, it was just a five-minute ride to their destination, with none of the attendant traffic.

The Pavilion was fully staffed with volunteers, but the riders were just starting to trickle in. Day Zero was the last day to complete all the required paperwork, attend a safety class, and drop off bikes. Ryan was pleased to learn the first safety meeting would be held at eight in the morning. They walked their bikes to the designated area and waited for the class to begin.

This experience was pro forma for Ryan, who had attended five of them, but Jamie paid such rapt attention that Ryan actually had to laugh at her. The main theme of the meeting was the inherent danger of the ride. They would be using heavily traveled highways and roads that would remain open to vehicular traffic. The riders received tips on how to safely cross the narrow bridges—some barely wide enough to accommodate two trucks—that were on their route.

After the meeting, they zoomed back to the Pavilion to pick up their packets, and found the hall pass that enabled them to go directly to registration. Once there, they picked up their registration materials and went directly to the tent assignment station. The line was still quite short, and they were processed in a few minutes. Next they took their bikes over to the parking area. They affixed their numbers to the frames and handed them over to the very friendly volunteers.

Next stop was the merchandise area. Jamie bought a long sleeved T-shirt in each of the colors available. "I want to sleep in these all year to remind me of how we got to know each other," she said when Ryan expressed surprise at her purchases. Ryan had to buy a tiny little T-shirt in bright yellow for Caitlin, but that was her only purchase.

As they started to walk away from the merchandise area, Ryan spotted her partner trying to stuff another couple of items in her backpack. "What'cha got there?" she asked, knowing Jamie's tendencies all too well.

"Never you mind, sweet cheeks," she replied airily.

It was only ten, and they were finished. They walked around for a while just checking out all the people, but after a bit Ryan remarked, "Do you know what I would really love to do today?"

Jamie pursed her lips in thought. She looked up at the sky as if seeking the answer and finally replied, "Whatever it is, I bet it involves another blonde."

"You already know me too well," Ryan replied. "You're my favorite blonde, but Caitlin is a close second."

"Here's my phone, call and see if her busy schedule will permit a visit."

Their young playmate was indeed available. Tommy was at home alone with her, and he willingly relinquished possession of his daughter. They arrived at around eleven o'clock and whisked the giggling baby away moments later.

When they returned to the house, they decided to just stay close to home. They needed to pack and take care of any last-minute details and, even though Caitlin couldn't help, she was certainly entertaining. When they got into the house, Conor immediately snatched the baby away, tossing her in the air and carrying her all over the house as he sang one of her favorite songs. The girls took the opportunity to head downstairs and start to get organized.

Ryan had stressed the importance of taking as little as possible with them. Although their belongings would be carried for them, they still had to fetch them from the trucks each night and return them in the morning. Ryan warned that sometimes the truck was a very long ways away. They decided to take four day's worth of biking gear. They each brought one pair of padded ankle length pants. Jamie brought three pairs of knee-length padded shorts and four quick-drying jerseys, one long-sleeved and three short. Ryan wore padded cotton under shorts, so she brought three pairs of those and just two pairs of unlined bike shorts. She also carried four jerseys, one long-sleeved, two short and her new sleeveless jersey. Next came their thin sleeveless gore-tex vests and lightweight nylon shells. They each added a few pairs of underwear and four sports bras. They had purchased some new quick-drying thin socks, and these were added to the pile. Ryan had suggested Jamie bring a swimsuit for the beach in Los Angeles, which she dutifully did.

They also needed some regular clothes for the time spent hanging around off the bikes. The weather was very unpredictable, so they each brought a fleece jacket and a pair of heavy sweats. Ryan packed two pairs of her baggy nylon shorts and a couple of tank tops. She added two T-shirts and a pair of Teva sandals, and she was set. Jamie had a harder time deciding, but she finally settled on a couple of pairs of shorts and four T-shirts. She agreed the Teva sandals were a good choice, so she added hers to the pile. She packed an additional extra-large T-shirt to sleep in. She asked Ryan suspiciously, "What do you have to sleep in?"

"This is my last week wearing my underwear to bed," she intoned solemnly. "After this week, it's all nude all the time."

They decided to pack most things in heavy-duty trash bags first to insure that they wouldn't get wet. "I don't know how it happens, but the first two years, half of my clothes were wet when I put them on," Ryan said. "Nothing feels worse than clammy nylon on a cold morning."

Ryan had a checklist from previous years that she amended as needed. They carefully ticked off additional items one by one until she was satisfied they would have everything they required. Finally they got out their gear bags and began to load them up. Jamie had a ton of experience in packing for long trips, and she even gave Ryan a few pointers. They were finished packing by the time Conor brought the sleeping baby downstairs. "Do you guys want some lunch? I was gonna go down to the Italian deli to get a combo, how about you?"

"I'm in!" Ryan replied immediately.

"What's a combo?" Jamie asked.

Ryan slid her arms around her friend as she said to Conor, "She's been all around the world, but the poor little thing has never had a combo." They both shook their heads sadly.

"We'll remedy that oversight right now," Conor said as he handed her the baby. "I'll be back in half an hour."

With Ryan's help, Jamie sat back against the headboard with Caitlin nestled into her chest. Ryan lay down on her side, facing Jamie. She patted the soft little terry cloth covered back as she slowly said, "Lucky, lucky baby," while casting a sly smile up at Jamie.

"You're not treated so badly either, Ryan," she chided as she pushed her dark head down onto her lap. She stroked the raven locks as Ryan closed her eyes and let the contentment seep into her. Seconds later Ryan joined her cousin in sleep.

Conor stopped abruptly in the doorway as he caught sight of the happy little group. "Should I come back later?" he asked in a whisper. Jamie just smiled and shook her head. "The big one will be up in a second, and the little one won't hear a thing." As predicted, Ryan stirred as soon as she heard voices. She gazed up at Jamie with a look of pure love on her face, sat up and gave her a very tender, heart-felt kiss. Jamie looked surprised as she said quietly, "Conor's here."

Ryan turned around and caught sight of her somewhat embarrassed brother. "Get used to it, Conor, you're gonna see a lot of smooching around here from now on."

Conor had brought plates, knives, napkins and sodas as well as the promised sandwiches. Ryan removed the wrappings from both of their combos as Jamie supervised. "You're dripping on your desk," she observed.

"It's worth it," Ryan replied. As she brought the huge tomato sauce-covered sandwich up to Jamie's mouth, she instructed, "Bite." Jamie did and seconds later a pleasure-suffused smile covered her face. "Meatball and sausage together?" she asked with her mouth still half full.

"Don't forget the mozzarella," Ryan chided her as she took a big bite herself. They alternated bites of the same sandwich until Ryan popped the last bite into her partner's mouth. She then started on the second sandwich, very pleased when Jamie declined any more.

"I finally figured it out," Conor said with satisfaction as he watched Ryan eat.

"What's that?" Jamie asked.

"I figured out why Ryan's a lesbian."

"This I gotta hear," Ryan laughed.

"It's a clever ploy to get more than half of any meal. If you were with a guy, he'd want some of your food, just like you do with Jamie."

"Okay, wise guy. That explains me, but why is Jamie gay?"

He looked perplexed, as he answered. "That one I'll never figure out," he said. "But she clearly is, because if she were straight she could have had me," he laughed as he successfully ducked a quick backhand from his sister.

Caitlin woke up shortly after lunch was finished. She was all hot and sweaty from her nap, and she cried and fussed as they quickly changed her diaper. Conor got up to fetch a bottle and warm it, as Jamie tried to calm her down. She stood up and bounced her on her hip, talking soothingly into her little pink ear. Ryan just watched with pleasure as Caitlin slowly quieted and began to play with Jamie's face. She was trying to insert her fist into Jamie's mouth when Conor returned. He gently removed her from Jamie's grasp and laid her back in his strong arm with her bottle. Caitlin crossed her little feet and rested her head against Conor's chest and sucked lustily.

"You do have a way with women," Jamie observed as Caitlin gazed up at him adoringly.

Around five o'clock Ryan called Tommy to see when he wanted the baby back. "Oh, don't bother. Annie can stop by on her way home from work. She can be there by six. Is that okay?"

Ryan agreed, and she and Jamie took her out for a little walk. Rather, Jamie had a little walk. Ryan strapped Caitlin into her three-wheeled jogger stroller and ran up and down the hills of the Noe Valley with maniacal glee. As they passed her again and again, Jamie heard the wild giggles of the baby and the equally wild laughter of her partner. After a half-hour, Ryan was more winded than Jamie had ever seen her. She was forced to bend over at the waist for a long while, trying to suck air into her lungs. Jamie put a hand on her back and grasped the stroller with her other hand. Ryan was covered in sweat, and the heat radiated off her in waves. Caitlin was ready for more as she bounced in her seat trying to scoot the stroller forward.

Ryan finally stood up and raised her hands in surrender. "That's it, Caitlin. The express train is through for the day. We're taking the local from now on." She took the stroller handle from Jamie and started to walk down the hill in a more sedate fashion. But Caitlin would have none of it. She continued to thrust herself forward, craving speed. Her little grunts turned to whines, as she demanded that her needs be recognized. Ryan finally rolled her eyes and took off again. "You're turning her into a thrill seeker, just like you!" Jamie warned as they flew by once again.

After another fifteen minutes of frantic activity, they arrived back at the house. Ryan was surprised to see her Aunt Maeve's car as well as Tommy's. Jamie carried the baby as they entered the house, where they were surprised to see Maeve, Tommy, Annie and Kevin. "Surprise!" they all yelled. Conor, Brendan and Martin all came out of the kitchen to join in the greeting.

Jamie looked at Ryan in puzzlement. Martin finally spoke up, "It's a send-off party for you two. We wanted to make sure you had a good meal before you start." After he got a better look at Ryan he asked in alarm, "What have you been doing, Siobhán?"

She did look a sight. Her face was a deep pink, her bangs were plastered against her forehead and her marine blue T-shirt was drenched with sweat. All eyes turned to Jamie, who looked like she had just been sitting in a chair. Ryan finally piped up, "Caitlin and I were doing wind sprints on the hills. She's obviously in better shape than I am, because she's as cool as a cucumber," she teased as she pinched her little pink cheek.

"You go take a shower, young lady, or you'll catch your death," he ordered.

Ryan nodded and went downstairs. Jamie entertained questions about their training and her nerves until Ryan returned, looking much refreshed. She wore a navy blue polo and a pair of khakis along with a well-worn pair of penny loafers. As soon as she entered the room she snatched the baby from Jamie and put her on her shoulders for a quick little horsy ride.

"You know, Ryan, you get her used to a level of activity none of the rest of us can duplicate," Annie chided her.

"That's all part of my evil plan. She needs to come to me for her adrenaline rush," she said as she took off even faster around the house spurred on by Caitlin's giggles.

"Has she always been like that?" Jamie asked Martin.

"From the day of her birth," he admitted. "We were lulled into complacency by Brendan here. He was a perfectly lovely little baby, content to be cuddled and carried and cooed to. Then Conor came along, and we thought we would lose our minds," he said as he shook his head. "He was in constant motion, every minute. Rory made us think that Conor was just a fluke. He was so much like Brendan, so calm and peaceful." He smiled at the memory. "Then we finally got our little girl. I assumed she would sit on the front porch in a little white dress playing with her dolls," he sighed heavily. "But I swear, she was twice as bad as Conor ever was. She never showed fear of anything in her life, Jamie. I used to take her to the station when she was just Caitlin's age. All the guys would take turns sliding down the pole with her just laughing her head off. They'd all be tired, and she'd be begging for more."

They all shared a few more memories of the young Ryan, causing Jamie to smile broadly at her from across the room. Ryan came and stood next to her, putting an arm around her shoulders. Jamie leaned over and quietly whispered, "We're going to adopt. I can't take the risk that your energy level could be genetic."

Ryan just laughed as she gave her a little squeeze.

Conor had picked up some delicious homemade pasta sauce at the deli that afternoon as well as some fabulous crusty Italian bread. Dinner was pasta with meat sauce, a big green salad and the bread. As usual, Ryan cleaned Jamie's plate after she was finished with her own. "Do you do that in restaurants?" Conor asked out of curiosity.

"Yep," Ryan replied.

"Not always," Jamie corrected. "When we had lunch with my grandfather not only did she not eat off of my plate, she also carried on a lucid conversation. And she didn't once close her eyes and moan like she usually does when she eats something really tasty."

That brought a laugh from everyone, as Martin said, "I'm glad you can put on manners when you're out in public, darlin'."

"Thanks, I think," she replied scowling.

Before all of the guests left, Jamie saw Ryan huddled in the corner with her aunt. She had a serious expression on her face, and she was nodding intently. After a minute, Maeve patted her on the cheek and leaned up to kiss her. Ryan reminded them all of the spot where they would meet, and everyone promised to be at The Fort the next day to see them off.

It was almost nine by the time everyone was gone and the kitchen was properly cleaned. Jamie had taken on Rory's tasks in his absence, and she found that within a day or two her little jobs seemed like they had been hers for years. As they made their way downstairs, Jamie heard her cell phone ringing from its resting place in her purse. She extracted it and hit the talk button on the fourth ring. "Hello," she said breathlessly.

"Hi, Jamie," responded the deep voice on the other end.

"Jack! How are you?"

"I'm fine. Is this a good time to talk?"

"Uhm … sure. What do you want to talk about?" She made eye contact with Ryan, who went back upstairs to give her some privacy.

"Are you at home? I could call you on that line if you'd rather."

"No, I'm not at home. Let me call you right back," she said. He quickly agreed.

She took several deep breaths to settle herself and then sat down on the bed to dial the still-memorized number. He picked up on the first ring. "Are you at Ryan's?"

"Yes, I am," she replied, no longer concerned with his reaction.

"Are you living with her?" he asked quietly.

"Just this week, to get ready for the ride. I couldn't stand to be around Cassie another minute, so I came over here," she said, knowing that wasn't his real question.

"Yeah, Cassie called me a few weeks ago," he admitted. "Ever since then I've been wanting to call you, but I've been kind of afraid to."

"What did she say?" Jamie asked, knowing the answer.

"The details aren't important," he said graciously. "But the bottom line was that you were with Ryan now." After a quiet pause he asked, "Is that true?"

After a moment's hesitation she said, "I'm happy to talk to you about my life, but I hope you'll keep anything I tell you in confidence."

There was total silence for a long minute, then he said sadly, "I'm sorry you think you have to ask that. I thought you knew me better than that."

She winced as she acknowledged her paranoia. "I'm sorry, Jack. I didn't mean to hurt your feelings. It's just that I'm going through kind of a difficult time, and people who I thought were friends have betrayed me. But you're right; I never should have assumed that you'd hurt me."

"I never would, Jamie," he said quietly.

"I'm sorry. Really. I'd give anything to have avoided hurting you. I swear that as soon as I started to get a handle on my feelings, I was honest with you." She paused to gather her courage. "The answer to your question is that I am with Ryan now. And I hope I always will be."

"Are you happy with your choice?" he asked after a short, uncomfortable silence.

"You know ... I feel like I'm beginning to be completely comfortable with myself for the first time in my life," she replied. "I'm just so sorry that I didn't know myself better before I met you. It would have saved us both a lot of pain."

His voice trembled as he asked, "Did you know when we were together?"

"I didn't have a clue in my conscious mind. I must have had some pretty big subconscious clues. I mean, I was drawn to take that class, even though I told myself it was because of the time it was offered." After a beat she added, "That's another thing I'm sorry about. You knew something was going on, but I refused to acknowledge it. I wish ... I wish I had. For both of us, but especially you."

"I had a cold terror in my gut the night Cassie told me about that class. I think I had some suspicions even before that happened, but I was afraid to admit them to myself."

"Why do you think you were suspicious?" Jamie asked, amazed that he was admitting his own doubts.

"Well, I'm certainly not the world's greatest lover," he said with a self-effacing laugh, "but you just didn't respond to me in the way that I was used to. I kept telling myself you were just inexperienced, but you weren't … passionate with me. That never made sense, because you were so passionate in everything else you did."

"Yeah, that about sums it up," she admitted. "I loved you, Jack, but I couldn't summon passion for you, and that's not because of you. I'm just not oriented that way."

There was another short silence then he added, "I hope you find your passion with Ryan. I really do."

She fought back the tears as she replied, "I think that's the nicest, most generous thing anyone has ever said to me. Thank you for that. You don't know how much that means to me."

"I wish it could have been me, Jamie. No matter who you're with, I want you to be happy. I truly mean that."

"If I were going to be with a man, it would still be you, Jack. I hope you know how much I did love you. But I couldn't commit my life to you and not feel the physical connection that people in love need to have."

"Do you have that with Ryan?" he asked tentatively, needing to know the answer even though he feared it.

She considered telling him the question was too personal, but she felt he deserved the truth. "I do. I really do. This is right for me, even though it's taking a lot of time adjusting to it. I've been unconsciously fighting this for a long time. Now I have to be who I am … no matter what."

"It's funny," he said reflectively. "After I talked to Cassie, I spent a couple of days letting her get to me. I don't want to repeat what she said, but she's under the impression that Ryan has some kind of unnatural hold over you." As Jamie tried to interrupt, he continued, "But after a few days, I let reality in and thought about who you were. Jamie, you couldn't be talked into ordering a dinner that you didn't want. You're nobody's fool, and I don't believe that even someone as appealing as Ryan could get you to do one thing you didn't want to do."

"Thanks for acknowledging who I really am. Not only didn't Ryan push me, I really had to convince her that this was right for me."

"You had to convince her?" he asked, with Jamie detecting a bit of surprise.

"Yeah, I did. There's one other thing I need you to know. No one was more supportive of your and my relationship than Ryan was. She only cared that I was happy, and she spent the better part of the year trying to get me to see that all of the problems we had were my fault too. I swear she never undermined you, Jack. She's not that kind of person."

"Thanks," he said. "She certainly didn't make a friend of Cassie, but that doesn't reflect badly on her." He laughed a little. "I don't know why Cassie thinks she's my inside source, but I'm sick of her!"

"I think she'd like to take my place," Jamie said.

"As what?" Jack laughed at his small joke. "I prefer to be with kind, considerate women. Cassie's not in that group. You are."

"Thanks," Jamie said, her voice catching. "I'm really happy now. I just hope you find someone who loves you as much and supports you as much as Ryan loves me."

"I do too, Jamie. And I hope I can find someone that I love as much as I did you."

"I hope so too, Jack. More than anything," she said fervently.

"I'll let you go now. The reason I called tonight was to wish you the best of luck on your ride. I just want you to know I'll be thinking of you every day and sending you good thoughts."

Jamie lost her battle with her emotions this time. "Thank you, Jack. That means a lot to me," she said through her tears. "Thanks so much for calling."

"Anytime, Jamie. You tell Ryan to take good care of you next week."

"I will, Jack. Bye," she said as she hung up.

At nine-thirty, Ryan poked her head into her room and saw Jamie lying on the bed, staring up at the ceiling. She approached her gently and sat on the edge of the bed. "Are you okay?" she asked as she lightly grasped her hand.

"Yeah, I'm fine. I'll tell you about it tomorrow. Now, I just want to go to sleep," she said with a tired little sigh.

"Do you want me to go upstairs, and you can just stay here?"

"Okay, if you really don't mind," she replied sleepily. "I want to smell you on the sheets all night long," she said as she squeezed a pillow and was rewarded with the familiar scent.

"Sleep tight," Ryan said as she kissed her tenderly and rubbed her back. "I'll wake you up at four-thirty, okay?"

"Is it just me, or does that seem early?" she asked as she sat up and started to strip out of her clothes.

"It is a little early, so you go to sleep quickly," Ryan ordered as she turned her head while Jamie slipped into a T-shirt.

"Would you lie down with me and hold me for a few minutes?" Jamie asked. "You always calm me down so fast."

"Of course I will," Ryan said as she climbed into bed and wrapped her in her arms. In less than five minutes, Jamie was limp and breathing rhythmically. Ryan carefully extracted herself from the dangerously tempting spot and climbed the stairs to Rory's room.

At 4:35 a.m. Jamie felt a warm body slide into bed next to her. She scooted backwards until she was plastered up against the comforting form. "That was your last night of sleeping alone," Ryan said softly, "did you enjoy it?"

"No. I missed you all night," Jamie muttered. "I want you next to me for the rest of my life."

"That's a request I'm only too happy to fulfill," Ryan said as she rolled her friend over and started to give her a brisk rub to get her blood moving. After a minute or so, Jamie reluctantly struggled to her feet, and got into the shower while Ryan carried their bags upstairs. Fifteen minutes later, they were ready to go. They both wore the California AIDS Ride 6 official jerseys with the sponsor's logo brandished across their chests. Ryan was both pleased and slightly disapproving as Jamie handed her the jersey while they were getting dressed, but she swallowed her reticence about accepting the near-constant presents and thanked her sincerely. Martin and Conor were just finishing up their coffee as Brendan came in the front door. He gave Ryan a hug as he sleepily asked, "Couldn't you guys take off at around nine, just once?"

Ryan laughed and hugged him back. "I know it's early, but it really means a lot to me that you come to see us off."

"You have to drag that bike 560 miles, getting up early isn't really much of a sacrifice," Brendan said, as he gave her another little squeeze.

Ryan got down on the floor to give Duffy a hug, "You take care of Da and Conor while I'm gone, Duff. It's gonna be just you boys all week, so try to stay out of trouble." Duffy looked up at her sadly, recognizing the signs of her departure. Jamie joined her, getting a lick on the face in the bargain.

They tossed their gear into the bed of the truck, and they all climbed in. "I'm glad I bought the crew cab," Conor said as Brendan climbed into the back with the girls.

"You know, I don't remember ever having a normal car. Did we, Da?" Ryan asked.

"No, not during your lifetime," Martin said. "Your mother and I had a nice, little, normal Ford when we were married, but by the time you arrived, it was clear we had to switch to a bigger vehicle. We've had either a van or a truck ever since."

"Have you ever owned a car, Ryan?" Jamie inquired.

"Nope. All I've ever had were bikes. I got my first one when I was sixteen, and Da almost had a fit!"

"Yes, and I still blame you for that," Martin said as he poked Conor in the arm. "You're the one who had to start with the blasted things."

"It's not my fault Ryan had to imitate everything I did," Conor replied defensively. "Besides, she should thank me. I think she gets half her dates because of that bike."

"Then maybe we'd better get rid of it," Jamie laughed, "because your dating days are over."

"I've never given up anything so willingly."

Chapter Sixteen

They arrived at Fort Mason at around five-fifteen. Even though Jamie usually got up early, and considered morning her favorite time of day, she had never claimed to be a morning person. Today was a perfect example of that dichotomy. What she loved about mornings were periods of quiet contemplation while watching the sunrise or writing in her journal, but the scene that greeted them when they disembarked from the truck didn't in any way remind her of the thing she most liked in the morning—stillness. She was completely unprepared for the overwhelming number of riders, bikes, families, volunteers, news trucks, police officers, and spectators that greeted them. The noise level and general anxiety that flowed from the crowd was actually a little overpowering for the inexperienced woman, and she found herself gripping Ryan's hand much harder than normal.

"Nervous?" a calm voice whispered in her ear.

She managed a quick nod, embarrassed that such was the case.

"It *is* a big deal, Jamie. We've worked really hard to be able to do this, and it's only natural that you have butterflies in your tummy." Looking around she added, "It is pretty overpowering, isn't it?"

"I was in St. Peter's Square in Rome on Easter morning once," she replied thoughtfully, feeling better since Ryan agreed that her anxiety was expected, "but this is a close second."

They finally found the gear drop off point. After they checked that the bags were properly tagged, they went to their designated meeting place to say hello to the rest of the family. Maeve and Kevin were already there, but Tommy had yet to arrive. "Do you think you can eat yet?" Ryan asked Jamie. "I know you don't like to eat very early, but you have to today."

"Yeah, I could get some cereal down. Let's go get some now, so we can watch the opening ceremonies with everyone." They found the breakfast line and settled on oatmeal, bananas and raisins. Jamie agreed to forego coffee and settled for apple juice. Ryan added two bagels and some cream cheese to her selections. They sat at a long table, chatting with the other riders. Ryan knew a lot of the participants, and people stopping by to greet her continually interrupted her meal.

"Do you know most of these people from before the ride?" Jamie asked when they had a minute alone.

"No. I met them all on one of the previous rides."

"I can't believe the way you can remember all of their names," Jamie marveled. "How do you do that?"

Ryan looked thoughtful for a few minutes. While she thought, Jamie mused that she loved the fact her partner took even a simple question so seriously. "I only know the names of people I bonded with for some reason. I've had five different tent mates, and I've ridden with different teams through the years. This is actually the first time that I'm not with a team."

"How does that work?"

"There are lots of different groups that train together, and are sometimes sponsored together. Bike shops, hospitals, small businesses and even schools sponsor teams. I don't like to stick with a team for more than one year, though," she admitted. "I like to get to know a lot of people, and that's harder to do if you're with the same group all of the time."

Just then a very attractive woman, who looked like she knew Ryan rather well, approached and straddled the bench, facing her. "Hi, Ryan," she said in a very friendly tone. "Long time, no see."

Ryan smiled easily and greeted the woman. "Hi, Carly. It has been a long time. How'd your training go this year?"

"Not nearly as well as last year. You brought out the best in me on those training rides," she said with a suggestive smile. "So what have you been up to?"

Ryan gave her a brilliant smile and put her arm around Jamie's shoulders. "I've been busy falling in love. Carly, this is Jamie."

Carly looked a bit taken aback, but she rallied and extended her hand to Jamie. "I've got to admit, I'm surprised to meet the woman who actually tamed this wild cat," she said as she patted Ryan's leg.

"Oh, she isn't that wild," Jamie said with a forced smile.

"That's what you think." Carly got up, pausing just a second to pat Ryan's cheek in a familiar fashion. "Take care, girls," she said airily, walking away.

"You don't know everyone you've introduced me to as well as you know Carly, do you?" They both watched the attractive woman saunter away.

Ryan blushed deeply. "Uhm, not *all* of 'em."

Jamie just laughed, shaking her head, "I don't know how I'm going to keep you interested in me after all of the other women you've known."

Ryan slipped her arms around her waist and kissed her deeply for several minutes. "I don't even notice other women any more. You're more than enough woman to satisfy me for the rest of my life."

Jamie's blush rivaled Ryan's as she whispered, "We're in a pretty public place, you know."

"I know. I'm just trying to stop any more old flames from disturbing us."

Jamie pinched her hard on the side. "So you just kiss me to keep people away?"

"No, I kiss you to make my knees weak." She kissed her again, lingering longer than she normally would in public. "What people do with this informative display is their choice."

When they returned to the meeting spot, everyone was there. Caitlin immediately reached for Ryan, who gladly accepted her. The baby was wearing her new T-shirt, and she looked positively adorable. She had on a little baseball cap that Ryan had bought her not long ago, and after she gave Jamie a sloppy kiss, she happily sat on Ryan's shoulders to watch the parade of people.

Another ex-lover happened by, this one much more polite. Ryan introduced Jamie and, as the woman looked from Caitlin to Jamie, she finally asked in surprise, "Is this your baby?"

Ryan laughed as she introduced the rest of her family and indicated Caitlin's parents. The woman wished them well and went to find her riding partners. "Well, that went better than the last one," Jamie said.

"I really tried to date nice women, but once in a while I didn't screen them properly."

"I've seen you in action, Ryan. I think your screening process was a little lax," she said as she playfully jabbed her riding partner in the stomach. "Unless you think an eyebrow wiggle is a sufficient screening tool."

"Oh, you really *do* have my number, don't you?"

"I most certainly do. So don't try any funny business."

At six-thirty, the Opening Ceremonies got underway. Willie Brown, the Mayor of San Francisco, and a large number of the Board of Supervisors were in attendance. The gay and lesbian community was a big supporter of the mayor, and the elegant, handsome African-American man genuinely returned the affection. He spoke extemporaneously for a few minutes, then various members of the ride team and the San Francisco AIDS Foundation said a few words. After the speeches were finished, a hush settled over the crowd as the directors of both the San Francisco AIDS Foundation and the Gay and Lesbian Center of Los Angeles came onto the stage. Six volunteers somberly guided a riderless bike up the center aisle through the throng. The quiet grew heavier as the assembled crowd paused to remember exactly why they had dedicated themselves to participate in the ride.

The speaker began, "This morning we begin a magical journey. A journey of exploration, a journey of wonder, a journey of commitment. A journey we make together. To see what exists beyond what we thought we could accomplish as individuals. To see what exists beyond the limits commonly ascribed to humankind.

"To open the treasure chest that is ours when we meet on common ground.

"To find a new horizon that will give the world a glimpse of a different, kinder, magical way to live.

"Please turn your eyes to the center lane, and witness the bicycle being led down the path. This bicycle has no rider. See the empty space above the seat and the pedals. See the empty space behind the handlebars.

"The empty space inside the helmet that hangs at the side. See that empty space, and remember.

"Let us together remember the friends, and the loved ones, that we have lost to AIDS. This year, last year. Years ago. All of them, still in our hearts and our minds. Remember their faces. Remember their laughter. Remember their lives, their hopes, and their dreams."

Jamie looked up sharply when she heard a small quiet cry, almost like a wounded animal. Turning quickly, she saw her partner bent over, trying to compose herself, but having absolutely no success. Before she could move toward her, Maeve put both of her arms around the crumpling body and pulled Ryan's head up to her shoulder. Her body shook with deep, wracking sobs as she allowed herself to be comforted like a small child.

As much as she wanted to reach out to Ryan at that moment, something stopped her. She took a few deep breaths, feeling Annie's arm drape around her waist, and in that moment, she knew what it was. She hadn't known Michael and neither had Annie. As much as the two women might empathize with the pain of losing a beloved young man, neither of them could know how that loss had felt to their loved ones. This was a pain that could only truly be shared by those who had experienced it.

The speaker continued: "Remember their love. Let us feel all of them with us right now. Among us. Looking over us. Their hearts overflowing with joy this morning and proud that we were their friends. As we embark on this courageous endeavor, let us use this moment to invite them to come with us, to keep us safe, to carry us up the difficult hills. Through the rain. And against the wind. To be there with us when the road is difficult.

"To be there with us, when we feel like giving up. Let them give us strength, let them give us joy, and let them give us the courage to continue. Their spirit is here to ride with us. Let us carry it, keep it, and let it fill up the empty space, until there is no empty space.

"It's time, everyone—the moment is here. Make this everything you have ever hoped it could be. With our brothers and sisters who have been lost to AIDS, together, we begin California AIDS Ride 6."

As Jamie stood in the throng, she felt a swelling of emotion in her chest that became almost painful as these last words were uttered. In that moment, she felt prouder of herself than she ever had in her life. Not just because she had worked so hard, although that was part of it. Rather, she was proud that, for once in her family's history, someone had tried to make a difference in someone else's life. Not with money, since that was no sacrifice at all for a family such as hers—this was a sacrifice of her time and her effort and her safety and her will. She was about to challenge herself to do something that was going to be difficult, and she was doing it out of love for people she didn't, and probably never would, know. She was doing it for the tens of thousands of people in California who were affected by this deadly disease. Yes, she was doing it for Ryan and the rest of the O'Flahertys, to show her support for their loss, but she was primarily doing it to show that people with AIDS mattered, and would continue to matter, until the scourge was completely and irrevocably destroyed.

There was not a dry eye amongst the O'Flahertys, each of them focusing their thoughts on their beloved Michael. Ryan raised her head as Maeve fished out tissues from her purse, and they all spent time composing themselves. Ryan leaned in close to her aunt and whispered something that was greeted by a smile and a kiss on her cheek as the smaller woman reached up and captured the last few tears with her fingertips.

Ryan indicated with a nod of her head that it was time to get in line to retrieve their bikes. Another round of tears accompanied their departure, and this time Jamie was a full participant. When Martin hugged Jamie, he leaned over and whispered, "Take care of my little one, Jamie. This is very hard on her."

"I will, Martin," she promised.

They were just about to sneak away to join their assigned group when they heard a pathetic "No!" come from Caitlin. Ryan dashed back to kiss her and give her a squeeze, and then she jogged back to Jamie's side. "God, that's hard to do," she muttered as she looked back to see a screaming Caitlin frantically trying to extricate herself from Tommy's grip. Jamie was still too choked up to reply, so she merely gripped Ryan's hand more firmly.

After they got their bikes, they checked their tires, made sure all of their tools and supplies were in their packs, and put on their helmets. Ryan actually did most of the work since Jamie's hands were shaking too badly to be of much use. When Ryan made her stand still while applying another layer of sunblock to her face and neck, Jamie felt like she was receiving final inspection from her commanding officer before the big battle began.

At seven-fifteen the first riders pulled out to the strains of blaring, inspirational music and the cheers of the assembled throng. Because of the huge number of riders, it took quite a while before they could move. Ryan kept offering encouraging glances, but Jamie knew her body wouldn't calm down until they were underway. Her heart was nearly beating out of her chest by the time they started, but once they took off she began to feel better when her rubbery legs could actually propel the bike. Hundreds and hundreds of people lined the street leading out of Fort Mason, all of them waving and cheering the riders on. The thought crossed Jamie's mind that riding a bike in a huge crowd was not really easy to do in the best of circumstances, but with her eyes continually filled with tears in an outpouring of emotion, it was nearly impossible. Luckily, they were going quite slowly and no decisions had to be made. They just moved with the crowd and let the energy and the positive vibrations carry them along.

After a few minutes, the riders started to separate, and it became easier to concentrate on maintaining proper position and pedal cadence. Jamie lost herself in the process of riding, letting her mind go blank except for the sensation of pedaling. She kept a low level of awareness for the condition of the street and the distance she was from other riders, but for the first time that she could recall she was in a deep level of concentration, where everything just flowed. Every fifteen minutes her watch alarm buzzed, and she grabbed a water bottle and drank, but even this interruption didn't disturb her focus. As they left the city, her concentration started to flag, and she spent some time just looking around.

Ryan was just ahead of her, and she focused on her for a few long minutes. She quickly learned that watching Ryan from this vantage point was not a good idea. She found herself being nearly hypnotized by the twitching of Ryan's butt when she stood on her pedals, and she was forced to jerk her attention away. *Are you suicidal?* she chided herself, focusing on the other riders and passing scenery.

They stopped at the first pit stop about thirteen miles out. It was crowded, but Ryan stated that this was an anomaly, and that subsequent stops would be less hectic. The crowds didn't dampen the cheerfulness of the volunteers who handed out snacks and water. They greeted each rider with a smile and offered encouraging words. Ryan methodically took the water bottles and added powdered drink mix from her pack. After she was satisfied with the mix, she poured them into the three bottles that each of them carried on their bikes. "You're going to be a fanatic about that stuff, aren't you," Jamie grinned as she watched her scientist work away.

"You betcha," Ryan agreed, her mouth curling into a tiny smile as she concentrated on pouring. "And as proof, we're not leaving until you drink every last drop of this down." She handed her partner the bottle and supervised her consumption with a smile at her compliance. The day was still cool, but Ryan knew dehydration could occur during the coolest weather, and she was not going to let that happen to her partner on her watch.

Jamie started to get onto her bike, but Ryan insisted they move away from the crowd and take a few minutes to rest. "But it's only thirteen miles," Jamie complained. "We've done lots more than that without a break."

"I know. But this is different. Now sit down here and let me massage your thighs for a minute."

The little orange bike was dropped like a hot rock. "Why didn't you say so in the first place?"

Ryan started to work on her thighs, smiling to herself when Jamie's lids started to droop almost immediately. "Boy, you're easy," she grinned as she picked up the pace, trying to invigorate her.

"I know," she moaned. "You start rubbing me, and I'm powerless to stay awake. It's just so calming."

"It's good to be calm when you're riding in a huge pack like this. How are you doing with the traffic?"

"Uhm, pretty good. It was dicey coming out of the city, but once the road started to open up I kinda got into it. It makes you feel like you're part of something, you know?"

"I do indeed." Ryan gave her a little slap on each leg. "Let's rock!"

They took off again, riding in a fairly large group until they reached the second pit stop. The first thirty miles of the ride was through dense urban clutter, but when they arrived at Stop Two they could see more rolling, open scenery before them. Jamie knew that one of the worst hills of the ride was coming up, and she wanted to ask for reassurance, but she felt childish about it. Ryan went to wait in the long line for the Porta-Potty, giving Jamie a stern glance when she said she didn't need to join her. When she returned, Jamie was working on her second bottle of her drink mix. Ryan began her lecture, but Jamie held up her hand to stop her, "If you don't have to go to the bathroom at every pit stop, you're not drinking enough!" she said sternly. They both laughed as she forced herself to drink three bottles of her drink mix and eat a banana and some trail mix. When she finished, she trotted over to get in line for the Porta-Potty.

When Jamie returned, she gave Ryan a kiss and said, "Thanks for taking care of me."

"I've never had a more pleasurable job." Ryan began to rub the tension from her partner's shoulders. "Big hill coming up, huh?"

"Yeah."

"Nervous?"

"Uhm ... a little."

"No need to be." Ryan leaned over and kissed her cheek. "It's strenuous, but not nearly as bad as some of our training up in the hills. Guaranteed."

"Thanks," Jamie murmured as she turned and wrapped her arms around Ryan's damp waist. "You can always tell when I'm nervous, can't you?"

"Oh, I don't know if *always* is the right word. But you give off some physical cues that are pretty telling."

"Really? Like what?"

"One big one," Ryan said, hopping back on her bike, "you stop talking!" Her laughter flowed back over her shoulder as she stomped on her pedals trying to avoid the dreaded pinch.

The four-mile climb up Highway 92 was tough going for almost everyone. The day was beginning to heat up, and the highway was quite narrow. As they labored up the hill, Ryan dropped back to ask if Jamie minded if she let out a little speed on the way down. "You go right ahead," she panted. "I'll catch you later." As she gave her a smile, she added, "I want you to have fun today. Do what you need to do to get your juices flowing."

"Well then I'd better hold back, because the quickest way to get my juices flowing is to stay very close to you." The flashing white smile that accompanied this sentiment made Jamie wish they could stop for a moment and share a kiss, but she didn't want to interrupt her momentum, so she satisfied herself with blowing a kiss to her grinning partner.

Following Ryan up the long, steep grade, she gave silent thanks for all of the hours of hard training they had put in. She was actually quite proud of herself and spent a few minutes just feeling the power of her legs as they propelled her continually uphill.

They reached the crest after what seemed like an hour. Jamie heard her partner let out a whoop of pure excitement as she stomped on her pedals, hurling herself down the steep hill. She followed at a much saner rate of speed—nonetheless, she was flying down the hill at thirty-eight miles per hour.

After they had leveled out a bit, they turned onto Highway 1. Ryan pulled over and stood just off the wide bike lane, waiting for Jamie with a huge grin on her face. Jamie pulled up next to her and watched her grin turn to a smug little smile as she wiggled one eyebrow at her. "You're the fastest, you're the coolest," Jamie said in a singsong fashion.

"I'm glad you think so," Ryan said smugly as she gave her a hug. "'Cause I am."

After the successful scaling of the big hill, Jamie was more than ready for the next twelve miles before lunch. As she quickly found out, the seemingly flat terrain was deceptively hilly. She began to dread every dip since she knew that a hill would quickly follow, but she concentrated on her cadence and let herself enjoy the lovely scenery, trying to take her mind off the effort she was expending. They arrived at the lunch stop and practically wrestled to be first in line. For the very first time in their relationship, Jamie ate everything on her plate and was actually looking around for more. Ryan stared at her as she finished off her second apple with a flourish. "I've created a monster. A hungry monster."

There were still plenty of snacks available, and Ryan grabbed a couple of energy bars to tide her over. After three more bottles of water, a short thigh massage, and a few kisses, they were ready to go again.

The ride down the homestretch was aided by a nice tailwind the entire way—even though they had to cover fifty miles, the distance seemed much shorter. Nonetheless, it was three-thirty by the time they rode into the large city park in Santa Cruz, their home for the night. The volunteers had prepared the area beautifully, clearly marking every area.

Their first task was to find the security area for the bikes. Jamie was impressed by the system they had installed to keep track of all three thousand bikes, obviously not an easy task. The area was segmented into large sections, with each one named after an international city. They picked Madrid, one of Jamie's favorite spots, and quickly hung their bikes from the tall saw horses placed there for that purpose. Actually, Ryan hung both bikes, as the sawhorses were really quite tall.

Jamie was ready for a long nap, a hot Jacuzzi and an hour-long massage—however, before she could partake in two out of three, they had to find their assigned camping spot. They were given #J-22, and Ryan showed Jamie how to find the spot by using the small markers placed near the ground. After locating their spot, Ryan generously offered to go wait in line and get a tent and all of their gear. Jamie considered the offer for less than a second before she gratefully accepted. She wandered off to look for the shower trucks as Ryan gamely stood in line for a tent.

She finally found the shower truck after spotting a number of people with wet hair and scrubbed skin coming from one direction. Regrettably, the line was long, but she knew that she would feel better once she got the road grime off so she stayed in line. It moved rather slowly, and there were still five people in front of her when Ryan jogged up carrying her toiletries, a swimmer's towel and a change of clothes. Jamie smiled brightly at her thoughtfulness. "I was just standing here knowing I should leave to get my stuff, but I was too tired to move."

Ryan helped her pull off her bike shoes and socks, when it became obvious that Jamie's legs were too weak to support her in an off-balance position. With a kiss, Ryan went to the rear of the now very long line and waited patiently while Jamie neared the front. Luckily, moments after she gained her spot, a buddy from the first ride got in line behind her.

"Pretty early to already be waiting on your tent mate hand and foot, isn't it?"

Ryan turned and barked out a laugh, hugging the grinning woman who stood behind her. "Melinda! I haven't seen you since the last ride. How've you been?"

"Good, very good in fact. Jared started school this year, so Stacy and I have been able to start working the same shift."

"Wow, I can't believe that," Ryan said. "I still remember how anxious you were on the first ride. I've never seen someone search out public phones like you did."

"Well, waiting for your lover to have your first child *was* a pretty big deal," she reminded her.

"She was only seven months pregnant," Ryan said, smiling. "Is Stacy here?"

"Oh yeah, she's around here somewhere. Jared is with my mom for the week, back home in San Jose. I'm sure he'll come back thoroughly spoiled, as usual. So, who's the cutie you were waiting on?"

"I can't disagree with the description, but she's a lot more than my tent mate," Ryan said. "She's my," Ryan paused for a moment, trying to decide on the proper term, "partner. Jamie's my life partner."

"*You!* You're in a relationship?"

"Hey," Ryan objected, hurt by the amazement in her voice, "I need love too, you know."

"Uhm-hmm," she said suspiciously. "You've never seemed to be lacking in that department."

"Oh yes, I have," Ryan said. "I've been starved for love, Melinda, but gorging on sex. There's no comparison."

"You really are in love," she said slowly, still slightly amazed.

Jamie came back and gave Ryan a kiss. "I feel so much better," she said wanly.

"This is an old friend," Ryan said. "Melinda, this is Jamie Evans. Jamie, Melinda Stone."

"Good to meet you," Jamie said as she extended her clean hand.

"*Amazed* to meet you," Melinda murmured, still astonished that Ryan had entered into a committed relationship.

Ryan shot Jamie a glance and said, "Melinda's known me since the first ride. She's seen the annual changing of the guard."

"I see," Jamie drawled good-naturedly. "Did she ever introduce any of them as her lover?"

"No, never. It was always more like, 'This is … what was your name again, honey?'"

Ryan gave her a playful cuff for that comment. "I have never, in my entire life, referred to a woman like that."

"Just kidding, sport," Melinda agreed. "But it was always obvious that they were just passing through. I get a completely different feeling from this one, though," she conceded as she smiled at Jamie's proprietary hold on Ryan's dirty, sweaty body. "If she can hug you when you're that grimy, she must be in for the long haul."

"The longest," Jamie agreed as she kissed the dirt-flecked lips smiling down at her.

After a brief chat, Ryan asked Jamie for her dirty clothes, which she dutifully handed over. "I'm going to do laundry when I'm finished," she said. "Do you remember where our tent is?"

"J-22," she replied decisively.

"Very good," Ryan said as she patted her on the head. "Go take a nap after you drink another bottle of water."

After her showering and laundry duties were done, Ryan headed back to the tent. She found Jamie sprawled across both sleeping bags right in the middle of the floor. She didn't have the heart to wake her, so she went in search of something to do, or, even better, something to eat. An hour later, she opened the tent flap and crawled in next to her sleeping partner, cradling her close. After a few moments Jamie started to awaken. She sniffed a few times, then she rolled over and sniffed again. "I smell …" She licked around Ryan's mouth for a moment. "Mexican food." After a moment, she sat up in surprise, "Hey! Did you eat dinner without me?"

"Only my first course. I've got plenty of room for seconds."

"C'mon," Jamie said as she crawled out of the tent. "I'm starved!"

The long dinner line snaked along all too slowly for Ryan's unsated stomach. Jamie smoothly diverted her attention when she asked, "How do you think today went?"

As was her fashion, Ryan paused and considered the question, and her answer, thoroughly before she replied. "I was very, very pleased with how today went. The day just flew by, mostly because I was so focused on you. I've had a lot of friends and a few bedmates that I cared about on the ride, you know. But none of them captured my attention like you did today. It was a very pleasant diversion," she decided with a big grin.

"You're too sweet," Jamie beamed as she stood on her tiptoes for a kiss. "But I don't like the inequity of attention you've been lavishing on me. I want to make you feel better, too."

"But I feel fine," Ryan assured her. "I'm used to this kind of pace, so it's really not that big a deal for me."

"Still, tomorrow we share shoulder rubs and leg rubs. You're not getting out of here without some pampering."

"Oh, all right," Ryan muttered in mock disgust. "You're so hard to live with!"

"I know. And you're such a saint to put up with me."

"It's just an act of mercy. You're like the little dog that followed me home. If I don't take you in, no one will."

"Ggrrrrr," the feisty little stray replied.

"Was today like you expected?" Ryan asked while they worked on their desserts.

"Yeah, I was totally ready for the physical aspects," Jamie replied, after taking a minute to consider her answer. "But you didn't give me any idea of how ... well ... gay it was." She chuckled softly.

"You didn't know most of the people would be gay?"

"No, no," Jamie laughed. "I mean gay! Like festive."

"Oh, yeah, it is pretty darned festive."

"Yeah, I didn't realize that so many people would decorate their helmets, and wear costumes. I swear I saw a bunch of guys dressed like flamingos!"

"Yeah, that's pretty common on the ride. That's one of the nicest things for me. People can really be creative. A lot of guys even dress in drag."

"I can't imagine doing this in full make-up," Jamie laughed. "But whatever floats your boat."

They finished dinner by seven o'clock and spent a little time wandering around the tent city, Jamie marveling at all of the amenities. People were diligently working on ailing bikes in the repair area, every available masseuse was hard at work, and the medical trailers had a long line of people seeking relief from various minor injuries. There was even a small general store selling necessities. The entertainment started just as it was getting dark. Jamie was interested, but also very willing to go to bed right then. So they compromised by deciding to watch for half an hour, and then go to sleep.

After only a few minutes, Ryan excused herself. "I've got to go do something. Can you find the tent?"

Jamie nodded her assent as Ryan took off. After twenty minutes she made her way back to their temporary home. It was just eight-thirty when she crawled in to find Ryan lying on her side in a fetal position. "Ryan, what's wrong?" she asked in alarm as she crawled up right next to her.

"Cramps."

"Oh, you poor baby. Did you take anything?"

"Yeah, I just took some ibuprofen. I'll be okay in a while."

"Do you usually hurt like this?"

"No, not very often. I felt a little twitchy earlier, and I should have paid attention and taken some pills then. If I knock them out right away, I don't have any trouble. When I let them really get to me, it's much harder to get rid of them."

"Isn't there anything I can do? How about a massage?"

Ryan rolled over onto her back as she smiled up at her partner. "You'd really like to help, wouldn't you?"

"Yeah, it's hard to see you in pain and not be able to do anything."

"Well, sometimes it helps if you can just put your hand here," she said as she placed Jamie's hand right above her pubic bone. "And then kind of rock me."

Jamie did as instructed, rocking her very gently as she put firm pressure over her uterus. Ryan let out a deep sigh as the pressure began to relieve her cramping. After a long while Jamie asked, "Does one of your ovaries hurt more than the other?"

Ryan nodded, "Yeah, the right one." Jamie moved her hand over to the right side of her abdomen. She probed with her fingers for a moment until Ryan let out a little gasp. She then applied pressure to this area and kneaded until Ryan's face relaxed and she looked much more peaceful. "Boy, you have a great pair of hands there," Ryan said gratefully as Jamie climbed into her outstretched arms.

"Do you feel better?"

"Much," Ryan said as she kissed her tenderly. Jamie responded to the kiss, and slowly the intensity began to escalate.

"I thought about sleeping with you all day," Jamie murmured into her ear as they took a break.

"I thought about you too, but sleeping wasn't involved," Ryan replied with a leer as she placed more searing kisses on Jamie's smooth lips.

"For a sick girl, you sure do kiss good." After the passion between them rose another notch, Jamie began to notice that Ryan's body was relaxing in direct proportion to the increased beating of her heart.

Jamie wrestled the sleeping bags from under her now limp body and tossed the joined bags over the two of them. Placing one last tender kiss on her moist lips, she wrapped her arms around her. "Good night, Ryan," she whispered into her ear.

Ryan forced one eye open and looked at Jamie with a questioning glance and a tilt of her head.

"That's enough playtime, sweetie. We both need to rest. We've got a long day tomorrow."

"Okay," Ryan sleepily agreed, "But I don't think I can sleep before it's even fully dark out."

"Fine," Jamie soothed, whispering into her clean pink ear. "You don't have to sleep. Just relax for a little while." Moments later, she felt Ryan fall into a deep sleep in her arms.

Just after two in the morning, Ryan woke from an insistent pressure in her bladder. She struggled out of Jamie's embrace, as well as the sleeping bag, and searched for her sweats with her hands. When she found them, she slid out the tent opening and fumbled her way into her clothes. She had left her sandals outside the tent, and she stepped into them on the way to the bathroom. It was quiet at the campsite, but the ever-present security personnel were on duty. She made it a point to walk by each person she saw to say hello and thank him or her.

As she approached the medical trailer, she realized that more than her bladder was causing her pain, so she stopped in to request some more ibuprofen. The woman on duty gladly fulfilled her request, also giving her a tampon. When she was finished, she made her way back to the tent, realizing that she hadn't put her normal beacon on the top. She had learned through experience that finding your tent out of fifteen hundred identical ones on a dark night was no picnic. She usually put a light stick on the top of the tent when she left, but she'd been so groggy that she'd forgotten. She used her innate sense of direction and eventually found the 'J' section. To her relief, finding #22 was not too hard. She undressed outside and kicked her shoes off before climbing back in and settling down next to her lover.

She was moments from sleep when she heard a soft voice grumble, "I have to pee."

Using every bit of her self-control, she took a deep, even breath and asked, "Do you want me to go with you?"

"Do you have to go, too?" Jamie asked hopefully.

"Yeah, I have to go too," she replied, out of nothing but love.

After they completed their pit stop, Ryan stopped at the medical trailer again to snag an energy bar. The ibuprofen wasn't sitting well on her empty stomach, so she munched on the bar on the way back. This time the light stick was clearly in place, signaling them home.

After they climbed back into their little nest, Jamie automatically put her hand over Ryan's uterus and began to rock her gently. Ryan gazed at her sleepy green eyes in appreciation as Jamie mumbled, "You look like you don't feel so good." Ryan just nodded and closed her eyes, willing herself to focus only on her partner's healing touch. Within minutes she was sound asleep.

Chapter Seventeen

The muted, but insistent, stirrings of the huge camp woke Ryan just before dawn. She felt surprisingly good considering she had cramps, had slept on the ground, and had ridden ninety miles the day before. She had an insistent need to go to the bathroom again, but before she did, she gently woke Jamie by lightly rubbing all over her body. Jamie nestled up against her, muttering a small protest. "Come on. You've gotta get up. There's a cute little orange bike that wants you to take it to King City."

Jamie pried her eyes open and yawned. She stretched every muscle and joint before she sat up, blinking groggily. She turned to Ryan as she ran a hand through her wild hair and asked solicitously, "How ya feeling?"

"Pretty good, all things considered. I can't believe how much better I feel just sleeping next to you."

Jamie gave her a big smile and leaned over to offer a hug. Ryan gladly accepted, and they held each other lovingly for a few moments, allowing themselves to wake up fully. Ryan let go reluctantly as she slid out of the tent. She pulled on her sweats and dragged her gear bag out with her. After rummaging through the bag for a few minutes, she found the outfit she wanted to wear and then got ready to head to the shower. "Are you going to take a shower in the morning, too?"

"I normally don't. But it's probably good for my cramps."

Jamie kissed her goodbye and gently patted her seat. "I'll take the tent down and get us packed, then we can go eat breakfast and get you some more pills."

"I'm going to try to do without any more pills," Ryan said. "I'll bring some along in case I really need them, but they make me feel lightheaded and I don't want to lose my concentration."

"Can I give you a little tummy rub during our pit stops?"

"I can't think of anything I'd like better. Oops, one thing I forgot," she said, digging into her bag again. "Bring your swimsuit!"

After they pulled their bikes out of Madrid, Ryan worked on their water bottle mix. They were all loaded up by just before seven, but right before they left Ryan had to make another pit stop. Jamie patiently waited for her, getting a sheepish little grin when she returned. "I have to go constantly when I get my period," Ryan admitted.

"Speaking of periods," Jamie said as they left the campground, "After I get mine this month, I'm going to stop taking the pill."

Ryan looked at her quizzically, "I didn't know you were still taking them. I guess I assumed you stopped after you broke up with Jack." Ryan felt her stomach do a little flip as she considered the only obvious reason Jamie would continue to take the pill.

"Yeah, but I stayed on them because I wanted to regulate my period so I'd be sure not to get it during the ride. I thought ahead for a change," she said proudly, causing Ryan to let out a sigh of relief.

"That's pretty darned smart."

Jamie didn't understand why this little discussion had caused Ryan's face to light up with delight. As the grinning woman surged ahead of her, singing a happy tune, she forgot the question entirely and just took in the view.

The first fifteen miles of the day were problem free. The road was well paved, and they were both able to make good time. The first pit stop was at the Monterey Bay Academy, overlooking Sunset Beach and the stunningly beautiful Pacific Ocean. It was a memorable setting and caused Jamie to pull her tiny camera from her seat pack to take a few pictures.

"I've got to get a shot of this gorgeous vista," she said as she focused on her partner.

"Uhm … Jamie, the ocean is that way." Ryan jerked her head in the correct direction.

"Ocean? What ocean? You're the only scenery I'm interested in."

After the photo session, they enjoyed the view longer than they normally would have at the first stop of the day. Ryan even agreed to lie down and let Jamie work on her abdomen for a while, and she had to admit that she felt better. After forcing down two bottles of water, they took off again.

Pit stop two was also along the ocean, and they removed their helmets and let the breeze dry their hair as they rested on the ground. Ryan lay with her head on Jamie's lap, while Jamie worked her magic on her still tender tummy. After the stop, they continued on Highway 1 for quite a while, and then cut inland through fields of flowers and artichokes. They were no more than a few miles from the ocean when it became obvious that early June in California farm country was pretty darned hot. They followed some little-used agricultural roads, riding smoothly until they reached their lunch stop.

They pulled into a very shady state park and got in line to pick up lunch. Ryan looked at Jamie and asked with a twinkle in her eye, "Are you really hungry?"

"Yes, I'm starved, Ryan. Go ask them for another lunch. I plan on eating all of mine," she said as she narrowed her eyes and placed her hands protectively around her bag.

"That's not why I asked. There's a neat spot not too far from here where we could have a more private picnic, so I thought we could eat a little now and a little later."

"Don't you mean a lot now and a lot later in your case?"

They ate half of their lunch, but stayed until they could force enough fluids down before continuing. They had to manage a long, rather steep slope to climb into the Salinas Valley. It was slow going, but they both handled it well. When they reached the crest of the hill, they sped down it until they crossed a one-lane bridge. Ryan was in the lead, and she motioned for Jamie to pull over. They peeked over the edge to see about a dozen people in the Salinas River, skinny-dipping.

"Uhm, Ryan?"

"Hmm?"

"Is that where we're going?"

"Yep."

"It looks awfully cold."

"How can you tell that from here?"

The smirk that greeted that question soon turned into a full out smile, as Jamie teased, "You really don't know much about men, do you?"

They walked their bikes down to join the other riders then continued on foot for about forty yards until they came to a more protected spot. Ryan yanked off her jersey and shorts, revealing a totally hot suit that made Jamie's mouth water. Her top was a Lycra sports bra in a brilliant white. The bottom, of navy blue Lycra, began just under her navel. From the front it had the appearance of a thong, as it was cut up very high on her legs. As Jamie slowly walked around to the back, she saw with some regret that both cheeks were covered by the fabric. Only about an inch of material held the front and the back panels together at her waist, and Jamie spent a moment wondering how long it would take to chew through the barrier. "I take it you like my suit," Ryan said teasingly as she regarded Jamie's open-mouthed stare.

"I'd like it better if I could take it off you." Jamie's eyes were half-closed while she ran her hands over the firm abdomen.

"You are the randy little one, aren't you?"

Her hands stilled immediately. "I ... I guess I am. I never thought of myself that way, but it's practically all I think about when I'm with you."

"I think it's adorable," Ryan said, wrapping her arms around her and giving her a squeeze. "Hey, I showed you mine, now show me yours." She tried to snag Jamie's jersey to remove it, but her partner danced away.

"I don't have mine on yet. Give me a minute." As soon as she started to strip, she caught Ryan trying to peek. "Turn around," she chided. A few minutes later she said, "All ready," and Ryan turned around to perform her own little staring ritual.

"Wow," was all that Ryan could get out, and even that one word was strangled. The suit was absolutely perfect for Jamie's body. It was made of a shimmery deep blue and emerald green material that almost looked metallic. The top was a skintight tank top with tiny spaghetti straps, and it stopped just above her navel. The bottom, in the same fabric, covered her rather modestly except on the sides, where two little ties were all that held the suit on her body.

"I have never," Ryan said in a whisper, "ever, wanted to pull a string as much as I do right now." Her hands roamed over the slick material, and her fingers paused on the little ties. Jamie removed the tempted digits and placed them firmly on her waist. Ryan gave her a brilliant smile as she said, "I had no idea I'd benefit so personally when I offered to train you. I really should give you back every dime I took from you." She ran her hands up the tautly muscled abdomen, feeling each dip and curve with her thumbs. "I just can't believe how hot your body is. I knew you had the potential to look really good, but I didn't foresee this." She continued to run her hands lightly all over the firm body.

Jamie wrapped her arms around Ryan's neck as they kissed tenderly for many long minutes. She finally pulled back and asked, "Are we gonna swim or make out?"

"I guess we're gonna swim," Ryan replied glumly as she dropped her head to her chest. Jamie lifted her chin with two fingers to see the twinkling eyes as Ryan yelled, "Let's get wet!" and, throwing Jamie over her shoulder, jumped into the ice-cold river.

They both screamed in shock from the cold as they tried to catch their breath. When Jamie recovered, she jumped onto Ryan's back, dragging her under the water. When Ryan shot back up a second later, she sputtered and dove for her friend. The next few minutes were spent dunking each other and playing wildly in the cold water.

After they had burned off their excess energy, they took turns floating on their backs. Jamie had to support Ryan's effort since her body was too dense to float on its own. They lazed about in the water for a good half-hour before they regretfully decided they needed to get back on the road.

Ryan had brought her swimmer's towel and a set of underwear. She got dried off quickly and dressed then she gave Jamie the towel as she went to collect the rest of their lunch. Jamie dressed in private, and when she emerged from the trees she saw Ryan sitting on the ground with a happy smile on her face. "I'm gonna think about you in that suit all day long. It's gonna be a long forty miles," she added as she shook her head.

As predicted, the last forty miles were very hard. They fought a headwind most of the way, and by the time they arrived at camp they were both totally exhausted. They were too tired to even think of a shower, so they set up camp together and stripped to their underwear for a nap. Mere seconds passed before they were both soundly asleep.

After waking, they were relieved to find that the shower line was quite short since most people were at dinner already. They were clean and refreshed when they joined the crowd just before six. Ryan went through the line first, and when Jamie finished she looked around to find her standing by a table full of people. "Hey, honey," Ryan called out, beckoning to her to join her.

Balancing her heavy plate, she walked over to the group and stood patiently while Ryan made the introductions. There were twelve people at the table, an even mix of men and women. Jamie tried to catch all of the names, but her hunger was winning out over her politeness. "Can we join you?" she asked, sitting down before anyone had the chance to say no.

"Of course," a pleasant looking woman named Naomi said. "We were just telling Ryan how much we miss her at the Y."

"Y?" Jamie replied through a mouth full of food.

"I worked at the YMCA for a few years while I was in high school," Ryan said as she shoveled her own dinner into her mouth.

"Ryan got us all involved during the second ride," Naomi said. "She dragged us over all the hills of the city. The ride was nothing compared to her training!"

"Don't I know it." Jamie agreed wholeheartedly.

They spent the meal chatting about friends they had in common and the ride in general. Jamie was charmed to watch her partner in this setting, and she realized she had never seen Ryan around a group of people she wasn't related to.

When Ryan was in public, or with people she didn't know well, she maintained a rather dignified air. She wasn't stuffy or remote, even with strangers; she invariably exhibited a polite interest. But there was a definite distance that she obviously felt more comfortable with. With this group of former coworkers and training partners, she was just like she was at home—funny, relaxed, outgoing and constantly teasing everyone at the table.

After they finished their spaghetti dinner, they took their leave to walk around the perimeter of the camp. They found a picnic table far away from the other campers, and they sat on the bench to chat. After a few minutes, Jamie began to get cold so Ryan sat on the table, scooting back as far as she could while Jamie snuggled between her legs.

She rested her head back against Ryan's shoulder and let out a heavy sigh. "This is bliss," she murmured. "You know, I had no idea how it would feel to be with you twenty-four hours a day."

"And?" the deep voice rumbled behind her. "What's your verdict?"

"Twenty-four hours a day isn't nearly enough."

"Is that right?" Ryan drawled as she quickly leaned forward and kissed her partner on every inch of exposed skin she could get her lips on. Jamie giggled and squealed wildly, but stayed right where she was, determined to weather the pleasurable assault.

"Yes!" she yelled as she jerked away from the ticklish torture. "I need more. Much, much more."

"I do, too," Ryan's now soft voice floated by her ear as she wrapped both of her strong arms around Jamie's waist and squeezed her tightly. "A lifetime with you isn't going to be nearly enough."

Jamie rested her head against Ryan's shoulder and languidly stretched for a moment. "I feel so good."

"You're not stiff?"

"Oh yeah. I'm stiff and my butt feels like it's pounded veal, but I'm so happy to be out here with you that none of that matters at all." Ryan's arms were still holding her firmly, and she spent a moment gazing at the muscular limbs. Tilting her head slightly to nestle more closely, she began to trace the protuberant muscles and tendons with the tip of her finger. A surreptitious grin crossed her lips as she felt her buff partner unconsciously tense the already firm muscles. *Showoff*, she laughed to herself. She secretly loved the fact that Ryan was proud of her hard earned muscles and liked to display them.

"Ryan?" she finally asked, breaking the peaceful silence.

"Hmm?"

"Do you mind if I want to talk about Jack's phone call?"

"Of course not," she said, even though she could have very happily lived the rest of her life without ever hearing that particular name again.

In fits and starts, Jamie related the story of her former fiancé's call. It was hard for her to organize her thoughts, but she got it all out eventually. "Boy, that was a generous thing to do," Ryan said with genuine admiration. "I can see why you picked him. He sounds like a really decent guy in many ways." She privately thought there were ways in which he was also a total jackass, but she didn't think this was the proper time to bring that up.

"He is, and that's why I felt so guilty about how I treated him. He deserves someone who can really love him."

"Everyone deserves that, but not many get it. We're both very lucky in that way," she added with a winning grin that Jamie could just see a corner of.

With a note of hesitation in her voice, Jamie asked, "Would it bother you if I went to his graduation next Saturday?"

"Bother me? Why would that bother me?" Ryan asked, truly perplexed.

"Well, it's our last day in Pebble Beach, and I hate to take time away from us. But I was with him all through law school, and I just feel it would help me get some closure on the relationship."

"I don't mind a bit. I respect you for wanting to make a gesture like that. Losing one day is not that big a deal," she said as she gave her a gentle squeeze. "We do have the rest of our lives to spend together." *I sure didn't do the math on that one*, she grumbled to herself. *I didn't realize she wanted to knock a day off our honeymoon.* But now that she was committed, she could hardly turn back.

Turning around more completely, Jamie pulled back just a few inches and stared directly into Ryan's eyes for several minutes. Ryan didn't say a word, although she felt like an impressionist painting as the gaze continued. "Sometimes I can't believe how generous you are," Jamie murmured. "You honestly amaze me."

As she leaned forward to offer a heartfelt kiss, Ryan thanked her mouth for having stayed shut at just the right time.

"You know," Jamie said reflectively, after they separated, "I wanted to ask you about your cousin and why the opening ceremonies affected you so strongly. Do you mind talking about it?"

"No, I don't mind," Ryan said softly. She was quiet for a long time, obviously gathering her thoughts. As her face clouded with long held pain, Jamie deeply regretted bringing up the topic, but it was too late to pull back now so she snuggled closer, trying to offer solace with her body. Ryan finally began, "You know my mother died when I was seven. The family found out about Michael's illness just a few months before her death, although we found out later that Michael had known for several months before he told anyone."

"He was afraid, huh?"

"No, he wasn't. That's not how he was at all. He was the most self-confident guy you'd ever want to meet. He knew his mother would be supportive and that his father would go ballistic, but he held off because my mother was so sick. He didn't want to add to the burden." A few tears rolled down Jamie's cheek, and Ryan sniffed a few times. She kept her head so close to Jamie's that she could feel her words coming through her body.

"He finally had to tell because he had to be hospitalized. The adults didn't tell us what was going on. They said he was going on vacation." She laughed bitterly at her own words. "I freaked out just because he was gone for a couple of weeks. When my mother was in her last months, either Aunt Maeve or Michael was at the house around the clock. He was twenty-one at the time, just starting his senior year at USF, and we all idolized him. He did whatever Da asked of him—babysitting for me and Rory, helping us with our homework, making a meal for us, anything.

"Even though the adults knew, my brothers and I were clueless that he was ill. He had Kaposi's Sarcoma, and even though he had lesions, they were hidden under his clothes. As the year went on, it became clear that something was wrong—especially to me. Even though I was young, I'd become hypersensitive to everyone's health. I watched over every person in the family, looking for signs there was something wrong with them. A few months after my mother died, they told us he was going on vacation again, but I knew they were lying. I totally freaked. I can remember screaming at Da and Aunt Maeve, begging them to tell me the truth." She took in a few deep breaths, trying hard to maintain her composure. Jamie stayed as still as she could, knowing that revealing this pain was a very difficult thing for Ryan to do, and not wanting to break the moment.

"After a few minutes they looked at each other. I can still remember the look on Da's face when he told me Michael was going into the hospital. I immediately jumped to the conclusion that he was dying, and I was inconsolable." She closed her eyes and took a deep breath before she could continue.

"They kept telling me he would come home and be all right, but I could tell from their eyes that they were lying." She paused for several lingering minutes, and Jamie thought she might stop talking, but she finally shuddered slightly and continued. "I think the hardest thing was that I stopped trusting the adults to tell me the truth.

They hadn't told me he was ill, and I didn't trust them when they said he would get better." She gave a sad little smile as she added, "I guess I was right on that one."

Now Jamie couldn't help herself. She pulled away from Ryan's embrace and climbed onto the table, taking the position that her partner had just held. She sat up as tall as she could and clutched Ryan's head to her breast, gently kissing the top of her dark head. Ryan sucked up the affection like a sponge, and it seemed to help as she got her second wind and continued. "Anyway, he did recover from that bout of K.S., and he had a good year or so. He just began to fall apart, one piece at a time. Even after all this time, it still boggles my mind," she whispered. "It was like his body was decaying while he was still walking around. Like his brain was alive, but his body was already dead." She shook her head slowly as she tried to erase the images from her mind but, as usual, she was unsuccessful. "He lived for five years after his diagnosis, which was remarkable for that time—but he was truly unrecognizable for the last year. During his last months, he didn't even know any of us," she choked out as she began to cry. "It was so horrible, Jamie," she cried in pain. "So horrible."

Jamie held on as tightly as she could, but Ryan was nearly limp with her grief. She ended up collapsed against her partner's chest, great heaving sobs wracking her body. Jamie was gently rubbing her legs, giving her silent support.

To her surprise, when Ryan calmed a bit she continued with her tale. "Hearing those words when they brought in the riderless bike just took me back to that time," she whispered. She hugged Jamie's arms tighter around her body as she added, "I know Da and Aunt Maeve thought they could spare us the pain of knowing about Michael, at least for a little while. But I learned something very valuable through that experience. Kids know. They're very intuitive little beings, and hiding things from them just backfires. I hope I have the guts to be honest with my children even when difficult issues come up."

"Our children," Jamie gently reminded her as she kissed her tear-stained cheek. "Our children," she added for emphasis. "I feel the same way," she vowed. "I'll try my best to be honest with our children, even with painful issues."

"I'm not angry with Da for what he did," Ryan said. "I was only seven, and I'd just lost my mother. He was having a heck of a time with me, anyway."

She sighed deeply, and Jamie couldn't resist the urge. "Why was he having trouble with you, honey?"

"Jesus, Jamie," she muttered, blowing out a frustrated breath. "I was a little girl, and my mother had been desperately ill almost my whole life. She was in and out of the hospital, lost her hair to chemo, spent hours vomiting after her treatments. I can't … I don't think I'll ever be able to make you understand what that was like. So losing her and having Michael get sick sent me into a tailspin. I had to be attached to someone around the clock. Aunt Maeve had a dying son at home, but she nearly lived at our house. Aunt Moira came for almost a month, and it was another blow when she left. My other aunts helped out a lot, but they all had kids around our age so it was really hard for them, too. I just attached myself to Aunt Maeve. I couldn't sleep unless she sat on the edge of my bed and rubbed my head. I know that it was hard for Da, but I just couldn't trust him to be there every night. It must have been so hard for him to know what to do with us. And he loved my mother so much; it had to be devastating for him to go on without her. I just can't imagine," she said softly as she started to cry against Jamie's shoulder.

After a while, Ryan raised her tear-streaked face and looked at Jamie with a forlorn expression, "It makes me think of losing you," she choked out as she began another round of sobs.

Jamie just patted her and spoke soothingly into her ear. She knew there were no words to assuage Ryan's sorrow, so she tried to comfort her with her mere presence. Ryan quieted down after a long while and sat up slowly to get the kinks out of her back. Turning to her partner, she delicately captured the tears on her face as she gazed up at Jamie with a look of pure love on her face. "Thanks for just letting me get that out. You're the only person outside of my family that I've ever let see that side of me." She dropped her head to Jamie's chest again as she added, "You make me feel so safe. You made me feel like I felt when my mother held me."

"Pardon?" she asked confusedly.

Ryan sat up abruptly, then got to her feet and started pacing. "That's it!" she said excitedly. "I get it! I really get it!"

"Get what?" Jamie asked, thoroughly confused. "What do you get?"

"The reason that I never let anyone get close enough to really love me! I was afraid to let another woman make me feel that way." she nearly shouted. "But I trusted you; I really trusted you! I knew you wouldn't hurt me, and I let myself feel that connection again with you. Thank you, Jamie. Thank you!" she said with an overwhelming sense of relief as she grasped her by the shoulders.

Jamie was dumbfounded. She knew how Ryan felt about her, but she had no idea what an important role her love for Ryan was serving. As she thought about it, she realized it made perfect sense. Ryan could only love someone who she trusted to reach her in that dark, broken space. She wouldn't let most people try, because she was so afraid of being hurt by another loss. Only because she trusted Jamie implicitly was she willing to risk being this vulnerable, and it was only through sharing her pain that she was able to let in the comfort she so desperately needed.

Jamie felt so honored to be trusted so thoroughly that she was at a complete loss for words. Ryan had obviously used up all of her cogent thoughts also, because she just wrapped her arms around her and held on tight. They sat on the table top in a solid embrace for a very long while. It was fully dark when Ryan pulled back and gave her several small kisses, finally taking her hand and guiding her back to the tent where they snuggled tightly together in sleep.

Just like clockwork, Ryan's demanding bladder woke her up at two. She lay there for a moment trying to get her bearings and to remember to put the light stick out. She searched around for a tampon and was just starting to crawl out of the tent when she stopped to look at her lover. Jamie was sound asleep with a look of quiet contentment on her face. Ryan thought of how much she loved the gentle, caring woman, and how she would do nearly anything for her. She smiled sweetly as she thought of how freeing it had been to talk about Michael so openly. *I love you more than I can say,* she thought with another fond gaze. *But I'm not going to let you wake me up two minutes after I get back to sleep. Love has its limits.* She gently woke her partner and said, "I'm going to the bathroom. Why don't you go with me?"

Jamie just nodded mutely and crawled out of the tent compliantly. *Not bad,* Ryan thought with satisfaction. *Not bad at all.*

Chapter Eighteen

J amie felt Ryan begin to stir as soon as their neighbors made a sound. Soft hands soothingly patted her back until she turned and grasped her partner tightly. "You have the sweetest ways of waking me up," she murmured into Ryan's ear as she snuggled up close.

"And you cuddle up to me so nicely," Ryan said as she rubbed Jamie's body all over, "that it makes me want to stay in bed all day."

"Have you always liked to cuddle?" Jamie asked softly, turning to gaze into Ryan's bright eyes.

"Yeah, I've been addicted to touch my whole life. How about you?"

"Well, I wasn't cuddled much as a child and I had to be careful with Jack, so I suppose I'm just now developing my cuddling abilities."

"What do you mean you had to be careful with Jack?"

"Uhm … sure you want to talk about this?" Jamie asked, assuming that hearing about intimate matters with Jack might be hard for her partner.

"That depends," Ryan said, sitting up and bracing her head on her hand.

"On what?" Jamie asked, as she turned onto her side to mirror her lover's posture.

Ryan smiled and trailed her fingers down Jamie's cheek. "On whether it bothers you to talk about it, of course."

"Oh … so only my opinion matters, huh? I don't think so, sweet cheeks," she insisted as she pinched one of the sweet pink cheeks at her disposal.

"Okay …" Ryan said as she flopped onto her back. "Here's the deal. I want to know everything about you. I want to know about every factor that has influenced, molded, pleased, dismayed, saddened or impressed you since the moment you slid from your mother's womb. Whether the topic is painful or funny it's important to me, and I wanna hear about it if you wanna talk about it."

Jamie had moved over and was now leaning over Ryan's face. Placing a whisper soft kiss on her forehead, she said, "I feel the same way. If it happened to you—I'm fascinated."

Ryan sat up and gave her a kiss as they both assumed their earlier positions. Propping her head up again Ryan asked, "So … you were saying?"

"Right … well … okay, I remember where we were. It's like this. If I rubbed up against Jack very much in the morning, he'd want to have sex. Well, actually," she blushed, "he wanted to have sex even if I didn't rub up against him much, so I learned to get out of bed quickly if I wasn't in the mood. Not like it is with you," she whispered as she leaned in close. "Now I want to stay in bed all day, and this is probably the most uncomfortable bed we'll ever share!"

"Far be it from me to turn down sex in the morning, but it's not my peak time," Ryan said. "And even if it were my favorite time, I wouldn't want you to have sex just to please me. So you can rub up against me all you want. You can also say no anytime, so don't feel like you have to run away to avoid me."

"I don't think I'd mind having sex with you in the morning," Jamie whispered seductively into her ear as her hand began to stroke Ryan's back.

"Mmm, maybe I am a morning person." She slid her hand under Jamie's T-shirt and began to rub her back in slow, delicate circles.

Jamie sat up abruptly, her eyes wide with alarm. "You'd better stop that right now, Ryan! My back is a total erogenous zone."

Ryan gave her a delicate little kiss as she withdrew her hand. "That's good to know, but don't tell me any more of your erogenous zones. I want to find them all by myself … manually," she said with an evil grin. "So, what's your favorite time to get busy?"

"I'm not sure what my preference is," Jamie said. "I've never really been the one controlling sex—I was usually the one responding." She looked at Ryan quizzically, "What's your favorite time?"

"Every day at three o'clock in the afternoon, I'm ready to rock," she said decisively. "But I'm totally flexible. I'm sure I wouldn't have any trouble accommodating you at any time of the day or night," she added, as she kissed Jamie again and began to slide out of the tent. She indicated her shower supplies and asked, "Same deal as yesterday?" Jamie nodded her assent and began to organize their supplies while Ryan made for the showers.

The day was starting out cool, but they expected very warm weather later in the morning. After their usual breakfast, they headed out. They passed through a neatly manicured little town in the middle of lush farmland. As they pedaled along, Ryan told Jamie about her third ride when the temperature had reached one hundred seventeen degrees going through this valley. "It was really brutal. A lot of people had to get picked up by a support vehicle and taken to the next campground. It was a very tough day for everyone. I don't think I've ever consumed so much fluid—I was drinking twenty ounces every fifteen minutes—and even with that, I passed two pit stops without having to pee."

"What are they predicting for temperatures today?"

"It'll still be hot, but it's not supposed to be much over ninety."

"Goody," Jamie muttered.

Ryan had warned her they would face a major hill early in the day, and after about fifteen miles they encountered the beginning of the upward slope. They slowly began to climb a five-mile grade of between two and four percent. They pumped along steadily, making good progress, but then the real hill began. It was two miles long and ranged from a six to an eight percent grade—a real thigh buster. Ryan stayed really close and encouraged Jamie all the way up. "You're doing good, not much farther, keep pumping, pull on your upstroke, that's it, you can do this, Jamie, come on!" she exhorted.

They made it to the top together, where the cheering crew greeted them. Music played loudly on boom boxes, and they noticed that a number of riders had joined the crew to encourage other riders up the hill. After they got their breath, they stayed for a while to cheer on those behind them. Jamie got her camera out and took a few pictures of the triumphant riders cresting the hill. When they got ready to leave, Ryan just wiggled one eyebrow as Jamie laughed and patted her on the back. "Go on, speed racer. I'll see you at the second pit stop."

Ryan took off, pedaling furiously, and was a blur in seconds. Jamie just shook her head as she watched her fly, and then prudently began her own descent, finding herself cruising down the five-mile drop at a fast thirty miles-per-hour.

The next pit stop was at an Army base, and the crew was dressed for the occasion in fatigues and other military paraphernalia. Jamie found Ryan lounging on the ground, eating a banana and drinking a large bottle of Gatorade. She was chatting with a woman who looked to be around thirty, a little stocky, but obviously very full of life. Ryan greeted her partner with a big smile as she patted the ground next to her. "Jamie, I'd like you to meet an old friend of mine. This is Karen Joncas." She draped her arm around Jamie as she said, "I did pretty well for myself, wouldn't you say?" She smiled smugly at her friend.

Karen regarded Jamie with a long look as she pointed at Ryan and said, "I never thought I'd meet the woman who could snag this one." She smiled broadly as she continued, "I'd say you both did pretty well for yourselves."

They chatted for a few minutes until Karen was ready to leave. "You two take care, now. You'd better double up on your vitamins, Jamie," she said with a laugh as she pedaled away.

Jamie raised one eyebrow and threw Ryan a mock glare. "And that was?"

"Uhm ... my tent-mate from the first ride?"

"Ryan, did you sleep with every person you shared a tent with?"

"Gee, Jamie, it gets cold out at night. You wouldn't want me to freeze, would you?" she asked as she batted her blue eyes ingenuously.

"So does Karen think I'm just the girlfriend du AIDS Ride 6?" she asked with a sharper tone than she intended.

"No. She thinks you're the woman I love," Ryan replied, sliding closer. "She thinks you're the woman I'm gonna be with for the rest of my life." Her arms wrapped around Jamie's torso as she nibbled on her neck. "She thinks you're the last woman I'll ever do this with," she said reverently, kissing her deeply.

"Oh ... well ... that's better," Jamie murmured, now completely placated.

Ryan nuzzled her ear for a few seconds as she whispered, "Did you see me fly down that hill?" Jamie's response was limited to a nod as Ryan took her breath away with a dizzying series of kisses. "I was going forty-two miles an hour," she breathed right into her ear. "Doesn't speed make you hot?"

Jamie pulled back a bit as she tried to focus her blurred vision. "You make me hot at any speed," she replied with a sultry little grin. "But unless you want to give these guys a real show, you'd better calm down, tiger."

Ryan agreed to cool off as they sat back to watch the crew do a competent rendition of "In the Army," a takeoff on The Village People. As they prepared to leave, Jamie indicated that she was feeling tender on the insides of her thighs and Ryan offered to get some butt balm for her from the medical trailer. She accepted the offer and waited in line for an available privacy tent to apply the ointment. Ryan gallantly offered to help with the application, but Jamie just laughed at her and gave her a kiss.

When they were back on the relatively flat road, they had the opportunity to ride side by side for a while. "Karen didn't look like your usual type," Jamie said reflectively.

"Oh? And what, may I ask, is my usual type?"

"Well, most of the women I've seen you with are young, and hot, and really cute."

Ryan gave her a beaming smile. "My, aren't we stuck on ourselves?"

"I don't mean me, I mean the other women I've seen you with," she protested defensively, a bit embarrassed.

"In your case, I'd say young, hot and gorgeous is more apt. But I honestly don't really have a preference for a particular physical type. I'm much more attracted to energy than looks. And Karen has great energy. She and I actually became pretty good friends, but she moved to Sacramento, so I don't get to see her often."

"But why is every woman I've seen you with young, hot and cute?" Jamie persisted.

"Well, given my dating history, first impressions were fairly important," Ryan admitted. "I'm a sucker for a pretty face, too, but I've been with many women who wouldn't be called attractive in the traditional sense. The best-looking woman in the world wouldn't attract me if she was listless or lethargic or boring."

"So, do you like me because I'm peppy?"

"You're the total package. Brains, energy, looks, sense of humor, and most of all," she said over her shoulder as she picked up speed, "lots of dough!"

Jamie really had to pound it to catch her mischievous partner, but she finally tracked her down about four miles outside of the lunch stop. The blacktop of Highway 101 was beginning to heat up, and the temperature was rising quickly. Ryan had shed her jacket, and Jamie had to consciously slow her heart down when she saw her in her new sleeveless jersey. It was a bright orange with vivid yellow designs that looked like little whirlpools. It flared just a bit where it skimmed the waistband of her shorts, accentuating her trim waist. Jamie intentionally lagged a bit to watch her muscles move as she pedaled up a slight incline. In addition to her recent discovery that she was most definitely a breast woman, Jamie had been surprised to discover that she was a back woman as well, and, luckily for her, Ryan had the nicest back she had ever seen. Every one of the muscles was fully developed and they popped out when they were under stress. But even with the impressive musculature, the back was not at all bulky looking—it was sleek, and firm, and taut when stressed, but when relaxed it felt smooth and soft. Jamie thought it was Ryan's best feature, but she decided that she should reserve judgment until she had seen all of the assets properly displayed. She started to let her mind wander to their upcoming honeymoon, but her reverie was interrupted by the lunch pit stop.

They were pleased beyond words to have the crew misting them with cool water as they pulled in for their meal. Ryan spotted a man she knew, and took Jamie over to say hi. She greeted him warmly and introduced Jamie. "Jason, I want you to meet my partner, Jamie." She went on to explain that she had met Jason and his lover, Eric, when they were part of her training group for AIDS Ride 4. She looked around as she asked, "Where is Eric?"

"He's riding solo this morning. He should be along soon, though. Have a seat and join us for lunch."

Ryan looked confused, but she sat down and waited for further explanation. Just then a woman approached, holding her lunch bag in one hand. Her other hand was encased in a substantial cast. "Ryan, Jamie, this is Ellen. She's riding with me this morning, and Eric is on her bike."

Ryan looked at her wrist with a questioning glance, and Ellen explained, "I took a tumble yesterday and landed right on my wrist. I fractured it, but the medical team got it casted for me. It didn't feel too bad today, so the crew helped me find all the tandem riders, and they all agreed to let me take a shift on the back where I don't have to use my wrist. Jason took the first shift; I think it went pretty well. What did you think, Jason?"

"I think I'm going to trade you for Eric permanently," he laughed. "You pedal just as hard, but you're a lot lighter."

They enjoyed their lunch together, exchanging stories of the ride and little things they'd seen. Jamie snapped a few pictures as they prepared to leave, then they rode through the cool mist one last time.

It was quite warm now, and as they went up a small hill, Ryan unzipped her jersey. The deep zipper stopped just above her navel and it clearly exposed her yellow sports bra to Jamie's very interested eyes. The vision of the dark woman straining as she pedaled up the hill, sweat flying from her body, and all of that luscious, exposed, tanned skin was almost too much for Jamie's heart to take. She forced herself to take the lead for the first time all day, just to regain her focus.

As they pulled into pit stop four, Jamie noticed a man pulling a child carrier, just like Caitlin's. "Ryan, can you bring a child on this ride?" she asked, rather dumbfounded.

"No, he's not carrying a child. He pulls that empty carrier as a memorial to all of the children who've died of AIDS. See the 'Positive Pedaler' flag on the back of the carrier?" she asked, indicating the flag that some riders with AIDS displayed.

"Oh, Ryan, that's so sad," Jamie said, her eyes welling up with tears.

Ryan just slipped her arms around her and held her for a few minutes. "So much loss," she said quietly.

After their stop, they rode in reflective silence until they reached the last stop of the day, Mission San Miguel Archangel. Located just twelve miles out of camp, this beautiful two hundred-year-old church had been restored and lovingly maintained by the Franciscan Friars. The friars had generously offered their grounds for the pit stop and had even set out hoses for riders who wanted to cool down. After they sat in the shade for a while, forcing fluids, Ryan said she needed some time to go into the church. She didn't ask Jamie to accompany her, so Jamie remained outside to stretch her back on the shady ground. After a good fifteen minutes had passed, Jamie went into the gift shop to buy some postcards. She peeked into the church and saw Ryan, deep in thought, sitting on a chair in front of an imposing statue. It dawned on Jamie that it must be a statue of St. Michael, and that Ryan's late cousin must have been named after him. She paid for her cards and went back outside, leaving Ryan to her prayers. After another fifteen minutes, she went inside to check on her partner.

Ryan was in the exact position she'd been in earlier. She was sitting in a straight-backed chair that she had pulled up in front of a very large marble representation of a battle-clad-angel who held a massive sword against the neck of the groveling devil that was curled up at his feet. She was leaning forward, with her torso braced by her elbows, which rested on her thighs. Head slightly bowed, eyes closed. Moving to her side, Jamie gently placed her hand on Ryan's dark head and pulled it against her hip. Ryan nuzzled against her, indicating her acceptance of the touch. "Mind if I join you?"

"Please," Ryan nodded, opening her eyes to gaze at her partner.

"Feel like talking?"

Her bottom lip stuck out for a moment as she considered her answer. A short nod followed and even though that wasn't a rousing yes, it was enough to assure Jamie that she wasn't interfering.

"I was just thinking how ironic it was," Ryan said as she turned her gaze back to the statue.

"How ironic what was?"

"How ironic it is that I feel his spirit so strongly here." Turning to Jamie she explained, "He was no fan of the Church."

"Really?"

"Really," Ryan said clearly, smiling at her memories. "I was still a kid when he died, but I recall him talking about it quite a lot—especially in his last year ... while he was still cogent."

"What did he say?"

"I think he held back a little with me, to tell you the truth," she recalled. "I was still in choir and I was an acolyte so I was really connected, and I think he was afraid of harming my relationship with the Church. His father, my Uncle Charlie, couldn't come to terms with Michael's sexual orientation. They fought—a lot—and it made the whole situation so much worse. My uncle was very old school about religion. He had been taught homosexuality was a sin and he was not going to let Michael die without doing his best to get him to repent. But Michael didn't buy into that at all. After a particularly nasty fight one afternoon, he looked at me and said, 'Ryan, I always want you to remember that God loves you just the way he made you.'"

"That's sweet," Jamie said. "Do you think he knew ... about you?"

"Oh yeah," she laughed. "He never said anything, of course, but I was a baby dyke from the time I was in diapers. Anybody who was sensitive to gay kids would have known. But he said something else that day. He said, 'God is with you everywhere, Ryan, although he seems to be mysteriously absent in the Catholic Church.'"

"Hmm," Jamie said. "Do you think he grew disenchanted with the Church when he discovered he was gay?"

"No, I think it was before that. Actually, I'm sure of it. He was a very bright guy, very much into philosophy and theology. Theology was actually his major in college. He kept a journal from the time he was sixteen or so, and a couple of years ago Aunt Maeve let me read them. Wow," she said with a laugh. "He was more than a little disenchanted, but it got worse when he came out, and much worse when he contracted AIDS. He thought the Church was a willing participant in the genocide of gay men worldwide because of its rigid stance against using condoms. Plus, he was angry with the Church for refusing to ordain women, not allowing birth control, and a dozen other issues."

"That does sound like he was more than a little disenchanted," Jamie laughed softly. "Did his feelings influence you?"

"No, not at the time," she said. "I needed the security of the Church at that point in my life. And Michael was usually very gentle in his criticism around me. By the time I read his journals, I had reached my own conclusions," she smiled. "My feelings now follow his pretty closely, but I still enjoy going to Mass. I just look at it in a different light now."

"Tell me how you look at it?"

Ryan grew pensive for a few minutes. When she spoke again she turned to Jamie and related, "Now I view going to church as a chance to be with other people who are seeking some spiritual answers. I like singing the songs, and the prayers are nice too. It makes me feel very connected to our ancestors," she said. "I sometimes get an image of prehistoric man, trying to make some sense out of his life, looking to the stars or the moon or whatever it was that they worshiped. I don't think we've made much progress from that point, to tell you the truth. But it's somehow reassuring to be with other people who are trying to answer some of their own existential questions."

"So you don't feel like a Catholic?"

"I'd have to say that I believe about one percent of what the Church considers dogma, so I'm sure the Church doesn't consider me Catholic," she explained. "But it is the faith of dozens of generations of O'Flahertys and Ryans, so I feel culturally Catholic."

"Did you make that term up?" she asked as she patted Ryan's leg.

"Probably," she admitted. "Some people refer to 'Cafeteria Catholics' as the people who pick and choose which parts of the faith they believe. But I believe so few of them that I'm basically fasting."

"But doesn't it bother you to go to Church, given how you feel about it?"

"No, I actually enjoy myself most of the time. It feels very familiar and usually quite reassuring. I like to recall my childhood, when I believed every word. It was a very peaceful feeling, and going to Mass sometimes lets me recapture that."

"I want to go with you sometime."

"I'd love to take you," Ryan said as she gave her a very generous hug. "Thanks for coming to get me." A shy grin crossed her face as she squeezed Jamie's thigh. "It helped."

After the stop, Ryan seemed in a much lighter mood, and they tossed teasing comments back and forth as they rode the last twelve miles. Jamie would occasionally try to zoom ahead, putting on as much speed as she could generate. Of course Ryan could easily best her, no matter how concerted her efforts. But the effort was always worthwhile when Ryan passed her, pedaling furiously, her muscled rear high off the seat, twitching with effort. *Mmm, maybe that's my favorite body part*, Jamie thought as Ryan blew past one more time.

They pulled into the Mid-State Fairgrounds in Paso Robles just before two. This was considerably earlier than they had finished the previous two days, and they decided to shower and nap before dinner. Jamie showered first, as had become custom, while Ryan set up camp. After her shower, Ryan slipped on a white tank top and a pair of vivid blue print running shorts. When she returned to the tent she tried to quietly crawl in to join her lover, who Ryan expected to be sound asleep. She was surprised, but enormously pleased, to find her wide awake, wearing only a light blue cotton tank top and matching panties. She was lying on her side, her elbow firmly planted, her head resting on her open hand. "Hi," she said in a sultry tone as she wiggled one eyebrow.

Ryan was a bit taken aback, but she rallied quickly, assuming a similar tone. "Hi, yourself. You look like something's on your mind," she said as she crawled up right next to her partner, mirroring her pose.

"Something is. Wanna guess what it is?" she asked as she started to trace light patterns on Ryan's arm.

Ryan closed her eyes to soak up the sensation. "I think I have a pretty good idea."

"Tell me," Jamie teased as she continued to play with Ryan's sensitized skin.

"I think you want to move our honeymoon up a few days." Ryan shivered involuntarily at the delicate touch.

That response seemed to jolt Jamie back into reality. She shook her head as she moaned, "God, Ryan I don't know what I want. I mean, I know what I want, and I really want it now. I really, really want it now. I ... I ... I've just never felt like this. Sleeping with you at night and waking up in your arms just makes me want to touch you ... everywhere. I think about it all day long," she groaned as Ryan moved closer and cradled her in her arms.

"Shh, it's okay, Jamie. It's okay," she said soothingly, as she lightly patted her back.

"I just feel so confused," she mumbled into Ryan's chest. As she pulled her head back, she added sternly, "And you're not helping matters in that tiny little outfit." As she ran her hands up and down Ryan's back, she moaned again in frustration. "No underwear, either?"

"I thought we were going to sleep. Would you like me to put some more clothes on?"

"No," she muttered, "you're a total hottie no matter what you're wearing."

"Uhm ... I'm sorry?"

Jamie looked at her seriously and finally asked, "Can you help me figure out what I want?"

"I think I can. Let's go back to when you decided you wanted to wait until our vacation. Why did you want to wait?"

Jamie looked embarrassed, but she gamely replied, "I know it's kind of silly. But I've built this up in my mind, and I really want it to be special. Does that make any sense to you?"

"Of course it does. I've told you it means a lot to me too. I want to look back and remember our first time together for the rest of my life."

"So you don't think I'm just being silly about this?"

"Not at all," she said. "I want this to be an experience that'll be burned into your memory."

"But what do *you* want? I feel that all of our discussions about sex focus on me."

"To be honest, when you first told me of your feelings I was worried that it'd be too hard for me to wait. I mean, I'd been with Tracy for three months by then, and I was really getting twitchy." She let out an embarrassed chuckle. "But I think waiting's really been good for me. With Tracy I wasn't sure of my feelings, so I was pulled in both directions. But with you, I'm absolutely certain that you're the woman for me." She sat up to better organize her thoughts. "This might sound weird, but it's been a little like Lent for me." Jamie gave her a quizzical grin, encouraging her to go on. "During Lent you deny yourself some things that you like, and you really try to focus on the important lessons of the season. With you, I've had to deny myself some things I really, really like. But that self-denial has made me focus on my feelings for you outside of the sexual arena. I know that I'm more in love with you than I was in March. And I really think keeping our relationship less sexual has helped those feelings blossom." She leaned in and wrapped her arms around Jamie again as she whispered right into her ear. "Even though I want you with a passion that I've never felt for another human soul, I'm glad we waited."

"So, you agree that making love in a tiny tent in the middle of three thousand people isn't the most memorable setting?"

"It might be memorable," she grinned. "But I want the memories to be ours alone. I don't want our neighbors to remember our first time as well as I do."

"Well, you do have a point there," Jamie said as she listened to the people come and go in the surrounding tents. She could hear their neighbors talking about the day, and she was sure they were using a normal conversational tone. "Besides," she teased, "I'm kinda proud being your first tent-mate on the AIDS Ride to resist your charms."

"Okay, you've got me there. Now can we take that nap?"

As they snuggled up together, Jamie abruptly sat up and asked, "You had sex with every other tent-mate on the ride. Didn't people hear you?"

"Oh yeah," she said with a chuckle. "I always tried to wait until everyone else was asleep, but I'll admit that I got a lot of knowing looks from my tent neighbors."

"But you don't want to do that with me?"

"No, definitely not. It was just sex with those women, and having people hear us was no big thing. Actually," she said with a rakish grin, "since my neighbors were usually guys, it was kind of a competition. I was just doing my part to show that lesbians like sex too."

"That might be fun next year after we need a little spice," she said with a chuckle. "But right now some nice quiet romance is in order."

"Romance it is," she said with a few delicate nibbles of Jamie's tender neck. "But until then how about a nice quiet orgasm?"

"Not a bad idea," Jamie said, after a moment's thought. "Give me fifteen," she demanded, jerking her thumb in the direction of the tent opening.

After her forced exile, Ryan crawled back in and snuggled up behind her physically satiated lover. When they awoke an hour later, Jamie was half sprawled across Ryan, with her thigh wedged between the long, muscular legs. Her right hand had strayed up under the white tank top, resting on her rib cage, just below a tempting breast. They laughed a bit at their position when Jamie said, "My subconscious has a mind of its own."

"I think I'm gonna like your subconscious," Ryan whispered in a sultry tone as she leaned in for a kiss.

They were already waiting in line when dinner was served. Ryan was jiggling her foot and generally looking anxious for some minutes when the line began to move.

"Hey, are you okay?"

"Yeah, I'm just really hungry. I normally eat a bigger lunch than we get here, and it's starting to catch up with me, I guess."

"Why don't you go back for seconds at lunch?"

"It's kind of a delicate balance. I need to get enough fuel, but if I eat what I normally do, I'd feel too heavy. So I try to make sure I'm getting enough calories, even if I still feel hungry."

"You look like you've lost a couple of pounds," Jamie said as she ran her hand up Ryan's tummy. "Try to make sure you get enough tonight, okay? It's early enough so you'll have digested it before we go to sleep."

"I'll do my best."

After Ryan had tucked away more chicken burritos, rice, beans and salad than Jamie thought possible, they went for another stroll around the campgrounds. They stopped by a group of UPS drivers who were still handing out gear bags to riders who had come in late. Jamie asked, "Are they volunteers, too?"

"Yep. Not only are all of the drivers volunteers, they take their personal vacation to do this. UPS donates the trucks, which is no small thing, but the drivers really make this ride happen. They cart all of the food and water to all the pit stops, and they transport all of the gear from site to site. It's really a remarkable contribution."

They continued on their little stroll, meeting a few of Ryan's old friends in the process. When they were at the farthest point of the campground, they found a quiet spot and grabbed a picnic table. "I really like how you introduce me as your partner," Jamie said as she cuddled up against her partner's warm side.

"Well, since you're my first real significant other, I had to think about your title," she admitted. "Lover is way too one dimensional. Girlfriend doesn't sound serious or permanent enough. That left me with partner, mate, wife and spouse." She pursed her lips and cocked her head as she continued. "I kind of like spouse, and I really like mate. But they both would seem more appropriate if we had a public commitment to each other. So partner seemed the best term for us right now. What do you think?"

"I think it's so sweet that you spend time thinking about things like this so carefully," Jamie said, wrapping her arms around Ryan's neck and kissing her soundly.

"I looked them all up in the dictionary," the grinning woman added with a hopeful eyebrow wiggle.

"Then you clearly deserve more kisses." When she was finished bestowing the reward, she asked, "Would you like to have a public commitment ceremony?"

"Absolutely," Ryan said, clearly having given the issue some thought. "I'd like to tell every person I've ever known how much you mean to me." She placed a few sweet kisses upon her partner's lips, adding, "When we get back I'm gonna write a long letter to my very traditional grandparents to tell them the good news."

"Do they know you're gay?" Jamie asked, realizing that Ryan rarely spoke of her Irish relatives.

"We've never formally discussed it, but I think my Aunt Moira may have indicated that I was. Neither of them has ever asked me a question about who I'm dating or if I'm going to get married, so they must know something, since my granny is always on the boys about it."

"How old are they?"

"My grandmother is eighty, and my grandfather is eighty-five. They still live in the little town where my great-great-great grandfather was born. They're not very wise to the ways of the world, but my grandmother knows people. So I don't think they'll be overjoyed, but I think they'll come to accept it. My Aunt is very cool about it and all of my cousins know, so my grandparents can vent to them if it really bothers them."

"When did you see them last?"

"My Aunt and my cousin Aisling were here just last summer—about a month before you and I met. But my grandparents won't leave County Mayo for love nor money, so I last saw them two summers ago. I try to save up to go at least that often since they're getting up in years."

"So you should go this summer, huh?"

"Yeah, ideally I would, but I think I'm going to be terribly busy with a little blonde I know."

"Likewise, I'm sure," she said with a grin. "Did you go to Ireland often when you were young?"

"Yeah, I did. After my mother died, Da had a heck of a time keeping track of me during summer vacation. He enrolled me in every kind of sport, and gave me every kind of lesson to keep me busy, but summers were always hard for him. I always had too much time on my little hands, and I was always in some sort of trouble. So he would send me to my grandmother for anywhere from one to three months. I think he did it partly to give Brendan a break, actually," she laughed at the memory of her brother tracking her down all over the city.

"Wasn't it hard for you to leave your father for that long?"

"Yeah," she reflected. "The first time I went was the summer after my mother died. That was tough, but Brendan went with me, which helped a lot."

"Wasn't there any other option?" she asked timidly, hating the thought of her tiny partner being sent away so soon after such trauma.

"Oh, don't get me wrong, I wanted to go," she said quickly. "It was my idea. My Aunt Moira was here a lot during my mother's last year, and I grew very close to her. And my cousin Aisling is my age, and it was cool to be around my only female cousin for a whole summer. Plus, I think there was a bit of me that craved to be in my mother's country, in her childhood home, with her family. It made me feel closer to her somehow," she said with a small voice.

"I'm glad you could go," Jamie said softly as she draped an arm around her back. "But what did you do all summer?"

"Oh, lots of stuff. That first summer, both Brendan and I were pretty depressed. We spent a lot of time going through our mother's things that my grandmother had saved. It was sad in a way, but it let Brendan and me get closer. My mother was buried in the small church cemetery, and I made Brendan walk me down there every day, just to talk to her. My grandmother didn't like it, and she tried to dissuade us, but you know how determined I get," she said with a wry chuckle.

"That I do," she said fondly as she patted Ryan's back. "So what about subsequent years?"

"Well, Brendan was in high school the next summer, and he didn't want to go. Rory didn't want to miss a summer of music lessons, and Conor never had much interest in the small town life, so I went alone."

"God, you were only eight!"

"Yep. The plane ride was kinda scary, especially since I had to change planes in New York," she said with wide eyes.

"I thought they had rules about little kids flying alone!"

"Oh they do, but I looked twelve when I was eight and they didn't require I.D.," she said. "The flight attendants kind of took to me, and they made sure I was okay. I had an escort to the connecting flight, so it was safe and everything."

"Jeez, that still must have been freaky!"

"Yeah, it was, but it taught me that you had to make some sacrifices to get what you want. I wanted to go, and I had to put up with some scary things to get there. I really have to hand it to Da for letting me go. It must have been hard for him, but I really wanted it, and he let me."

"So did you just play with your cousins all summer?"

"Ha! I wish! No such luck when my grandmother's in charge. I had to take Irish lessons every morning at the National school. Aisling took them with me, so it wasn't too bad, but those masters wouldn't put up with any nonsense. The schoolmasters in Killala closely follow the 'children should be seen and not heard' dictum. Then we had to take Irish dance lessons three afternoons a week until we were in high school."

"Irish dance?"

"Yep. Aisling would never have done that on her own, but Granny force-fed me Irish culture the whole time I was there. She always said she had to make sure I didn't turn into a heathen, which, in her view, is anyone from outside County Mayo."

"God, school every day... did you have any fun?"

"Yeah, I got to play lots of sports. The competition was much better in soccer than I got here, so it really helped me as a player. Plus I got to play Irish football, which is kinda like soccer but you can use your hands. And when I was older, Aisling and I joined a hurling team, and that helped me with a lot of skills. I'd say that most of my skills as an athlete came from my time in Ireland," she reflected. "But it took months to get rid of my accent every year. I sounded like an immigrant until Christmas."

"I bet your family was wild to have you back."

"Oh, they were glad to have me back—for about a week," she laughed. "I ran them all pretty ragged, to tell you the truth."

"You really must have been a terror, Ryan. I can't imagine you with the energy of a little kid."

"It was frightening. Luckily, Da didn't think there was anything wrong with me. One of my teachers tried to convince him that I needed medication for my hyperactivity, but he told her I was just very high spirited, thank you very much."

"Good for him."

"When I was ten, I switched from staying with my grandparents to staying with my Aunt. The last extended time I spent there was right after the debacle with Sara. I went for the whole summer that year, and believe me, I was a mess. I didn't have the guts to tell my aunt at first, but I finally told her what had happened and she was totally great about it. She's been very supportive ever since. I know you'll like her."

"I like everyone who loves you, Ryan. That's the litmus test."

They walked back to the main stage to watch the evening's entertainment, settling down to watch a very funny comic amuse the crowd. Ryan was leaning back on her hands, and Jamie was nestled between her open legs with her head resting on her abdomen. Finally, she turned around and ordered, "Don't laugh so much, you're making me seasick."

Ryan put her index finger up to her lips, dramatically making the sign for quiet. But she was unable to keep her promise, and Jamie finally got up and sat next to her. After a minute she said, "Need more contact," and she scooted over behind Ryan to wrap her legs around her. Ryan leaned back against her chest, completely content, while Jamie slid her arms around her torso and leaned over to whisper, "Perfect."

Since everyone was already laughing non-stop, Jamie leaned over and began to tickle Ryan unmercifully. She had finally found two very sensitive spots on each side, about halfway between her waist and her armpits. Ryan writhed on the ground, trying to keep from screaming over the comedian, and Jamie finally relented. Ryan quickly got her revenge by stooping down and flinging her giggling partner over her shoulder, carrying her like a sack of potatoes over to the Porta-Potties for their last pit stop of the evening. Unbeknownst to them, every move they made was watched by a woman whose very angry dark brown eyes followed them until they were out of sight.

Chapter Nineteen

J ust before dawn, Ryan blinked her eyes open to the delightful sensation of being almost completely covered by Jamie's sleeping body. As she lay on her back, she reached down to run her fingers through the soft blonde hair that tickled her chin. Somehow, Jamie had wound up nestled between Ryan's spread legs, lying mostly on her side. The blonde head was resting on one plump breast, and her hand covered the other. Her hand twitched periodically, providing a nice gentle sensation that helped ease Ryan to full awareness. She softly stroked the golden head as she felt her begin to stir.

Jamie shivered and stretched as she slowly woke, looking up finally with a sly grin on her sleep-creased face. "Do you think we make love while we sleep?"

"I think it's a distinct possibility," Ryan said in her slightly raspy morning voice. "We do wake up in some pretty compromising positions."

"God! I wake up horny, I ride all day horny, I go to sleep horny. Then we roll around all night like bunnies, and I'm asleep. I miss all the fun."

"Maybe this is the lesbian equivalent to wet-dreams, like we just have to let off some steam, so we touch while we're asleep."

"Speaking of dreams," Jamie said, "have I told you about the dream I had on my birthday?"

"No, I don't remember you telling me about a dream that day."

"Oh, I wouldn't have told you then!"

"Oh ... one of those kinds of dreams," Ryan said as she nodded her head. "Do you want to tell me about it now?"

"Uhm ... I don't think telling you about it in detail is a very good idea. I think I'd be too tempted to act it out," she admitted. "Suffice it to say that it was the most erotic, sensual dream I had ever had in my life, and you, my love, were the featured player."

"How did you explain *that* to yourself? I mean, didn't it bother you that you were dreaming about a woman like that?"

"I have excellent powers of denial," she replied proudly. "I just convinced myself that seeing all the other women at the bar flirt with you put the idea in my mind. But

I do remember feeling bad that I'd never gotten that hot with Jack." She looked up at Ryan with a crooked grin, "Do you think I had enough clues?"

"I think your mind just processes what it can handle, a little at a time. I really think it's a good thing that you can be in denial a little bit. It makes things less overwhelming for you."

"Speaking of overwhelming, we've got ninety-five miles to do today, so we'd better get shakin'," she said as she gingerly extricated herself from Ryan's body.

Ryan hopped up and started to get her gear ready. As she exited the tent, she looked over her shoulder with a sexy little smirk. "Don't forget your swim suit today. You might need it."

They were both feeling pretty good, and the first few miles were quick ones. The initially flat terrain quickly became a long succession of hills and mountains, all leading to the coast. After the first pit stop they turned onto Old Country Road. They rode up and down some quick little hills, but Jamie was surprised by the three-and-a-half-mile, very sharp, very steep downhill that ended in a treacherous hairpin curve. Even Ryan took her time on this one, keeping her speed under control, staying just in front of her lover. As they leveled out, they passed the Whale Rock Reservoir. They hopped off their bikes and spent a few minutes just enjoying the magnificent view. Jamie asked another rider to take their picture, and she carefully posed Ryan sitting on top of one of the rocks, then climbed up and sat between her legs. Ryan draped her arms around her neck, and leaned forward so their cheeks brushed as they smiled for the camera.

A short time later, they came to another steep hill. They fought their way up and were rewarded with the pit stop being at the top of the hill for a change. Every day the crew at pit stop two had a different theme. Today's was White Trash Trailer Park. Everyone was cross-dressed in truly tacky clothes, with cigarettes dangling from overly made up mouths.

After the stop, they reached the largest of the morning hills. They climbed steadily and were greeted at the top by Scott, a famous AIDS Ride cheerleader. He had made a large sign that read, "Halfway to L.A.," which he hoisted up every time a rider crested the hill. Jamie got out her camera and took a picture of Ryan standing next to Scott with the glistening blue Pacific in the background.

After another hilly twelve miles, they came to the lunch stop. It was located in the parking lot of a typical mini-mall. The grocery chain located there had provided fruit and other snacks as a generous donation, but the most amazing thing to Jamie was the large number of local residents who had come out just to greet them. Three little girls walked around shyly with plates of home made cookies for the riders. Their mother watched from a distance as the girls were fussed over by everyone they encountered. Ryan, of course, got down on her haunches and spoke to each of the girls, asking them how old they were and thanking them for their gifts. Jamie snapped a picture while Ryan wasn't looking, thinking that her little gesture captured her personality perfectly. As Ryan stood, a woman approached her, reached into her purse and handed her a wad of bills. Ryan's mouth dropped open as the woman said, "It's all I have, but you people are worth every dime," and she leaned over and gave Ryan a kiss on the cheek.

Ryan turned to Jamie, her mouth still open, and a stunned look on her face. Jamie helped her organize the money, and they found the crew chief to ask her to hold the donation until they could give it to the ride staff later at camp.

Ryan was still a bit dumbfounded by this unexpected gesture, and as they ate their lunch she said, "One thing this ride does for me every year is that it lets me store little things like that in my memory. When people are jerks, or worse, during the year, I pull one of these little events out and think about it. It always makes me feel better, and it reminds me that most people really are nice."

"I'm going to have a nice surplus of sweet memories, too," Jamie readily agreed.

Leaving lunch they headed back inland to San Luis Obispo, a lovely little town that Ryan sometimes stopped in for a break. But this year she had other ideas in mind. After leaving the town, they headed back to the ocean, but the typical cool breeze was absent this calm day. It was beginning to warm up, and as they reached the outskirts of town, Ryan asked over her shoulder, "Would you like a little break?"

Jamie knew that all of Ryan's breaks included some form of pleasure, so she happily agreed. To her eternal satisfaction, this stop proved to be far more pleasurable than most. They exited onto Avila Beach Drive and rode for just a few blocks before Ryan signaled and turned into the Sycamore Mineral Springs Spa and Resort. Jamie's eyes anticipatorily widened in pleasure as she gamely followed her partner. She pulled alongside and grinned up at her, saying, "Have I ever told you that you have the best ideas on earth?"

"I don't believe you have," Ryan said. "But I guarantee this will be one of the best hours of your life." She bent and kissed the tip of her nose, adding a happy grin as she asked Jamie to hold her bike while she went inside.

Curiosity got the best of the smaller woman, and she quickly secured the bikes and walked into the office after her partner. Ryan was deep in negotiations when she sidled up next to her. "A view is nice," the dark-haired woman said, "but I'm more interested in tranquility today."

"The most tranquil spot we have is probably Oasis," the clerk opined. "But it's a big one. It can hold forty people."

"Sounds good," Ryan decided as she extracted a few folded, and quite damp, bills from the hidden pocket of her shorts. "You might want to let those dry out before your touch them," she politely informed the clerk, as she grasped Jamie's hand to lead her to their tub.

The smaller woman was bubbling with excitement as Ryan led her to the path that caressed the hillside. They climbed up a short distance into the dense undergrowth that nearly obscured the wooden steps leading to the individual tubs. Towering oaks and massive California sycamores fringed a lovely small garden, filled with roses and star jasmine. The beautiful plants emitted a sweet scent that diminished quickly as they continued to climb. By the time they reached the platform that held their tub, the strong, acrid scent of sulfur filled the air, and Jamie cocked her head and asked, "Natural springs?"

"Yep," Ryan agreed. "A hot sulfur mineral spring lies about a thousand feet down." She opened the redwood door that guarded their haven, and Jamie gasped in surprise and elation.

"Honey, it's wonderful!" she enthused as she took in the gently flowing waterfalls that cascaded into the pool. The little room could have been lifted right from a tropical island with its in-ground rock walls and lush green plants. Jamie tossed her arms around her partner's neck and leaned back in the embrace, smiling up at her sweetly. "Wanna go naked?" she asked with just a hint of a flush covering her cheeks.

Ryan's slowly shaking head and gentle smile answered her question.

"No?" Jamie asked, perplexed that her bold partner would want to wear a suit.

"No. Definitely not. That'd be like taking a child to Disneyland and making her stay outside the park. Looking at your beautiful body without being able to touch it would be torture of the highest degree."

"You say the silliest, sweetest things to me," Jamie replied, standing on her tiptoes to bestow a kiss.

"All true, hot stuff, all true."

They modestly turned their backs to change into their suits and when they were ready, they held hands to climb into steaming tub. Simultaneously, they let out a hiss of pleasure as they sank in up to their ears. "Oh, God, this is heaven," Jamie purred as her eyes fluttered closed, and she dropped her head back against the wall.

"If this is what heaven is like, I can see why you have to be good to get there," Ryan agreed completely in a lazy, relaxed drawl.

The water was deep for Jamie so she eventually sat on Ryan's lap. Practicality quickly gave way to passion, and soon they were engaged in a torrid make out session they were barely able to control. Leaning heavily against her partner, Jamie finally moaned, "Can you imagine the awesome sex we're going to have?"

Ryan closed her eyes, letting her mouth quirk into a satisfied smile while slowly nodding her head. "I imagine it several dozen times a day. When I'm awake, when I'm asleep ..."

"You don't have to imagine for much longer," Jamie whispered. "Monday will be here before you know it."

"The minutes will seem like years," Ryan gently corrected. "Maybe decades."

After they had soaked for a good long time, Ryan hopped out and laid a towel on the redwood deck. She reached into her little pack and pulled out a bottle of massage lotion. One eyebrow wiggle had Jamie climbing out of the tub, ready to be rubbed. Ryan worked on her partner's thighs, butt and lower back, effectively removing all signs of fatigue from the overstressed muscles.

Jamie just grunted in pleasure all through the session. When Ryan was finished, Jamie summoned all of her strength and managed to give Ryan a similarly thorough rubdown as grateful repayment. When her muscles were nice and loose, Jamie lay down next to her, drawing her into her arms and kissing her for a few more minutes. They were deep into their enjoyment of each other when Ryan's watch alarm chirped. "Five minutes before our hour's up," she regretfully informed her blissfully relaxed partner.

"Buy us another hour," Jamie begged pathetically.

"Okay," Ryan dutifully agreed as she hopped up, but her progress was stopped by Jamie's hand gently grasping her ankle.

"We can go. I'm just … I'm so relaxed I can't imagine having to hop back on that bike."

"I know," Ryan agreed as she extended a hand to help her up. "You don't regret stopping, do you?"

"Regret? How could I regret the most wonderful hour of my life?" she asked with a wide grin. "You, a steaming hot tub, you, a tranquil tropical setting … did I mention you?"

"Yes, you did," she grinned. "I feel very appreciated."

"Well, you should. Because I appreciate you more than words can express."

"The feeling is decidedly mutual," Ryan said, turning around to shimmy back into her bike clothes.

When they were finished, Jamie stood still for Ryan's chronic re-application of her sunscreen. "This little pink skin is too precious to burn," she said as she kissed her on the nose.

When they left the springs, they headed back inland. The terrain was very flat in this agricultural valley, and they were chatting contentedly until Jamie spied a very steep hill in the distance. "What's that?" she asked as casually as possible.

"That's Little Agony," Ryan replied with a grin.

"Uhm … where's Big Agony?"

"You'll see. I do want to warn you though, Jamie. This is a very, very steep hill. It's almost impossible to go more than five miles an hour, so I want you to consider just walking up it. It's only about a quarter-mile long, but it's narrow and heavily traveled."

"What are you going to do?"

"I'm gonna bust my thighs," her buff partner said with an evil grin.

Ryan was right about the hill being very steep. It was about a twenty percent grade, the steepest by far of any they had encountered. The vast majority of the riders had chosen to walk up the hill, given the traffic and the narrow shoulder. But Ryan just put her head down and powered right up it. She actually didn't go a whole lot faster than the walkers, but her slow pace let Jamie ogle her for a while, so they both ended up happy.

At the top of the hill, many riders had gathered to cheer on their compatriots. Ryan was smiling broadly when Jamie finally crested the hill, and she gave her a kiss for her caution.

After the hill, another quick descent brought them to the last stop of the day. The sight of an entire Girl Scout troop that had come out to greet them charmed them both. Jamie caught an adorable interchange with Ryan and a whole group of the kids with her camera and then submitted to Ryan's order that she also pose. "Good thing you guys have on your uniforms," Ryan joked. "Or I wouldn't be able to tell which of you was my friend."

"Very funny," Jamie scowled as the nine-year-olds who surrounded her ineffectively tried to suppress their giggles.

The last fifteen miles of the day were flat and blissfully quick. The women pulled into the park to the cheers of hundreds of riders, crew, local residents, and community leaders all acknowledging their efforts. It was the largest welcome they had experienced yet, and neither could resist adding to the ranks. So, as tired as they were, they joined the crowd to welcome home their fellow riders, cheering them on for a long time.

They joined yet another of Ryan's old teams for dinner. This group, of almost twenty people from San Francisco General Hospital consisted of nurses, orderlies, technicians and a couple of doctors, all of whom kidded and teased Ryan unmercifully for finally finding a lover. During a fantastic tortellini dinner, they debated strategy for the next day. They only needed to cover fifty-five miles—quite a short distance compared with the usual ninety plus miles—but eleven of those miles were devoted to just one hill. They also had to face "The Wall," a really steep climb, right at the end of the day. "So do you want to power through the day and get to the camp really early, or would you rather take it easy and slow?" Ryan asked.

"Are there any cool places we could spend an hour or two?" Jamie asked, knowing that if such places existed, Ryan would know of them.

"Yeah, we actually stop for lunch at the Zaca Mesa Winery. It's a beautiful spot with lots of trees and shade. We could go on a tour if you want, but I don't think we can afford to sample the fare."

"What's tomorrow night's camp like?" Jamie asked, trying to gather all of the pertinent info before she made up her mind.

"It's the nicest one on the whole trip. Real showers and real toilets. And it's a beautiful setting, too. A gorgeous lake called Cachuma."

"Why don't we try to do both? Let's leave as early as possible, stop for a while at the winery, and then ride hard for the rest of the day. Then we should get in early to get one of those real showers."

"You are a genius," Ryan said reverently, giving her a sweet kiss.

"Don't eat my dessert," Jamie ordered, as she got up to stand in line for a Porta-Potty.

"Oh-oh," a nurse named Barbara said under her breath as Jamie walked away.

"What?" Ryan asked idly, still concentrating on Jamie's rear.

"Here comes trouble," she said a little louder.

The object of her concern made a beeline for Jamie, falling in right behind her in the slow-moving line. "Does your girlfriend know about your … past?" Barbara asked Ryan as tactfully as possible.

"She knows the truth," Ryan nodded. "But my version of the truth and Tiffany's probably don't have many similarities." She turned to Barbara and said, "I think I'll have to do some damage control later. I'd better go get some more cookies. I might need my strength!"

The purposeful woman slipped into line behind Jamie and tapped her on the shoulder. "Tiffany Grable," she said, as though the name should mean something to Jamie.

The blonde regarded the confident-looking woman who stood before her. Dark wavy hair, cut to just shoulder length, very dark, almost black eyes that radiated heat but not warmth, attractive but sharp features that curled into a smirk as Jamie extended her hand. "Jamie Evans."

"Are you the girlfriend of the week, or did you buy the line about going for a longer ride?" she asked, sarcasm dripping from her words.

"Uhm, Tiffany, is it?"

"Yes."

"Don't dis my lover," she snapped, green eyes flashing. She turned and stalked back to the table where twenty-one pairs of eyes tried not to let her see they were watching her. She flopped down heavily onto the bench and shook her head. "She must have had me confused with someone who gives a damn," she pronounced as she looked at the empty plate in front of her partner and demanded, "Where are my cookies?"

After a stop to replace the purloined cookies, they strolled around the campgrounds, walking near a large duck pond in the center of the site. They sat on the ground and watched the ducks forage for dinner for a long time. They didn't speak much, being content to just be in each other's presence.

They hadn't discussed Tiffany's display, since there were so many other people around, but Ryan knew it had to be bothering her partner. "Wanna talk about it?" she asked gently.

"What, that idiot?"

"Yeah, didn't that bother you?"

Jamie sat and contemplated her reply. Finally she turned to Ryan and said, "Not really. I mean, to be honest, I'd be pissed if you made love to me and then dropped me as soon as the ride was over."

"But I never led her on …" Ryan began, but Jamie cut her off.

"That's how *you* are, Ryan. *You* weren't invested, and you told them the truth. But most women aren't that way. They believe your signals more than your words. And knowing you, your signals were pretty encouraging."

"So are you angry with me?"

"No, of course not," she said quickly. "I know how you behaved before we got together. I know you were honest, but I also know that a lot of women must not have believed you. I feel sorry for them because I know how easy it is to fall in love with you," she said, giving her a sweet smile. "But just because someone is mad at *you* is no reason to get in *my* face. That's completely uncalled for."

"She didn't know who she was tussling with," Ryan agreed as she gave her partner a squeeze.

After several moments had passed, Ryan lay down with her head in Jamie's lap. As the nimble fingers began to slide through her long black locks, giving her a little scalp rub for good measure, Ryan warned, "You'd better be careful, there, Jamie."

"Why, is this one of your erogenous zones?"

"Well, it can be," she admitted. "But it's a surefire knockout when I'm tired."

"This puts you to sleep?" she asked as she continued the rub.

"Like a blow to the head."

"And just how many blows to the head have knocked you out?" she teased, tapping her skull playfully.

Ryan silently counted in her head, finally replying, "Five, I think."

"Jesus, Ryan!" she nearly shouted. "How did they happen?"

"Gee Jamie, it's really not all that hard to knock yourself out," she explained logically.

"Ryan, I don't know another person who's been knocked out once. So how did you get so lucky five times?"

"Well, let me think now. I got a doozy of a concussion when I was about ten. We were skateboarding down Lombard, and somebody cut me off. I flew over one of those little flowerbeds and landed right on my head. If I hadn't had on the helmet that Da made me promise to wear, I would have bit it."

"My God!" she said as she tenderly rubbed the skull lying in her lap. "Did you have to go to the hospital?"

"Oh yeah, paramedics, ambulance, the whole nine yards. I don't remember any of it, of course, but Da and the boys have never joked about it, so they must have really been scared."

"How long were you in the hospital?"

"Just overnight, I think," she said. "But I was pretty out of it for a while. I had headaches and vertigo for a couple of weeks. It was really pretty scary. But the worst thing was that Da wouldn't let me use my skateboard for months. I had to run like the dickens to keep up with my buddies."

Jamie shook her head and rolled her eyes as she considered that Ryan's perspective and hers were quite different regarding the worst part of the incident. "When did he relent?"

Ryan chuckled as she related, "I'd been saving up for something special, and I bought one of the first pairs of rollerblades sold in San Francisco. I really wasn't very competent on them, and he caught me trying to go down Noe on the darned things. He went right into his room and handed me back my skateboard. He said at least on a skateboard I could jump off and be on solid ground."

"How many sleepless nights that man must have gone through," Jamie muttered, patting Ryan's grinning cheek. "Now I'm afraid to ask, but what were the other times?"

"A couple of years later, I took a flying kick to the head in karate class. That laid me out for a few minutes, but I didn't tell Da, so I didn't have to go to the doctor."

"We're definitely adopting," Jamie scolded. "Tell me the rest."

"I got kicked in the head playing soccer in high school. It wasn't that bad, and I didn't even lose consciousness, but the trainer wouldn't let me back in the game just because I didn't know what day it was," she grumbled. Jamie shot her a disapproving glance, but she added, "We were behind," as if that explained everything.

"Okay, that's only three. Were the others from sky diving or cliff jumping?"

"Ooh, I've never sky dived, but I'd love to."

"Number four?" Jamie scowled.

"I was playing basketball, and a girl from the other team was on me all night. I don't know what her problem was, but she was really harassing me. Near the end of the game, I got the ball and went right over her head for a basket. As I turned around, she took the ball and heaved it right at me. It hit me in the back of the head, which wouldn't have been so bad, but I didn't see it coming and it knocked my head into the basket support. They said I fell like the building had dropped on me." She laughed at this image, but Jamie saw no humor in it at all.

"Hospital?"

"Yep. Just overnight for observation, though."

"Okay, give me number five."

"You sure?" she asked cautiously. "It's kinda bad."

"Yes, I'm sure. If it happened to you, I want to know about it."

She took a deep breath and blinked slowly a few times, causing Jamie's heart to pick up in anticipation of the obviously distressing story. "I was gay bashed," Ryan finally said, her voice just above a whisper.

"What?" Jamie cried, her shocked gasp seemingly a hundred times louder than Ryan's small voice.

"About a year ago," she continued. "Actually, it was the week after Gay Pride, so that would make it the end of June. I was on a date with a woman I was just getting to know. We were down in SOMA, going to a bar. We'd taken my bike, and she had her arms around me, just holding on—nothing sexual at all. When we got off, a group of guys came out of the alley and started hassling us. We were only about a block from the bar, but there was nobody around."

Unconsciously, Jamie began to gently rub her head to comfort her.

"I would have gotten back on the bike and run them over if I could have. It was obvious they were going to hurt us if they could. But I knew I couldn't get Kelly on with me, so I tried to talk them out of it. She was a lot smaller than I was, so they tried to push her around first. Things started to get out of control, and I made a mistake that haunts me to this day," she mumbled. "I showed my trump card too early. I took out the guy who was shoving her, but when I went to get the second guy a third one pulled a knife and put it to Kelly's throat. He said he'd kill her if I didn't back off. Of course, I had to, so two of them grabbed me, and made me watch while they beat her senseless," she closed her eyes and tried to blink back the tears.

Jamie couldn't say a word. She was just glad that Ryan wasn't looking at her so she didn't have to try not to look terrified.

"When they finished with her, they started on me. One of them had a pipe and they broke some of my ribs and bruised the rest, then they hit me on the head. That was the only time I was happy to be unconscious," she said as she shivered slightly at the memory of the pain.

"What happened then?" Jamie asked with a tremulous voice, afraid of the answer.

"Luckily they found us too repellant to rape, so they left us lying in the street. Somebody called an ambulance, and we were both taken to the hospital." She shook her head as she added, "It was so hard to see Da's face when I woke up. I don't think I'd seen him that upset since my mother died."

"How bad were your injuries?" Jamie asked, with a pale, frightened face.

"I had two black eyes, a non-displaced skull fracture, three broken ribs and a bruised kidney. They were afraid that my spleen was ruptured, but luckily it wasn't, and I didn't have to have surgery. I don't think there was a part of me that wasn't bruised. I looked like I'd been hit by a bus, and it took me most of the summer to be pain free. That's when my Aunt and cousin Aisling came to see me. It was pretty bad, and they were all worried, so they came to reassure themselves that I was going to be all right. I was just getting back to normal when I met you."

"What happened to Kelly?" Jamie asked, almost afraid to hear the answer.

"She was okay. She had tons of bruises, too, but nothing was broken. Obviously, it really freaked her out, and she wouldn't go out with me again. Not that I blame her," she added bitterly.

"But you tried to defend her!" Jamie said indignantly.

"I know," she said, in a comforting tone. "But I think I reminded her of what happened. Besides, I didn't feel like seeing anyone for a long time. I was afraid to let anyone touch me ... well, no, that's not true," she amended. "I was afraid to relax enough around people I didn't know to let them get close to me. It really bothered me emotionally, so I finally had to see a therapist for a while. She helped me see how it was just a random act, and there was nothing I could have done differently to prevent it."

"Now I understand why it was so hard for you when I was attacked," Jamie said quietly.

"Yeah, it was only about five months after this happened, so it was still pretty fresh."

"Your poor little head," Jamie murmured soothingly, stroking her hair again. "How could anyone hurt such a sweet woman?" she said, as she leaned over and kissed her all over her face.

"I don't know the answer to that. Some people are just filled with rage. There's not much you can do except stay out of their way."

"How long were you in the hospital?"

"Three days. They did every test known to humankind on my head. I had to tell them the truth about how many times I'd been unconscious. Boy, Da almost knocked me out again when he found out that I didn't tell him about those other times," she said, laughing.

"What did they find?" she asked a bit tentatively.

"Nothing much. There were a couple of spots that they could see had been damaged, but they're pretty confident I won't have any future trouble. But I really try to protect my head now when I do anything risky."

"You'd better," Jamie said. "I love every little synapse in that pretty little head." She leaned down again to kiss her forehead. "But Ryan, I want you to promise me something."

Ryan sat up and looked at her squarely. "What is it?"

"Please promise me that you'll never keep things like that from me. I don't want to see you hurt, but if you ever do hurt yourself, promise me that you'll tell me."

"I promise I'll tell you. And I already made that promise to Da, so I really have to keep it, or I'll have both of you on my tail."

"I can't imagine how hard it must have been for you to be laid-up for so long," Jamie said, unable to imagine her hyperactive partner sitting still for very long.

"Yeah, it was hard in some ways. I spent a lot of time in Lincoln Park, just looking at the water. I couldn't walk much because of the ribs, but there are some great spots out there where you can sit and contemplate life. When I could move around without too much pain, I started to go out to Land's End. I love it there—I think it's the wildest place in the whole city."

Jamie smiled to herself, acknowledging that her partner would logically seek out the wild parts of any locale. "What did you think about?"

"Oh, I don't know. I guess I thought about the randomness of life—and how lucky I am."

"Lucky?" Jamie asked, thinking she would probably not feel lucky to be beaten half to death.

"Yeah ... lucky," Ryan said. "I can think of fifty countries just off the top of my head, where every day is a struggle just to survive. I could have been born in Bangladesh and been sold into slavery as a young child. I could have starved to death in a Rwandan refugee camp. I could have been shot or crippled in any number of ethnic or religious civil wars. I was hurt … both mentally and physically … but I've been so blessed to be born in this country, in this age, and to my family, that I just couldn't let myself wallow in that pain. That's what got me through it. I just counted my blessings."

They both grew quiet then, letting the story settle a bit. Jamie still ran her fingers through the dark hair, but her touch was even more loving and gentle than before. Ryan blinked up at her and asked, "What are you thinking?"

A heavy sigh preceded the answer. "I was thinking of how many times you've been hurt in your life. How often terrible things have happened that you didn't deserve."

"Bad things happen to everyone," she said. "Nothing you can do about it."

The small hand stilled completely as her rough voice choked out, "There is when I'm the one who hurts you."

"What?" Ryan cried, jerking into a seated position. "What are you talking about?"

"*I* hurt you, Ryan. I hurt you worse than the people who beat you up because I knew you and loved you. I hurt you by going back to Jack," she gasped out between wracking sobs.

"Jamie, we've been over this," she soothed. "That was a hard time for you …"

"And it wasn't for you?" she asked with a bitter tone. "How does that make up for how I hurt you?"

"It wasn't easy," she agreed as she pursed her lips together in memory of the pain it had caused her. "But I'm glad you did it."

"You can't be!" Jamie replied forcefully. "No one could be glad to have someone jerk them around like I did you." She shook her head forcefully, eyes closed tightly. "I'll never forgive myself for doing that to you. I used both you and Jack, and I did it only to make myself more comfortable. It makes me sick when I think about it."

"Jamie," she soothed, pulling the resisting body into her embrace. "Granted, you did hurt both Jack and me, but I don't agree that you did it with any malice. You were doing exactly what I told you to do."

"What do you mean?"

"Look, honey," Ryan said. "I'd rather be hurt that way before we got too involved, than to have you have doubts about your choice. Lesbianism wasn't a choice for me. I was either going to have sex with women or be celibate. But you probably could have stayed with a man and been reasonably fulfilled sexually. If you had a guy who pleased you in every other way, it would have probably even made up for the spark you lacked physically."

"And?"

"And your short time with Jack showed you in the most compelling way that you were ready and able to take the risk to be exactly who you are … with no compromise. I honestly think that if you hadn't given it another try, you might regret your choice when things get tough—and I guarantee things will sometimes be tough. It's not always easy to be different, as my poor fractured skull can tell you."

"You're really not disappointed or angry with me?" she asked in a tiny voice.

"Are you disappointed or angry with me for inadvertently leading women on?"

"No, I'm not. It bothered me at first, but I'm okay with it now that I really know you."

"I'm definitely not angry or disappointed in you, either. I was hurt, but sometimes you do hurt the people you love. Forgiving is part of loving. They both have to exist to make any relationship work."

"And I so badly want ours to work," Jamie agreed fervently.

"It will, baby, it will."

While they lay in bed that night, Jamie traced the tiny knots on her lover's torso that marked her broken ribs. She bent and kissed each bump, then placed Ryan's head on her chest and began to rub it gently, soothing her to sleep.

Chapter Twenty

As the first rays of sunlight hit the tent, Ryan woke in a comfortable little nest. She was spooned up against Jamie with her face pressed against her back. Her left arm was behaving itself, nestled between their bodies, but her right arm had snuck down across her partner's torso where her hand was firmly wedged between Jamie's legs. She slowly extracted her hand from its little haven and placed it on the much less dangerous terrain of her waist. The movement caused her partner to stir, and moments later green eyes looked up at her in question. "Is it time to get up?"

"If you want to get going early it is," Ryan said, nuzzling her neck.

"Okay, I'm up," she said as she struggled to her knees. "Hey, c'mere." Ryan had turned around to crawl out, so she backed up. Jamie ran her hand up and down her torso. "You're losing weight. You're all concave here," she said, patting her tummy. "We've got to get some more food into you."

"I'll have an extra bagel for breakfast. And I'll bring some GU today. That'll give me another five hundred calories."

"Goo?"

"Gu is a little tube of a flavored energy replacement. Each one is a hundred calories, and it's fat free. It's just an energy source that doesn't upset my stomach, but gives me some easy calories."

"Do you like them?"

"Given how much I love food, I'd prefer to get my calories the old-fashioned way. But I'm really sick of energy bars, so I haven't been eating enough of them. And too much lunch really upsets my tummy, so this is my only option."

"You'd better take care of yourself, because you're going to need every ounce of energy you can get your hands on next week. This ride is nothing compared to what I'm going to do to you!"

"You really are a little sex maniac, aren't you?"

"You're just going to have to wait and see," Jamie said as she kissed Ryan right on the tip of her nose.

Ryan was already well into her breakfast when Jamie finally joined her. She was chatting with an Irish couple who had come from Dublin just to do the ride. She introduced Jamie, and they all chatted for a while. The couple got up, wishing them both a good ride, giggling as they left. "Why was that funny?" Jamie asked.

"We were just joking about that before you came up. 'Ride' is slang for making love, and they just find it funny that people are always wishing them good sex."

"Do you know a lot of Irish slang?"

"Yeah, I do. My cousins always had to give me a crash course every summer to teach me the current terms, and I'm sure a lot of what they taught me goes in and out of style just like here, but I can figure most things out when I hear it in conversation."

"Will you take me to Ireland with you sometime?"

"I can't imagine ever going without you."

They got started really early, pedaling out of Santa Maria just before six-thirty. The first fifteen miles were a breeze—flat road, good pavement, and no traffic. They pulled into the first pit stop just as a huge truck from an L.A. television affiliate did. "We're getting close. The media's here," Ryan observed.

"I couldn't imagine saying this before this week, but I don't want this to end, Ryan," she said with a catch in her voice.

"I know just what you mean. I always start to feel like this by day five, but this year it's worse. I just feel like we're in such a blissful little cocoon. People take care of all of our needs, we're together twenty-four hours a day, and we can be as affectionate as we want … it's really been idyllic."

"I can't think of a better way to start our life together."

Ryan proved to be correct when she described the Zaca Mesa Winery as a gorgeous little place. They ate their curried chicken salad sandwiches in a beautiful setting, surrounded by vibrant grapevines then found a spot under a small grove of tall trees, where they decided to take a little nap. Ryan had brought a shiny metallic space blanket that they spread out after they had cleared the area of rocks and twigs. Ryan rolled up their jackets and made an adequate pillow for herself while Jamie was perfectly content to use her favorite human pillow—namely, Ryan's shoulder.

Moments later they were both sound asleep. Jamie soon had her leg thrown over Ryan's pelvis, and an arm draped across her torso was next. By the time Melanie saw them, they looked as though they were welded together. She reached into her fanny pack and snapped a few pictures of them, grinning the whole while.

They slept for over an hour in the cool shade. They were both groggy when they woke, but the rest had done them good, and they started off again around noon. Heartbreak Hill was their first real obstacle of the day. It was just over a half-mile long, but was about a twelve percent grade, so it was challenging. They both rode up without stopping, and Jamie felt a good bit of satisfaction as she powered up the last fifty yards.

They zoomed along for another four miles or so until The Wall. This little beast was a full one and a half miles of at least a six percent grade. Ryan knew Jamie was tiring a bit, so she offered her an inducement. Jamie was constantly begging Ryan to sing to her, and while she usually indulged her requests gladly, she had yet to sing a note on the ride. "I'll make you a deal," Ryan said mischievously, as they took a water break just before the hill. "I'll stay behind you and sing a song. I'll keep a nice, steady pace. But you'll only be able to hear me if you stay in front. So I'll serenade you up the hill, but I'm not repeating any of the verses, so keep moving," she said as she poked her in the butt.

Jamie took off, trying to keep an even pace. Ryan began her song, a long, lyrically dense story about a young maiden who is seduced by an old flame who intentionally gets her lost on the back of Rare's Hill and has his way with her after they drink a nip or two. Jamie missed an important verse as Ryan passed her at one point, but she pressed her lips together in concentration, lifted her butt from the saddle, and cranked for all she was worth until she was back within earshot. They crested the hill to the cheers of many other riders and crew, and as they pulled over to join the crowd for a bit, Jamie gave Ryan a heartfelt kiss for trying so hard to make the hills fun for her.

As they approached the campsite, Jamie mused to herself that Lake Cachuma was one of the most glorious sights she had ever seen. She knew the place was actually not the stuff of postcards, but the lure of real showers made it seem like a showplace. The only drawback was that they weren't allowed to swim, but that was a small sacrifice, given the lovely setting. Their first stop was not to look at the scenery however, it was to find that porcelain and take a real shower. They were among the first in line, and they soaked up the hot water like manna from heaven. They were both careful not to use too much, since they knew everyone else needed a turn, but every drop was delicious to their dirty bodies.

They got into the tent in their T-shirts and panties and fell into a deep sleep in a matter of minutes. As they woke, Jamie thought nothing had ever felt quite so good to her as snuggling together with their clean, shower-scented bodies and fresh clothes. A light breeze blew through the open tent flap, and Jamie couldn't resist tasting the toothpaste-fresh mouth right next to hers. She kissed and nibbled and sucked on that sweet mouth for many minutes. Ryan tried her best to control the escalation of passion, but as usual, she failed miserably. Jamie wound up straddling her hips, grinding against her with overwhelming need. Ryan took pity on her and whispered, "Do you want me to leave you alone for a while?"

But Jamie merely pressed her lips together and shook her head in frustration. She rolled off her hips and once again started kissing her partner deeply. Ryan eventually came up for air and whispered, "Honey, you seem so frustrated. Are you okay?"

But Jamie held steadfast—frustrated beyond belief—but steadfast. She bent down again for another round of frantic kissing, seemingly trying to physically merge with her partner. After a long while she rolled over onto her back, panting deeply. Ryan leaned over and asked solicitously, "Is there anything I can do to help you?"

Jamie blinked up at her and shook her head, a tiny smile finally gracing her lips. "I'm gonna assume that was rhetorical," she chuckled. "Because we both know that you could help plenty."

"Well …" Ryan drawled, "I don't like to boast, but I do have some experience in these matters."

"Save your experience until Monday," Jamie said, as she flopped down onto her back. "I can use all the help I can get."

"Don't think I'm laughing at you," Ryan insisted as she chuckled deeply. "But I think you're gonna prove to have a certain natural gift." She placed a few final kisses on Jamie's swollen lips and added, "I predict that you're going to be a real phenom. Now give me five minutes alone or I'll be fidgeting all during dinner!"

After they loaded up on dinner, they walked around the lake. They found a deserted little spot near the banks of the placid lake, and sat down to chat. After a while, Jamie asked, "Have you given much thought to our living situation?"

"Yeah, I have. I don't think I can live without you, even for one night, so whatever we do, I really need for you to be with me."

"I agree completely," she said. "But what would you be comfortable with? Would you consider moving in with me?"

"That makes the most sense. But I'm worried about moving out completely. I know Da probably seems really independent to you, but I think he'd be lost without me around. So I'm kind of torn."

"Well, we have the house to ourselves until September. I want to go to summer school, so it makes sense to stay in Berkeley during the week. But I'd be willing to go back and forth on the weekends if he's serious about letting us sleep together at your house."

"Would you really do that for me?" Ryan asked with a look of wonder on her face.

"Ryan, I'd carry you back and forth to Berkeley if it would make you happy. I love you, you big goofball."

"Okay, okay," she laughed. "It does make the most sense to stay in Berkeley during the week since I have to work every day. But we could go to my house on Friday evening and stay until Monday morning. Would that be okay with you?"

"Yeah, then we can see Caitlin and have Sunday dinner with the boys. I'd really miss Sunday dinner."

"You really do understand my connection with my family, don't you?"

"Yeah, I do, but I have a connection too, and it's important to me to spend time with them."

"You know, if I were to design a girlfriend, she wouldn't be as perfect as you are," she said contentedly, as she gave Jamie a brilliant smile.

"Well, that settles the summer. Let's see how it goes and then decide later what we want to do during the year."

"Okay," Ryan agreed. "Let's just make this the best summer we've ever had."

"It already has been, for me."

"This does bring up one little tiny issue, however," Ryan said.

"What's that, hon?" Jamie asked lazily.

"I think your parents are going to have a few questions. Have you given any thought to telling them about us?"

"Uhm … no," she admitted. "I've been so focused on the ride and everything that I haven't really thought about it. But I guess I do have to do it at some point."

"Yeah," Ryan drawled. "And given your mother's visit, I think that point might be soon. You really should think about how you want to do it … and when," she added.

"Okay, as soon as we're back from our honeymoon, I'll start discussing it with Anna. At least then it'll be too late for them to protect my lesbian virginity," she said with a giggle.

"It certainly will be if I get a vote!"

Day Five was the night of the traditional rider talent show. Jamie pestered Ryan to sing, but she firmly refused. "I'm saving my voice for the woman I love," she said. "I only perform for an audience of one."

They had a great time watching the show. Several people had marvelous voices, and a few professional-quality drag acts had everyone howling. One guy was a terrific juggler, and a few really talented guitar players rounded out the high quality talent. A few people with more enthusiasm and guts than talent really made the night fun, though. It was great to see people feel so much a part of the community that they didn't mind exhibiting their foibles.

They were in bed by 9:00 and asleep by 9:01. The next day was going to be a tough one—emotionally, it was their last night of camping—physically, the Gaviota Pass awaited them.

Chapter Twenty-One

A sharp, tingling sensation woke Ryan just a bit after dawn. She groggily tried to focus, but quickly gave up and settled back into sleep. "Ouch," she said moments later, as her eyes flew open, and she found the source of her discomfort.

Jamie's hand was lying on her breast, thumb and index finger curled around a very hard nipple. As her hand twitched reflexively in sleep her fingers compressed, sending a wave of sensation through the tender nub.

Ryan was about to remove the offending appendage when the hand flattened out, changing the sensation from pain to comfort. Jamie was sprawled across her body, her golden head resting on her chest. Ryan did a quick inventory and found that one of her own hands had strayed into forbidden territory, and she slowly extracted it from its resting place inside the back of Jamie's panties. Just as she slid her hand out, green eyes locked onto her "Caught ya," she said mischievously.

"You'd better check on your own hands before you go throwing stones."

Jamie did, blushing deeply as she removed her hand from its soft pillow. "Sorry," she said sheepishly.

Ryan lifted her chin with two fingers. "Jamie, you never have to apologize for touching me. Don't ever be sorry for expressing your love or your desire."

"I ... I ... I'm not sorry that I touch you, I'm just sorry that I tease you. I know this is hard for you. God knows it's hard for me, too," she added with a laugh. "I had no idea how hard it was going to be, though. I almost exploded yesterday afternoon."

"I hate to admit it, but this is one thing the nuns were absolutely correct about."

"What's that?" Jamie asked, wondering how nuns figured into this discussion.

"They said that the easiest way to get into trouble was to be in a compromising position with someone. They said it was just too easy to go that next step. They called it 'avoiding the near occasion of sin'."

"There's nothing sinful about how I feel for you," Jamie said.

"I couldn't agree more," Ryan said as she gave her a tender good-morning kiss. "Although some of the things I want to do to you are positively wicked," she added.

After they had packed up, they sat down to breakfast, where Jamie was quite surprised when Ryan ate only a bowl of oatmeal. "Are you feeling okay?" she asked solicitously, as she gently placed her hand on Ryan's tummy.

"I feel marvelous. I'm just saving room for something," she added mysteriously.

"Well, if you're saving room for something, I know it's gotta be good. I won't eat much either."

Minutes later they left Lake Cachuma, and enjoyed a relatively flat, quick pace. They hadn't even reached the first pit stop when Ryan signaled they had reached their destination. They had just entered Solvang, a terminally cute little Danish-style village. Nearly every shop was open, even though it was just after six. There was a constant stream of riders going into a sporting goods shop, and Ryan pulled up in front. "Watch my bike for a minute, okay?" she said over her shoulder as she walked inside.

She emerged moments later, carrying an aerosol can of bike polish. Jamie looked at her quizzically and said, "This is what you saved room for? Petroleum-based solvents aren't really good for you, honey."

Ryan shook her head solemnly and said, "No," as she pointed at a little bakery with a faux windmill on the roof. "That's what I saved room for."

Jamie's eyes lit up as they walked their bikes over to the little shop. The aroma was overpoweringly good, a mix of coffee, cinnamon, sugar and just about everything else Jamie loved. The display case was packed with freshly-baked goods of all varieties. Most were familiar to Jamie, who had spent some time in Denmark two years before. She searched her memory for which of the pastries had been her favorites, finally deciding that, judging from the aroma, she couldn't go wrong no matter what she chose.

Ryan was leaning over the case and Jamie was actually afraid she would drool on the clean glass. She sidled up to her and said admiringly, "You manage to top yourself almost daily in the surprise department, Ms. O'Flaherty."

"Shh, I'm concentrating," Ryan said with mock severity. "I've only got ten bucks on me, and I don't wanna make a mistake."

"Ten bucks! Ryan, most of these pastries are only a dollar. Are you really going to eat ten of them?"

"Unless I can get you to create a distraction while I grab an armful, yes, I'm only able to eat ten of them."

"You know, I can never tell when you're kidding about things like this," she said good-naturedly. "But if you're serious, I've got some major cash on me, so have at it."

As it turned out, Ryan was kidding, but not by much. She ate a cheese and a cherry Danish, two cinnamon crisps and a light little cream puff, while Jamie limited herself to a cherry Danish and a cinnamon crisp. They each had a delicious cup of coffee, their first of the trip. After they had finished, Ryan jogged off in search of a bathroom. Jamie got back in line and bought three more pastries for her lover to snack on later in the day. She was hiding them in her bike bag when Ryan returned, energized and ready for the day.

They rode only a few more miles until the first pit stop. They spent a few minutes drinking water, as Ryan advised Jamie of the impending problems climbing the Gaviota Pass.

"This next one is kind of tough," she warned. "It's a long seven miles with anywhere from a two to a five percent grade. But the real problem is the narrow shoulders on a couple of bridges. I get off the bike, turn around, and make sure that no trucks are coming. If it's clear, I ride across if it's a long bridge, or I sprint across if it's short. Promise me that you'll be careful, okay?" she asked seriously, placing her hands on Jamie's shoulders and looking intently into her eyes.

"I promise I'll be careful. I don't have the thrill-seeking gene like somebody I know," she replied, as she found her favorite tickling spot and gave it a few good twitches.

Ryan's prediction was accurate. The climb was not really all that bad, but Highway 101 is busy every hour of the day. Jamie hated having the semi's fly past her on the narrow road, but she summoned all of her concentration to focus just ahead of her, knowing Ryan would keep an eye out for the road ahead.

They dismounted and walked their bikes across two of the small bridges, then rode across a longer one, after waiting for traffic to break. When they reached the top of the pass, there was a brake test area for trucks, so they knew a big downhill was coming. For a change, Ryan didn't go down at breakneck speed. She stayed just in front of Jamie, all the way down the four-mile drop.

They reached the second pit stop at mile forty-four. Today's theme was Bath Time, and all of the crew wore shower caps, towels and slippers. They rested for a while, since the stop was later than normal because of the pass. They were now right on the ocean and they would stay close to it for the rest of the ride. The cool ocean breeze and cooler temperatures were refreshing, but Jamie knew they came with a price—they would be riding into that breeze for most of the rest of the ride.

They pedaled through the wind, and finally arrived at their lunch stop—the University of California at Santa Barbara. As they rode along the beautiful, eucalyptus-lined streets of the campus, they were greeted by dozens and dozens of elementary school kids, college students and local residents who came out with signs and banners welcoming them to Santa Barbara. Jamie fought tears every time they encountered a spontaneous display like this. She knew Ryan really appreciated it, too, from the adorable grin that she always wore when she waved back.

The cycling team from the college was on hand to welcome them at the lunch site. "Jeez, look at the thighs on that woman," Jamie said in awe as they sat on the grass eating lunch.

"Her calves aren't bad either," Ryan said with an appraising glance that began at the woman's head and slowly traveled all the way down to her feet.

"Hey," Jamie said as she poked her in the ribs. "Keep those looks for me, kiddo."

"Everything I have is for you. My interest is purely professional."

After a moment Jamie turned and faced Ryan squarely, "Do you really think I'm gonna be enough to keep you interested for the rest of your life?"

"Where did that question come from?" Ryan asked, slightly perplexed by the unexpected query.

"I don't know," Jamie replied defensively. "I just didn't like the way you looked at that woman."

"Then we need to talk about this," Ryan said. She sat up straight and put her hands on Jamie's knees. She closed her eyes for a moment to compose her thoughts, and when she opened them she gazed deeply into Jamie's eyes. "I pledge my fidelity to you alone. I'll never touch another woman in a sexual way. I swear to that, and I'd never make such an important promise that I couldn't keep."

"I know, Ryan," she said as she wrapped her arms around her neck. "I'm sorry. I'm just feeling sensitive today."

"No, don't brush this aside," she insisted. "I really want you to understand this. I think you and I are different in this area, and I want you to understand me." She pulled back from Jamie's embrace and held both of her hands. "I love women. I love just about everything about women. I get a lot of pleasure out of seeing a beautifully built woman. But I look at other women like works of art. My pleasure comes from seeing their bodies, and the way they carry themselves. I don't objectify them or think about having sex with them any more though. I just admire the female form. I don't think I can stop doing that, and I'm not sure that I would, even if I could," she said resolutely. "But you're the woman I want to be with. You're the woman I want to touch intimately. You're more than enough woman for me, and you always will be. I find everything about you beautiful. Not just your face or your body. It's your spirit that I love, and that will always be the same, even when we grow old." She slid her arms around her partner and kissed the tears coursing down her face. "You're the last woman in my life," she whispered, bending to kiss her tenderly.

"Oh Ryan, you are so sweet to me," she said through her tears. "Thank you for putting up with my insecurities."

"I don't understand why a jewel like you is insecure, but I don't consider talking about things like this 'putting up' with you. We're still getting to know each other. And I want to spend the rest of my life getting to know you … at the cellular level," she said with a crooked little grin.

"Only you could weave biology into an expression of love," Jamie said teasingly, kissing Ryan on the nose. "And I hope you know I don't doubt your love. I just get insecure when I think of the other women you've been with. I just worry that I won't measure up."

"Jamie, Jamie, Jamie," Ryan said, hugging her close. "I've been eating from McDonalds and Burger King for all these years. You're the finest five-star restaurant in the world compared to those other women. I could never miss those empty calories. Each meal was indistinguishable from the next." She rocked her slowly in her arms and added, "You, and only you, are what gives me true sustenance."

Jamie fought back the tears again as she kissed Ryan's face, "I truly think that you are the sweetest woman on earth."

After lunch, they rode on the lovely system of bike paths that traversed Santa Barbara. Ryan explained how far the system went, and showed Jamie some of the spurs that cyclists could take to cross town. "How do you know so much about the system?" Jamie asked.

"I was down here a couple of years ago for a tournament, and I stayed on campus. I borrowed a bike and rode all over when we weren't playing."

"What kind of tournament were you in?"

"Basketball."

"I didn't know you played basketball," she said with surprise.

"Sure you did. I told you one of my concussions was during a game."

"But I didn't understand that you played on a real team. I thought you were just fooling around. Was this in high school?"

"Nope. College."

"You played college-level basketball?" she said suspiciously. "And you've never mentioned that you played?"

"Guess not," she said over her shoulder as she took off with a laugh.

It's gonna take me years to get all of her secrets out, Jamie thought. *But I'll get 'em eventually.*

Their next stop was the town of Carpinteria. The Rotary Club, the city council, several hundred residents, a radio station and a large group of local merchants were there to greet them. Big boom boxes provided loud music, and as people milled about waiting for massages and food, a number of people danced energetically to the booming sounds of the music. They were right on the beach, and they watched paragliders, surfers and body boarders work the waves. Jamie was happy to just plop down and take a rest, but Ryan was buzzing with energy. She spotted her old friend Karen, and motioned her over. They chatted for a while, and when it became obvious that Ryan was wired, Karen asked, "Hey Jamie, do you mind if I work some excess energy off your girlfriend?"

"I guess that depends on how you plan on doing that," was the dry reply.

"Just a little dancing is all."

"Be my guest," Jamie said with a flourish.

"Do I get a vote?"

"Nope," Jamie and Karen replied simultaneously.

Karen took her hand and led her over to the largest boom box. They started to jump around energetically, bleeding off energy. Jamie watched with fascination, thinking, *I don't know what's better, dancing with her or watching her dance.*

After they were back on their bikes, Jamie said, "You know, it was fun watching you dance. You and Karen really look cute together."

Ryan cocked her head at her as she replied, "It didn't bother you to see me with her, did it?"

"Not at all. I meant what I said. It was cute." After a beat she added, "Why didn't you want to date her seriously? She really looks like your type, now that I've been around her."

"She's too much my type," she admitted wryly. "We would've driven each other crazy. She has more energy than I do in some areas, and she had even less interest than I did in settling down with one person. She slept with someone else on the ride!" she said indignantly.

"Why did that bother you?"

"Because we were having sex every night. I'm not used to people looking elsewhere while I'm actively bedding them," she said. "And it was in our tent. I had to go sit on a picnic bench, and wait for them to finish so I could go to bed. Then, to add insult to injury, she still wanted to do it with me later that night."

"And you, of course, said no, right?" Jamie asked innocently, as she batted her big green eyes.

"Well, she obviously wasn't satisfied, so I had to show her what she had missed," Ryan explained with a wry chuckle.

"It doesn't bother you to talk about your old flames, does it?"

"No. Does it bother you to hear about them?"

"No, it doesn't," she said reflectively. "I like thinking about what a player you used to be. And I stress the 'used to be' part of that statement."

"My membership in that group has been voluntarily and irrevocably terminated."

The next twelve miles were torturously slow ones. The wind had freshened and blew in their faces the entire time. It seemed as though they had done the entire ride in one day rather than six, and the remaining miles loomed ahead of them like an unbreachable wall. Ryan rode directly in front of Jamie, trying to be a foil, but it really didn't help much. Several times during the worst of it, Jamie rued her decision to take on this adventure, but after a few minutes of grousing, she would look up ahead and see her determined partner grinding away, and her mood would improve immediately. They rested much longer than normal at the last pit stop, dropping to the ground under the shade of a small tree after they had consumed two bottles of sports drink. Neither spoke for the entire time they lay there, and after a good half-hour's rest, Ryan stood and extended her hand, pulling Jamie to her feet. They headed out for the last ten miles of the day with grimly determined faces.

They arrived at Buenaventura State Beach significantly later than normal. Both felt more tired than sweaty, so they skipped their evening shower and took a quick nap. The nap was actually more like a quick coma than anything else, since neither heard their boisterous neighbors setting up camp, singing Streisand tunes at full volume.

Almost as soon as they left the tent, Jamie could sense that the mood over the camp had a different feeling than every other night. They stood in the longish line observing the assembled riders. After a few minutes, Jamie tilted her head up and said, "I've been trying to think of what this reminds me of. I think I've got it."

"What's that?"

"It feels like the last days of high school," she decided. "You know, you're all aware that it's almost over, and you know that even though you claim you'll stay close, it will be the last time you will see some of your acquaintances."

"Yeah, I guess it does," she agreed halfheartedly.

"It's not like that for you?"

"I didn't have any friends by the time I graduated from high school," she said flatly. "And the thought of never seeing most of my classmates again was pure bliss."

Turning in her direction, Jamie placed her hands flat against Ryan's chest. The look on her face was one of sheer incredulity. "Ryan, everyone loves you," she insisted. "I know you had troubles, but surely …"

"No. No one," she declared, her face impassive, but her eyes reflecting the lingering hurt.

"But how …"

"Not now, Jamie. This night is hard enough for me without dredging that stuff up."

For the hundredth time, Jamie mentally rebuked herself for her unerring ability to find topics that greatly upset her partner. *Quit prying into her past so much,* she chided herself. *She tells you plenty, but she only does it when she's ready. Leave the poor thing alone.*

Trying one of the two things that always seemed to brighten Ryan's mood, she peeked down the table and commented. "Mmm, brownies for dessert."

"Where?" Ryan asked sharply.

"Right over there." She pointed, indicating a large platter nearly filled with the treats. "I'm not really in the mood for chocolate tonight," she said with a casual dismissal. "You can have mine."

A sweet smile and a little squeeze of her hand greeted her offer. "It's okay. I'm not mad at you for asking about my life. You don't have to give me cookie reparations."

"Would you like my brownie?" Jamie asked.

"Mmm, let's just say this for the record. When I turn down a brownie, it's time to take me to the emergency room."

"It makes me happy to make you happy. So do us both a favor, and accept my peace offering, okay?"

"Hrumph! The lengths I have to go to please you!" she muttered, trying to hide a grin.

"St. Ryan of Mayo," Jamie decreed. "It's got a ring to it."

"Mmm, I think I prefer St. Ryan of Killala," she decided. "The town could use the tourist business my shrine would bring in."

"Yet another saintly act, always thinking of others."

After they received their food, they were searching around for a place to sit when a voice called out, "Hey, 'O'".

Ryan looked around and identified the speaker, then turned to Jamie to ask, "Mind if we sit with the wild girls?"

"Ahh, no, I think I've shown that I have a soft spot for wild girls."

They walked over to a table of six women. Jamie guessed they were a little older—in their late twenties to early thirties—and they clearly knew Ryan well. She went from woman to woman, kissing each on the lips, before she began to introduce her partner. "Jamie, this motley crew is a small part of the Lavender Menace, one of the teams I trained with a couple of years ago. Everybody, this is Jamie Evans, my ..." she cast a devilish grin at her partner before decreeing, "fiancée."

"What?" the women responded, almost in unison.

"Yep. We're tying the knot on Monday," she related. Ryan caught the shocked look on Jamie's face, but she just beamed a smile at her and gave her shoulder a little squeeze.

The assembled women spent quite a while dragging the whole story out of Ryan. Jamie sat at her side, responding to direct questions, but finding herself very happy just to watch her partner interact with the group. She recognized at least one of them from the off-road ride Ryan had taken her to up on Mt. Tam, and as she regarded each of them, she had to admit that they were the most stereotypical looking lesbians that she had seen Ryan with. They all had very short hair, much shorter than her own, and two of them had hair of a color rarely found in nature. Their casual poses allowed her to detect that at least three of them didn't shave their legs, and all of them had some type of body ornament, either tattoos or a visible piercing.

Even though she hadn't met a lot of Ryan's friends, she decided that, based on looks, her partner wouldn't have a lot in common with these women, but there was some deep bond that reflected her connection to them. She was a little more boisterous and a lot more full of herself—boasting about her conditioning, and her preparedness for the ride—but it was all done with such a teasing, playful sense that it was very well received. It took a minute for the realization to dawn on Jamie, but she finally recalled what it reminded her of. *It's like any group of jocks*, she mused. *They build themselves up and tear each other down, but it's done with an affectionate teasing that's really cute*, she decided. *Yet another side of the enigmatic Ms. O'Flaherty*, she thought affectionately as she watched her perform.

"So, Ryan," a woman named Cathy said. "I hear Tiffany's been looking for you. Hey!" she cried when her neighbor poked her in the ribs. "O's cool with it, aren't you?"

"Yeah, it's fine," she agreed with an amused chuckle as she slung an arm around her partner. "Jamie already told her to take a hike."

"Good for you, Jamie," a woman named Brenda opined. "She's trash!"

"Oh, she's not that bad," Ryan said, always trying to give people the benefit of the doubt.

Six pairs of eyes rolled at that comment. The women struggled to their feet, patting Ryan and Jamie on the back as they passed. "We'll see you two over at the stage," Brenda said. "We want to catch all the announcements about tomorrow."

"Okay, see ya," Ryan said as they departed.

"Tying the knot?" the amused voice at her side softly wafted up to Ryan's ear.

"Yep. That's exactly how I think of it."

Jamie snuggled close and slipped her arm around her partner's waist. "Why haven't you told me that?" she asked. "I mean, I know we've both been looking forward to next week, but I didn't know …"

"You didn't know how much it means to me emotionally?" Ryan asked as she turned to look at her.

"No, no … I guess I do know that," Jamie said. "I'm not sure what I mean. Maybe it just surprised me to hear you talk about it in those terms."

"Just because we're not having a ceremony doesn't mean that it's any less meaningful for me." Ryan grasped her hands. "This is our honeymoon. I'll admit that I didn't spend much time thinking about my wedding day when I was young, but the commitment still means a lot to me. You've held my heart for a very long time. But on Monday, I'm giving you my body too. This means more to me than I can say."

Once again her partner's ability to take her breath away had Jamie struggling to calm her heart. She found herself unable to answer at the moment, her words uncharacteristically abandoning her. So she turned her head and leaned heavily against Ryan, letting the emotion pass between them for a long time.

She jerked into an upright position, however, when Tiffany passed right in front of them, chortling with some comrades as she did.

Jamie smoothed her hair into place and passed her brownie over to her partner along with a kiss on the cheek. "I think it's so sweet that you don't trash people," she said, very pleased that Ryan hadn't even commented on the woman's presence.

"Oh, I do," Ryan laughed. "I can be positively wicked. They just have to hit a hot button. Tiffany didn't ever do that."

"Do you have any idea why she's so angry with you?"

"Yeah, a pretty good idea," Ryan said, as she nibbled on her gooey brownie. "Partly it's just her personality. She's very confrontational—always ready to pick a fight. She works at San Francisco General now, with a lot of the people we met the other night, and she's never been well liked there. I met her on one of the bike rides up in Marin. She wasn't at the hospital when I trained that group."

"So she hangs out with the women we met tonight?" Jamie asked, trying to fit the snotty woman into the friendly, relaxed group that she had just been introduced to.

"Kinda. She doesn't really fit in with this crowd, but she was in the group when I volunteered to train them for the ride."

"You trained the whole group?"

"Yeah. Nothing like I did with you, though. I just helped them with the actual riding part. Many of them were mountain bikers, and they were unfamiliar with road bikes and how to get ready to do a long trek like this. We used to go on long rides on Saturday and Sunday, and then get dinner together. Tiffany knew how I was—without a doubt," she insisted. "Everybody knew I was sleeping with Alisa. Remember her?"

"Yeah," Jamie grimaced, the image of the lovely Latina kissing Ryan after the off-road ride on Mt. Tam still burned into her brain.

"Right. Anyway, Tiffany knew that, but she still tried to get me to go to her apartment after almost every dinner. I went a few times—really—just a few times," she insisted. "I was still seeing Alisa, and she knew that, and everything seemed fine. When we got our registration packets for the Ride, she asked if we could bunk together. That seemed fine with me—I actually didn't care who I slept with. Well …" she blushed and added, "you know what I mean. But she obviously thought it meant something. The night before the ride ended she told me that she wanted to be exclusive with me. I didn't feel the same way at all, and I tried to explain that in a gentle way, but she was furious. I actually thought she was going to hit me. I went to watch the entertainment, hoping she'd cool down, but when I got back to the tent all my stuff was laying in a heap outside the flap. Luckily, they let me sleep in the medical trailer, or I'd have had to sleep on a picnic table!"

"Wow, she *was* furious," Jamie agreed her brow furrowed slightly. "Did you ever talk to her again?"

"I tried to," Ryan explained. "When we got home, I called her several times, but she never picked up and she never returned my calls."

"Her loss, sweetie," Jamie decided. "If you didn't love me, I'd still want to be your friend. I'd take whatever little piece of yourself you'd give me."

"I give you everything," she said with a very serious look on her face.

"I know you do, love. And it's the best gift I've ever received. Someday I hope I'm worthy of it," she added, leaning in for a gentle kiss.

"I don't give myself away to someone who I don't think is worthy of my love," Ryan assured her. "You're the woman I want … heart and soul."

"That's just what you've got," Jamie agreed, tasting the rich chocolate that lingered on her partner's smiling lips.

They began to make the rounds, saying goodbye to everyone they recognized. Each stop took a few minutes, as Jamie snapped photos of people she hadn't yet captured. They had all obtained their commemorative booklets for the closing ceremonies, and they had their new friends sign the booklets as a keepsake. The stop at Karen Joncas' table took quite a while as they chatted companionably. Jamie got a particularly cute shot of Karen sitting on Ryan's lap, giving her a big kiss on the cheek, as her grinning lover smiled right into the lens.

When they got up to leave, Karen said, "I hope you can cook, Jamie, because slim here is down about fifteen pounds by my estimate." She gave her friend a pat on the butt to test her theory. Grabbing a handful she amended her estimate, "Maybe twenty."

Ryan laughed and admitted, "I'm a little low. I've been having a tough time getting filled up, especially in the mornings." She was about to add something to her statement when she caught the glint in her former lover's eyes. "Don't even go there!" Ryan ordered, playfully cuffing her on the head.

When they had spoken to everyone around the dining area, they made their way to the stage. Ryan loved this night, as they were all able to say thank you to the volunteers and organizers of the ride. But it was always very bittersweet, and she knew this year would be worse than most, since she had been so emotionally vulnerable throughout the week. The tears flowed freely when the various crews were introduced for a rousing thank you. Jamie's hands were sore when they had finally thanked the hundreds of men and women who had made the ride the wonderful experience it had been.

They walked around the camp perimeter one last time, hand in hand, silently soaking up the experience. When they returned to their tent, the emotion was still too high to speak, so they held each other for a long while, each reflecting on the experience. Finally, Ryan gave her partner a chaste kiss on the cheek, mumbling, "It's too tempting tonight," before she rolled over with her back to Jamie and went to sleep.

Chapter Twenty-Two

Her eyes opened slowly as dawn broke over the mountains. Disoriented, she shook her head to try to get her bearings—nothing felt familiar as she tried to fully open her eyes in the still-dark tent. Her face was resting on something smooth and warm, but it didn't feel quite right. She knew she was intertwined with her lover, but the parts didn't seem to be in the right order. Finally adjusting to the light, she could begin to make out where her head lay—on a firmly muscled thigh—and she felt with her hands until she could discern that Jamie was indeed facing in a different direction, with her head resting on Ryan's abdomen. *That's why I have to pee so badly*, she thought absently.

As soon as this thought hit her cerebral cortex, she shot straight up, causing Jamie to do the same. They sat, wide eyed, facing each other for a few seconds, trying to make sense of their strange positions. Finally, Ryan just shook her head, as she struggled to find her shower gear. "I need a honeymoon," she grumbled, as she crawled out of the tent into the misty dawn.

When Jamie had packed up the tent for the last time, she stood in line to put their gear on the correct truck. They were going to the closing ceremonies, but a number of people were not, so there were different trucks for the different destinations. Since their things would be delivered based on last names, they decided to put Jamie's name on everything. That way, when Mia came to find them, their gear would be together.

Ryan came back from the shower looking grumpy. Jamie pulled her aside and sat down with her at a picnic table. "You know, I think Mia would understand if we just went home tonight. We could be in Pebble Beach by midnight."

Ryan just shook her head, still wearing a frown.

"We could go to a really nice hotel in L.A. We could stay for a couple of days if you want," she offered. "That would be a perfectly acceptable compromise."

The frown remained, as the head shook again.

"Tell me what you want, sweetheart," she cooed, running her fingers through the dark tresses.

That brought a smile to the grumpy-looking face. "I don't think you've ever called me that before," Ryan said shyly as she looked up, blue eyes twinkling through dark bangs.

Jamie considered that, then said, "I think I have, but if I haven't, I should. You *are* my sweetheart," she soothed, pulling Ryan's head down to kiss her thoroughly. "Now tell me what you want, and I'll do my best to give it to you."

"I want to be with you, and I want to wait," she moaned as she leaned into the contact. "My head's all clouded. I don't think very well when I'm turned on all the time. I don't have enough blood going to my brain," she pouted.

"You poor baby," she murmured softly. "Your head's all cloudy and confused, huh?" she asked, gently kissing the cloudy head.

Ryan just nodded slowly, still refusing to meet Jamie's eyes.

"Are you all grouchy 'cause you're horny?"

Another little head nod.

"How can I help you? I'll do anything you want," she soothed into her ear.

"Anything?" she said as she pulled back and allowed her blue eyes to search Jamie's carefully to determine her sincerity.

"Anything."

"You'd go back in the tent and have sex until they threw us out?"

"Absolutely," she said. "And when they threw us out, I'd take you to the first motel we passed and do you until you begged for mercy."

Ryan stood and stretched. "Okay, you don't have to do anything."

"What?" Jamie asked, truly confused.

"I feel better knowing that you take me seriously. As long as I know you'd go out of your way to make me feel better, you don't have to," she said, as though this was an obvious answer.

"Has anyone ever told you that you were a little quirky?"

"Get in line," Ryan said, narrowing her eyes in a playful glower.

They left the campground later than they would have liked. Today's ride was only seventy miles, but it was fairly hilly, through lots of traffic, and they expected the wind to be in their faces the whole day. Ryan was still feeling out of sorts, and her demeanor was off enough to cause Jamie some serious concern.

When they approached the first pit stop, Jamie came over and put her hands on her partner's shoulders. "Ryan, tell me what's wrong."

She looked down at the ground for several minutes. Jamie wasn't sure if she would answer her at all, but she finally looked up. "I don't know," she said as she shook her head.

"Something must be wrong. You've barely said a word to me since we left camp. Now tell me how you're feeling."

"I really don't know what's wrong," she said, a hint of an edge in her voice. "But I don't like to feel like I'm under a microscope, so just give me some space, will you?" Jamie's head jerked back at this totally unexpected rebuke. Her feet didn't want to move, so she stayed right where she was, still grasping Ryan's shoulders. But her grouchy lover shrugged out of her hold and stalked over to a group of trees, dropping to the ground dejectedly.

Exasperated, Jamie walked over to the line for the Porta-Potties. Ryan stayed where she was, looking miserable. After she was finished, Jamie hopped on her bike and took off without even looking for Ryan. *I really don't want to snap at her*, she thought as she pedaled along, *and I'm afraid I will if I stay close. It's obvious she's cranky about the ride ending … I guess she just doesn't deal with this much emotion too well.* She had gone about two miles when she paused at the top of a small rise and saw Ryan, back in the distance, riding alone. *She must just need to have some time alone to get a handle on how she feels,* she thought. *She'll probably be better by the next rest stop. And by then, I'll have given myself a little pep talk so I don't get angry with her if she's not.*

She didn't see her partner for the rest of the sixteen-mile trip to pit stop two. After getting a power bar and some Gatorade, Jamie sat down to wait. She felt a lot better than when she had left the earlier stop. She knew Ryan was just having an off day, and she felt much more able to be supportive after giving herself a talk.

After twenty minutes, she began to worry. She looked all around the incoming riders, finally spotting the one familiar face that she would have preferred not to see. Nonetheless, she approached the woman who had taunted her about Ryan at the opening ceremonies. "Hi, uhm … Carly, isn't it?"

"Yeah, hi …"

"Jamie."

"Right, hi, Jamie."

"Did you happen to see Ryan on your way in?" she asked, trying to sound casual.

"You know, I think I did. I saw someone off the side of the road by that hill by Point Mugu. I kinda thought it was Ryan, but that just didn't make sense for her to be taking a break there, so I didn't stop. Do you think she's okay?" she asked with concern.

"Yeah, I'm sure she's fine," Jamie said with much more confidence than she felt. "Thanks for the info, Carly."

"I'm feeling really good today," Carly said. "I'd be glad to ride back there and check on her."

Jamie was touched by this generous offer. "That's very sweet of you, Carly, but if she really needs it she can catch the SAG van."

"They'd have to hog tie her to get her in that van, Jamie. If she's not here in a few minutes, I'll go back."

"Thanks," she said, as she let out a relieved sigh. "That's very generous of you."

"Hey, no big deal," she brushed off the compliment. "I should apologize to you for being bitchy on the first day. I was just jealous that you nabbed her."

"I understand," she said sincerely, as she grasped Carly's arm. "No hard feelings. I'll go look for her and let you know if I can't find her."

Ten minutes later, Jamie spotted her in the distance. Carly was just getting on her bike to go back, so she thanked her again and sent her on her way. Ryan pulled in looking worse than Jamie had ever seen her. She was the color of chalk, her skin was sweaty and cold and she was shaking so badly that she could hardly stay upright.

"My God, Ryan!" she gasped as she helped her off her bike. "What's wrong?"

"I don't know," she moaned. "I just don't feel good."

"Let me help you sit down," she offered, placing her hand on her waist.

"I don't want any help," she snapped, her temper in good shape even though nothing else was.

"Ryan, we need to go over to the medical trailer," Jamie said as she tried to drag her along.

"Unh-uh," she said firmly as she stopped walking and dug her heels in to the dirt.

"What do you mean 'unh-uh'?" Jamie cried, incredulous that her normally reasonable partner was being so unreasonable. "You're going over there Ryan, and then we're gonna get SAG'd the rest of the way."

"Unh-uh!" Ryan said, sounding much more like Caitlin than herself. "I'm riding, and that's final."

With a heavy sigh, Jamie sat down on the ground and looked up at her wobbling partner. "Sit down right here and tell me exactly how you feel," Jamie ordered, her patience beginning to flag.

Ryan heeded her wishes and allowed herself to collapse right at Jamie's feet. She hit the ground with a thump and immediately stuck her head between her raised knees, obviously struggling not to vomit. Jamie began to lightly run her fingers down her spine, trying to reassure her. It took quite a few minutes, but Ryan finally gathered herself enough to begin her story. "I didn't feel right from the time I woke up. I'm tired and listless, and my stomach's upset. I threw up everything I had for breakfast just after the first pit stop." She paused to stare at the ground, "When you ditched me," she added quietly.

"Oh, sweetheart, I didn't ditch you! I felt like I was irritating you, so I just tried to give us both some space. You didn't act like you wanted me there, Ryan, but I'm so sorry you felt like I'd left you."

"I was sick, and you didn't even care that I was sitting on the side of the road barfing my guts out," she said with a pout weighing down her lower lip.

"I couldn't be sorrier, Ryan," she soothed as she cradled her face with her hands. "I hope you can forgive me. I feel so bad that I wasn't there for you the one time that you needed me."

"I need you all the time, Jamie. I just needed you more than normal today," she said, her lower lip starting to quiver.

It felt like a vise was tightening around her heart, and Jamie struggled not to burst into tears. Her normally stoic partner was so terribly fragile and vulnerable that she just wanted to cradle her like a child and rock her until she felt better. "What can we do now?"

The fragile child remained for just another moment or two. Then Ryan's analytical mind kicked in, and she began to try to identify the needs of her usually responsive body. "I need a pretty long rest, and I need to force as much fluid down as possible. I really screwed up my electrolyte balance when I threw everything up and then had to ride without any fuel," she admitted glumly. "But if I can suck down some GU and keep it down, I should be okay in a half-hour or so."

"What do you think happened?" Jamie asked as Ryan leaned back on one arm and sucked deeply on a bottle of Gatorade.

"I think I just woke up on the wrong side of the tent," she said with a wan smile. "The last day of the ride is usually hard, and I think I just let it get to me. I was feeling out of sorts, and I didn't pay close attention to what I was doing. But I think my big mistake of the day was drinking that energy drink they had at breakfast. I should have checked the carbohydrate level, but I'm guessing it was over the maximum I can tolerate, which is eight percent. If I drink anything higher than that, I always get sick to my stomach." Jamie checked her skin again and found that it now felt normal to her touch. "So I think I'm kinda bonking from not getting enough calories, plus add the too-sweet drink and you've got trouble."

"Well, you're looking a lot better now. How do you feel?"

"I feel better. I don't feel sweaty and clammy any more. But I knew I was in trouble when my bike shorts felt too big today. I don't know how much weight I've lost, but I couldn't really afford to lose any. I know that's the biggest problem."

Jamie put her arms around her and hugged her tight. "Are you mad at me for not being there for you?"

"No, I was being kind of a jerk. I don't blame you for wanting to be alone," she said as she stared down at the ground.

"Please don't think that. I thought you were right behind me. I just assumed we needed a little break from each other. I'd never leave you if I thought there was a chance that you needed me."

"Okay, let's just put this behind us and try to get through the rest of the day. I think I can go again."

"No, not yet," she insisted. "I want to make sure that drink settles in your tummy before you try again. I screwed up once today, and I'm not going to let that happen again."

Ryan leaned her head back and gazed at her lover with an appreciative glance. "You didn't screw up. I'm kinda hard to be around when I don't feel well. It's really not your fault."

"You're never hard to be around. I just have to learn your cues better."

"Well, if you figure me out, be sure to tell my father," Ryan said with a small smile. "He's been trying for twenty-three years."

After another twenty minutes, they decided to give it a go. "I'm going in front of you to try to block a little wind," Jamie said. "We'll get through this. You and I ... together."

Ryan looked up at her with her first real smile of the day. "I know we will."

The pace they kept was much slower than normal, but Ryan stayed right on Jamie's tail all the way to lunch. When they pulled off, she dropped right to the ground and stayed there until Jamie brought her lunch back. Jamie pulled her up just enough to be able to eat, and propped her up against her outstretched legs. Ryan got all of her lunch down, albeit slowly, and then she drank her own sports drink mix, getting down two full bottles before she announced she was ready.

When they left, Jamie looked around at the assembled crowd. This was their last meal together, and she felt a lump in her throat just thinking about it. Ryan noticed her expression, and she leaned over and said, "I'll miss this too," hugging her.

"It's like the world's biggest family," she said as a few tears escaped. "There are the relatives you love, the ones you're not so crazy about, and the ones from out of state, who you don't see much, but you're all connected in a deep way. I never want to lose this feeling."

"You don't have to. Some of these people are my closest friends even though I only see them once a year. Your family will be here next year and the year after that. There will be some new faces and some will be absent, but the feeling remains, Jamie, I promise you that."

She closed her eyes for a minute, reflecting on Ryan's words. "Thanks," she murmured. "That helped."

They only had thirty miles to cover after lunch. On a normal day, Ryan could do that in an hour and a half—max, but they stopped frequently—very frequently—along the way to drink from their water bottles and eat a power bar. Jamie was nearly obsessed with making sure her partner was well, checking her temperature at every stop and forcing her to drink until she needed to use the facilities. She was so focused on checking her mirror to make sure Ryan was following that she nearly gasped in amazement when she realized they were cruising down Ocean Avenue in Santa Monica. Turning away from the beach, they headed towards Brentwood. Jamie had been to this area several times with her parents since they normally stayed in Bel Air when they visited Los Angeles, but she had always been in a car or an airport limo when they had traversed the winding, tree-lined streets on those trips. This was an altogether different experience, and she found herself smiling widely as they powered down the street.

Since the distance to be covered was short, the riders were bunched closer together than normal. A steady stream of riders passed them, quite a few turning in the saddle to give them questioning glances at the slow pace they were maintaining. But Jamie responded to each look with a smile and a thumbs up sign, and the riders continued on their way. As they followed the pack, her heart started to beat faster as they approached Century City.

This small, neat section of Los Angeles boasted a dozen high-rise office buildings, many restaurants, and a nice outdoor shopping mall—but that was all. It was really quite tiny, not more than four blocks square. Nearly every major law firm was either headquartered here or had an office in one of the high rises, and she could see the tower where her father's L.A. office was housed. She had learned on an earlier visit that the neighborhood used to be a part of the 20th Century Fox back lot. Many productions had been filmed on the property, but when Fox overspent on *Cleopatra*, the Richard Burton/Elizabeth Taylor film, they found themselves in such a cash crunch that they had to sell the lot to developers just to stay solvent. The lot was cleared and the buildings went up quickly, transforming a quiet little tree-lined neighborhood into a bustling business district filled with BMWs and Mercedes.

Just shy of Century City, they took a quick turn and headed towards the staging area—Beverly Hills High School. *So here we are in 90210*, she smiled to herself.

As they drew near, they were greeted by hundreds of family members and local residents, but the people were spread out over a very large area, and she struggled with her disappointment for a while. *I thought it would be more special*, she thought with a mental pout. *It's really nice that some people came out though … I guess it's just to hard to get jaded Angelenos out of their swimming pools on a lovely June day.* Looking into her mirror, she saw that Ryan looked pretty normal, although her fatigue was evident. *This must be what she expected*, she reminded herself. *This is her sixth ride, after all.*

As they rolled into the athletic fields to park their bikes, she did her best to put her disappointment aside and focus on Ryan. *She never mentioned what the last few miles were like*, Jamie recalled. *And if it were going to be special, she would have teased me with it—just to keep me going.*

Ryan actually allowed her to help get her off the bike, and it was evident that even the act of swinging her leg over the frame was an effort. They parked their bikes with all of the others and found a quiet grassy spot to lie down. It was only two, and they weren't due to begin organizing until three, so Jamie propped herself up next to the bleachers on the football field and Ryan put her head in her lap. She ran her fingers though the shiny tresses for just a few minutes before Ryan was sound asleep.

She studied her lover like a precious work of art, watching her steady intake of breath, seeing the little twitch of her eyelids, the slight pursing of her lips. She watched in annoyance as her dark eyebrows furrowed when a passerby was speaking too loudly and nearly woke her. She wanted to yell "Quiet!" but that seemed a little counterproductive, so she held her tongue and just gave a small scowl to people who had the nerve to come too close.

Continuing to run her fingers through the dark hair, Jamie thought of how sad Ryan had looked when she felt she'd been deserted. *If I've learned one thing on this ride, it's that my sweetheart needs a lot more care than she'll ever let on. I swear that I'll never ignore her again if she seems under the weather.* She had learned a valuable lesson, and even though it was painful for both of them, she was grateful she had been shown this vulnerable side of her stoic partner. She'd learned that Ryan was truly a terrible patient. She knew her body better than anyone Jamie had ever met, but when it started to fail her she fell into an intense state of denial. Jamie vowed that she would pay better attention to the small signals and not let Ryan's brusqueness cause her to turn away.

Glancing around idly, a shiny object hidden inside Ryan's helmet caught her eye. She pulled the helmet over and tilted it to get a look as a laminated photo fell out. Jamie reached down and turned the small, concave photo right side up. Gazing back at her was a very attractive young man who looked to be in his mid-teens. A broad smile graced his friendly, open face. He looked fit and strong, and appeared to be on the verge of growing into a powerful body. His hair was a deep auburn, and the sun showed deep red highlights in the straight, medium length locks. His muscular arms were raised in a classic weight-lifter's pose—fists clenched, biceps tensed. He was standing with his legs slightly spread to support the weight he carried upon his shoulders. That beaming weight was a young Ryan, no more than five or six years old. She mimicked the young man's pose, showing off her smooth, thin arms. They looked like they were having a marvelous time, and both wore the untroubled, carefree faces of youthful innocence.

Jamie stared at the photo for a long time, realizing immediately that the young man in the picture was Ryan's cousin, Michael. *This must have been taken before Ryan's mother died*, Jamie mused. *And before Michael contracted AIDS*, she added grimly.

There was something so appealing about the twosome, that Jamie couldn't stop looking at the photo. It was hard to pin it down, but it was obvious these two were more than cousins, more than friends. *I don't think I'll ever really understand what this young man meant to her*, she thought. *But I know that he was one of the biggest influences in her life.* Looking down at her sleeping partner she thought, *I'm so sorry you had so much pain at such a young age, sweetheart.* She continued to run her fingers through the dark hair, wishing for nothing but peace and joy and love for the precious woman lying in her lap.

Ryan didn't move from her position for a solid hour. At a little after three, the ride staff began to hand out special long sleeved T-shirts. The riders would parade down the street in groups, separated by color, so Jamie had to extricate herself from Ryan to fetch the same color T-shirts for them both. She picked up her head to wake her, but not a muscle in the tanned face flinched, so Jamie placed the dark head on the ground, jogged off to grab the shirts, and was back before she stirred.

She looked down at her and decided to do the one last thing that Ryan was obviously too ill to do for herself. Struggling through the assembled bikes, she found Ryan's and performed the simple task with love.

There was a lot of noise from the nearly three thousand people assembled and the plethora of announcements over the public address system, but still Ryan didn't move. Jamie was beginning to worry when she finally stretched and groaned at three-thirty on the dot.

Jamie had replaced Ryan's head on her lap, and the blue eyes finally looked up at her groggily. "Where are we?" she asked through a parched throat.

"We're at the high school. Don't you remember?" she asked with concern.

"Oh, yeah, I remember," Ryan said as she closed her eyes again.

"We're going to be moving in a few minutes. Can you get up?"

"Yeah. I just need another drink."

Jamie scrambled up and fetched a water bottle for her. She sat up and drank the entire thing down without stopping. "I feel better now. Thanks for taking care of me. Last year's tent-mate would have kicked me as she walked over my unconscious body."

"Well your current and future tent-mate loves you completely."

The ever-cheerful crew called them to order and organized them by T-shirt color. There were about four hundred and fifty people in each color of the rainbow flag— blue, red, green, yellow, purple and orange. They had been assigned purple, and they lined up on their bikes with the others. "I've never been part of a flag before," Jamie said with a grin.

"I think you look adorable as a little rainbow stripe," Ryan pronounced, bending to kiss her. Her eyes were twinkling again, and her color was completely normal by the time they hopped back on their bikes.

They rode slowly—extremely slowly—until they reached the Avenue of the Stars. "What's the holdup?" Jamie asked, as the crush of riders around them became a little claustrophobic.

"Can't say from here. I guess we'll find out when we round this corner."

As they negotiated the last turn of the ride, Jamie nearly fell from her bike at the sight before her. Their slightly elevated position at the crest of the street showed the massive throng below them, and as soon as they saw the crowd, the cheering and applause assaulted them. The six-lane major thoroughfare was the main road through Century City, and the nearly three thousand riders filled the massive street from curb to curb. The wide sidewalks were absolutely packed with well-wishers and family members. They were about three-quarters of the way back in the procession, and Jamie could see all of their fellow riders slowly pedaling up the street with the cheering crowd waving and clapping. The noise was overwhelming, and the emotion from the crowd fed the weary riders and brightened the spirits of every single one of them.

Turning to her partner with her heart thumping in her chest, she cried, "You knew!"

"Yep. I knew," Ryan replied with a blinding white smile. "But I wanted you to savor it for yourself."

"I love you, Ryan O'Flaherty!" she cried out as she threw her head back and howled with delight.

When they were no longer able to move forward, the street was filled with the multicolor jerseys looking very much like the world's largest rainbow flag. The announcer asked the crowd to welcome them home, and the noise grew even louder as Ryan turned to her and said, "Remember all those exercises I made you do on your pecs?"

Jamie nodded, a bit confused.

"Well, here's why!" she cried as she and every other rider picked up their bikes and held them high over their heads. Jamie fought back the tears as she grabbed her bike by the frame and powered it over her head. The emotion that flowed through the crowd was so strong it was almost palpable. Ryan gave her a luminous smile, leaning forward just a bit, kissing her soundly, bicycles held high over their heads. "I'm so proud of you, Jamie," she said as the tears rolled down her beautiful cheeks.

Jamie just had to lower her bike to the ground. She had to wrap her arms around this wonderful woman right this moment. She hugged her with every ounce of her strength as she murmured, "You're my hero, Ryan," as she kissed her again and again.

Moments later they were drenched by all of the riders squirting their filled water bottles up into the air. Jamie had wondered why Ryan had insisted on throwing away their energy drink and filling their bottles with water, but once again she was glad for her preparedness. They squirted each other and shot their extra bottles high into the air, blowing off some of their excitement in the process. The cheers of the crowd were almost deafening as the sound reverberated off the towering high rises that surrounded them on every side. The applause seemed to rise in waves, flowing over the now energized throng like a gentle caress.

Ryan looked at Jamie with tears in her eyes as the speakers began to address the crowd. "You polished my bike," she choked out in a mixture of delight and gratitude.

"Of course I did. It was important to you, and anything that's important to you is important to me."

The crowd grew quiet, and Jamie saw the riderless bike being led forward by representatives from the various crews. She didn't want Ryan to have to watch or listen to this in her weakened state, so she wrapped her arms around her and whispered right into her ear the entire time that the tribute was being read. She whispered how proud she was of Ryan for struggling through a very, very hard day. She thanked her for all of her help and encouragement in getting her ready for the ride. She thanked her for all of the tips she had given her on the way. She thanked her for the nightly massages she had received. She thanked her for being such a good friend, and most of all, she thanked her for just being herself.

She pulled away as the speech ended. Ryan was crying hard, her shoulders shaking from the effort, but she perked up as they joined together to thank the crew who had made the ride happen. They all chanted "Crew, Crew, Crew," as the smiling men and women ran down the raised center platform, filling it for nearly two blocks.

A few more quick speeches, and they all joined together to sing *America the Beautiful*. Jamie was sure some people were not crying, but she didn't see any of them. When the song was finished, everyone struggled to regain their composure for a few minutes, and then they started to mingle trying to find friends and relatives who had come to welcome them.

Ryan was struggling to get her emotional bearings, but as friends and former teammates approached them from all sides, Jamie could actually see her normal mood return. After just a few minutes, Ryan was joking and laughing with the near-constant stream of people who stopped to wish them well and pledge to see them again next year.

They moved forward very slowly in the crowd, finally finding themselves about a hundred feet from the huge stage that stretched across the wide street. Out of the corner of her eye Jamie saw a woman dash across the stage and yank the microphone from its stand. Tugging on Ryan's sleeve, she asked, "Isn't that your friend?"

Ryan turned her attention away from the man she was speaking with and looked up to where Jamie pointed. "Yeah, that's Brenda all right. I wonder what she's up to?"

The impish-looking woman was hard to ignore even among all of the distractions. She had followed the style for the last day, decorating her bike helmet as many others had. But Brenda's look was quite distinctive. She had two Barbie dolls attached to her shiny black helmet, engaged in an act that Mattel clearly hadn't intended for the little plastic figures. Jamie had a hard time prying her eyes away from the happy-looking identical lesbian twins on Brenda's head, but her amplified words finally yanked Jamie from her musings.

"HEY!" she yelled at full volume. "Is this on?"

The amused crowd yelled back, "YES!"

"Okay! Most of you don't know me, but there's a very special pair of women out here today. One of these women has been a tremendous inspiration to me and to dozens of other riders. She and her partner are tying the knot on Monday, and I want you all to join me in wishing Ryan O'Flaherty and her lover Jamie the very best from everybody connected with AIDS Ride 6. Come on guys, let's show 'em that we love them!"

As Jamie stared at Ryan in amazed silence, the rest of the Lavender Menace ran onto the stage. Seconds later, they were joined by each of the teams Ryan had trained over the years. By the time two women from the crowd grabbed the stunned lovers and dragged them up to the stage, there were at least seventy-five people packed onto the platform.

Jamie had never seen her partner so overcome with surprise. Ryan actually looked frozen as she was pushed along the group, receiving a hug and a kiss from each of her friends and training partners, but as the minutes wore on she loosened up a bit and started to enjoy herself.

The crowd still packing the street was thoroughly taken with this spectacle, and even though most of them didn't know anyone on the stage they quickly joined in the fun, clapping and yelling out their congratulations.

Someone found the musicians who had played *America the Beautiful* and convinced them to come back up on stage, instruments in hand. A few instructions from Brenda, and they launched into the requested song. As the crowd heard the opening chords, they began to join in until everyone was singing:

> *Going to the chapel and they're gonna get married*
> *Going to the chapel and they're gonna get married.*
> *They're in love now and they're gonna get married.*
> *Going to the chapel of love.*

Brenda knew Ryan rather well, and she shoved the microphone into her hand, urging her to sing the lead. Ryan hesitated for just a moment, but when she saw Jamie's dancing green eyes looking up at her, she accepted the microphone and sang,

> *Birds will sing ... sun will shine ... I'll be yours and you'll be mine.*
> *Monday's the day, we'll say 'I do' and we'll never be lonely any more.*

The crowd joined in for the chorus once more, the ranks of singers swelling as more and more people got in on the fun. Ryan sank to one knee in front of Jamie and soulfully sang, "Yeah ... yeah ... one more time ... going to the chapel of love!"

Jamie dropped onto Ryan's leg and tossed her arms around her neck, leaning in for a very public, very enthusiastic kiss. The crowd cheered loudly, demanding more. As Jamie pulled back slightly, Ryan's dancing blue eyes twinkled impishly as she said, "Can't disappoint the crowd now, can we?"

The beaming smile and head shake were precisely the answer Ryan wished for. Several more joyous kisses followed, with Jamie finally leaning against her partner as she vowed, "I've never been happier in my life."

"You ain't seen nothin' yet, love!" Ryan promised as she wrapped Jamie in her arms and gave her a kiss that satisfied both the cheering crowd and her beaming lover.

The End